LANDER

LIMINAL SKY: OBERON CYCLE BOOK 2: LARGE PRINT EDITION

J. SCOTT COATSWORTH

Published by
Other Worlds Ink
PO Box 19341, Sacramento, CA 95819

This book is dedicated to my grandmother Joyce Peterson, who was also a writer, and who passed away before my first story publication. She passed down her writing talents to me and would be so proud of how far I've come. Love you, Grandma P.

It's also dedicated to my husband Mark, who always has my back.

CONTENTS

VOLUME 1

ACKNOWLEDGMENTS

I want to thank all the people who made this book happen.

First, my husband Mark, whose belief in me continues to amaze me, and my mom, who helped kick me in the… well, let's just say she encouraged me to get back to writing at a time when I needed it.

I'd like to thank my beta readers—Angel Martinez, Sadie Rose Bermingham, Jenni Lea, and Mary Newman. Thanks also to Lynn West, my publisher, who believes in me and this story.

And finally, thanks to my readers who read and enjoyed Skythane and are ready to follow me to the ends of the world and beyond.

OBERON

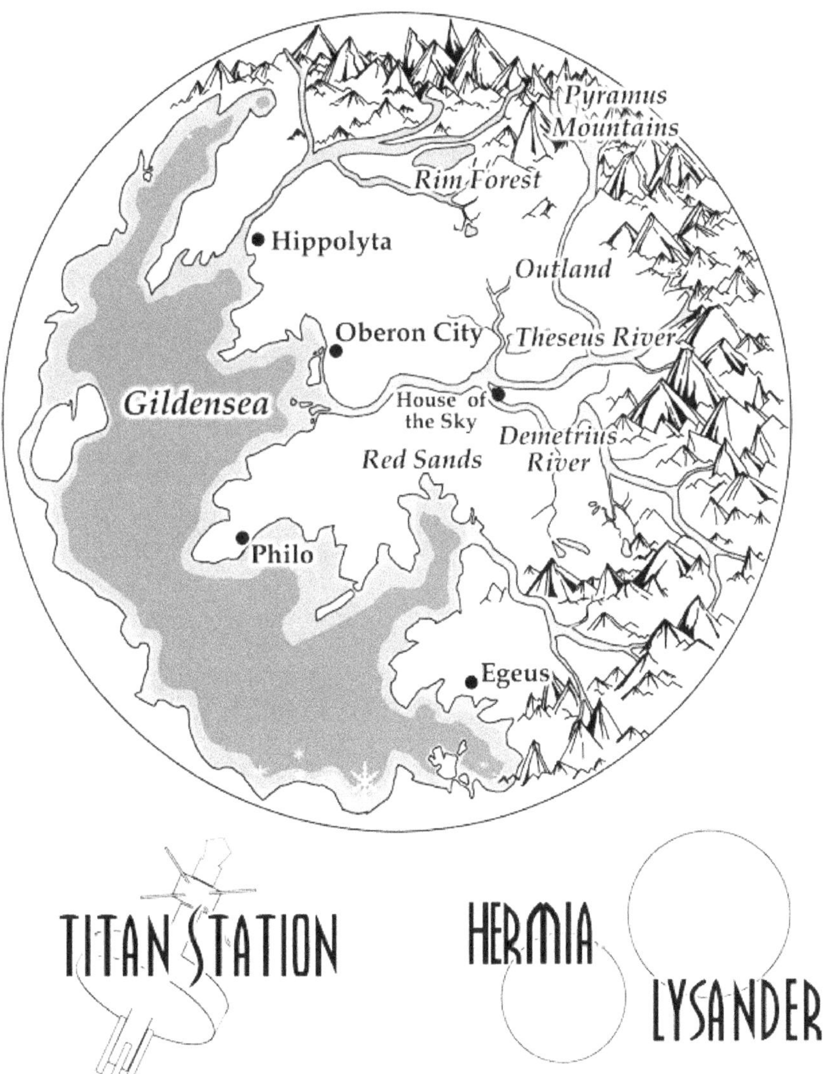

TITAN STATION

HERMIA

LYSANDER

TITANIA

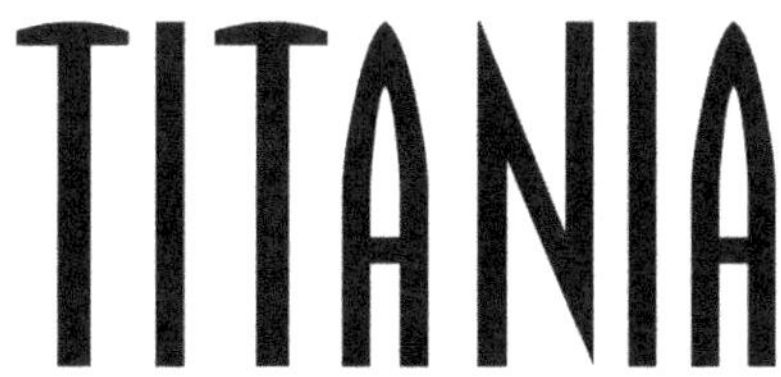

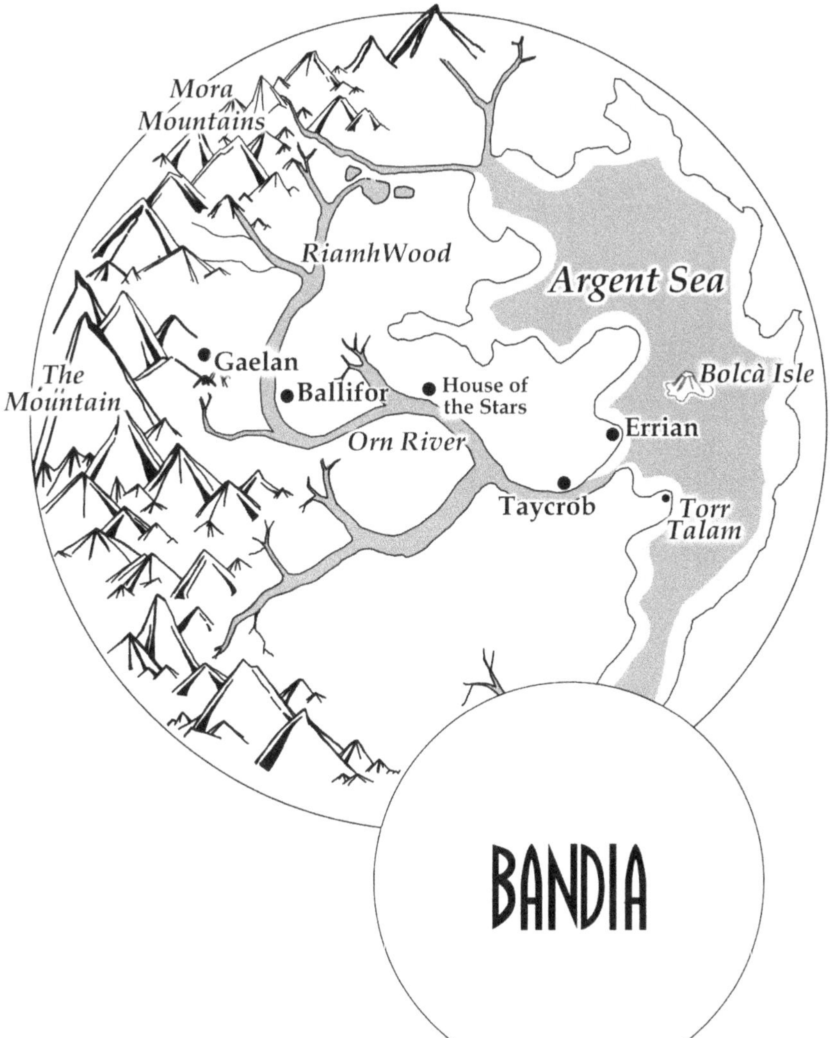
Mora Mountains
RiamhWood
Argent Sea
The Mountain
Gaelan
Ballifor
House of the Stars
Bolcà Isle
Errian
Orn River
Taycrob
Torr Talam
BANDIA

FOREWORD

As we get ready to close out 2020, our world has been turned upside down by Covid-19. Black Lives Matter marched in the streets demanding justice for our black citizens. Climate change brought us hurricanes, fires and floods. And every day seemed like it lasted a week. Or a month.

I'm on my own personal author journey, having taken back most of my books to publish them under my own banner, and in 2021 I'll start releasing new work again.

Lander was another first for me, the first time I ever released a sequel. It's something I am immensely proud of, especially since I didn't take the expected path with the Alix-Xander-Jameson triangle. I think the book is stronger for it.

The story also features three kick-ass female characters, including Jameson's ex fiancée, Jessa, someone whom I hope you'll come to love.

So dive in… and get ready for Ithani, the final book in the trilogy!

VOLUME ONE

PRINCIPAL CHARACTERS (GLOSSARY AT END)

Alia: Guard in Gaelan

Alix Preston (PA Erissa): Xander's ex, a lander man missing for a year

Danielle (Dani) Black (PA Hera): One of the lander enforcers in Gaelan, daughter of Danner Black

Davyn Sléite: Xander's Gaelani name

Jameson Havercamp (PA Angie): Psych from Beta Tau who comes to investigate pith shortage on Oberon

Jessa: Jameson's fiancée on Beta Tau

Kadin Tamain: The chamberlain of the House of the Moon

Lyrin Madainn: Jameson's birth name

Morgan: Mysterious child Xander finds on Oberon

Mylin: Young skythane girl who helps Xander

Quince Farrai (PA Ari): Xander's skythane friend who joins the quest

Robyn Sléite: Queen of the Gaelani and mother to Xander, and Quince's former lover

Rogan Horth: Syndicate boss who has history with Xander

Venin: Guard in Gaelan

Xander Kinnson (PA Ravi): Skythane who works in Oberon City, embarks on a quest with Jameson

PROLOGUE

The course of true love never did run smooth....
War, death, or sickness did lay siege to it,
Making it momentany as a sound,
Swift as a shadow, short as any dream;
Brief as the lightning in the collied night....
The jaws of darkness do devour it up:
So quick bright things come to confusion.

—William Shakespeare, *A Midsummer Night's Dream*

THE SUN was rising angry and red over the half world as
the Oberon shuttle came around to give its one pas-

senger the view it was most famous for—the Split. Jessa stared at the naked, broken edge of Oberon, fascinated.

She was the only one making the journey down to the surface, and it had cost her a pretty penny to buy her way onto this trip. Titan Station had been jam-packed with refugees fleeing the planet. Her Jameson was down there somewhere, maybe taken hostage by the locals, for all she knew. He'd dropped off the grid, and she meant to find him and bring him home.

The shuttle shook violently, and Jessa grabbed the arms of her seat. Something was wrong. The craft jumped, as if pushed upward by a giant hand. She closed her eyes, praying to God to get her to the ground safely.

The cabin shuddered, and for a moment she thought her teeth would be rattled out of her skull. Then as suddenly as it had begun, the turbulence was over.

She opened her eyes and peered out the window.

The impossible had happened, and her eyes refused to accept it for a moment. The Split was *gone*. The planet was suddenly whole, round. Impossibly *normal*. *What the hell?*

Boiling clouds spread upward and outward from the ground, and thunder and lightning exploded all around her in a cacophony of violence. Fierce winds and heavy rain buffeted the shuttle as the storm over-took them.

"Please hold on," the pilot said over the comm. "We're taking this shuttle down as quickly as we can in these unexpected conditions."

Unexpected conditions. The world had gone mad. The cabin was plunged into darkness as the lights failed and the clouds blotted out the world. What had Jamie gotten himself into? What had he gotten *her* into?

A lightning bolt passed within a couple meters of the wing with a deafening *boom*, lighting up her world in a monochrome flash. There was no way this thing would make it to the ground. *I'm going to die here.*

The shuttle shook again as if in the grip of some vengeful god. The lights came on and then went off again in the cabin, and something audibly cracked. "Oh God oh God oh God oh God…." She forgave herself for using the Lord's name in vain, just this once. He would understand, given the circumstances.

She closed her eyes and willed herself to be calm, shutting out the turbulence. *I can do this.*

Strangely, the ship's course smoothed out. She opened her eyes. Sunlight once again streamed into the cabin. The shuttle had come out of the fury of the storm to settle into an even descent path.

Jessa closed her eyes. "Thank you, Lord." She sent a

little prayer heavenward. Maybe it wasn't quite her time. *Not yet.*

She looked out the window. Oberon City was spread out below them, as gritty a black-and-white place as she'd ever seen. The shuttle swung past it to find its landing place at the spaceport on the edge of town. Grim towers soared over black pavement, and one whole section looked like it had fallen into utter ruin.

As they made the turn, she got a good look at the monster tempest approaching the city. It was a storm on a scale she'd never seen before, its thunderheads raising up kilometers into the sky, their skirts black as the void.

She'd need to find cover as soon as she got through customs, but at least she'd survived the landing. She said a small prayer of thanks.

Jamie, you better be in a serious heap of trouble.

1
———

THE GATHERING STORM

Jameson savored the kiss, his arms around Xander, the way they fit *just right*. They were finally together, and Titania and Oberon were one again.

Erro, Quince had called this new world. Like the skythane god of the sun, the one Errian and the Erriani were named for.

For the moment, *everything* was right in his life, and he never wanted it to end.

A cold drop of water on his cheek brought him out of his reverie. He glanced up. Storm clouds were piled high and were swiftly overtaking them. Rain began to pour out of the sky like a waterfall, and thunder echoed in the clouds as the valley went dark, sunlight smothered by the onrushing tempest. Nearby trees thrashed about in the wind, their purple leaves fluttering in distress.

"What the hell?" Xander said as the winds picked up and ruffled the feathers of his wings. He stared up at the black sky.

"The Split!" Jameson shouted over the howling of the wind. He mimed the two halves of the world, each with their own atmosphere, suddenly being forced together in the middle. "When the Oberon half shifted, all the atmosphere it brought with it along the Split was forced up here!"

A bolt of lightning struck a nearby tree, crisping it to ashes and standing Jameson's hair on end.

"Run!" Xander shouted.

Jameson's vision swam, and a memory slipped into his conscious mind from that *other* part of him. It was a high-ceilinged cavern that was more like a faery palace than a cave, a place where he'd stolen away with a lover more than once.

His stomach heaved at the displacement, and he clenched his hands. *That wasn't me.* They were someone else's memories.

"Follow me!" he shouted at his four companions—Xander, Quince, Kadin, and Venin—and ran toward the cliffs that were rapidly fading to invisibility behind the rain. He pushed down the memory-nausea, tasting bile in the back of his mouth.

Alia was missing.

He'd last seen her as they had fled the Mountain, when it had begun to collapse. Jameson looked around wildly, but she was nowhere to be seen. "Where's Alia?" he shouted at Kadin as they ran. Thunder shook the valley.

Kadin shook his head, mouthing, "I don't know."

Rain swirled all around them, coming down so fast that it pooled on the ground and ran in rivulets downhill toward the lake that was now half-filled with the broken remains of the Mountain.

Mud made his footing treacherous. Jameson clambered up the hill, using roots and rocks that offered a firmer surface than the naked ground. The wind tugged at his wings, threatening to flip him over. He pulled them in tightly and glanced back to be sure the others were following him through the tempest.

Jameson reached the cover of the forest, plunging under the protection of the canopy. The trees here were tall and thin with white bark trunks and broad purple leaves that were being shredded by the storm.

The thunder boomed constantly now, loud as a shuttle engine at close range, and lightning strikes were coming every few seconds all around them. *Thank God it's only a few hundred meters—*

A flash and *boom* and he was flying backward into Xander, sending them both crashing down in the mud. Jameson's head slammed against the ground hard, and he blacked out.

He opened his eyes, with no sense of how much time had passed. His head was spinning.

He untangled himself from Xander, who said something he couldn't hear, pointing.

The world had gone silent.

"I can't hear you!" he shouted, but it was barely audible. *God, I hope this isn't permanent.* There was no time to worry about it then.

They started off again toward the cliff face. He got a glimpse of it every now and then. The trees blocked some of the rain, enough for him to strike a path toward the cavern he remembered.

Xander followed.

The world around him was strangely mute. Jameson was separated from it by the peculiar, deadening silence. They staggered through the nightmare forest of burned, fallen, and broken trees.

A monster tree trunk crashed directly in their path. Jameson jumped back and pulled Xander hard to the left to detour around it.

At last the cliff face appeared ahead, lining the southern side of the valley. He threw himself forward at a dead run, praying not to be struck down by lightning. God—or the gods?—seemed to favor them. They reached it safely after coming out of the deadly forest. The cliff face was white like chalk, and water was pouring down it in a thundering deluge all along its length. *So much water.*

Jameson stopped and looked around, casting about for something he recognized.

The standing stones. There were two tall stones that guarded the entrance to the cavern he sought. If he closed his eyes, he could see them, staring blankly into the valley below. His stomach lurched again, and he pushed the memory aside.

The trees had fallen away behind them, leaving them exposed to the full fury of the storm. He could only see a few feet in either direction. If he had to guess….

"This way," he shouted, but it sounded small and tinny inside his head. He ran along the cliff wall, searching for the standing stones. The entrance was here somewhere. It had to be.

Then the statues materialized out of the rain like ancient sentinels, tall and slender, the rock worn smooth by weather and the ages. Who or what they depicted, he had no idea.

He beckoned his friends to follow, but only Xander was there. "Where are the others?" he mouthed.

Xander looked around wildly. "I don't know."

Jameson grabbed Xander's hand and pulled him inside, plunging through the wall of water that cascaded down across the entrance.

A few more steps and they were out of the rain and inside the safety of the cavern.

LIGHTNING STRUCK TEN METERS AWAY, and Alix clapped his hands over his ears. It left a strong, acrid smell hanging in the air, fraying his sensitive nerves. *God, I* hate *this world.*

Wind howled all around them, and the rain flew by sideways in the semidarkness. They'd come out of the tunnel from near the work camp to reach Titania. Greeted by Alia, who had spotted them far below as the world had shifted, they were all soon swamped by the ferocious storm.

Alix scrambled over the wet rubble, clambering from rock to rock, trying to reach somewhere more stable. He took the lead with Tucker right behind him. Robyn and Alia brought up the rear.

The world—worlds—he had known, Oberon and Titania, were now one. *Erro,* Robyn had called it.

He couldn't wrap his head around it. He was a simple soldier, not an astrophysicist, though his mother would have been happier to have him home studying the stars.

He'd seen the Pyramus Mountains before the storm had closed in. It was impossible. They were part of Oberon, not Titania. The Split, where he'd languished for weeks, working in the amalite mines, was gone too.

He shook his head. The skythane had been right about the whole *shift* thing after all.

Xander was one of those skythane. His beautiful, damaged Xander. *Fuck, why'd I ever leave him?*

Water trickled down Alix's back under his shirt. He was a wet mess all over. His clothes were soaked and clammy, and he was miserable. He climbed over another half-shattered boulder, wondering where the hell the four of them were now. This ruined landscape resembled no place he'd visited on either half of Erro.

The ground shook, an ominous rumble filling the air.

Alix looked back. An avalanche was descending upon them. "Ruuuuuuun!" Small bits of scree slipped past him, nipping his ankles, as the rest of the slide crashed toward them. Alix scrambled down the broken hillside as the roar built into a crescendo. He slipped, fell, and slid on his ass down the pile of rubble.

Alia sprang into the air, buffeted by the powerful wind, and pulled Robyn, the queen, with her up and out of harm's way.

Wish I had that option. Alix skidded twenty meters downhill, trying to find purchase in the loose rubble.

The avalanche subsided, leaving him shaken but alive. *Thank God.* He came to rest against a large boulder and stood, checking his body. Other than a few scrapes and scratches, he seemed to be in one piece.

He stared up the hillside as Alia and Robyn came back to ground. Displeasure was evident on the queen's face, probably at having to be saved by someone else.

Alia ignored her. "Where's Tucker?"

Shit. Alix clambered back up the loose slope, ignoring the ache from the various cuts and bruises he'd sustained in the fall. "Tucker!" he called over the rain and wind. They weren't safe there, but he wouldn't leave a man behind.

"Alix." Robyn pointed to the edge of the slide.

One arm and the edge of a red shirt were visible, sticking out from under a large rock. The man's fingers twitched once and then went still.

Alix looked away. "Goddammit." He'd seen far worse on the campaign in Gaelan, and he hardly knew the man. Nevertheless, the man had been under his charge. He hated losing someone, and it could just as easily have been him. *I'm sorry, Tucker.* He knelt and laid a hand on his arm. "Into the void," he whispered.

"We have to keep going. There's nothing we can do for him," Robyn shouted over the howling of the wind. "The Mountain is still settling. We're not safe here."

Alix nodded. *The Mountain.* So that's where this was? The once-beautiful valley, reduced to a pile of wet, crumbled stone.

He knew where they needed to go. If they could get to where Dani stashed the bi-wings, they might make it to Gaelan once the storm abated. "Come on." He stood and started back down the broken mountain.

Gaelan.

The occupation had started out simply enough, with Dani and her rangers as a support force, there at the will of the king. As the year wore on and the occupation tightened, things had gone downhill. His fellow soldiers were subjected to regular acts of disobedience, small and large, and relations with the *wing men*, as the invaders called them derisively, had quickly soured. "*Lander-boy*," they'd called him and spat on him, though he was probably about as far from his boyhood as he was from his life's end.

In the end, some of the OberCorp rangers and enforcers had taken matters into their own hands. More than a couple wing men lay buried in shallow graves, just outside the city. That was a black time in Alix's life, one he still regretted.

Dani Black, the leader of the Lander occupation force, had called him into her room. She wanted his help capturing Xander—Prince of the Gaelani—and hadn't *that* been a surprise. He knew how to pick 'em.

His left leg was sore. He glanced at the back of his calf. He'd scraped it up on the slide downhill. Something had sliced clean through the material of his trousers. Nothing to do about it at the moment.

His refusal to help Dani had gotten him sent to the mines—days of backbreaking manual labor and nights alone in a cold, dark cell.

He closed his eyes, trying to remember Xander's touch. The smell of him, the taste of him when they kissed. The arch of his back and the fluttering of his wings as he reached climax. God, he missed that touch.

Now he was free, and in company with two of the skythane—the young woman, Alia, and the Queen of the Gaelani, who had lost her wings. Fate was laughing at him. He would find Xander and apologize for the things he'd done.

They descended another slope of loose scree. The rain was continuous, pouring in heavy sheets.

Robyn lost her footing and slid down the slope past

him. Alix grabbed her arm, pulling her back up onto her feet. "Careful."

She nodded but said nothing in reply. She was cold to him. She had her reasons.

Alix wondered what had happened to the others who'd fled the mines, both on foot and in the escape balloons. Surely they hadn't fared well in the storm, if they had even managed to escape the Split. If not, they were entombed beneath a couple hundred trillion tons of rock.

They reached the bottom of the slope after another hour. The boulders were more widely placed here, making it easier to get around them, and the howl of the wind lessened slightly.

Robyn's emerald eyes narrowed. She looked like he was a bug she wanted to squash.

Alix shivered.

Alia fell in beside him as they navigated the boulder field.

"Where did you come from?" he asked Alia over the sound of the wind and the rain.

"What?" she asked, looking up at him.

She was beautiful enough, with fine features and honey-blonde hair pulled back and tied behind her neck in a long braid. There was a hardness in her brown eyes. She'd seen things that had marked her soul. She had golden wings, though they were damp and matted down with rain and mud.

He'd always had a thing for wings, but his heart belonged to Xander. Maybe, if he were still single…. "Where… did… you… come… from?" he tried again, louder this time.

"Gaelan," she shouted back with a weak smile.

"I mean, why were you *here*?"

She shook her head. "What?"

He sighed. It was still too loud for a conversation. He'd have to wait until the storm settled down to get some answers.

He closed his eyes and drifted into a quieter place, holding on to the image of Xander's face.

I'll see you again soon.

XANDER STARED at the torrent of water pouring over the cavern entrance. Somewhere out there, Quince and the others were lost in the storm.

"What happened to everyone else?" Jameson shouted, putting his hand on Xander's shoulder.

"I don't know. Last I saw them was before the lightning strike." How had things changed so quickly?

Jameson started toward the exit. "We have to look for them!"

Xander pulled him back.

Jameson's eyes were wild.

He squeezed Jameson's hands, trying to reassure him. "Hey, calm down. There's nothing we can do right now."

"We already lost Morgan." Jameson's eyes pleaded with him. "I can't lose the rest of them."

Xander shook his head. "It's no use. We'll never find them in this tempest. They're seasoned veterans. They can take care of themselves. We'll go looking after the storm passes." The loss of Morgan weighed on him too, though he was less and less certain that Morgan had been a human boy at all.

Jameson looked doubtful.

Xander felt it too, but there really was nothing they could do. "Hey, it's gonna be all right." He pulled Jameson to him, enfolding the two of them with his wings. Jameson was soaked, but Xander didn't care.

Jameson nodded against his chest. "You're right. Gods, I know you're right. I'm sorry. I thought we were done with all this."

Xander held him out at arm's length. "Gods, huh? We're doing the plural thing now?"

Jameson gave him a half smile. "Trying it out? When in Rome…."

"How's your hearing?"

Jameson cocked his head. "It's better. But everything sounds muffled."

Xander nodded. "I can tell."

Jameson blushed. "Am I talking too loud?"

"Just a little."

Jameson smiled sheepishly. "It's weird. It feels like my ears are full of water."

Xander kissed him gently. "It'll pass." He looked around the cavern at last, his eyes gradually adjusting to the dim blue light.

The place was a faeryland, filled with rows of golden stalactites and stalagmites, like the bulwarks of an eldritch castle. Each one was a miracle of minute detail, like candle wax dripped from above. The whole cavern was lit by a turquoise-blue glow.

Xander looked around for the source. It came from pools of water on either side of the cavern. The scintillating light shimmered along the walls, creating complex, ever-changing patterns.

"Look, Jameson… it's beautiful." They were both a muddy mess. "We're stuck here until the storm blows itself out. Why don't we get cleaned up and try to rest? Then we can figure out what to do next. We have a long flight to Gaelan." He was still shivering from the rain.

"A bath sounds like heaven." Jameson let Xander lead him to one of the glowing ponds.

"Do you think it's safe to go in?" Xander asked, pulling off his boots and testing the water with his toes. It was warm.

Jameson looked queasy, but then he smiled. "They called them faery ponds. There's a microscopic organism that makes the light. It's harmless, but beautiful." He grinned. "Romantic, even."

Ah, that's how you knew this place. "You've been here before, haven't you?" he said, slowly and clearly, gesturing to indicate Jameson and the cavern. His own generational memories were still fleeting, occasional things.

Jameson's smile fled. He shrugged. "Not me personally…."

"Shhh. I know." If he closed his eyes and focused, he could see this place too, but he seemed to be able to block them out when they were inconvenient. "Too many memories." Xander pointed at his head.

Jameson nodded. He looked relieved. He reached out and pulled Xander close, his hands warm on Xander's waist.

Xander slipped his arms around Jameson and kissed him once, twice. He wrinkled his nose. "You're filthy and you stink! So do I." He held up his shirt as proof. It was covered in mud stains.

Jameson laughed. "We can fix that."

He helped Jameson unlace the sides of his shirt,

pulling it off to reveal the naked skin underneath. Jameson returned the favor, his hands lingering for a moment before withdrawing to pull down his own pants.

They shucked their wet and dirty clothes and descended into the water. It was surprisingly warm, silky and smooth around Xander's waist.

The pool was about three meters across and sloped down to about a meter deep at the far end. There was a warm, gentle current drifting past Xander's legs, and the stone beneath his feet had been worn smooth by water and time.

Xander washed the grime off his skin, and it drifted off into the water around him.

Jameson pulled him in deeper and gestured for him to lower his head.

Xander lay in Jameson's arms, and warm water washed over him, carrying the mud and dirt out of his hair. Jameson massaged his scalp, pulling away the twigs and bits of gunk he'd accumulated on the mad run through the forest in the storm.

Xander's desire threatened to overwhelm him at Jameson's gentle touch. He dipped his face into the water and rinsed off. It was *so fucking good* to get clean.

He shook his head, splashing Jameson, who shot him an aggrieved look.

The look turned into a wicked grin, and Jameson splashed him back. Then they were going after each other and laughing, a fine mist of water flying through the air.

Damn, it's good to hear you laugh again. Xander grabbed Jameson and kissed him, harder this time, and Jameson's body responded. They fell back into the water, and Jameson was hard against him, his own need naked before Xander's desire.

After all that had happened, Xander needed to feel human and alive again. He tugged Jameson back to the shallow part of the pool and pulled his skythane down on top of him, Jameson's skin warm against his own.

He kissed Jameson's neck and nibbled on his ear, eliciting a low moan.

Jameson wanted this as much as he did. He could tell.

For a long, slow, ecstatic hour, Xander forgot all about the storm.

2

——————

NEED

Quince was *flying*, and Robyn was beside her, as if the last twenty-five years of misbegotten history and separation had never happened.

A seemingly endless sheet of ice lay beneath them, white as far as the eye could see, glimmering under Titania's red sun. It was cold out, bone-chillingly so.

To her right, a mountain range carved up the otherwise seamless landscape of white, one peak after another, ending in a tall crag that reminded her of nothing so much as the Mountain, before it had fallen—taller than all the rest, perfect in its symmetry.

As they approached the great peak, a low booming filled the air, like the sound of a giant drum. Once, twice, three times it sounded.

The huge mountain shuddered, cracks appearing on its sides. Great slabs of ice and snow slid down its skirts, forming massive avalanches that set up a thunderous noise as the debris buried the valley below.

Then the mountain itself split open with a deafening crack *that went on and on like the judgment of the gods. A fierce golden glow shone from inside, and she could feel the heat of it even at a distance.*

As they reached the mountain and flew overhead, Quince could make out a small figure perched on one of the split peaks, head in his hands, peering down at the light below. He looked up at her, his face a mixture of anticipation and fear.

Morgan.

His emotions struck her like a lightning bolt. Terror. Anger. Need. "Help me, Quince!"

QUINCE WOKE WITH A SHUDDERING GASP, flailing around in the rain until she remembered where she was, trapped in the storm.

Morgan was alive. She didn't know *how* she knew it, but she believed it with every fiber of her being, and he *needed* her. Something terrible was coming.

The storm still raged around her. She tried to get up as the relentless downpour pelted her, but her left leg was lodged under something. She felt blindly through the deluge until her hand reached the object…. It was rough, like wood. A fallen tree or branch, then.

"Help!" she shouted into the storm. The rain and thunder drowned out her voice. "Can anyone hear me? Jameson? Xander?"

No one came.

She tried again to pull out her leg, but she was blinded by the rain and couldn't see how she was trapped.

Had anyone noticed she was missing? Venin? Kadin? The boys?

She sighed. There was nothing else she could do but wait out the storm. The gods knew it couldn't last forever.

She turned her head to the side and laid a wing over her face to protect herself from the falling rain as much as she could, and closed her eyes.

ALIX LED his party over the foothills that sat at the base of the Mountain. The fallen trees were thick here, slowing their progress as they scrambled over and under logs through the tormented hellscape. At least the rain washed some of the dirt off.

Robyn paced him now. The queen looked at him

from time to time, her arched eyebrow saying, more than a torrent of words, what she thought of him and his kind. He was probably an idiot for staying in skythane territory after what landers like him had done in Gaelan. He could have hightailed it back the other direction when the worlds came together, but he felt a strange responsibility toward the queen and her people.

He stared at her for a moment, but he was the one who turned away first.

The rift between skythane and lander went deep, and the subjugation of Gaelan hadn't helped matters any.

The rain had slowed, and the worst of the thunder and lightning had moved on, but Alix was sick of being cold and wet.

"You were one of *them*," Robyn said unexpectedly, her voice carrying over the downpour. Her tone left no doubt what she meant by *them*. Even soaked to the skin as she was, she retained her regal bearing.

He nodded. No point in denying it. "Yes, ma'am, I was."

They locked eyes again, and the weight of her judgment fell on him like a blow. She stared at his hands, roughened from the work camp. "Why were you sent to the camp?"

He looked back at her, surprised. *Not judgment,*

then. Not yet. "I stood up to Dani. I told her she was wrong to use Xander that way." He lifted a fallen tree branch out of her way.

Her eyes narrowed. "What did she plan to do to my son?"

Her tone sent chills down his spine, like the screech of metal on metal in space. One wrong move and death came in for a visit. You could take the queen out of the castle… "She wanted to drug him with pith, and then use him to take over Gaelan."

Robyn hissed. "She would have killed us all."

Alix laughed harshly. "Apparently." Without Xander, the shift wouldn't have happened, and if the shift was real, he was guessing that Oberon-adjacent space was a damned inhospitable place to be right now. Solar flare and all.

"I *may* have misjudged you." The words sounded like they were being dragged out of her.

He looked back at her, surprised. The queen didn't apologize. Ever. "Thank you."

Robyn held out a hand.

He took it. She had a firm grip. If she knew half the things he'd done in Gaelan in the name of keeping the peace, she might feel differently, but now was *not* the time to bring them up. It seemed they had common cause, at least for the moment.

"So what happened to your wings?"

She looked down at her hands, her face suddenly pale. "They were… removed. Most painfully. Dani wanted answers." She turned away, but he pulled her back gently.

"I'm sorry… Your Highness?"

"Just call me Robyn. I'm no longer the Queen of the Gaelani."

"Robyn, then. Dani Black's not *human* inside. Not like most of us." There was a darkness in the woman that she seldom let show. He shuddered. What she had done to Robyn…. "Did you tell her what she wanted?"

Her returned glare could have melted ice. "No. Not a word."

It would have been understandable if she had. "Then how did she know about Xander?"

Robyn shook her head. "I don't know. I'd guess there's a traitor in Gaelan."

Alix nodded. "It would seem so. Do you know who?"

"I have my suspicions."

Alia had been following right behind them, apparently listening to the whole exchange with a bemused expression. "You know Xander?"

"Yes." Alix crossed his arms. "We were close. Lovers.

Before I was hauled off to Gaelan by Dani with her crew."

"He can't be far from here. I was with him and Jameson before I found you—"

"Jameson?" the queen interjected.

"You'd know him as Lyrin, Your Highness."

"Wait, Xander's *nearby*?" Alix grinned. Some habits were hard to break. He'd known his lover would be coming to Titania, but they were at least a day's flight from Gaelan. What was Xander doing *here*? Was *this* where Xander had brought the two worlds together? It might explain the destruction of the Mountain.

Alia nodded. "The storm came quickly after the shift. They can't have gotten far."

Xander is here. *Somewhere.* His heart beat faster at that thought. He remembered Xander's touch, the taste of his mouth. His beautiful wings. Alix used to love running his hands over those black feathers, feeling them slip between his fingers. He sighed.

The bi-wings were suddenly less important.

He set off again, and the others followed. He was going to find Xander if he had to swim all the way to him through this drowning valley.

Who the hell was *Jameson*?

· · ·

*Q*UINCE WAS SOARING *above the ice again, the mountain below her cracking open to reveal its golden glow.*

Morgan looked up at her, his gaze beseeching her. You have to save me.

Pain twisted her gut at the memory of his passing. He'd become the key they needed to shift the world. He was gone, vanished in the midst of the unimaginable power he had unleashed. She'd seen it happen.

Yet here he was, calling to her. His need *pulled at her soul.*

*Q*UINCE OPENED HER EYES, focusing on the wing that protected her from the rain. She was tired. She'd already crossed the world—twice—to save it. She wasn't sure she had any more fight left in her, and yet Morgan's insistent little voice pried at her conscience. *You have to save me.*

"There you are."

Quince lifted her head, spitting out mud. She sat up as far as she was able and spread her wings. The rain had lessened, and she could see a few feet in each direction. It was a dismal vista.

Venin stood over her. "I've been looking for you. Are you okay? I got separated from the rest of you and found a place under a fallen tree to wait out the worst of it." He knelt next to her.

She nodded. "I think so. My foot's trapped." She wiped mud off her face, aware she must be a frightful mess.

"Let's see what we can do about that, shall we?" Venin gave her an encouraging grin and went to get a better look. "Hold still." He straddled the trunk and tried to pull it up, his dark blue wings fluttering at the strain. He was quite handsome, his muscles straining with the effort. Too bad it was wasted on her.

"Any luck?"

"This thing's heavy. Let me see if I can find something to lever it up."

Quince's stomach rumbled. How long had she been out here in the storm? At least she could do something about her hunger. She pulled off her pack and rummaged through it, finding a roll and some cheese she'd brought from Gaelan. She missed the MREs and more civilized food. Still, it was *food*.

She offered Venin some, but he declined. "Any sign of the others?"

"Not since we were separated." He picked up a big stick and snapped off some of the smaller branches.

Where would they have gone? She'd grown up a long way from here and wasn't sure if she'd ever ventured this far west before. "Are there any other landmarks around here, besides the Mountain?" Well, that was gone now.

Venin brought his stick to the fallen tree. "Not much, no. There are some caves along the edge of the valley. Old statues too. Ruins of the ancients, I think."

She nodded. "Jameson was leading us to shelter."

Venin looked at her strangely. "How would he know about the caves? He's an offworlder."

She laughed ruefully. "It's a *long* story."

He shrugged. "Okay, let's give this a try." He stuck the branch under the trunk and tried to get enough purchase to lift it up just a little. It moved up a few centimeters, then came crashing down as Venin's grip slipped on the wet wood.

Quince gritted her teeth. "Gods, that hurts!"

"Sorry. Let me find a better spot."

He wedged the branch in.

The weight of the trunk on her leg was an agony.

Venin pushed down on the branch, and the trunk inched up again, five centimeters, then ten.

Quince pulled her leg out carefully. Scraping it along the bark, she cried in pain and frustration. At last it came free.

The branch in Venin's hand snapped, sending him flying backward onto his ass. He spread his wings to cushion his fall.

"You okay?"

"I'll live. I'll take some of that food now, though." Venin came to sit next to her and took a chunk of cheese.

Quince pulled her leg close to look at it in the rain. It was scraped up rather badly, but she'd live. Blood blended with water and ran down to the muddy ground.

She couldn't shake the dream. Or had it been a vision? It *couldn't* be true. She'd watched Morgan vanish before her eyes inside the Mountain. He was *gone*.

Her gut told her it wasn't that simple.

Morgan *was* still alive. Whatever he was, he still existed.

Why he had chosen to reach out to her, she had no clue. Xander would have been a more likely choice, or even Jameson. If she'd had her way, he would have been killed the first time she'd seen him, and the whole world would have paid the price for her action.

Now she had a chance to make it right.

ALIA RETURNED from the still-dangerous sky to share her news. "The valley is mostly impassable. The Mountain's collapse filled in the lake, and fallen trees have made most of it a nightmare to traverse on foot."

"Worse than this?"

She nodded. "It's like a giant bramble patch."

Alix remembered hiking through this country when he'd arrived here with Dani and her squad. It had been beautiful then, a long lush green valley around a turquoise-blue lake, surrounded by hollyhock and púca trees.

It had taken them hours to make their way over the edge of the mountain rubble, slipping and sliding through a rocky landscape that had dumped him on his ass more than once. He was ready for a break.

The rain cleared away ahead of them, giving him a momentary view of the valley below. The lake was no more, buried in a pile of rubble. The trees had been knocked down for kilometers, looking like matchsticks. Beyond the end of the old lake, a new one had formed as the rain filled up the valley bowl—a brown, roiling mass filled with fallen tree trunks and other debris.

Robyn came up next to him. She pointed to the southern edge of the valley. "The way is clearer up there, along the cliff walls."

The limestone walls had offered some protection from the winds. Alix nodded. "So we skirt the valley and hope to run into Xander's party. If they survived." That was convenient. It was also where the bi-wings were stashed.

Alia nodded. "If the others survived, they would have tried to make their way out of this mess."

"We'll head for the wall there—" Alix pointed to a spot closest to where they stood. "—and then follow it eastward."

He considered it less and less likely that anyone could have survived the storm down there. Xander was tough, though. He'd had to be, after some of the things he'd gone through. If anyone could make it through, it would be him.

Did Xander still *need* him, like he had back on Oberon?

Alix wondered how the citizens of Oberon City were faring through all this. Was Titan Station still up there?

They started down the slope toward the edge of the valley as the rain closed in once again, blocking the view. How long could it go on?

As water sloshed around inside his boots and churned the already soaked ground, Alix decided he hated the fucking rain too.

QUINCE STRUGGLED up the slope toward the cliff, trying to see far enough ahead to find a protected spot where they could rest.

Venin let her put an arm on his shoulder, supporting her. She was grateful for the kindness.

She'd considered flying, but the rain and wind were still heavy enough to make that a really bad idea. She'd been lucky to get off with just a sprained ankle in her last fall. What if she broke a wing?

For a brief moment, the rain let up.

Quince looked into the gray sky and then back the way they'd come. The shimmering air parted to reveal the ruined valley, half-filled with water from the storm.

She hoped Xander, Jameson, Kadin, and Alia had survived. "The prophecy never mentioned a flood," she grumbled and turned back toward the ridgeline.

Venin laughed. "Prophecies are notoriously vague. Let's keep going. We're almost there."

He seemed solid and steady. She needed both at the moment, though she'd never admit it.

They resumed their climb as the rain descended again in heavy sheets. Venin helped her clamber over slippery logs and boulders. She'd scraped up her knees several times, and the blood now flowed freely down both legs along with the rainwater. Her cuts were small enough to pose no immediate danger of blood loss, but she'd be lucky if they didn't get infected.

At last they reached the white cliffs that ran along

the south side of the valley. The limestone disappeared into the mist and rain above. "Which way?"

Venin shrugged.

"West it is."

They found a rock hollow about a hundred meters along the cliff face, with an overhang deep enough to give them respite from the rain. Quince pulled out her pulse pistol and used the laser sight to provide enough light to check for inhabitants. There were whipcats up in the mountains, and who knew what else. Luckily the hollow was empty, with a deep loam of leaves and dirt to provide them with some cushion.

"It'll work."

"Looks like heaven to me." Venin let her go in first.

She stooped and made her way under the protection of the cliff.

She was itching to return to Gaelan. The shift had many practical consequences, including the fact that OberCorp now shared a world with Errian and Gaelan, the skythane nations. The corporation was a clear and present danger to both, and the denizens of the Slander wouldn't be far behind. She had promised Rogan a shitload of pith, after all, that she'd failed to deliver.

They'd have to do something about all those things, and figure out how to shift the damned Oberon half of the world back to its own universe once the flare was over. Otherwise the misplaced landers would soon take over all Titania—Erro now—and the skythane nations would never be the same. It looked like she was going to be needed, after all.

Until the storm passed, they were stuck.

She opened her carry sack and pulled out some more of her rations, and Venin did the same. She was still hungry. It had to be late afternoon, maybe? She'd lost all track of time in the rush from the Mountain and during the storm.

She took a bite of the remainder of the bread and dried fruit they'd brought with them. The bread was soaked through, but it filled her stomach with nourishment, and for that she was grateful.

They watched the rain fall outside.

"I've never seen a storm come up so hard and fast." Venin chewed on some bread.

She offered him her canteen.

He shook his head and held up his own. "I brought something stronger."

"What is it?"

"Mothrot, my mother called it. It's a home-brew liquor, and it'll take the sting out of just about anything. Want some?"

"Yes, please." She had a lot of sting to lose. She took the flask and sipped it. It was about the vilest thing she had ever tasted. "Oh my gods, what's in this?" She stared at the canteen with disgust.

He laughed. "Wait for it."

"For what?" Then a warm feeling of contentment began to spread through her gut and out to her fingers and toes. "Oh man, that's nice." She looked at the canteen with new appreciation. "What's in it?"

Venin grinned. "You don't want to know. Splash a little on your wounds too. It'll kill just about anything."

She did. "Damn, that burns."

He winked at her in the dim light. "That's how you know it's working."

An errant breeze blew a splash of rainwater into the rock hollow. Quince laughed. "I imagine this storm is all the atmosphere on the split side of both worlds, forced out by the shift. Unintended consequences and all."

Venin nodded. "There's a whole mountain-sized pile of rubble out there that could fit under that header. What happened back there?"

Quince shook her head. "I don't know. Something new. I still don't understand how Morgan vanished. Or what he was."

"Maybe a sneach?"

Quince shook her head. "I thought so at first too. But now…. He had his own agenda. But he helped us when we needed him most." She could still see him, there between Xander and Jameson, pulling the worlds together. Then vanishing as if he'd never been.

"There are stranger things than we know in the world." Venin held up his flask. "More 'rot?"

"No thanks. That little bit did the trick, I think. Tell your mother thanks for me the next time you see her."

"Wish I could. She's been dead three years now."

Well, shit. "Sorry."

He squeezed her shoulder in response.

They sat in silence for a while. Quince pulled out a clean, damp shirt from her carry sack and used it with some rainwater on her legs, wiping off her wounds as best she could. They were shallow—mostly just scrapes, but she longed for some warm water and soap to truly clean them out. The mothrot would have to do, for now.

City life had made her soft. Time to harden herself up again.

3

MEMORY SHIFT

QUINCE WAS sure she'd heard *something*.

Venin was slouched over next to her, snoring. She frowned. Men were always falling asleep on her.

She touched his shoulder.

He startled awake. "What?"

"Voices," she whispered. *Jameson and Xander? Or Kadin?* She crept to the edge of their rock shelter, wincing as that put pressure on one of her scrapes. *There.* Coming from the west. From the direction of the Mountain.

She stood up outside the shelter and stared into the rain. It had to be close to nightfall—hard to tell in the dim light of the storm. It was quiet except for the wind and the *drip drip drip*.

One hand went to the hilt of her pulse rifle, which she'd tucked into her belt.

Nothing. She shook her head. *Must be effects of the mothrot.* She was about to crawl back into the shelter when a winged form appeared out of the rainfall.

"Alia!" Quince surged forward and hugged the woman. "Gods, it's good to see you. I was worried we'd lost you."

Alia squeezed her arm. "It was a near thing. But I brought company."

Quince looked over Alia's shoulder. Impossibly, Alix was there. Xander's ex. He shouldn't be. Couldn't be, and yet….

"Hello, Quince." Alix flashed her a smile. "Long time."

"Alix…." Then Quince's gaze strayed past him to the woman who stood with them. *Holy shit.* "Robyn…. Heaven and Erro," she managed, stumbling across the intervening space to squeeze Robyn tightly. "Oh my gods, it *is* you. You're alive!" She held Robyn out at arm's length, hardly daring to believe her eyes. She reached out to touch Robyn's face, afraid it was just a mirage. It was real enough, her skin not as soft as it had once been, but firm, real.

Robyn smiled weakly. "Hello, Quince."

Quince laughed and kissed Robyn hard, her heart bursting with joy.

Robyn's arms went around her waist, and they stayed like that for a long time. A warmth spread through her gut that was even better than mothrot. She wanted to dance, to scream, to fly.

"What in the three hells are you doing here?" Robyn asked when they separated. "I didn't expect to find you tonight." *Or ever*, her face said. It wasn't just the rain. There were tears in her eyes. Quince was sure of it. Not that Robyn would ever admit to such a thing.

"Someone had to get this thing done." She'd been sure Robyn was dead, that this moment would never come, and yet…. "What am *I* doing here? What are *you* doing here, and what happened to your wings?"

"That's a discussion for another time, when we have some privacy." She squeezed Quince's hand. "You have shelter?"

Quince nodded. "It's small."

"We'll make do. Alix here is looking for Davyn—Xander, I guess you call him now." Her brow furrowed. "Maybe you can tell us what happened here?"

"Of course." She shot a look at Xander's ex. His sudden appearance could be bad for Xander and Jameson. Very bad. Fate was laughing at her—she was sure of it. "Come on inside. Let's talk."

Quince sat next to Robyn, unsure what to say. So much time had passed since they'd seen one another. And Robyn's wings…. By the Split, had Dani done that to her?

Venin, Alix, and Alia fell in together, talking about the storm and the shift.

Robyn seemed ill at ease. Her normal air of command was gone, replaced by something else. Exhaustion? Defeat? She seemed deflated, like a wilting flower, her dark hair hanging around her head in damp clumps.

"I thought you were dead," Quince managed at last, reaching out to touch Robyn's face.

The queen looked at her, her green eyes meeting Quince's for a brief moment. Then she turned away. "I wished to be. Many times."

Quince nodded. "So did I. I almost got my wish, in Gaelan."

"The enemy?"

"It's over. Your son took back the city."

Robyn would have been so proud to see it.

Robyn's face lit up. "And Dani?"

"Imprisoned. I… what happened to you? Did she…?" She couldn't finish the sentence.

Alix squirmed uncomfortably next to her.

Quince glared at him. He knew, or at least had an idea, what had happened. What role had he played? She brushed that thought aside for the moment. *This* was more important.

She eased forward on her knees and took Robyn's hands in her own. "What did they do to you?"

For her answer, Robyn burst into tears, startling Quince. "Later," she whispered, wiping her eyes and re-asserting some of her former haughtiness. "When we're alone."

This was *not* the Queen of Gaelan she had known, but it *was* Robyn. She had been broken, and that broke Quince's heart. She threw her arms around her love, fingers interlocking behind Robyn's back.

"It's okay. You don't have to." She rocked Robyn, burying her face in Robyn's hair. "We're together again. That's all that matters right now."

Robyn squeezed her tightly. "I'm sorry. I'm such a mess."

Quince snorted. "Have you seen the rest of us?"

That earned her a soft laugh. "Yes, you've really let yourself go since the last time I saw you."

Quince laughed out loud this time. "You gave me quite the task, you know. What? You wanted me to show up with my shoes shined and my hair put up in a braid?"

"Of course not." Robyn was suddenly serious. "You did it, Quince."

"*We* did. Lyrin and Davyn did it."

"Where *is* Xander?" Alix's voice cut through the confined space.

Quince and Robyn shared a glance. Quince squeezed Robyn's hands and let her go. "They were with us, but we were separated by the storm. They can't be far."

"They?"

"Xander and Jameson." Quince waited for the inevitable questions, but Alix just nodded. Either he knew more than he was saying, or he was biding his time until he and Xander were reunited. "He let you go, Alix," she said, more sharply than she intended. "You left him, and he finally gave up waiting."

Alix's eyes narrowed. That had hit home.

"In any case, it's too dark to go out looking for them now. We can try at first light, if the storm has abated."

Robyn nodded. "Good idea." She leaned against Quince and rested her head on her shoulder.

It was cold, damp, and cramped in the rock hollow, but Quince was content.

Jameson kissed Xander again, his passion fading, but his ardor for the man still in full bloom. It was good to find time for the two of them in the middle of madness.

Xander was at rest, peaceful as he floated on the surface of the water, his eyes closed and his muscles slack. His black wings trailed off below into the glow of the pond. He looked more like an angel to Jameson than he had since the first time they'd met.

Images flashed in his head—this place, other people, other times. He squeezed his eyes shut, willing them to go away.

Reluctantly they subsided. Jameson stood to get out of the water, shaking his head as if to dry his hair.

Xander pulled him back down for one more kiss. "What's the hurry? I can still hear the storm roaring outside."

Jameson growled. "I'm hungry. Don't you ever get your fill?" He *should* have told Xander about the memories. He knew Xander saw them too, sometimes, but Jameson didn't want to ruin the moment.

"Apparently not." Xander let him go. "But I like to watch your backside, so I guess this is *some* kind of compensation."

"Pervert." Jameson smiled to himself. He was still sore from their exertions, but it was a good kind of sore.

He climbed up to the rock floor next to the pool, using one of the columns to steady himself. Something skittered across the edge of his vision. A bat? Or something like it? He looked after it, but it had vanished.

He went to pull his pants back on and wrinkled his nose. His clothes were filthy.

He opened his pack and grabbed a fresh set. He pulled on his underwear first, then laced up his shirt while Xander watched appreciatively. Getting dressed had been a hell of a lot easier before he'd gotten his wings. To compensate for his lack of skythane clothing, they'd raided the king's closet, and it had been a challenge to find anything without a fur lining or silver buttons. King Theron had been a big man too—thick in the middle, if his clothes were any indication. Frowning, Jameson cinched his belt tight to hold up his pants.

"It suits you." Xander smirked, getting out of the water and giving Jameson a full-on view of his beautiful body. He was muscled, but not overly so, his stomach firm and his body sleek. He was perfect.

Jameson felt a surge of love for Xander. He took full advantage of the unguarded moment, enjoying the show. Xander's well-defined abs and his lopsided grin were almost enough to entice Jameson to give it another go, but the memories were messing with his head, and he really was *hungry*.

"Let's eat." Xander pulled out his own change of clothes and sniffed them.

"A little damp?"

"Yeah. Mildew from all the rain. Still, it's better than the alternative."

He grinned. It was a shame Xander needed to wear anything at all. "Um, food. Yeah. Sounds good."

"We need to be ready to leave as soon as the storm lets up." Xander pulled on his pants. "That means keeping up our strength. Getting fed, getting some sleep…. I want to look for Quince and the others, and my people need me back home. Things will be confused in Gaelan after the shift."

My people. Jameson had his own people too, somewhere across the continent. "Things will be crazy in Oberon City too, I'd imagine."

Xander nodded. As he finished dressing, Jameson took a look around the cavern. It was maybe fifty meters across, and half that deep, and there were dark shadows at several places near the back, leading off to other caves or rooms.

He wondered how far this cavern system went. His new gift—or curse?—wasn't specific on details like that, though sometimes memories sprang wholly formed in his head.

Back home on Beta Tau, caverns could stretch on for hundreds of kilometers. The Great Rift system went on for at least three hundred and fifty, meaning it was theoretically possible to get from New Davos to Arctus without ever going aboveground.

He closed his eyes, trying to *remember* this place. The ability seemed to come and go randomly, but there had to be a way to summon it up at will. It had come to him when he needed it, but not of his own volition.

Again, there was a flickering, like something fluttering past in his peripheral vision. This time it slipped past on both sides. He looked around wildly, but there was nothing there. Not bats, then. He was losing his mind.

"What are you thinking about?" Xander asked. "You seem a little… distracted."

"You didn't see that?"

"What?"

"Never mind." He sighed. "It's probably just this place. I… *remember* it, but I don't."

"I know. Since that kiss, it's been hit and miss for me too."

Jameson nodded. *That kiss.* The one at the House of the Moon, when memories had flooded through him, through Xander, like a torrent. It had been the second time for him, but for Xander….

"Do you ever… see things that aren't there?"

"Sometimes. Quick images. Like brief overlays of the past on the present."

"Do you see them now?"

Xander looked around. "No, nothing now. You?"

"No. I…." He stopped. Something was moving at the edge of his vision. He looked around. The cavern seemed to shift, becoming brighter. There was a weird fluttering, as if a hundred dark wings were flapping just out of sight.

"Jameson, you okay?"

Everything went fuzzy for a moment, and his stomach clenched in protest. When he could see again, golden light flickered from candles placed all around the room. Where had they come from?

He turned back to Xander, but Elyra stood there instead, grinning at him, leaning forward, her breasts like two perfect moons under her vest. "You came. I've been waiting for hours." She pulled him close. He could smell her musky perfume, feel her long raven-black hair brush against his cheeks as their lips met….

The world shifted again.

The cavern was dark, lit by only the smallest blue illumination from the pool, and he was all alone. The deep, keening sadness of loss cut him with a sharp physical pain. In his left hand was a bloody dagger, and his right cupped his torn intestines.

Shift.

A massive furry creature with eight arms and long

teeth like a saber-toothed tiger rose up with a growl, and six eyes stared at him over its wrinkled snout. It swiped at him with a hairy paw tipped with sharp claws and he danced away....

Shift.

He was out of breath, gasping for air, and covered in sweat. He held on to one of the rock columns for support, staring over his shoulder. Surely they hadn't followed him all the way back here.

There were shouts behind him, in the main cavern, and he took a desperate gulp of air and pushed himself onward, toward the darkness at the back of the cavern....

Shift.

He/They/We were joined, feeling a sense of peace and harmony at their union. He/They/We fed on the nutrients in the water, joined body and mind, and mused about the world outside and the events of the last few days. Each part of He/They/We shared its experiences out in the world, the others they had encountered before returning with their knowledge to enrich the whole. The time of the Great Move was coming....

Shift.

Xander stared at Jameson, alarmed.

Jameson was frozen in place, his eyes twitching as if he were in REM sleep, but they were wide-open, jerking back and forth as if Jameson were watching a tridimensional. It was one of the creepiest things Xander had ever seen.

"Jameson, you okay?"

Jameson didn't respond. He seemed to be locked away inside himself.

Xander grabbed him by the shoulders and shook him. "Jameson! Talk to me." This was wrong. *Jameson* was wrong. "Tell me what's happening to you."

Jameson's eyes turned to look at him, but there was no recognition there. His mouth moved soundlessly.

Xander's gut twisted. "By the Split, Jameson, snap out of it!"

Jameson's eyes remained blank, but Xander read the fear in them. Jameson stood there, arms slack at his side, his mouth open and drooling.

Xander slapped Jameson hard across the cheek. "Come on, man, wake up!" It had no effect. There had to be a way to shock him out of this, whatever this was.

Shock. He had to find a way to give Jameson a shock. Xander knelt and rummaged through his carry sack, coming up with his pulse rifle. That should do it.

He turned down the intensity of the pulse as low as it would go, so it would send a good jolt through Jameson's system. Then he took Jameson's hand. "Hang on there, my prince."

Maybe he should test it first. If he caused Jameson any harm, it would kill him. He turned the weapon and fired it into the pool. The water bubbled but didn't boil. "Looks about right." Xander put the barrel against Jameson's palm and closed his eyes, one arm holding Jameson's, the other tucked behind his back.

He hesitated. What if the pulse hurt Jameson? It was set to stun, so it should be fine, but sometimes, if your heart was bad….

Xander had been pulsed as a kid, when his master Rogan had wanted some amusement. It hadn't killed him, though it had left his nerves jangling for days.

He had to do *something*, though. This couldn't be good for Jameson. "Here goes." He squeezed the trigger and the pulse passed through him, a not-unpleasant vibration, up and down his spine as he took the pulse second-hand.

Jameson collapsed, and Xander caught him, lowering him gently to the ground. He set the rifle down next to them. "Jameson, are you okay?"

Jameson's body was limp as a rag doll. Xander's heart thumped against his chest. *Oh God, I've killed my prince.*

Xander knelt next to Jameson and lifted his eyelid.

His eye looked… normal? Whatever that was, under the circumstances. At least he was still breathing.

Xander relaxed a little. It frightened him how much he'd come to care for this man who'd been a stranger just a few weeks before. It wasn't like him. Not since Alix. "You probably need to sleep it off," he said softly, and pulled Jameson's sleep sack from his carry sack and laid it out. With a bit of effort, he managed to get Jameson moved onto it. He didn't try to get Jameson undressed.

His eyes… like he'd been in the grip of a dream. Memories?

These memories were going to be a problem if they couldn't find a way to get them under control. He hated seeing Jameson helpless like this.

Xander finished dressing himself, took a deep draft of water from his canteen, and refilled it from the torrent still pouring down at the cave entrance. Then he lay down next to Jameson and put his head on his shoulder.

"You scared me there, little robin."

Jameson wasn't the only one who remembered *things*.

"Sorry, sparrow."

He sat up. "You're awake?"

Jameson was looking at him through slitted eyes. "Tired. Very tired."

"That's okay. You sleep. Time enough for talking tomorrow." Xander felt a huge sense of relief.

He needed to be in Gaelan. Things were surely *happening* out there, and he was their king. He should be with his people, but Jameson was clearly in no condition to travel, even if the storm let up. Tomorrow would come soon enough.

They needed Morgan here to heal poor Jameson. The thought flashed through his head, and Xander closed his eyes, feeling the familiar pain in his gut. The boy was gone. He'd given himself up to save their worlds. Xander still didn't know what that meant.

He leaned over and hugged Jameson. "Rest."

"Okay." Jameson snuggled into his sleep sack.

They fell asleep as the rain continued to pour down outside.

Jameson moaned. Every muscle in his body ached, like he'd been running a three-day marathon, or maybe had been used as a punching bag. He opened his eyes.

Xander was sitting next to him, staring down at him. "Welcome back to faeryland. How are you feeling?" Xander's face was framed by the cavern's blue light, his brow furrowed.

Jameson lay still for a moment, assessing his condition. "Like I got hit by a shuttle," he decided, growling. "What happened? Where are we?" He tried to sit up and regretted it immediately.

"You went into some kind of memory loop, I think…."

"Oh God." He remembered it now—one after another, and no way out. "It was like an oncoming train, memory upon memory. All of them about this place…." He grasped Xander's arm. "I don't think all those memories were human."

"You mean they were skythane?"

"No." He gave Xander a sharp look. "Skythane is still human. It was the weirdest thing." He tried to assemble his thoughts. His brain was still groggy. "I was someone else. *Something* else, maybe. I don't think I was male or female, not like we understand it."

"Not all humans fit neatly into one gender or another, you know."

Jameson nodded. Even that made him ache. "I know. I've worked with transgender, nonbinary, and gender fluid clients. That's not it. This place, this planet—it has a long history, going way back before we arrived here." He thought about the waygate and the strange forces that seemed to hide the House of the Stars.

"I'd agree with that."

Jameson tried to get up but failed miserably.

"Hey, don't push yourself too hard. You just went through a mental trauma."

Jameson nodded. He forged ahead with his thoughts, though, too excited by the idea to stop. "Who do you think split the world in two? Who created the keys? Who built the waygates? You know it wasn't the skythane."

Xander shook his head. "I don't think so either. We *do* have a long history here, but I don't think skythane ever possessed that kind of power or technological savvy."

Jameson pushed himself up slowly this time. As long as he didn't move too fast, the pain in his head stayed at a bearable level. He remembered. Xander had taken care of him, had made the memories stop.

Xander stooped to help him. "You sure you want to get up?"

"No. Sit. Just sit." Getting up sounded way too complex a challenge.

Xander helped him get himself propped up against one of the intricate rock columns that rimmed the pool they'd bathed in.

The blue light gave everything a monochrome appearance. Jameson looked at his hands as if they weren't his own. They looked cold and dead.

"It's been a hard couple weeks." Xander sank down next to him.

Jameson knew what Xander meant, but he was reluctant to talk any more about the memories. Or about Morgan. "Sorry. It's just—"

"I know." Xander let it go. "So we need to talk about what happens next."

"Yeah, probably." His stomach grumbled. "Is there anything to eat first? Might help me think straight." He was *starving*. The memory loop had really taken it out of him, and he'd been hungry to begin with.

Xander grinned. "Yeah, I think I have something." He pulled up his pack and rummaged through it. He came out with some bread and dried fruit and handed it over to Jameson.

"How'd you knock me out of the loop?" His memories—the real ones—were vague.

Xander blushed. "I, um, shot you with a pulse rifle?"

"Holy shit, seriously?" Jameson laughed despite himself. No wonder he hurt all over.

"In my defense, it was on low."

"Yeah, that's what every lover likes to hear. 'Sure I shot you, but I set it to stun.'"

Xander chuckled. "Well, it did the trick." He ate a mouthful of fruit, a thoughtful expression on his face. "So… we saved the world, apparently. What next?"

Jameson grinned. He munched on his bread, considering. The world had shifted under their feet, literally, and things would be in chaos out there. "We're heading back to Gaelan first, right?"

Xander nodded. "We need to secure the city. Ober-Corp may come after us soon."

Jameson had been thinking the same thing. "Shifting the world was just the beginning, I guess. We've been so focused on it." It had been all they had been working toward since they left Oberon City, even if he hadn't known it then. There were a lot of things he hadn't known then. He closed his eyes, thinking about all the moving pieces out there. "Now we have to keep everyone from killing each other until we can figure out what comes next." He looked up at Xander. "Easiest would be shifting the whole damned Oberon half back where it came from." He shook his head. Funny how he now considered moving an entire world *easy*.

"Won't work. The mountain is gone. Morgan is gone too, and the *rocthane* key is broken. Unless there's another way."

It was too much for Jameson to take on at the moment. "What do you think is happening in Errian?" He tried to picture Erro, the new world they found themselves on, where Oberon and Titania were one. "From what I can figure, it's not that far from Oberon City now. The Erriani are my people. I should be there—"

"Wow." Xander stared at him.

"What?"

"That's the first time I heard you describe them that way. Hell, it's the first time you've admitted to being skythane at all."

Jameson shrugged. "I guess it is. No use denying it now." He was what he was, and he was tired of fighting it. *Look where that got me.*

"Guess not."

They ate in silence, each lost in his own thoughts. The only sound was the muted howl of the wind and rain outside.

"Do you think anyone else died?" Jameson said at last into the empty space. The thought had been gnawing at him.

"When? With the shift?"

Jameson nodded. "I've been thinking about it. There must have been miners out on the Split. Damage in Oberon City. Maybe an incoming shuttle…."

"Probably. But look, people were dying already. That shuttle that crashed by the banks of the Theseus, *before* the shift—how many died then? And how many more would be dead now, if we hadn't—"

"I know, I know." It all made rational sense. Still, the

bodies of the dead weighed heavily on his conscience. Those people had no choice in the matter.

He was an adult, though, and a prince, no less. Or a king? He'd weighed the risks and made his own choice. He would have to learn to shoulder that too. "I never planned for this."

"Neither did I." Xander pulled him close, and Jameson rested against the man's warm chest, feeling his strong heartbeat. For a little bit longer, he could hide from his responsibilities in Xander's strong arms.

"So, what do we do now?" Jameson looked up at Xander. His lover was staring off into the distance.

"The best we can."

4

A FAMILIAR FACE

Sometime during the darkest part of the night, while the rain still fell outside their little shelter, Quince finally found a few moments alone with Robyn, or as alone as they could manage, tucked together in the deepest part of the rock crevice away from the downpour. The rain continued, though slower now, a steady purr of white noise.

It was pitch-black in their shelter. Quince couldn't even see the outline of Robyn's face, but her touch told her Robyn was there.

"I can't believe it," she whispered, aware the others had fallen into an exhausted sleep. She was tired herself, but she'd waited twenty-five years for this moment. "You're *really* here."

"Yes," Robyn whispered, her voice thinner than Quince remembered. "I didn't know if you would ever return. I had to keep faith."

Quince couldn't see it, but she was sure Robyn was making the symbol of the two gods, tapping her right fist against her heart twice. She pulled the queen's slender form against hers, her wings encompassing the two of them. She found the place where Robyn's wings had attached to her back, the rough, wounded skin there a reminder of the pain Robyn had gone through. Was likely still going through.

Robyn started to pull away from her touch.

"Hey, it's okay. It's just me," Quince whispered, pulling her close again.

"I'm ugly and broken now." Robyn took a deep breath. "She stole my wings, Quince. She made me into this."

Quince shook her head. "You're not ugly to me." She took Robyn's head gently in her hands and kissed her, and Robyn responded, drinking her up like a woman too long without water.

Quince let her have her fill, pouring love and solace through the bond they shared. It felt so *good* to be connected once again. To be a part of *we*. To close the long, lonely Oberon chapter of her life and leave it behind.

At last Robyn came up for air. "Oh gods, I missed you, Quince."

"I know. But we did what we had to." If not for that sacrifice…. Quince shuddered to think of what would have happened to them all. "We will find Davyn. Find them both, after the storm." She paused, debating whether to bring up Morgan. His face floated before her in the darkness, calling to her. "Robyn, I have to tell you something."

Robyn tensed up in her arms. "What? Is there someone else?"

"No, nothing like that. Well, something like that. There was a boy—"

"A boy? Well, that's unexpected." Some of her haughty queenly tones had returned.

Quince laughed, covering her mouth quickly so as not to wake the others. She took Robyn's little joke as a good sign. "His name was Morgan. I don't know what he was. But without him, things would have gone badly."

"Morgan?"

Quince nodded. "Xander… Davyn found him in a farmhouse on Oberon, but he was much more than he seemed…." She launched into the tale, although she conveniently omitted the whole I-almost-killed-the-boy part. She was still ashamed of her mistake.

Robyn listened, interjecting thoughtful questions here and there, as the rainfall outside gradually tapered off.

When Quince was done, Robyn was silent for a long time.

"What do you think?" Quince asked.

"You thought he was a sneach?"

"Maybe. At first. Now, I don't know. I saw him, Robyn. Twice, in dreams."

"When?"

"Today."

"Maybe it's just your emotions, working themselves out—"

"You were there too. In the dream. I had these visions before you found me again, and you were there. You had these beautiful, iridescent wings."

"Then you know it was false." The bitterness crept into her voice again.

Quince sighed. "I'm so sorry about what she did to you. But he needs me. I have to go after him."

Robyn put a hand on Quince's face. "That's what I love about you. Always so eager to chase off after the helpless, to charge into danger." She kissed Quince again, her lips lingering for a moment. "We can talk about it some more tomorrow, my love. We both need some sleep."

"All right. In the morning."

Robyn curled up, her head on Quince's chest, and Quince wrapped her wings around them both in the darkness to keep them warm.

Tomorrow.

Morgan's face floated in the darkness before her, mouthing her name.

XANDER STARED out into the early morning sky. The rain had finally ended, leaving behind a muddy, sodden mess of downed trees and other debris. The clouds seemed to be on their way to breaking up.

"You sure you're ready?" he asked over his shoulder.

"I'll be all right." Jameson was lacing up his shirt. Xander turned and leaned against the cavern wall to enjoy the show.

The golden wings suited Jameson. He wasn't muscle-bound, just lithe and beautiful, his red hair adding fire to the mix.

"What are you looking at?" Jameson asked, sounding annoyed.

"Just appreciating the view."

"I'm a mess. I can't wait to get back to Gaelan and get a bath."

Jameson had really taken to the whole water bath

thing. Xander had to admit, they were much more satisfying than ionic showers. But there were a lot more things waiting for them there than just getting clean—issues that urgently needed their attention.

They'd search for Quince and the others first. He hoped they'd all made it to safety.

Jameson finished getting dressed and gave him a quick peck on the cheek. "Ready if you are."

Xander nodded. One of the statues had collapsed across the cavern entrance. The featureless head stared up at him as he climbed over the rubble. He wondered what its face had looked like, and who or what had carved it. He breathed in the air. It was fresh and clean. The clouds *were* breaking up, and Titania's red sun was starting to peek through.

That begged the question. With the world back together again, Quince had told them they were now on Erro, but where had that name come from? Had the planet had another name of its own long ago, before it had been split, given to it by whatever had lived here then?

Jameson joined him, whistling at the sight below. The valley was half-full of muddy water, slowly draining out through a massive logjam. "Gaelan must be in trouble…."

Xander nodded. "Much of the city is built up

against the cliffs, and the House of the Moon is strong and on high ground. But there *will* be flooding. We should go."

He launched himself into the sky and Jameson followed, climbing an updraft behind him. From above, the destruction was even more evident. No one had lived there, but he despaired of finding Quince and the others under all that debris. If they were still alive.

They had to be. He refused to think otherwise. They hadn't come this far to lose her now. They would need her knowledge and her iron will in the days to come, while they figured out what to do next.

Oberon City lay in wait for them, the Slander and OberCorp like twin spiders who would eventually come to hunt the skythane, to take control of both Errian and Gaelan. The occupation of Gaelan had shown that. They were likely momentarily stunned by the shift, but that wouldn't incapacitate them for long.

Someone there already knew about Titania—that was evident from the occupation force. He had to get home and prepare Gaelan to fight once again.

He followed an updraft, circling around a few more times, hoping to see some sign of their friends. "Maybe they've already started home." Funny, when had he begun to think of Gaelan as home?

"Maybe so. But I would have thought they'd be out

searching for us too…. Xander, look!" Jameson pointed at a spot along the cliff side not far from the cavern entrance, which was now just a patch of black far below.

There was movement and a flash of color. "I see it." He fell into a dive, the wind whistling past his wings, tucked against his back. Quince. It had to be Quince. *Please let it be Quince.*

He saw her white wings before he could see her face.

He spread his own wings to slow his fall and landed right in front of her, ignoring the others with her to pull Quince into his embrace. "You're alive!"

"A little scratched up," she said gruffly. "But I'll live."

Jameson alighted behind him and ran forward to hug her too. "Don't ever do that to me again." He held her for a long moment and then looked around. "Where's Kadin?"

Quince shrugged, frowning. "We lost him in the storm."

Xander looked at the mass of mud and fallen trees scattered across the valley. "Maybe he headed back to Gaelan," he said doubtfully.

"Perhaps." Quince laid a hand on his arm. "Xander…."

Xander turned to look at the others who were with her and froze.

"We have some unexpected company."

"Alix." The man was just as Xander remembered him, as he had been on the tri-dee, all those thousands of times he'd watched that last video. "Holy crap, Alix!" He embraced the man who'd been his lover, his savior, and hugged him hard, feeling himself tear up.

Alix smelled of dirt and sweat, his clothes *crunching* under Xander's embrace, but he was still one of the sweetest things Xander had ever seen. And yet…. "What the hell, Alix?" he asked as they separated. "How could you leave me all alone like that, without another word after that stupid transmission?"

Alix smiled that lopsided grin he only used with Xander. "I had no choice. I was called up and sworn to secrecy. But I'm here now."

Xander refused to let Alix charm his way through this one. "We'll talk about it later." He got a good look at him. "You're a mess. There's a place nearby where we can get you all cleaned up."

Someone cleared their throat.

Xander turned to find Jameson glaring at him. "Right. Sorry. Alix, this is Jameson. Jameson's my…. We're together now." *Split it, I'm an idiot.*

Jameson came up next to him and put his arm around Xander's shoulder.

Someone was jealous. *But holy shit. Alix.* Alix, who he'd spent a year letting go. Alix, who was supposed to be dead. Dani had told him the truth in the end, after all. Or part of it.

Alix extended his hand. "Good to meet you, Jameson." His narrowed eyes said otherwise.

This was going to be trouble. Xander could smell it.

"Davyn."

It took him a minute to realize that was *him. Who would call me that?* Xander turned to find a woman staring at him. A lander woman. She looked familiar. *Who are you?* He knew that face.

She strode forward, regal as a queen, and in that moment he *knew* her.

A memory struck him. His own, this time.

His mother, pulling him back from the rail before he'd had wings. Cradling him in her arms in the House of the Stars, the day she let him go.

His mother, here and now, her arms around him, hugging him fiercely.

He hugged her, and felt the rough skin and scabbed nubs where her wings had been.

She winced at the touch.

"You're my mother—"

"Yes. Shhh, my little sparrow." Her hand rested lightly behind his head, and she held him against her warm shoulder. "You're home."

Despite himself, he began to cry.

. . .

JAMESON STOOD by in stunned amazement as Xander ran to hug Alix.

Alix, the man who was supposed to be dead. Where the hell had he come from? Why was he there? Jameson's stomach twisted in knots.

Alix had been, at the very least, an accomplice in the subjugation of Gaelan. He'd broken Xander's heart, something Jameson had found even harder to forgive. The man had left Xander all alone with no word for a year. *Like I left Jessa?*

And yet, Xander didn't seem to care.

"Ahem."

Xander introduced them. At least he blushed at his oversight.

The man's hand was callused, his grip firm, and the glare he gave Jameson sent a shiver down his spine. He did not want this one as his enemy. Alix could have been a space marine, thick as a truck, his red hair cropped close in marine style.

He looked like he knew where to bury the bodies so they'd never be found.

Funny how Xander had never mentioned Alix was a redhead too.

Quince slipped up next to him. "Don't worry, Jameson. Xander's meant for you, not him," she whispered in his ear, squeezing his arm encouragingly.

I hope so.

The next shock hit him harder than he would have imagined.

"Davyn."

"Who is that?" he asked Quince, but he thought he already knew. That brow, those eyes, her haughty demeanor….

"That's Robyn. She, Alix, and Alia found us last night. Robyn and Alix escaped from one of the labor camps on the Split."

His feelings were decidedly mixed at the reunion. Just like that, Xander had his ex and his mother, two people who still apparently cared for him more than anyone else in the world.

Jameson was all alone. His own parents weren't really his, and anyhow they were light-years from here. His own mother, Andra, was gone. He closed his eyes, visualizing that moment again, when Danner Black's knife had slashed through her neck.

He could still see it in his head, as fresh as if he'd witnessed it himself the day before. He turned away, leaving Xander to his reunion.

He was happy for Xander. Really, he was. They'd feared Robyn was dead, and here she was, although without her wings. There was a story there, a painful one.

She was alive, though. That was the important part. Jameson was happy for his love, and yet, he'd never see his own mother again.

Quince must have seen the flicker of pain on his face.

"I know, little robin, I know."

"Where's Kadin?" he asked her.

"No one knows."

"Who did this to you?" Xander's angry voice rose above Jameson's pain and roused him from his reverie. Robyn had turned around and pulled down her shirt. Where her wings had been, there were two ragged stumps covered in scabs.

"It's not important right now…."

"Was it Dani?" he demanded, his hands in fists at his side.

She looked away, her eyes downcast. "Yes. She had it done. It's called the *Cattorah*, a ritual punishment we used to practice for rapists and murderers."

"I'll kill her. I'll fucking kill her." Xander looked like he was about to hit someone.

Jameson took one of his hands. "We'll deal with her." He gently turned Xander's face toward his. "She *will* get what she deserves, but right now we have to get back to Gaelan." He couldn't quite bring himself to call it home. It was Xander's home, but he hadn't yet figured out if it was his.

Xander looked angry, confused. "She tried to kill Quince. She wanted to hurt you, too, and she did… this to my mother." He pointed at Robyn, who seemed embarrassed, pulling her shirt up to cover her wounds.

Jameson tried to imagine what it would be like to lose his wings—the keys to flight that had opened the door to the sky for him. Worse, to have them savagely cut off his back. He shivered.

"We'll make Dani pay for this," he promised again, pulling Xander close.

Xander hugged him back, but he was tense, drawn tight like a bowstring.

Over his shoulder, Jameson caught Alix staring at them. The man's face darkened, and he looked away.

Oh yes. He was going to be trouble.

5

———

RETURN

Jessa managed to flag down a private taxi drone from the hotel. She was the only guest at the Galaxion, and the staff seemed really nervous.

As the drone lifted off the rooftop of the hotel, crowds of people gathered in the streets below. The shouts reached her, even at fourteen stories above the ground. She keyed in to local news coverage on the drone's screen. The signal was spotty at best, but it showed news footage of the crowds, many carrying signs that said The End is Near and OberCorp, Where Are You?

The drone dropped Jessa off in front of the Ober-Corp HQ. She was surprised her cred was still good there. Apparently the local economy, also known as

OberCorp, was proceeding as though nothing strange were happening.

Her time as a reporter for her local tri-dee station, and her more recent anchor experience, stood her in good stride there. She knew where to go to ferret out information, and she had a friendly face that people tended to trust implicitly.

She'd spent the last night at the bars looking for information, stun whip at her side, and had only had to use it four times. Not bad on a backwater world like this.

People were talking. The world had changed. She'd seen it herself in the bumpy shuttle ride down. Wherever the missing half of the planet had been for all these years, it was back now.

There were sightings of strange birds along the Gildensea. Small quakes shook the city at odd intervals, and the sun was red.

Those who had survived the Split had blown into town with tales about a last-minute warning and the huge storm that had come up from nothing.

Jessa had plugged into the local grid to look for any trace of Jamie, using the skills she'd learned as a reporter, ferreting out the news that others wanted to hide.

There was a public log of Jamie's arrival, and then nothing. Wherever you went, you left a trace in the grid.

It was nearly impossible not to. Not unless you were really good at it, which Jamie was not. He was great at being a psych, but a miserable failure at tech arts.

Which meant someone else had erased his tracks.

All roads led to OberCorp.

The structure was massive—as tall as the city's fabled arcos, but set apart in a quarter of its own, surrounded by a lake like a protective moat. The building shone with plas and steel, glimmering in the sunlight.

The protesters had been kept outside the moat, shouting across the water.

She took a deep breath, running her hands through her newly shortened hair. She'd managed to pick up a pair of camspecs and had paired them to her AI, Jessica. A deft insertion of her credentials into the grid and she was a Galactic News Service reporter, there on the heels of a hot story.

What that story was, she hadn't yet decided. It would come to her.

She put on her confident face and entered the doors, ready to find her man.

XANDER AND JAMESON held each other tightly.

Alix looked away.

Jealousy stabbed deep in the pit of his stomach,

seeing Xander with this other man, followed by a nauseating wave of guilt. After all, he'd been the one who'd decided to leave, and he'd broken Xander's heart.

Xander had chosen someone else. It was really that simple. So why couldn't his heart accept it?

"We should get moving," he said gruffly, looking at Quince. "OberCorp will figure out what happened soon enough, and then you'll see an invasion of both Errian and Gaelan with ten times the firepower as the last time."

Quince nodded. "He's right. We need to get back to Gaelan, sooner rather than later. Hopefully the storm will be causing problems for the landers too, but we can't count on it."

Xander sighed. "No rest for the weary, right?"

"'Fraid not." Quince clapped him on the shoulder.

"Alix and Robyn can't fly." Jameson looked directly at him. "Maybe we should leave them behind, send someone back for them later?"

"Absolutely not," Quince and Robyn said in unison.

Alix smiled. "We won't have to. Dani stashed some extra bi-wings nearby, in case of need."

"Bi-wings?" Xander looked at Robyn, who nodded.

"The landers used them sometimes, when patrolling Gaelan with their pulse rifles."

Alix nodded. "She had them brought through the same tunnel we used to get here."

"Tunnel?"

"OberCorp found a way in from Oberon to Titania that didn't require a waygate. There's… well, there was a tunnel in the Split that connected the worlds."

"That explains a lot." Xander rubbed his chin. "Where are these bi-wings?"

"Up here a little farther. There are caverns under these cliffs—"

"We know," Jameson said sharply. "I found one of them."

"Good." The man clearly didn't like him, but Alix could live with that.

"Let's not fight amongst ourselves." Xander glared at Jameson. "You can clean up there before we move on."

Xander seemed to have matured a lot since Alix had left him. Alix looked at Jameson with newfound respect. Maybe he had been a good influence on Xander.

Alix sighed. He'd been gone so long. It wasn't Xander's fault he had fallen for Jameson. "Let's go, then." He was getting impatient. If he was going to make his case to Xander, he had to get him alone, and that wasn't going to happen among that motley group out there in the wilderness. Alix turned to lead them along the cliff face toward the cave where the bi-wings had been stashed.

He hoped they were still there. If not, he might yet get stuck cooling his heels while Jameson and Xander flew off into the sunset.

The cavern entrance was only a few hundred meters away. The day was already warming, the sun coming out to start drying the ruined valley. As he walked, he breathed in the morning air. It was thick and humid, but still cool.

It was a shame this beautiful valley had been all but destroyed, but he feared it wouldn't be the last place to see such devastation.

They approached the cavern entrance. One of the old statues had fallen, but the other still stood as a marker on the right side of the opening.

"They're in there?" Xander asked with a frown.

"They were."

Alix followed Xander over the pile of debris and caught a whiff of his scent and struggled to ignore the effect it had on him.

He caught both Quince and Jameson staring at him speculatively.

Damned busybodies. Frowning, he ducked into the cavern.

The caverns were as beautiful as he remembered

them, with ponds lit by a strange eldritch blue glow. They'd camped out there the first night after they'd come through the tunnel, bathing in those warm ponds. A couple of the guys had gone off to do what military men will do on a long campaign, but Alix had found a semiprivate corner to retreat to, sick with the knowledge that he'd left Xander behind with no explanation.

He shook his head clear.

"They were back here." Alix led the group to a semi-hidden passage that connected to a smaller cavern. He turned sideways to slip through the rift and emerged into a space a third the size of the main cavern. This space had one pool, which lit the sculpted walls, making them look like melted blue wax.

Tucked against the back wall were five bi-wing packs. "Bingo."

The others filed in behind him.

He picked up one of the packs, looking it over. It was shaped like an oversized backpack, with a hard plas shell. It was superlight and powered by amalite. Wouldn't be much more of that mined, he reckoned, with the Split… unsplit.

"They look like they're in good enough shape."

Xander picked one up. "These are military issue."

Alix nodded. "Dani had them shipped in from

Traxon. Useful on lighter gravity worlds and moons." He handed one to Robyn.

"How does it work?" Robyn was looking at hers like it was a snake.

"I'll show you." He brushed past Xander, and his arm tingled in reaction. He clamped down on his emotions hard.

Jameson, whoever he was, was skythane, like Xander. They had things in common that Alix couldn't hope to match.

Alix had to believe that Xander still loved him, though, somewhere deep down inside. He had to hope there was a way back into Xander's heart.

"Let's get you all cleaned up first," Xander said as they reentered the main cabin. "At least get those wounds cleaned out." He took Alix's hand and guided him to one of the ponds. "Jameson, want to help Quince?"

Jameson grumbled something that might have been a yes. Or maybe a fuck-you.

Alix grinned. He let Xander pull off his boots and socks. Then he stood and slipped off his pants, wincing as they stuck to the wound on the back of his left leg.

He noticed Jameson staring from the other end of the pond, where he was cleaning off Quince's legs.

"I'm not going commando, if that's what you're worried about." Although his underwear *could* use cleaning….

"Don't even think about it," Xander hissed, and guided him to sit on the edge of the pond. He pulled a rag out of his carry sack and waded in barefoot to stand in front of Alix. He knelt, looking at the wound. "This is gonna hurt."

"I can take… fuuuuuuuuuuuuck!" Fire blazed in his leg as Xander cleaned out the wound with fresh water. Blood and mud ran into the pond, to be carried away on the current.

Xander seemed to be enjoying it. "Better a little pain now than an infection later." He pushed the cloth into the wound harder than Alix thought was strictly necessary.

Payback was a bitch.

When his legs were clean, Xander dried the wound and then bound it with a clean shirt. It wasn't too deep, thank the Split, but having it bound would help keep it protected. "Thanks." He wanted to kiss Xander so badly it hurt.

THEIR LEGS WRAPPED TOGETHER, *the sheet laid over them as they lay on their bed. Alix wanted to live in Xander's eyes, wanted to stay there forever, the rest of the world be damned.*

ALIX LOOKED AWAY. If Xander noticed, he gave no sign.

Instead, he asked the question that had been burning inside him since this whole soggy trek had begun. Had it really been just the day before? "What happened out there?"

"You mean the storm?" Xander glanced out at the sunshine that now poured into the cave.

"The storm. And the whole when-worlds-collide thing." He'd never believed the skythane superstitions about Oberon and Titania, but it looked like he'd been the fool.

Jameson sat down next to Xander. "The place where Oberon used to be is a solar flare hellhole at the moment." He put his arm around Xander's shoulder possessively.

"If we hadn't shifted Oberon here—" Xander gestured around at the cavern and Titania in general, "—most everyone and everything on the Oberon side would now be dead."

Alix snorted. "Guess you made the right choice." He had more questions, but he decided to bide his time.

Maybe he could corner Quince later. Jameson was shooting daggers at him with his eyes.

After they tended to everyone's wounds and cleaned up, Alix led them outside and then eastward along the base of the cliff, retracing his steps from the year before.

The air was starting to smell with the stench of decay, as the water drained away from the valley. It left behind a wet, desolate moonscape.

The contours of the valley, at least their end of it, were unchanged, thank the Split.

Quince came up to walk next to him as they climbed the trail cut into the bluff. "I wondered what had become of you," she said after a few moments.

"I was called up. I wish I could have stayed." That was mostly true.

"Maybe so. You should have at least told him."

Alix shook his head. "I couldn't. The company—"

"That's horseshit, and you know it."

Quince was right. He could have said *something*. Should have, in fact. "I… I thought a clean break was best. Maybe I was wrong. But I had no idea when I would be coming home. He would have come after me."

"He did anyway. He looked for you for weeks. Did you know that?" She side-eyed him.

"No, I didn't." He imagined Xander in the Outland, visiting their old campsites, frantic with worry.

"You just about broke him." Quince glanced over her shoulder at Jameson and Xander. "They're happy, you know."

"I don't believe it." He *couldn't* believe it. Just being in the same place with Xander again made him weak in the knees. Xander had *needed* him. He'd been the knight in shining armor, riding in to rescue him from Rogan, but the truth was that he *needed* Xander to need him. It gave him a purpose in life.

"Some friendly advice. Let him go. It took a hell of a lot to get them together in the first place…."

He stared at her. "A lot of what?"

"Nothing. Just time."

He frowned. There was more she wasn't telling him. "I still love him, Quince."

"I know." She put a hand on his shoulder. "If you truly do, let him be happy. Think about it." She squeezed his shoulder and then dropped back to talk to Robyn.

She was hiding something. He would figure out what it was, one way or another.

Quince growled under her breath as Alix walked away. She didn't trust him.

It wasn't just that he'd been part of the OberCorp

invading force in Gaelan. If Robyn had forgiven him for that, if it had truly been against his will… well, she supposed she could move past it too.

There was something else there.

Something about the way he'd looked at her when she'd mentioned how hard it had been to get Xander and Jameson together. It had been a slip of the tongue. She'd let herself be careless. They could never be allowed to find out about the pith she'd dosed them with.

She'd done it out of necessity. There simply hadn't been time for nature to take its course. They needed to be *connected*. In love. That much the *nimfeach* had told her, but not why.

Alix was suspicious of her, though, and she'd almost tipped her hand.

Quince fell back to walk with Robyn. She reached out to touch Robyn's cheek. "I still can't believe you're here," she said softly.

Robyn touched Quince's white wings. "Sometimes I wish they had just killed me."

Quince absorbed that as they climbed up a steep path cut into the cliff face. The limestone was fissured here and there, little redferns growing out of the cracks. Above, the sky was clearing as the remnants of the storm fled to the east.

"I'm glad they didn't," she said at last, and Robyn

looked at her with sad eyes. "I'm glad you came back to me."

Robyn squeezed her hand but didn't reply.

"I almost died too. When we fought to take back Gaelan. I was ready to go… but only because I thought it meant I would be with you again." She would have been all alone in death.

"Maybe we both would have been better off if we had died."

Quince stifled a retort. This was not the woman she remembered. Whatever had been done to her had wounded her more deeply than just the flesh.

The path led up the cliffside to a wide flat space that extended back a hundred meters to the foothills. The trees there had suffered less damage than their counterparts down in the valley, but it would be a long time before this region recovered from that terrible storm.

Alix was strapping on his bi-wing. It was a hybrid mechanism, with strong, flexible, extendable wings made of plas and biomatter, and an amalite core that, when unshielded, provided uplift as well as power for thrust. The wings, when extended, shimmered iridescently in the red sunlight, reminding Quince of insect wings… maybe a dragonfly's. They were like the wings in her dream.

"We should at least try to find Kadin," she told Xander.

He nodded. "We can fly over the valley and see if there's any sign of him."

"Did you say Kadin?" Robyn's eyes blazed.

"Yes. He was here with us when the Mountain fell." Quince frowned. "Why?"

Robyn *growled*. "Kadin was the one who cut off my wings."

"What?" Now Xander was growling. *Like mother, like son.* "That son of a bitch."

"All the more reason to get back to Gaelan with all possible haste." Quince felt sick to her stomach. All that time he'd been with them, working to subvert their cause.

"When I get my hands on him…."

"Keep it together, Xander. Let's just get back to Gaelan and find him." Quince returned to Robyn's side and helped her strap the wings to her arms like she'd watched Alix do with his.

When both had their bi-wings on, Alix gave a demonstration. "It's like being a superhero." He gave them a slight grin. He touched a button on the shoulder strap and lifted off the ground. "The amalite helps take the edge off the gravity here. Then you just use them like normal wings. Hitting the button again shields the amalite core and brings you down. If you get in trouble, the pull cord on your left shoulder, here"—he indicated the orange cord—"opens the parachute. Got it?"

Robyn was shaking.

"What is it?" Quince had never seen her lover like this. Robyn had always been a queen, sure of herself, defined by her power, her bearing.

"I'm not ready." She tried to pull the straps off her left arm. "It's too hard. I can't—"

"You can. Robyn, you have to. I'm not leaving you behind again." Quince cupped Robyn's face. "*They* did this to you. I can't take that away—the pain, the loss. But you are more than your wings. You always were." She hugged Robyn, cupping the stumps where her wings used to be. "You're still Robyn to me. The woman I fell in love with. I know this feels weird, alien. Frightening, even. But you can fly again this way. We can fly together. And I'll be right with you." She kissed Robyn's forehead, like she was comforting a child.

"Is she okay?"

Quince looked up to see Xander and Jameson at their side, both looking worried. "She will be." To Robyn, she said, "We can wait a few minutes…."

"No. I'm stronger than this." Robyn straightened her spine, and for a moment she was the woman Quince had known before, tall, strong, regal, her wings flared behind her. "Come on, Quince. Let's show him how the skythane fly." She tapped the button to activate the amalite core, and then leapt off the cliff, catching the wind and soaring up above the top of the cliffs.

Quince followed, the wind feeling wonderful through the feathers of her wings.

JAMESON PUT on his game face, the one he used to use with patients when they'd told him something particularly surprising or upsetting. *Never let them see you sweat.*

He was sweating profusely, though, on the inside.

They'd found no sign of Kadin, but that wasn't what was bothering him.

It was the memories. They'd never really gone away, even when Xander had shocked them into submission with the pulse rifle. They were a constant distraction, overlying the rest of the world like a thin gray film.

Now they fluttered around him like crows, or maybe shadows of crows, a host of them haunting his flight.

He didn't dare look directly at them. When he had done so as they climbed the cliff face, he'd been momentarily stunned as one of them unfolded itself in his head, stopping him in his tracks as he remembered this place, some eons before, through the eyes of someone or something other than himself.

Xander had bumped into him and knocked him out of it.

Jameson made an excuse about being tired—which he was—but ever since, he'd been careful not to engage with the memories again.

He couldn't keep this up forever.

Xander flew at his side, casting worried looks back at Quince and his mother from time to time. Ahead of them, Venin, Alia, and Alix had taken the lead.

"Do you see… anything weird?" Jameson asked Xander at last.

"Like what?"

"Memories."

Xander shook his head. "Not in a while, no. Why? Do you?"

Jameson wanted to tell him. Wanted to share the fear he had, the nagging feeling that something wasn't right in his head. But Alix was there now. What if Xander still loved him? Wanted to go back to him? Alix was strong and brave and beautiful. What if Jameson was too broken to keep his Gaelani prince's interest?

He couldn't voice it, not even to himself.

"No. I'm okay."

Xander smiled. "We'll figure this whole memory thing out. I promise."

Something dark flitted past Jameson's field of vision. He closed his eyes until it passed.

"You sure you're okay?"

Jameson nodded. "I'm fine." He could hold it together for a little while longer.

XANDER WAS DISTURBED by the level of devastation evident in the winding river valley below. The storm-caused flooding had wiped out the forest downstream from the Mountain, leaving a trail of mud and destruction like a vast brown scar on the land.

As they flew on, the cloud cover broke up, blades of sunshine illuminating the damage.

Almost as worrisome was the fact that Jameson was lying to him.

Xander could see the distress his lover was in. Was it the memories? Or agony over what had happened to Morgan and the people who had likely died when the world had shifted? Or Alix?

Maybe all three.

As if on cue, Alix turned and flashed him a smile.

Xander flushed.

He wasn't immune to the man's charms. They had a history, much longer than what he and Jameson shared.

And much shorter, in another way. Or shallower?

Xander still wasn't sure he bought this whole soul-mates thing. World shifting notwithstanding. He cared for Jameson. Hell, he probably even loved him. But they'd been thrown into this cauldron together, and it was hard to see what was real and what was simply shared hardship and experience.

Alix had *saved* him.

Xander touched his head, where the explosive charge that had defined his life for six years had finally been removed when Alix came for him.

Alix, whom Xander had finally written off after a painful year of not knowing.

Maybe Jameson was right to be worried.

When they reached Gaelan, he'd have to talk with both of them. He was with Jameson now. Surely Alix would understand.

As if all that wasn't enough, his mother was back from the dead too. Xander still wasn't sure how to deal with that fact, either. He'd been without one for so many years. Quince had filled the role, but she was more like a dear aunt.

Not that he'd ever tell her that. He'd get his fingers bitten off.

As the afternoon waned, they rounded the last bend in the winding course through the mountains, bringing Gaelan into view. What was left of the city, in any case.

Xander's mouth fell open as he took in the extent of the destruction. *Oh my God.*

The valley was awash in brown water, a mirror to the valley they'd left behind that morning. The winding course of the Orn was obscured by water and debris.

The aeries had fallen, every last one. Only the tower on Founder's Hill and the House of the Moon—the black castle that perched above the valley on its western edge—was untouched.

Jameson's mouth made a little O as they surveyed the scene. "Xander, I'm so sorry."

Xander reached out and squeezed his hand.

Skythane were everywhere, salvaging what they could, working in an organized fashion from the walls of the House of the Moon.

Xander and his companions alighted on the castle wall one after another. "Excuse me," he called to one of the skythane who had just landed with a bundle over her shoulder, a woman with dark eyes and wings.

The woman turned to see who called her and immediately dropped to her knees. "My lord." She dared a glance up at him. "You've returned." Then she saw Robyn and did a double take. "My lady?"

"This is no time for formality." Xander helped her up. "What's your name?"

"Teanna."

"Teanna—the flooding… it looks like it was bad."

She nodded. "There was a great wall of water that came down the Orn. It came in the late morning, thank the Gods, or there would have been more deaths…."

"More? How many were killed?"

"Maybe fifty?"

Xander swore. *This* was the price of his actions. A handful dead so thousands more could survive. This was the price his people paid to save the landers.

He had to remind himself that everyone would have died, skythane and lander, if he'd done nothing.

It might have been worth it.

"Who is in charge of the recovery?"

Teanna pointed to the courtyard of the castle. "Her name's Mylin, sir."

Mylin? "Thank you, Teanna. I am so sorry I wasn't here when it happened."

She grabbed his arm. "They say you left to save the world. Did you?"

Xander took a deep breath and sighed. "It's too soon to tell." He squeezed her arm and leapt over the wall to descend into the courtyard.

Mylin turned toward him as soon as he landed. "Xanderrrrrrr!" she called, and threw herself into his arms.

He loved that she didn't stand on formality with

him. "Hey there." He held her out at arm's length. "How did you end up in charge of all this?" Xander looked around the courtyard in wonder. In one corner, a crew was busy washing off salvaged materials. In another, foodstuffs were being stacked. In a third, a makeshift shower had been set up. In the fourth….

His stomach twisted, and he turned away. The last corner was filled with shapes wrapped in sheets and curtains and other assorted cloths.

"I… I don't know. It needed to be done."

He took her gently by the shoulders. "I am so proud of you," Xander said softly. He *should* have been there. He should have prevented this from befalling his people, but he was blessed with people like *this* in his absence. "I've brought some friends. Put us to work."

She nodded. "I could use some help with food collection. Most of the fields were destroyed, so I've got teams scouring what's left and looking for wild sources as well."

"The castle stores should be opened as well."

She blushed. "Already done. Kadin opened them, before he left with the prisoner—"

"Kadin?" He'd hoped the man was dead, buried under the muck and rubble of the Mountain. He'd run back here instead.

"Yes… he came back yesterday. He said your mission was a success, and that you'd asked him to take that woman to you...." She tapered off. "The OberCorp prisoners escaped too, last night. We would have gone after them, but this... seemed more important."

He swore. "You made the right choice." Always one step ahead of them.

Robyn had come to stand next to him. "Kadin's already gone?"

Xander nodded.

"Your Highness!" Mylin whispered and dropped to the ground.

"Get up, girl." Robyn extended a hand to help Mylin stand up. "The man's a traitor."

"What?"

"Kadin's the one who cut off my wings. At Dani's command."

Xander had been kicking himself for not seeing it sooner. "He was with me every step of the way." Kadin's sudden disappearance in the midst of the storm. The broken rocthane, the key that was supposed to help them shift the worlds. Dani's confidence even after she'd been captured.

Robyn's revelation had been a knife to his gut. He had trusted the man. "When did they leave?"

Mylin looked miserable. "Last night. I'm sorry— should I have stopped them?"

Xander shook his head. "He would have hurt you. You did the right thing." He hugged his mother fiercely. "I'm sorry. If I had known…." At least the cards were on the table now. "We'll deal with Kadin when we find him. For now, there's lots of work to do…."

"Xander!"

Xander turned to see Quince catching a falling Jameson, whose eyes were fluttering back up into his head. *Not again.*

"I think he's having a seizure," Alix said.

Xander shook his head. "It's the memories. It happened yesterday as well. I think they're too much for him." He wondered why they weren't affecting him the same way.

Quince nodded. "Help me get him to a bed."

Mylin got up uncertainly. "The castle is full of refugees, but I can find you a place. Follow me."

Xander turned to the others. "Alia, Venin, find out where you can be most useful. We'll see to Jameson."

Venin and Alia left, and Xander picked up Jameson by his shoulders and Quince took his legs. Together with Alix, they followed Mylin through the crowded hallways of the House of the Moon.

6

COUNCIL

ALIX FOLLOWED after Xander and Quince, trying to ignore the scowls and hateful stares he got from the skythane they passed as they made their way through the halls of the castle. He wasn't wearing his enforcer garb, but either these people recognized him from his time there, or they were just soured on landers as a whole.

He couldn't really blame them. They'd come as advisors to the king, promising to help modernize Gaelan. Within a few months, they'd become occupiers instead.

One man spat on him as he passed.

Alix closed his eyes. They had their reasons—even if he hadn't been personally responsible for most of the bad things that had happened. He was still a ranger.

He was also astonished that Xander was a prince here. The first time they'd met, Xander had been a pale, skinny thing, running courier duty for Rogan in the Slander. Alix had immediately wanted to protect the boy, but it had taken him three long years to find him again and to buy out his contract. By then Xander had been seventeen, but in some ways he had still seemed much younger, his development arrested when Rogan had taken him. He'd had a lot of anger issues.

Xander had grown into his full potential. It was strange to see the man inhabit the role of a skythane king. Xander had always been out for himself before anyone else, a lone wolf. It was a natural response to six years of sexual slavery.

Now that version of Xander was gone. Somehow, his new maturity only made him more attractive to Alix.

Quince had warned him to stay away, but how could he? The man he had dreamed about for a year, had missed like a ragged hole in his soul, was right there in front of him.

Alix was no fool, though. Xander was focused on his new love, and he would gain nothing by stepping in the middle of that. Especially when Jameson was in some kind of crisis. He would have to wait and see what developed.

"In here." Mylin led them into a small, bare room with a lumpy mattress.

"What is this place?" Xander asked.

"It's my room," Mylin explained. "I didn't want it. But some of the others insisted I have a place to come for an hour or two to get away from the madness."

Xander kissed her cheek. "I'm grateful."

It was a particular kind of grace, as if the whole place didn't belong to him to begin with. "Let's get Jameson down on the mattress." Quince and Xander laid Jameson down, holding him in place to keep him from thrashing about too much and injuring himself.

The man's face was flushed, his wings extended and shivering as if he were freezing cold, but his skin was covered in sweat.

"What's wrong with him?" Alix asked. He'd seen that look on men on campaign who'd been injured, but there wasn't a bruise or cut on him, as far as Alix could tell.

Mylin returned with an earthenware bowl and a cloth and used it to wipe his forehead. The cool water seemed to calm him.

"He's stuck in a memory loop," Xander said, as if that should make perfect sense. "He sees these past memories, things that happened wherever he is, and sometimes they overwhelm him."

"Whose memories? Looks more like a seizure to me." Xander wasn't buying into the native superstitions, was he? Though to be fair, Alix had seen his share of strange things on this half of the world.

Xander glared at him. "I have them too, but not like this."

"What?"

"The memories. You sounded skeptical. We just shifted an entire *world*. You have to learn to adjust your expectations for what's *likely* and *possible*."

That shut Alix up.

"This happened before?" Quince asked.

"Yeah, back in the cavern." Xander pulled out a pulse pistol. "This shocked him out of it."

Quince smiled grimly. "I imagine it would. But you don't want to go applying too many of those to poor young Jameson here. They could start to scramble his brain."

"I know." Xander winced. "So what do we do?"

Alix refrained from saying that it would be hard to tell the difference. "I might be able to help," he said instead, as surprised as any of them that those words came out of his mouth.

Xander and Quince turned to him, surprised. "How?" Xander asked, but he looked hopeful.

"I have some experience dealing with post-traumatic stress disorder and panic attacks." He pulled off his jacket and unbuttoned his shirt. He brushed off Xander's renewed glare. "I *know* it's not the same, but he needs to regain his focus on the here and now. I know a few things that might help." He knelt next to Jameson.

Jameson whimpered.

Alix had a hard time keeping up his anger at Jameson. In fact, for a moment he was reminded of Xander, the first time they'd met. Jameson was pale and helpless, out of control of his own fate. Alix growled under his breath. He did *not* want to have sympathy for this man.

Gently he took Jameson's hand and turned it over. Stunned, he hesitated.

Jameson's fingernails had a double moon—a second arc above the first, separated by a thin line. It was subtle, but he was used to seeing it in rangers who'd taken up the habit during the long occupation.

Jameson was a pith user?

Alix shook his head. It was none of his business. "Can you take the lantern out of here? It may be easier if he has less to focus on."

Robyn complied, taking it outside the door, and the room dimmed.

Alix held Jameson's palm to his own bare chest. "Jameson, can you hear me?"

There was no glimmer of recognition in Jameson's eyes.

Alix sighed. He had no guarantee that this would work. Still, it didn't hurt to try. "Jameson, this is Alix. I'm right here with you." He took a deep breath and breathed out just as slowly. "You have to focus, Jameson. Focus on me. Feel my breathing." He breathed in once, deeply, holding it for a long moment, and then out again. "I want you to breathe with me."

Alix put his other hand on Jameson's chest. "In. Out. In. Out. Focus on breathing."

He concentrated on his own.

"Is it working?" Xander peered over his shoulder.

"Shhhh." Alix's hand was warm against Jameson's beautiful chest. Jameson looked like an angel. He shook his head. He would not let himself be attracted to Xander's crush. "We're all here with you, Jameson. In…."

Jameson's chest lifted.

"Out."

Jameson's chest fell.

"That's good." Soon they were breathing together as one, connected skin to skin. It was as intimate a thing as he had ever experienced. "It's okay. Let the memories go. Just keep breathing."

Xander's hand settled on his shoulder, sending a new splash of warmth through his body.

At last, Jameson's eyes focused.

He looked up at Alix. "What… what happened?"

"You were stuck in your memories. The breathing helped you to get a grip and move past them." He lifted his hand off Jameson's chest and laid it down on the bed. The connection was broken.

"Thanks." Jameson's voice was raspy.

"Are they gone for now?"

Jameson looked around. "I think so."

Alix nodded. "Good. I can teach you how to cope with them, I think. If you want."

"Yes, please." Jameson closed his eyes. "So tired."

"He was tired last time too," Xander said. "I think these memory storms really take it out of him." Alix got up so Xander could kneel next to Jameson. "Sleep, my love."

Jameson nodded, and his head drooped to the side.

"That was nicely done," Quince whispered to Alix.

"Just part of my training." He was uncomfortable with the memory of Jameson's warm chest, of the look in his eyes when he'd woken up. He pulled her aside, out into the hall. "Can I ask you something?"

She stared into his eyes for a moment, and then nodded. "Shoot."

"How did Jameson and Xander shift an entire world?"

She laughed ruefully. "There are things you don't know about this world. It's ancient beyond the time of humankind. And we're not the first to live here."

He nodded. "I'd figured out that much. But still, Xander and Jameson… they're skythane. But they're still human."

Quince's face turned serious. "I'm not so certain of that."

"What do you mean?"

"I think they were both touched by something. Something that changed them fundamentally."

"Changed them how?"

"I don't want to say too much. But they have a destiny, those two." She poked him in the chest. "You'd do well to remember that."

He pondered that for a moment. It sounded like superstitious claptrap. But then so had the whole bit about shifting worlds. "What happens next?"

"How do you mean?"

"Do they send Oberon back once the crisis is over? Can they split the world again?"

She shook her head. "I don't know. The rocthane was destroyed."

"The what?"

"The key that made the shift possible. In the end, only intervention by an outside force made it happen."

She looked away. "We may all be stuck here in this new universe."

It was a lot to think about. "Thank you for filling me in." He glanced back inside the small room, where Xander and Jameson sat together. "I'll do whatever I can to help." He tried not to think of Xander's touch. His kiss.

Her gaze narrowed. He could see her thinking *what are you up to?*

Even Alix didn't really know.

Quince found Robyn outside the room, which was little more than a closet, watching Alix breathe with Lyrin in the weak flickers of lantern light. "You okay?"

Robyn shook her head. "I'm home, but I've never felt more disconnected."

"I know. It's… weird to be here again."

All of this had to be strange for her. She'd last held Davyn as a baby. He was both strong and humble, as a good king should be. This was clearly his kingdom now, not Robyn's.

Robyn was pale, like a wraith, a ghost in the halls, stripped of her wings and her pride. Quince pulled her close. "We'll figure it out."

Robyn nodded. "Being here… it brings back more than just good memories."

"Of course."

"It was brutal. The *Cattorah*. They held me down on the floor. Kadin sawed them off, one by one…. Moonrise help me, Quince, it was the most painful thing of my life."

Quince shivered. The *Cattorah* was something once practiced among the skythane dark ages, when their people had first come to Oberon. Criminals, murderers, pederasts had been *landed*, stripped of their wings and left to fend for themselves. It had been abandoned in modern times, because to *land* a skythane was tantamount to gutting their soul, a fate worse than death.

"You're alive, though. You're here with me now."

Robyn nodded. "I am. But I'll never feel the wind through my feathers, or spiral through the clouds under my own power again."

"You're still the queen. Wings or no."

Robyn laughed ruefully. "I suppose I am. Though Xander's the king now, so I suppose I'm a queen in retirement."

"Maybe so." Quince kissed her. "There are worse things to be. We'll work it all out."

. . .

XANDER GESTURED for them all to gather in the hallway, leaving Jameson to rest. He wished he could cuddle up next to his Errian prince, but there were decisions to be made, and time was drawing short.

Alix had surprised him. He'd gone out of his way to help Jameson come out of the memory storm, despite the fact that Jameson was with Xander now.

Why were the memories affecting Jameson so strongly? Where had they come from, and what did they have to do with the shift and the long, strange history of Titania and Oberon, of Erro?

He had no answers.

"Xander!" Someone was shouting his name, running down the hallway toward them.

He turned to find Alia all but barreling into him. "Slow down!" He was laughing. "Breathe."

"Sorry. It's…." She paused to catch her breath. "A lander ship just flew over the city."

Xander frowned. "Here on Titania?"

"There is no Titania anymore, remember?" Quince nudged him. "This is Erro."

Of course. "It's a surveillance mission." He'd known this was coming. Time really was running short.

Alix nodded. "I'd say so."

"Mylin, is there somewhere we can meet privately? We need to make some decisions, and quickly."

"I can find a place for you to talk—"

"You're part of this too."

"I… I don't…," she stammered.

She was stronger than she knew, and he wanted her there. "You've taken a place at the table. Don't back out on me now."

"I won't, my lord."

"Xander." He grinned.

"Xander." She beamed. "Come on. It's this way."

Every room along the hallway showed signs of habitation, although he suspected most of the skythane were out working to secure the city. "How many inhabitants are there?"

It was Robyn who answered. "About three thousand in and around the city."

Xander whistled. "That's a lot of mouths to feed."

"We're gathering as many of the scurf as we can find in a safe pasture above the city." Mylin opened the door to another room. The armory, by the look of it. The wall was hung with shields, and there were racks of swords and vases filled with arrows. There were also now a few pulse rifles.

"Scurf?"

"They're like cattle," Quince supplied. "Six legs, lots of meat. A little slow, but you gotta watch the horn." She put the lantern on a round pitted wooden table in the middle of the room and closed the door behind them. "Good choice." She nodded approvingly at Mylin.

"Thanks. I'm having some keff brought in to keep us awake."

Xander liked the Titanian version of coffee, though he missed the real stuff. "Pull up a seat." Xander grabbed a wooden crate that looked sturdy enough to hold him and sat down at one end of the table.

Everyone found a place to sit.

"Could Dani and Kadin have reached Oberon City yet?" Xander asked.

Quince frowned. "I don't see how. It's half a world away from here. Unless they were picked up by a hoversport."

"We can't rule it out." He scratched his chin. "Gaelan and Errian are in imminent danger. They may not have believed in the shift before, but OberCorp won't take long before they try to establish control over the new world order."

"Maybe they'll just leave us alone?" Mylin looked hopeful.

Xander shook his head. "I love that you think that, but I doubt it. They've been the aggressors, every time. When they first took over Oberon, we fled here, hoping they would leave us alone. Now they've come after us again, occupying this very city."

Alix frowned. "They see themselves as the rightful owners of Oberon… of Erro." He glanced at Quince, who nodded. "How in the hell did you pull this whole thing off, Xander?"

It was strange, having Alix nearby again, and he still wasn't entirely sure of the answer to that one. "It's a long story, one that started before we met. Though I didn't know it yet. The bigger question is, can we reverse it? If so, how long do we have to hold them off?"

Quince raised her hand. "The flare lasted at least a week the last time. Ten days to be safe."

Xander whistled. "That's a long time."

She stared at the table. "And we're not even sure if there's a way to undo the shift, now that the Mountain is in ruins."

That had been bugging him too. Why had the shift been accomplished without such destruction the last time, by Elyra and Daedus? Or had it? What if they couldn't reverse it and return things to the status quo? Were they forever cut off from their old lives, the Common Worlds, all of it?

Titania… or Erro… was his home now, but still—he wasn't sure how he felt about that.

"We're in no shape to fight them here," Robyn said,

drawing their attention. "I'm not sure it's even possible to stand up to them with blades and arrows and shields and a few pulse rifles, in any case. But as things stand now—"

"Ballifor," Quince whispered, but she had everyone's attention.

"What's Ballifor?" Alix asked.

"It was Quince's hometown." Xander frowned. "It was destroyed by some kind of bomb."

"Holy shit. With all the skythane here… it would be a slaughterhouse." Alix's statement hung in the air like a sword.

"Maybe so. But we have to remember that Ober-Corp's force isn't an army. It's primarily a security force, which gives us a chance if we can exploit it." He sighed. "In any case, I agree. We need to evacuate the city. What's left of it." He'd hoped things would get easier once they'd accomplished the shift, but they had only become more complicated. "What are my options?" He looked up at Robyn and blushed. "Perhaps you should be leading this discussion, Mother. You are the queen, after all." *Mother.* It was a strange word on his tongue.

She shook her head. "I lost the throne, and even if I had not, I would abdicate it for you now. The people look to you. You have to lead them."

"Fair enough, though I've got shit-all experience at it." He laughed ruefully.

"We could send them to the faery caves," Quince said.

"I'm listening."

"The mountains above Gaelan are riddled with caverns like the one you took shelter in. They were left by the old ones, or so the rumors go. Some of them are stocked, like the waystations, for times of need."

Xander got up and paced back and forth, thinking. "That sounds good. We should send children, the elderly, and the injured there post-haste." They would be out of harm's way, at least for the moment. He had enough death on his conscience.

"And the rest?" It was Mylin.

"We go to Errian."

ROBYN STOOD on the House of the Moon's battlements in the moonlight, wrapped in a white shawl, looking out at the destruction below.

Xander watched her from the shadows.

Fifty dead. That's what Mylin had told them, and that was on top of casualties elsewhere caused by his actions. It must be killing her too. "Mother."

She didn't turn around. "I'd hoped it would be you."

Xander came to stand beside her, surveying the damage in the silver light. Somehow the moonlight helped take some of the sting out of it. "It's hard to look at, isn't it?"

She nodded. "Hundreds killed by Dani and the OberCorp forces during their occupation. Every one of them a black mark against my name, and now this."

He wept for the destruction in the valley. The city had been broken, a tangled mess of stone and mud like the Mountain before it. Things would never be set back to the way they had been before.

"If I'm honest with myself, I'll admit that it had already fallen, long ago." She turned to look at him. "My time here is over." She put a hand on his shoulder. "You must rule over Gaelan now."

He put his hand over hers. "I don't think I'll be very good at it. I've made such a mess of things."

She pulled him close and cradled him in her arms. "Nonsense. I remember how it felt to hold you as a child, to want to protect you from all harm. How weak and dependent you were." She took a deep breath. "You're a grown man now, and everything I hoped you might become. You don't need me. Not anymore."

"I *do* need you," he protested. It was barely a whisper. He had a mother again. She soothed a rough place in his heart that had been barren for so long.

Robyn's eyes flashed with anger. "You don't. You've been gone from me for twenty-five years. Quince made sure you grew up strong."

He hugged her tightly and then let her go. "What did Dani do to you?"

Robyn snorted. "I lost my wings. Isn't that obvious?"

"It's more than that." He stared into her eyes. "Kadin must have cut something else out of you as well. Quince told me all about you, what you were like when I was a child. The woman she knew wouldn't just give up."

"I haven't given up." She pulled her shawl tighter around her as if seeking its warmth. "You have no idea what I've been through."

"Tell me, then." Xander touched her cheek with the back of his hand.

She turned away, shaking her head. "Another time. Don't worry about me. I'll find my way." She kissed his forehead. "I'm so proud of you. You will lead the Gaelani back to glory."

7

―――――

DREAMS AND VISIONS

Zaxxim flew on gossamer wings, their claw extended to touch the wingtip of one of their lovers.

Xiini flashed them one of their smiles, their skin nearly translucent and shimmering in the afternoon sunlight.

"Are you ready?" Xiini was beautiful, their skin aflame with sunlight, their pointed ears and lopsided grin making Zaxxim's hearts beat faster, their lower heart thumping against their stomach.

Zaxxim nodded. They took Xiini's hand, and Xiini pulled their key from their chest pouch.

Verrim flew on their other side, their violet crest quivering with excitement. They were a perfect triad.

Xiini twisted the key, and a waygate opened in midair

ahead of them. Together, the three of them dove through it, emerging over the Great Sea just as evening fell.

They released hands and spiraled down toward Bolcà Isle, a beautiful extinct volcano surrounded by tropical foliage, whose broken walls sheltered a crater lake, in the heart of the Great Sea.

The war would go on without them. They had earned a break.

A weekend away was just what they needed.

JAMESON WOKE SLOWLY. He had a splitting headache.

He opened his eyes. He was in a small dark room, somewhere in the House of the Moon, he guessed. The memories seemed to have fled for the moment, but the strange dream lingered in his head, as did the sensation of Alix's hand resting on his chest.

The man had helped him, something Jameson wasn't sure he would have done if their positions were reversed. And there had been something else there between them too—energy. An attraction.

He shoved that thought aside. Xander was the one for him. Alix was just…. Alix.

He slowly became aware of someone in the room next to him, the sound of soft breathing. He propped himself up and turned to look at who it was. His head throbbed in protest at the movement.

Xander.

He was seated against the wall on the floor, his black wings resting over him like a blanket.

Jameson watched him for a moment. He was so quiet, so peaceful like this. The cares of the world had slipped from his shoulders, and he was just Xander once again, not the King of the Gaelani.

"Hey," he said softly.

Xander stirred and opened his eyes, looking up at him. "Hi. You okay?"

Jameson nodded. "I'd kill for a pain-blocker," he deadpanned. He didn't suppose Gaelan had reached that level of technical sophistication yet.

"Yeah, sorry. None of those around here." He sat up, his wings slipping behind him. "I'm glad you're awake. How are the memories?"

Jameson looked around. "They seem to be leaving me alone for the moment." He rubbed his temples with his thumbs. "What did I miss?"

"OberCorp buzzed the city with a hoversport."

"That can't be good." The world was rushing on without him, and he'd have to play catch-up.

Xander shook his head. "We're evacuating the young and elderly to the faery caves—"

"Faery caves?"

"Like the one we holed up in."

"Ah. And the rest?" He scratched the spot between his wings, calming the itch there.

"We're going to Errian."

Jameson took a deep breath, and then nodded. "I'm needed there."

Xander looked him over appraisingly. "Are you ready for the responsibility?"

"For what?"

"To be their king?"

Jameson laughed. "How do you *ever* get ready for something like that? I still don't really believe it myself." He sat all the way up, ignoring the pain in his skull. "But here we are. It's not like either of us had a choice, right? Were you ready?"

Xander chuckled. "I'm still not." He stood and stretched his arms and wings. "Do you think you can travel?"

"I think so. What time is it?"

"A little after midnight. We helped get the refugees out of the city while you slept. We plan to leave with the rest of the Gaelani in the morning."

Jameson stretched his own wings. "You've raised me an army."

"I guess you could say that." Xander helped him up.

"Slowly. Headache, remember?" He got to his feet and put a hand against a wall as his legs threatened to buckle. "See? Good as new."

"Jameson, I'm worried."

"About how much time we have?"

"Yes. It will take us four or five days to get to Errian. OberCorp could have forces there in a fraction of that time."

"Maybe not."

"They're just across the sea, now. And they have hoversports."

"No, I know that." Jameson rubbed his forehead, wishing the pain would go away. "I mean, it might not take us a week to get there, at least some of us."

"Really? What are you thinking?"

"Take me to Quince. She'll be able to tell me if it will work, or if I'm just plain crazy."

Xander side-eyed him as he helped Jameson out into the hall. "What do you have planned in that strange off-worlder head of yours?"

Jameson managed a wan grin. "You'll just have to wait and see."

They made their way upstairs, emerging at last into the courtyard of the castle. Bandia shone silver in the sky, and a cool wind blew through the courtyard. Water trickled from the fountain in the center of the wide space.

The bodies were gone.

Xander noticed his glance. "They were burned, down by the river. My mother led the ceremony, invoking Gael, the moon god. It was quite beautiful."

That seemed appropriate. Jameson wasn't a follower of the skythane faith, but he didn't see what harm it would do to shoot a quick prayer up to the moon for those lost in the flooding.

"It's important that we honor the dead," Jameson said softly. *So many dead.* "Where's Quince? She's on watch, isn't she?"

Xander nodded. "She wouldn't have it any other way."

QUINCE SAT with her back against the balustrade, staring up into the starry skies of Titania. Drimm the Dragon stretched out lazily from star to star. It had been one of her brother's favorite constellations when they'd been children. His red eye glared at her with a magnificent malevolence.

She missed Dillan fiercely. The mention of Ballifor had brought it all back for her. The flight from Errian, the bomb that had destroyed everyone she'd known growing up.

Beside her, wrapped in a sleep sack, Robyn was sound asleep. They'd chatted for hours after the refugees had left, comparing life stories from their twenty-five-year interval. Quince had talked about caring for Xander. She'd left out the bits about Rogan. Robyn was too fragile for those at the moment.

When she was done, Robyn had said that it must have been hard for Quince, all alone on an alien world.

Robyn, in turn, told her of decades with a man she didn't love, and who didn't love her in turn. Waiting for the time to come when Quince could return to her, not sure it ever would. And about the dark time of the occupation.

The words had come flowing out of her, like blood from a perpetual wound. In the end, the words had slowed and then stopped, and Quince had taken her in her arms, wrapping her wings around Robyn's lithe form. Her lover seemed so much smaller, so fragile without her wings, without her confidence. Quince just held Robyn while she sobbed, her body trembling with emotions too painful to reconcile.

At last, Robyn had fallen asleep, and Quince had tucked her into a sleep sack to rest, hoping for some real healing. Robyn needed a new purpose, now that Gaelan had been taken from her. Something to live for. Quince did too.

She stiffened. She could tell that she was no longer alone.

"Thought we'd find you up here," Xander said softly.

She relaxed. "It feels good to get back out into the fresh air." Though with the new swamp below, this city wouldn't smell so good after a few hot days.

Quince stood and gestured for the boys to follow her away from where Robyn was sleeping. Let her get her rest.

"Jameson had an idea," Xander said when they'd put some distance between them and his mother.

Jameson shrugged. "Not an idea, so much as a dream or a memory. Maybe."

"Tell me." Quince was still unsure about where these memories came from. The gods? The nimfeach? But they'd proven accurate on more than one occasion, so she was willing to trust them. Besides, she had her own visions to tangle with.

Jameson looked at Xander, who nodded. "The keys that open the waygates, and the other keys, like the rocthane… are there many of them?"

Quince considered. Robyn had given her one of the smaller ones that allowed her to take the boys across to

Oberon. "I'm sure there *were* others. The rocthane's broken now—"

"I know. But the waygate keys?"

"Yes. There are others. Robyn might know more." She glanced back at where her love still lay. "I'd rather let her sleep now." She turned back to Jameson. "Why? We don't need them now. Oberon's *here*."

"I… saw something. Remembered it, rather. Last night. Is it possible the keys could be used to open waygates here too? From one place on…. Erro, to another?" His wings quivered.

Quince's mouth fell open. It was something she'd never considered. "I honestly don't know. Maybe?" It would change everything if it were true, and if they could figure out how it worked. It could give them a decisive advantage over the landers.

"What did you see, exactly?"

Jameson described his vision, the strange beings who had used one of the keys to shift themselves halfway around the world. "They were beautiful, Quince. Three of them. Like human butterflies. Or alien butterflies. I don't know. It's hard to explain."

Quince leaned back against the wall, staring up into the sky. What Jameson described… there were clearly forces at work here that she didn't understand. She closed her eyes. She could feel it—something reaching out from an ancient time to ensnare them all in something they couldn't hope to understand.

"I've seen them before. Or their like."

"Where?"

"The nimfeach."

"The creature who told you to flee?"

She nodded. "That and a lot more. They are beautiful. But they're more like ghosts than anything. Translucent. These beings, they were real? Corporeal?"

"I think so. It was a memory. Or a dream."

"Can I join you?" Alix appeared out of the darkness. "Sorry, I couldn't sleep." He looked longingly at Xander but said nothing else.

Jameson stiffened visibly. "We were just discussing the keys that used to open the waygates between Titania and Oberon," she said to smooth things over. "Jameson thinks they could do more."

"Where is yours, Quince?" Jameson asked.

She shook her head. "I don't know for sure. My best guess? The waystation where Dani and her team ambushed us. If she didn't take it."

"It's in the right direction, on the way to Errian. Can we stop there and look for it?" Jameson glanced up at Xander.

"I don't see why not." Xander yawned. "We'd better get some sleep if we're going to depart first thing in the morning." He looked around at the ruined city in the moonlight. "We'll rebuild this, Quince. One day, when things are back to normal."

Quince laughed harshly. "Whatever that is. I haven't seen normal for twenty-five years."

Xander nodded. "Yeah. Whatever it is." He hugged her. "See you at first light."

He and Jameson headed down one of the ladders to the courtyard.

Alix came to stand next to her, staring up at the cloudless sky, and they looked at the stars silently for a few moments. A cool breeze was blowing down out of the mountains. Quince shivered, then rubbed away the goose bumps.

"You sure Jameson's *memories* are real?" he asked at last.

"What do you mean?"

He glanced over at her. "Quince, he's a pith addict."

"What?" She shivered again, this time from more than the cold. He was getting close to a truth she didn't want him to know.

"You have to know. I saw all the signs. Hallucinations. Puppy-dog love. And his fingernails have the double moon."

He'd guessed too much. She had to deny it. "I don't know what you mean. He and Xander are in love. No puppy-dog about it. And the things he's remembered… they've been right, every time."

"As far as you know."

"As far as I know."

"And the fingernails?"

She shook her head. "Probably a side effect of the shift." It sounded lame, even to her.

Surprisingly, he nodded. "Maybe so. You'd certainly know more about it than I." He kissed her cheek, reminding her of the times the three of them had spent together when he'd been with Xander.

Maybe his intentions for Xander were questionable. But he'd always seemed like a good guy, if she'd read him right. That didn't make lying to him any easier.

"Get some sleep, Quince. I'll see you in the morning." Then he was gone.

She shivered. She had a bad feeling about what the new day would bring.

She returned to sit with Robyn, pulling her own sleep sack up over her shoulders and staring out at the darkness.

After a long while, she closed her eyes.

.   .   .

Snow, everywhere. The air crisp, searing her lungs as she breathed it in. She and Robyn landed on the broken peak, alighting like two imprean to receive their messages.

Morgan ran across the snow barefoot, gesturing for them to go, his face a mask of fear. He threw himself into her arms. "Quince, you have to go!"

"Not without you."

"It's too late. They are coming—"

"Who?"

"Ithani." He pointed at the split in the mountain.

The golden glow rose from the pit, and an alien music spilled out to melt the snow.

QUINCE AWOKE WITH A START. She was startled to find herself back in Gaelan.

It had felt so real, holding Morgan in her arms again. The boy had been scared to death of something.

The Ithani.

What the hell was an Ithani?

JAMESON PULLED Xander aside in the darkness of the courtyard. "I'm not really tired."

Xander's eyes twinkled. "What did you have in mind?"

"We have a few more hours before daylight, right?"

Xander nodded.

"I'd like to spend them with you."

Xander kissed him and led him back to the tiny room they shared.

Jameson was a good bit more tired by the time the sun finally rose over Gaelan.

8

————

DEPARTURES

Jessa sat in the OberCorp waiting room for a second time, tapping her white leather boot on the industrial carpeting impatiently.

The OberCorp folks had kept her waiting all day and then sent her packing with the promise of an appointment "tomorrow." So here she was once again. They'd figure out soon enough that she wasn't going away. Her time as a reporter had taught her how to be resourceful, tenacious, and creative to get her story.

She'd tried the bars again the night before. Someone there had offered to take her "to the Outland," an offer she firmly rejected. But she had managed to get some information out of him about the stars.

The constellations were *different*.

She'd laughed at that at first. How was it even possible?

But the man had been adamant and had shared some stills he'd taken on his various tours.

She was no astrophysicist, but they looked different to her, and that scared the hell out of her. What had happened on her shuttle ride down to the planet? Where the hell was she now?

She'd heard from someone else that the space station was gone too. There were no shuttles coming down or going up anymore. That much she was able to verify from the grid.

"Ms. Simpson?" The man peering out at her from the doorway to the corporate suites was thin as a scarecrow, dressed in a suit that looked two sizes too big for him.

She stood and pulled her carry sack up onto her shoulder. "Jessa *Smithson*, from GSN." She extended her hand. She'd practiced the alias over and over until it slipped off her tongue as easily as Althorpe, her real name.

"Oh, I'm so sorry." He took it, and she squeezed hard, making his eyeballs bulge out. "I'm Mattis Vinder. This way, please. Our publicist Tamara Fine is ready to see you."

"Thanks." She had no idea who Ms. Fine was, but

she *had* asked for someone in their PR department. OberCorp practically ran the planet, so they had to know *something* about Jamie.

"Follow me, please."

The hallway behind the door was total corporate. White translucent walls hung with oversized photos of Oberon—the Split, Oberon City, the arcos, the Gildensea. All the parts of the planet she was sure the company was busy raping and pillaging. On Beta Tau, all corporations were under church control. She crossed herself as inconspicuously as she was able.

The floor was carpeted in a color so inoffensively beige that it bugged the shit out of her.

They reached a hover tube, and he palmed open the door. "She's on the twenty-seventh floor. I'll send you up. First door on the right." He gestured for her to enter the translucent tube.

She balked, concerned about trusting her person to it on a planet like this. They didn't have many hover tubes on Beta Tau. Most of the buildings were only two or three stories tall. Still, she was supposed to be a well-traveled, confident, take-charge journalist.

"Sorry, I'm just a little worried about power outages, given all that's going on…."

"Understandable. But we have two backup generator systems here at the Tower. It's quite safe."

"Gotcha. Thank you for your help." She stepped into the tube and was whisked gently upward. It was actually a pleasurable experience, like being lifted by an invisible hand. There was no wind, just the walls of the tube passing by her, each floor marked by a colored ring.

She counted at least forty floors on the way up. Was this thing malfunctioning? She began to get nervous.

As she rapidly approached the top of the tube, she ducked, afraid her head was going to smash into it.

Instead, just past the last ring—purple—she came to a gentle halt, and the doors opened before her.

She stepped forward, and it was like she was standing on a circle of clear glass. Still, she was relieved when she put her feet on solid ground once again.

There was only one doorway in the small room she found herself in. The doors were twice as tall as she was, and they were made from a shiny, liquid-seeming substance she recognized instantly as amalite. The surface swirled and changed, combining and recombining into near-infinite patterns.

On Beta Tau, that much amalite would have cost as much as a small planet's annual economy.

Who had she been sent to see?

She looked for a doorknob or palm reader—some way to announce her presence.

She needn't have bothered. The doors swung silently open on their own.

"Please come in, Ms. Althorpe."

ALIX WOKE BEFORE DAWN, lying alone in a cot in an otherwise empty room that Mylin had found for him, with a small window looking out on the black cliffs behind the castle. Not the Galaxion Hotel view, but better than another night spent sleeping on the ground.

Actually, he preferred it this way. The sparse room suited his military training, as well as his need to punish himself for being a part of the ill-fated occupation that had torn him away from Xander. That seemed newly relevant now.

Alix slipped off the bed, dropping to the floor to do his morning push-ups. As his body moved mechanically through the exercise, his mind drifted back to his skythane man. He closed his eyes, remembering the last time they'd been together. The night before his mission had taken him away to another world.

Xander on his back, his golden chest heaving as Alix worked him over, bringing him to the edge before making him wait once again. Running his hands up and down Xander's smooth thighs. Making it last for hours.

Skythane were human in all the ways that mattered.

But more than the sex, more than the memories of Xander's beautiful form, he missed the aftermath, the long nights in Xander's arms. The musky smell of him after sex. The tender look in his eyes at being treated as a *someone*, not a *something*. The years of making up for what Rogan had done to him.

Alix pushed himself harder, faster, hoping to obliterate that sweet gaze from his mind, his muscles pumping, the stress mounting in his arms.

When he was done, he found his way to the closest washroom, using the cold water and soap there to clean himself up as best as he was able.

He was getting scraggly. He hadn't been able to shave in days, since they'd evacuated the work camp. He scratched the beginnings of his red beard.

He was no longer a ranger, and there were more important things to worry about at the moment. Like what his mother was up to on the other side of the world.

Xander was right to evacuate the city, if past history was any guide.

Alix wondered, too, how Jameson was doing. He wanted to hate the man who had taken his place, but it was hard when he'd seen the skythane in such a vulnerable place, when they'd shared such an intimate connection. Jameson's hand had been warm against his chest, and Alix had felt… something. Desire. Connection. Trust? He wasn't sure.

He still wasn't convinced Jameson's "memories" weren't the result of a pith addiction. The drug could make you believe strange things, among other side effects. He'd seen it in the rangers. More than one of his fellow soldiers had succumbed to the addiction, here where the stuff was made and was readily available.

He strode back down the hallway in his underwear, nodding to the skythane he passed on the way to his room. He had no body shame.

They'd apparently been instructed to be civil to him. At least this time, no one spat on him.

He reached his room and pulled his new clothes off the windowsill. Mylin had found some skythane clothing that fit him well enough, though it left his shoulders and arms mostly bare. It was a relief to have something better than prison clothes to wear. He pulled on the pants and laced up the shirt, as he'd seen the skythane do many times. The morning air was cool on the wing-holes over his shoulders.

Satisfied that he was as presentable and ready as possible, he headed down to the mess hall, intent on getting something to eat before they departed for Errian.

·   ·   ·

JAMESON TOOK A HUNK OF BREAD, some cheese, and a mug of keff and sought out his nemesis in the huge dining hall. The ceilings were at least eight meters high, and large iron chandeliers hung from huge wooden beams, lit with candles.

Jameson always felt like he'd stepped into a King Arthur tri-dee when he entered this place.

The place was half-full, skythane coming to get their last meal before abandoning their city. A sense of unease filled the room, with hundreds of low conversations being held between both friends and strangers.

Alix sat all alone in one corner, his back to the wall, concentrating on eating his morning repast. He looked rough around the edges. It suited him.

"Mind if I sit?" Jameson asked, trying not to notice how good-looking Alix really was, even when he was a mess.

Alix shook his head. "Suit yourself."

The man was handsome in that rugged space marine kind of way. Jameson could see how Xander had been attracted to him. Alix was ostracized here because of his lack of wings, and his part in the occupation of Gaelan. *Did you do things here you regret?*

Jameson imagined it was hard for Alix here, where most people instinctively hated him. He took a seat across from him, wishing for a good cup of coffee. There were still things about lander civilization he missed desperately—when this was all over, he'd suggest a few *improvements* in Errian.

He picked up the hunk of cheese and peeled off some purple mold. They'd promised him it was perfectly edible. Still, he sniffed at it distrustfully.

"Not exactly up to lander standards, is it?"

Jameson snorted. "Not really. Hey, how did you know?"

"I asked around. You're skythane, but you grew up offworld. Plus you talk like an offworlder. Traxon?"

"Beta Tau."

Alix nodded. "Religious, then."

"Lapsed." The bread wasn't much better, but it was food. They had an army to feed, after all.

"Ah."

Jameson worked up his courage, chewing on a bite of the hard bread. "Thank you for what you did last night."

"It was nothing." Alix leaned against the wall, staring at him over the table.

"Could you… would you teach me more?" The memories were behaving for the moment. They seemed worse when he was tired, broken down, when he didn't have the resources to deal with them.

Alix considered him. "We're not friends," he said at last. "You get that, right?"

Jameson nodded. "I'm sorry." He should have known better than to ask something of him, Xander's ex. "I shouldn't have bothered you." He picked up what was left of his cheese and his mug and started to leave.

"Wait." Alix grasped his hand. "I'm sorry. That came out wrong. I just mean that things are bound to be a bit weird between us, considering."

"Xander."

Alix nodded. "I didn't say I wouldn't help. You're important to Xander, and he's important to me."

He seemed to be telling the truth. "All right. I guess I can live with that." He finished the cheese, which had a decidedly fishy taste, and washed it down with keff, enjoying the flavor, sort of a coconut-herbal tea thing. He missed his morning coffee. "So what do I do when I feel a storm coming on?"

Alix leaned forward and took Jameson's hands. His hands were callused and warm. "There are two ways to go about it. The first is distraction. When you feel a panic attack—"

"A memory storm."

"Whatever. When you feel it coming on, focus on something outside yourself." He looked around the room. "This can be any number of things. Pick out something like that chandelier to look at, and count the candles. Some folks recite numbers out of order. Sometimes repetitive eye movements or gestures help. Some focus on measured breathing. That's what we did last night."

Jameson nodded. "It helped bring me back."

"It's a good exercise, but you're not always going to have someone there to help you breathe." He let go of Jameson's hands, but Jameson could still feel the tingle from where they had touched. "One of my friends visualizes a white light passing through his body, taking the panic—"

"Memory storm." Jameson was starting to get annoyed with Alix's insistence that he wasn't experiencing *real* memories.

"—away. But you're right, it's not quite the same, is it?"

Jameson shook his head. "I worked with patients with PTSD before. This is… different. It might induce a panic attack, though."

"Are you seeing the memories right now?"

Jameson looked around. He nodded. "They're always there, but they've pulled away. It's like a flock of crows circling overhead."

"I have an idea. Do you trust me?"

Jameson considered the question. "I guess I have to."

"Good choice. I won't bite." He grinned. "Pick one of the memories and concentrate on it."

Jameson's heart beat faster. "What if I lose control?"

"Give me your hand."

Jameson took Alix's hand again.

"Trust me."

Jameson nodded. "Okay."

"Pick one of the memories and focus on it."

Jameson looked up and found one of the "crows." He stared at it, and as if beckoned, it swept down, engulfing him in its darkness.

HE LAY ON A BED, naked, his wings spread lazily behind him, staring up at an intricately painted blue and gold ceiling.

A woman danced for him, also naked in the firelight, her sinuous curves twisting with an astonishing grace, making the room hotter than the fire could account for. The flames sparkled on gold flakes along the walls and ceiling.

He wanted her. Needed her. Was a moth drawn to her flame, her raven-black hair and eyes.

He rose from the bed and met her in three short strides, joining the dance.…

. . .

"Holy fuck!" His eyes focused on the trickle of blood that dripped from his thumb. "What did you do?"

Alix wiped his knife on his trousers, cleaning off the blood. "Just a test. Pain. That's one way out when you get locked up in a panic… memory storm."

Jameson sucked his thumb. "Seriously? Thanks for the lesson, but I think I can figure it out myself."

"You also might want to get clean."

"Clean?"

"You know what I mean." Alix winked at him and went back to his own meal.

Jameson had no idea what the man was talking about. "Um… not really?"

"Suit yourself. I'm here if you need me."

Fucking jerk.

The remainder of the Gaelani, those who hadn't been sent to the safety of the caves, gathered in the courtyard of the House of the Moon.

Xander surveyed them from the top of the wall, still amazed to find himself leading an army. Behind him, his companions had gathered, Jameson to his left and Alix to his right, a pointed distance maintained between the two of them.

Whatever mutual goodwill they had found the night before seemed to have evaporated.

Xander sighed. He was glad Alix was alive, he really was, but his presence there complicated things, at a time when Xander's life had already become hellishly complex. He missed his sleepless nights alone in his flat back on Oberon City. Now he had an entire nation dependent on his decisions.

He still wondered if he'd made the right call, evacuating Gaelan.

Quince put a hand on his shoulder. "A moment?"

"Sure." They stepped away from the balustrade, a few paces away from his… what were they? His court? His lieutenants? His advisors? "What's up?"

"I think you're doing the right thing." She rested a hand on his shoulder. "Robyn and I are so proud of the men you two have become."

"I hear a 'but' coming."

She chuckled. "You know me too well. And you know I'm a rational person—"

He side-eyed her.

"Well, usually."

Xander laughed ruefully and nodded. "Except where Morgan came into things." The loss of the boy still stung. Xander had felt stirrings of something—maturity, fatherhood?—when he'd had the skinny kid under his wing. A sense of what could be, someday.

Quince looked at him strangely.

"What?"

"It's just… I don't know how else to say it. I think he's still alive."

"What?" It was impossible. The boy had vanished. Imploded. Something. Been there onc moment and gone the next, and yet his heart hoped it was true. "What do you mean?"

"I've been having these dreams."

"Ah."

Quince grimaced. "Hence the whole I'm-usually-a-rational-person thing."

He nodded. "After the memories and visions Jameson and I have had, I'm loath to discount anything new. What did you see?"

She looked away. "I'm not sure. Something happening, up north, something he's mixed up in. I think he needs me."

Xander would have called bullshit on something like that just a few weeks before. Now he wasn't so sure.

"Could you manage without Robyn and me?"

There it was. He'd had precious little time to spend with his mother, but then again, neither had Quince. It was easy to see how the loss of Robyn's wings had wounded her badly, beyond the purely physical.

"I…. We don't know this world. Not like you do, memories notwithstanding. And Jameson…." He glanced back at his prince.

"I know. But this is important to more than just Morgan. I can feel it." She looked at their friends. "Venin knows every mile of the route from here to Errian. We talked it over at breakfast."

He trusted Quince. If she said this needed to happen, she had her reasons, even if there were things she wasn't telling him. Again. "If you think it's so important, I won't stop you."

She squeezed his hand. "Thank you, Xander." She reached up to give him a hug.

He held her tightly. "You be careful," he admonished her. "I've almost lost you more than once on this quest."

"I will. That goes for you and Jameson too." She looked at Alix. "He still loves you, you know."

"I know. We'll have to figure that out when there's more time and less rush."

"So, in a hundred years?"

He laughed. "Sounds about right."

She kissed his cheek and went to talk with Robyn.

He followed her. "Quince tells me you two are heading up north."

Robyn touched his cheek. "It's bad timing. I'd hoped to spend a little time with you. We hardly know each other."

"I know." He nodded. "I have this memory. On a balcony right down there." He walked over to the edge of the wall to look down, and she followed. "I tried to climb the rail, and you pulled me back and told me to be careful, because I didn't have my wings yet. You said 'You'll fly with them soon enough.'"

She smiled wistfully. "You remember that?"

"I do." He hugged her tight. "You be careful out there. I don't want to lose you again."

She hugged him and reached up to kiss him. "You boys be careful too." She squeezed him tight and then let go and went back to Quince.

Xander stared after her for a moment and then went to look down into the courtyard. The Gaelani there were milling about, some lacing on their flying leathers, others deep in conversation with one another. It was a motley crew.

He wished he had the big bell from Founder's Hill to command their attention. Instead, he bellowed, "Skythane, hear me!"

The crowd silenced, and one by one they looked up at him.

"These are difficult times for all of us." Many below had lost someone, in the fight to retake Gaelan or in the flooding after the *shift*. "You've opened your arms to me, and now I ask you to follow me again." Alia and Venin had helped Mylin spread the news of his plan the day before, but he felt it was best to speak to all of them, directly, as their king. "The Gaelan we knew is gone, destroyed by the flood. We will come back here to build it anew. But first we must face another threat." He paused to let that sink in. There were mutters and nods in the throng below. "Before long, OberCorp will send their forces against us, and after the shift, they are no longer limited in their access to Titania. We must fly to the aid of our brothers and sisters in Errian." He pulled a surprised Jameson to his side and held up his hand for the crowd. "Errian's prince stood with us. Now we must stand with him."

The crowd cheered.

"When this fight is over, we will return here to put up the towers of Gaelan once more. And Errian will help us."

There was more muttering at that.

"Listen! No more will we allow ourselves to be divided. Our two peoples, Gaelani and Erriani, have been manipulated by outsiders for long enough. Now we will stand strong together."

There was the sound of agreement below. He had them. "Are you with me?"

This time the cheer was twice as loud as before.

Jameson squeezed his hand. "Well done," he whispered, and kissed Xander's cheek.

Xander smiled. "Each of you has been assigned to a wing leader. Follow him or her, and we will reach Errian within the week." Maybe sooner, if Jameson was right about the key. "To the skies!"

The skythane host began to climb the ladders up to the castle wall, and flight by flight, they leapt into the air, leaving Gaelan on the way to Errian, on the shores of the Argent Sea to the east.

Xander and Jameson led the throng with their companions.

9

———

POISON

Quince and Robyn watched the rest of Gaelan's skythane take to the skies, emptying out the House of the Moon one flight at a time. When they were all aloft, the host slipped off to the east like a great flock of birds, slowly disappearing into the distance.

Quince turned away at last, pulling on her own carry sack and tying the straps. It was full of supplies for their trip north, including cold weather gear and a zero-C sleep sack she'd raided from the OberCorp supplies. Robyn had one too.

"Are you ready?"

Robyn nodded. She shouldered her bi-wings and gave one last sad look to the ruined city below. "It's my fault. Everything that happened here."

"You have to stop thinking that. All of us have been swept up in events beyond our control."

"Maybe so." She looked angry now.

Quince took that as an improvement over the deep sadness that had filled her the night before.

"Do you think it's my fault because I helped the boys complete the shift?" She put a hand on Robyn's cheek, turning it gently toward her. "By that logic, the flood was more my fault than yours."

"That's absurd." Her eyes flashed with anger, and Quince was heartened to see Robyn's old spirit return. "You don't control the weather."

"Exactly. And you don't control the landers, or the nimfeach, or the world at large."

Robyn held her gaze for a long moment. "You're probably right," she conceded at last. "But I can't help feeling guilty. It happened on my watch."

"And I love that you feel that way. But you have to promise me you won't try to… to end it. It would kill me too if I lost you again."

"I can't promise that." The pain in her voice tore at Quince's heart.

"At least promise me you'll talk to me first."

Robyn thought about it and nodded. "I can do that."

"Shall we fly?"

"I'm ready to be done with this place. Check my wings?"

Quince checked the straps. "They look good." She took Robyn's face in her hands and gave her a gentle kiss.

"What was that for?" Robyn asked when they separated.

"For being you. For being here with me when I thought I'd be all alone." She climbed into the embrasure and spread her wings. "Here we go." She leapt from the House of the Moon, leaving the castle behind her. Robyn soon followed, and they soared over the ruined city.

Only the Founder's Tower still stood in the valley below the castle. It was high upon a hill above the mud and muck and wreck of the aeries.

"That's something." Robyn pulled even with her, staring down at the tower.

"It was here first, and it still stands. Gaelan will be beautiful again, once all this is over."

They flew past the city walls and out over the purple canopy of the Riamhwood, turning north to skirt the edge of the Sléibhte Mora. The peaks were dusted with new snow from the great storm that had passed over them days before. Every valley was filled with fallen trees and mud, new wounds torn into the foundation of the world.

"What awaits us up north, Quince?" Robyn asked as they flew. Her color had returned. Maybe it was the flush of exercise, maybe the distance from Gaelan. Whatever the reason, she seemed more herself than she had in days.

Quince shook her head. "I don't know. Morgan needs me. That's all I'm sure of."

"Who is this Morgan, really?" They'd had precious little time to talk before.

"I don't know that, either." She gave a rueful laugh. "Xander found him… or maybe he found Xander, while we were separated on Oberon. He saved us, on more than one occasion. I'm certain he's not a little boy. Or… not *only* a human child. Beyond that…." The vastness of the Riamhwood threatened to overwhelm her. It stretched from the foothills all the way down to the sea, too far to see from their location. Down there, somewhere to her right, Xander, Jameson, and half of Gaelan were winging their way toward Errian on the shores of the Argent Sea. "I think he might be connected to the nimfeach."

"Can you trust him?" Robyn's eyes were narrowed.

Quince shrugged. "Without him we'd all be dead."

Robyn looked away. "There are worse things."

Quince didn't contest that.

They flew on for the rest of the morning. The air was fresh and crisp, washed clean by the storm.

Around midday, they found a spot on the slopes of one of the mountains that looked out over the woods below. Whirills sang in the branches of the trees below them, and the sun through the leaves warmed Quince's shoulders.

Quince brought out her canteen and some of the hard tack. She handed it with a few dried berries to Robyn, who took them with a half smile.

"I remember when we used to steal away," she whispered, her gaze lingering on Quince's face as she nibbled on their lunch.

"That was a long time ago." Quince tried to remember how she had felt, with the attention of a queen on her. She'd been so young. It had been flattering to be singled out, by fate and by the queen, for such special attention.

"Do you ever regret it?"

"What?"

"The choices we made."

"Ah." Her flight from Titania with Jameson and Xander…. Lyrin and Davyn. "Sometimes. I wish there'd been another way. We've all suffered for it."

Robyn nodded. "I wish I'd never been born to royalty. That I'd been born in a little village to a blacksmith and a seamstress."

Quince laughed. "Close enough to where I started out, and yet, here I am with you." She finished her berries and washed them down with a swig of lukewarm water, handing the canteen over to Robyn. "We were chosen, by fate or the nimfeach—or both. Once that happened, I think our chance at a normal life was over."

"Probably. At least I found you in the bargain." She leaned over and kissed Quince tenderly.

The touch of her lips was like fire. Her face burned, and an electric sizzle raced up Quince's spine.

She broke away, embarrassed. She should be in better control of herself than that. Besides, they had little time to waste.

Robyn frowned.

"We have a lot of ground to cover." Quince turned away first. She brushed the crumbs off her hands and put away the canteen. "Ready?"

"Whenever you are."

She regretted the biting tone in Robyn's words, but there was nothing to do about it now. They really did need to go.

She spread her wings and took off into the sky, and Robyn followed.

· · ·

As afternoon shaded into evening, the host from Gaelan reached the waystation where Quince, Xander, Jameson, and Morgan had stayed the week before. Jameson blushed as he saw the place, far below, where he and Xander had first consummated their relationship.

They landed on the rocky top of the island. Xander was surrounded by his new lieutenants.

"I want the camp set up along the southern side of the Orn." Xander took in the denuded banks of the river. The floodwaters had mostly subsided, but the river was still partly clogged with fallen trees. "Far enough from the water to be safe, just in case. No fires, everyone under tree cover. We can't avoid being seen with this many skythane when we fly, but we can make it harder for them to find us at night."

"Should we forage for more food? Our supplies will run out before we reach Errian." Venin glanced toward the east. "There are hoarberries, auxen, and verils in these woods."

"Perfect." Xander had no idea what two of those three things were. "Just remember, be careful." Xander looked at Jameson and Alix. "We'll join you shortly."

"Yes, Your Highness." Venin bowed, and he and Alia took off to direct the rest of Xander's host.

Xander sighed, and Jameson laughed. "You're not going to win that battle."

"You're probably right." He leapt off the ledge, swooping down to the waystation, and Jameson and Alix followed.

Xander alighted on the broad terrace that fronted the waystation itself. It was just as he remembered it. He'd been standing there just a few short days before with Quince, staring up at Titania's sun. How much had changed in a week.

He and Jameson went inside, looking for Quince's carry sack.

Outside, Alix closed his bi-wings and followed.

The room was untouched, except for their bags, which had been rummaged through. "We may be out of luck." Xander picked up his own carry sack.

Strangely his old pulse pistol was still inside.

Jameson held up a holo. "Jessa," he said, by way of an explanation. "Why didn't Dani's men take these?"

"This wasn't Dani. It was Morgan."

Jameson looked to him questioningly.

"*He* rummaged through the bags. Remember, he brought us our clothes? Maybe Dani was sloppy and didn't come down here to check."

"Maybe so."

"Is this Quince's bag?" Alix asked, holding up a third carry sack.

Xander nodded. "Is the key still there?"

Alix pulled out the contents, including some clothes, the jar of salve, and finally the key. "Is this it?"

It was a smooth round sphere made of amalite. Jameson took it and held it up to the light. The surface of the metal squirmed and twisted. "Looks like it."

"Do you know how to use it?"

Jameson shook his head. "I…." He stopped, getting that faraway look Xander had come to associate with a memory storm.

Xander steered him toward one of the cots. "Breathe, Jameson. In and out."

He put his hand on Jameson's chest like he'd seen Alix do, and Jameson's hand on his. "Follow me. Like this. In. Out." He demonstrated, and Jameson nodded, his eyes still strangely unfocused.

Come on, dammit. You can overcome this.

Elyra stretched her black wings, holding the key aloft. It was warm to her touch. She reached inside….

• • •

Jameson felt Xander's hand on his chest, felt Xander take his own.

The key began to glow, warming to her touch. It hummed, too, the vibration traveling up her arms. In her mind, she pictured the place she wanted to go.

Jameson breathed slowly, one breath in, one out.
"Are you okay?" Xander asked.
"I… I can see it."

She could smell the sea, hear the sound of the waves crashing against the massive stones of Torr Talam, near Errian. Hear the cries of the imprean as they soared over the sea, looking for fish among the waves.

"See what?"
"How she did it."

She pushed the image into the key, and the air before her spit and tore, opening a doorway between the House of the

Sky and the Argent Sea. Still holding the key, she leapt off the balcony and into the rift, to where her lover awaited her.

"Who?"

"Elyra. She knew how to use it." He was aware of being simultaneously in two places at once. Of being two people at once—Elyra and Jameson/Lyrin. It was unsettling, and yet it was a marked improvement on the whole knocked-out-by-memories thing.

"Good. Now come back to me. Jameson?"

The sound of the ocean waves faded away, and the waystation reappeared in his vision. Jameson's eyes focused on Xander's. "That was… better."

"Yeah?" Xander's brow was knitted.

"I was more in control. I think."

Xander nodded. "You didn't go into freefall, anyhow. That's something."

Alix stared at the vial.

He shouldn't do it. He'd watched Xander and Jameson over the last two days. They belonged together. Or at least, they fit together really well.

And yet… they should know. He would want to

know if someone had betrayed him. If someone had manipulated his emotions. Wouldn't he?

If they were strong enough, they would overcome it, and if not… "Guys?" he held up the vial. "Is this what I think it is?"

Xander took it and turned it over, looking at the black liquid inside. "Probably? It looks like the vial Quince gave to Rogan."

"Rogan, the Syndicate boss?" Alix growled.

"One and the same. It's a long story."

"Oh God, Xander." Alix pulled him close, hugging him tightly. "I didn't want you to ever have to see him again."

Jameson frowned, and Xander tensed under Alix's touch. He let go.

"I wonder why she had it." Xander pushed Alix gently away.

"Can I see your hands?" Alix asked.

Xander nodded, frowning. He held them out for Alix to inspect.

Alix turned them over and looked at his fingernails. "When did you take pith?" Alix asked.

"I didn't." Xander pulled his hands back. "I'm not a pith addict. Why would you ask me that?"

"I'm sorry. It's just—"

"What?"

"I hate to say this." He really did, but there was no going back now.

"Something worse than calling me a pith addict?"

Alix nodded. "Pith users show a few physical signs after using the drug for a prolonged period. One of those is double 'moons' in their fingernails. It's subtle…. You have to look for it."

Xander looked at his nails.

"Let me see." Jameson looked at Xander's hands. "He's right about the nails. I've seen it before, in patients. But why would Quince…." He curled up his own fingers to look at his own hands.

Alix knew what Jameson would find there. "Holy shit." He sat down hard on the cot.

"What?"

"Mine have the double moon too. That means…."

Alix knew what it meant. Pith was psychoamoratic. It could induce feelings that felt like love in its users.

Xander sank down next to Jameson, and they looked at each other. Alix could imagine their thoughts. *Does he really love me? Do I love him?* Jameson could see it mirrored in Xander's eyes.

"I'm going to give you two a moment." Alix backed out of the room, leaving them alone.

• • •

JAMESON STARED AT XANDER, replaying their time together in his head.

Their first kiss. The night right here at the waystation. The electric feeling he associated with Xander's touch. The *fated connection* they had.

"Is it all a lie?" he whispered at last.

"I don't know." Xander reached for Jameson's hand. The familiar electricity ran up Jameson's arm. He pulled his hand away as if it were burned.

"How do we know if this thing between us… if any of this is real?" He was cast away at sea. Loving Xander and coming out had required a leap of faith, a belief in the growing feelings in his heart. It was a repudiation of everything he'd been taught growing up, but he'd done it, had trusted his heart.

What if it was all just manipulation? Had Quince done this to them because she needed them to be together, at the end? Would any of this have come to pass without the drug?

The pith was like poison in his veins.

"Jameson… I—"

"I need some air." He got up and ran out of the room, leaving a surprised Xander behind. He ran past Alix and took to the sky, wanting to put some distance between himself and both of them.

He needed to be alone.

10

BOLT FROM THE BLUE

It was midafternoon, and the sun shone warmly across the world as if nothing had changed.

Quince wondered about that. Surely the turbulence of the storm that had all but destroyed Gaelan wasn't the last of the rough weather they were in for. Two settled weather systems had been thrown together as one, and it would take a while for it all to work itself out.

She wondered, too, if it was even possible to send the Oberon half of Titania back to the human universe, or whether they were all trapped in the Titania one forever. Well, maybe *trapped* wasn't the right word.

"River cat got your tongue?" Robyn asked, her brow furrowed.

"Just trying to make sense of it all."

Robyn laughed, and warmth spread through Quince's chest. It was the first time in decades she'd heard that beautiful sound. "Which part? The shift? Your friend Morgan?" She paused. "Me?"

"All of that and more. I should be back there with Jameson and Xander…. Lyrin and Davyn."

"Old habits die hard."

Quince nodded. The wind slipped past her wings, and the sun warmed her back.

"We could still go back."

"Can't. Morgan needs me." Quince frowned. The forest canopy was nearly unbroken below, a tapestry of greens and purples that tugged at her heart. She'd been away from Titania for too long.

It was Erro now. She remembered one of the old legends:

Split in twain as two lost souls
Erro now two simm'ring coals
Titania in her purple robes,
and Oberon his disaster sows….

"I misjudged Morgan and his importance before. I won't make the same mistake again." Morgan was the tip of the iceberg. She was sure of it.

Robyn looked troubled. "What do you think we will find?"

"I don't know. Something terrible, I fear. I—"

Pain lanced through her shoulder, and something was burning. "What in the Split?"

"Pulse rifle! Dive!"

A blaze of light shot past her right wing, and Quince obeyed Robyn's command. She tucked her wings back and plummeted, making herself a harder target. She wobbled in flight, her right wing radiating pain.

Next to her, Robyn also dove, her bi-wings pulled in too.

As they approached the canopy, Quince pulled up short to fly low above the trees, an action that caused her intense pain, making her gasp. Tears formed in her eyes.

Robyn was right behind her as they soared rapidly over the treetops, skimming the trees of the Riamh-wood. "How… bad… is it?" she managed.

"It looks like a glancing blow… some singed feathers, maybe a flesh wound. How does it feel?"

"Like someone shoved a hot poker into my wing."

"Fly for as long as you can stand it, and then we'll find a place to land. We need to put some distance between ourselves and those OberCorp bastards."

"You… sure it was them?"

"Who else?"

Some of the escaped enforcers. Quince nodded. "I can go farther." Each beat of her wings sent a shockwave of pain down into her shoulder.

They flew on, and Quince could feel concern radiating from Robyn, though she didn't say any more. That was a blessing. Quince was having a hard enough time just concentrating on flying, and every now and then, she flinched at the pain and dipped closer to the treetops.

At last, Robyn pointed ahead. There was a clearing by a small lake.

Quince nodded. *Just a little farther….*

The last of the trees passed beneath them, and then she was going down. She aimed for the shore but overshot it and plunged into the cold waters of the lake.

She sunk like a stone, opening her eyes to a world of bubbles and slanted green light. Startled yellow fish darted out of her way, and then she was clawing herself back toward the air, toward the sky.

She surfaced with a great gasp, and Robyn was there to help her to shore.

Together they crawled out of the water and onto a verge of purple grass that offered a soft place to lie down.

Quince just lay there for a few moments, letting her breathing slow, her eyes closed, willing the pain to stop.

Robyn put her cool hands on Quince's wing.

"Is it bad?"

"It could be worse." Robyn kissed her. "I'm going to start a fire so we can heat some water. The pulse cauterized the wound, but I don't want to risk an infection."

Quince grimaced. "Fire means smoke… unless you have croyol here? Or wrenwood bushes?"

Robyn shook her head. "Neither, I'm afraid. We'll have to make do with regular wood."

"They'll find us." The darkness underneath the canopy of the Riamhwood now seemed much more threatening.

"That's what I'm counting on." Her face was both terrible and lovely to behold in its anger. "We'll just have to be ready for them."

JAMESON FLEW UP and up into the sky, his wings lifting him until the island and the Orn River itself were mere spots on the curve of the world far below.

His new foundation had been severely shaken. One more sharp blow might shatter it altogether.

He'd given up so much of himself for Xander, for these worlds. This world. He'd let it erode at his sense of who he was until that old self had all but collapsed in a torrent of emotions and memories that weren't his own.

For the moment, they remained mercifully silent.

He was in love with Xander. He felt it. He knew it in his bones. He'd kept that part of himself at bay for so long. For years, a decade, even. His attraction to the man, at least, that much he could say was true. If he were honest with himself, he'd felt it the day they'd first met, and unless Quince had figured out a way to slip him some pith on the shuttle ride down to Oberon City, he was sure she wasn't responsible for *that*.

What about all the rest?

If she'd been steadily dosing the two of them, how could he separate what was real and what was the drug?

He soared in lazy circles high above the ground where all his troubles were distant, all his fears and cares and joys left behind far below.

He needed this space.

What if he'd thrown away his old life for something that was false?

Who was real? Jameson or Lyrin?

You always do this. When something was hard or new or scary, he ran away. From Beta Tau. From the enforcers he'd killed. From Xander, more than once.

He'd tried to break the pattern with Xander, and yet

here he was, literally running away once again at the first sign of trouble.

Surely Xander must be wrestling with this too. Talking it over with Alix.

Jameson's blood ran cold. This was just the opening Alix needed, just the wedge to push between them.

Jameson didn't know if all of what they had was real, but he sure as hell wasn't going to let Alix take it away before they had the chance to sit down and figure it out. *No more running.*

Decided, he tucked back his powerful golden wings and dove toward the waystation and Xander.

XANDER SAT DESPONDENTLY on one of the cots in the waystation's room, staring at the doorway through which Jameson had just disappeared.

"Dammit, Quince, what the hell were you doing?" He looked down at the bottle of pith in his hand. There was enough of the potent drug there to dose half of Oberon City.

They didn't *know* she'd been using it on the two of them. Not really. But it made sense. She'd needed the two of them together for the shift, and what better way to guarantee it than to make them both pith-happy and in love? *Fuckitall.*

"I'm sorry, Xan." Alix sat down on the cot next to him. "Give Jameson time. He's got to work this out too."

Xander looked over at his ex. Alix sounded sincere. "Was any of it real?" He shook his head. "Would he even have liked me without this?" He held up the bottle, looking at the black liquid inside. Black as death. "I was a total bastard to him when we first met."

"I don't know." Alix sounded uncomfortable. "It was so strange to see you two together. To find out you didn't wait for me—"

"I thought you were dead."

Alix nodded. "That's fair." He sighed. "Still, it hurt to see you two together. But… I was glad too. In a weird way. Glad you found someone to make you happy."

Xander snorted. "But did he really? Or was it this?" He stood and began to pace back and forth inside the small space. "I don't know anymore. Goddammit, I just don't fucking know!" He looked at the bottle once more and then hurled it against the wall. The glass shattered, and the black liquid splashed across the rock and dripped down to the floor.

Alix stared at him for a long moment. "I'm sorry." He turned away. "I shouldn't have mentioned it."

Xander took a deep breath. "No, it's better that we

know. That we figure this out ourselves." He lifted Alix's chin with his hand. "I'm glad you told me."

Alix looked up into his eyes and, in one smooth motion, stood up and kissed him.

Xander's eyes went wide, and he pushed Alix away. "Hey. That's not what I meant. I'm with Jameson."

"Oh God, Xander, I'm sorry." He backed away and stumbled over the cot. "I'm so sorry. It's just been so long."

Xander felt badly for Alix, he really did, but he wasn't the one who'd left. "I… I need to figure out things between Jameson and me first."

"No, I get it. I shouldn't have…." Alix turned to leave. "I'll give you a few moments."

Xander grasped his hand and pulled him back. He cupped Alix's face in his hands, looking him right in the eyes. "I'm glad you're alive. That you're here. It just *can't* be like it was before."

Alix grimaced. "I said I get it. I'll be outside."

Xander let him go and sat down on the cot, staring at the black liquid puddling on the floor. Quince had a lot to answer for.

Jameson would come back. He always did. Then they could talk this out.

The little cavern shook, and debris rained down outside the entrance. "What the hell was that?"

"Pulse rifle." Alix's voice came in from outside. "We're under attack!"

Xander slipped off his pack and pulled out his own gun. He slipped up next to the doorway. "Where?" he shouted.

"Across the river."

Xander peeked out the doorway, then pulled his head back just in time to avoid having it fried by the pulse beam that struck the back wall and fused a patch of rock. "They're not playing around." It had to be some of Dani's escaped rangers.

Hopefully someone from camp would notice what was going on, but in the meantime, they were on their own.

Xander crouched down and looked out the doorway again. Alix lay on the ground behind the short rock wall that surrounded the terrace. If he stayed low, he could get there too, and they could figure this thing out.

He lay on the ground and crawled out onto the terrace, flattening his wings as close to the stone-paved terrace as he could. Landers really had an advantage there.

He reached Alix without incident. "You okay?"

Alix shot him a grin. "I bent over to pick up a pebble. I was gonna throw it into the river. That first shot missed me by a hair's breadth."

"What do we have?"

"Two rangers, near as I can figure, on the far bank. No one up above us, I think, or we'd be screwed."

Xander nodded. "Here goes nothing." He popped above the wall and fired a haphazard shot into the trees on the far side of the Orn.

A pulse blast came in quick response, but Xander had already ducked behind the wall. The angle of it gave him a better sense where their attackers were.

"Just like our old hunting trips, huh?" Alix was grinning ear to ear.

"Not quite. Swamp bears don't fire back." He suppressed a grin of his own, not wanting to give Alix the satisfaction. "They're about ten degrees left of center."

A shadow slipped by them.

"Oh shit," Xander yelled, glancing up at the hill above them. "There's someone up there too."

11

——————

ATTACK

Jessa cursed herself for an idiot.

She wasn't supposed to curse, but as the daughter of a Christianist pastor, she'd done a whole lotta things in her life she wasn't supposed to, and her current situation deserved it more than most.

She sat in the back of a hoversport, the black transport vehicles in vogue for moving rangers and enforcers around this crazy little world. From what she could tell, they were basically a corporate army.

Jessa wished she really did work for GSN. There was a helluva story here. Unfortunately, GSN was a universe away.

When she'd walked into that office, she didn't know what she'd expected, but certainly not this.

"Welcome, Ms. Althorpe. I'm Lena Preston, CEO of OberCorp." The woman was tall and thin, her face angular and beautiful in an exotic, cold way. She wore a crisp business suit, and her green eyes were ice-cold. She held up a blade file. "So nice of you to join me. Please have a seat."

"I… I'm Jessa Smithson. I'm not sure who this Althorpe person is. I'm here from GSN—"

"Have a seat."

Jessa complied, not sure where this was going, or how Lena knew her real name.

"You know, you did a nice job planting that profile in the grid. It almost fooled me, which is why you were left cooling your heels down in the lobby all day yesterday." She got up, tapping the file against her hand, and circled around her plas desk. "But there was something about the name. Jessa. Jes-sa. You know how something tickles the back of your mind until it clicks?" She leaned back against her desk, tapping her manicured green nails against the plas.

"Honestly I don't know—"

"Oh, cut the crap. I know who you are. I even know why you are here." She set the blade file on the desk and waved her hand over it. A tri-dee of Jameson appeared, suspended in midair above the file. "I went back into my notes about the whole Titania affair, and lo and behold, Jameson had a girlfriend back on Beta Tau. A woman named Jessa."

"There are a hundred thousand Jessa's in the Common Worlds, maybe more."

"But only one of them showed up here."

It was time to drop the pretense. "All right. Assuming I am this Jessa Althorpe—"

"You are."

"It's fiancée, thank you. And what's the 'Titania affair'? Where is he? Where's Jamie?"

The woman nodded. "Good. I like it when people are honest with me." She sat back and interlaced her fingers over her chest. "I honestly don't know. Since the shift, we're running blind without satellite coverage."

"The shift?"

"Yes. We… that is, Oberon… seems to have been forcefully reunited with its wayward other half."

"I don't understand." What was the woman talking about? Surely they were no longer where they had been, but beyond that….

"When this world was split in half, thousands or hundreds of thousands of years ago, the other half shifted somewhere else. Now we too, apparently, are in that somewhere else."

Different constellations. "What does that have to do with Jamie?"

"He's one of the criminals responsible for it."

What the hell was she talking about? "Where is he? I want to see him."

"I don't know where he is right now. But I do know where he's *going* to be."

"And where's that?"

"A place called Errian." She leaned in and took Jessa by the chin. "And you're going to be my bait to catch him."

Now she was on a transport, part of a fleet sent to subjugate this place called Errian.

Jamie was on his way there too. Apparently.

She had to figure out a way to warn him. Despite what Lena Preston thought, Jessa was *no one's* damsel in distress.

THE EYELET-SHAPED ISLAND between the two arms of the Orn grew larger and larger as the wind at this lower elevation rushed past his wings, warming him up.

He'd decided. He would talk it out with Xander. It was what he should have done right away, but he found he was still prone to running when things became difficult. He needed to break that pattern, once and for all.

There was a flash of light below, followed by a rumble.

What the hell?

Then another.

Pulse rifle discharge. Someone was attacking the waystation.

Two more blasts, this time from the terrace. That would be Xander and Alix?

Jameson had the advantage. No one was expecting him. He could slip off to camp, bring reinforcements, and overwhelm their attackers.

Then he drew close enough to see the ranger crawling across the rocky outcrop that was the backbone of the island, toward the waystation. Xander and Alix were probably focused on the assailants across the Orn. If Jameson didn't take action now, they might both be dead with pulse bolts through the back by the time he returned with help.

He spread his wings and slowed his fall, turning toward the far bank of the river. If he planned it right, he'd be able to sweep the man off the heights from behind, but he'd be leaving himself open to pulse rifle fire from the others. *Cross that bridge.*

The ranger had just reached the edge of the plateau and was aiming his rifle when Jameson swept up behind him, skimming the ground like a hawk. He'd gained better control over his golden wings in the past two weeks, and he smiled with grim pleasure as he closed on his prey.

The man must have heard something or seen his shadow, because he twisted around at the last second, but it wasn't enough to save him.

Jameson grabbed him by his black shirt and threw him over the edge, soaring back up into the sky as the man's body plummeted to the ground below. He waited for a bolt of pulse fire to take him from the far bank.

Xander pointed. "It's Jameson!"

Someone screamed, and a body dressed in the black of the enforcers hit the ground in front of them with a sickening *thud*.

"We have to give him cover!" Alix shouted. He popped up and started laying down fire toward their attackers' position in the forest.

Xander joined him, and a broad swath of vegetation blew to blackened bits, showering the waters of the Orn with debris.

The ruckus must have captured the attention of someone at the campsite, because soon the sky was swarming with skythane.

Their allies fired a few more shots before their attackers were dispatched. None among the skythane were injured. A great cheer went up as the last man was killed.

Xander was breathing heavily, finding it hard to believe he was still alive. He stood and surveyed the carnage. The riverbank would recover, but the dead men… their families would mourn them when they didn't come home.

He turned to look at the man whom Jameson had killed.

His neck was broken, twisted at an odd angle, his eyes open and staring at the sky. A puddle of blood oozed from underneath his chest.

Jameson alighted next to them. He glanced at the man's body and then turned away, looking green around the edges. "Are you two okay?" he asked Xander. "I saw him about to shoot you, and I just acted." He threw his arms around Xander.

Xander hugged him back, but with considerably less enthusiasm. "Yeah, we're okay. Thanks for taking him out."

Jameson seemed to sense the change. He pulled back, holding on to Xander's shoulders, and looked him in the eye. "We should talk."

Xander nodded. "Alix, would you mind giving us a little privacy?"

He expected his ex to balk.

"Of course. I'll head back to camp and let them know what happened here. I'll see you there?"

Xander nodded. "We'll follow you shortly."

Alix strapped on his bi-wings and then leapt off the wall of the terrace, swooping across the river toward camp.

"Let's carry the body inside. No point making it easier on Dani and her crew if they come to see what happened."

Jameson nodded, and they hustled the man's body into the waystation. Xander did a quick check of the man's pockets, but there was nothing of interest. He'd probably carried a pack and left it behind somewhere.

The pulse rifle had been bent on impact and was useless. Fortunately, he had the one he'd brought with him from Gaelan.

Jameson stared at the black stain on the wall, then looked at Xander with a frown. "Pith?"

Xander nodded. "I was angry. I still am." He looked at Jameson. The man still *looked* the same. Xander still *felt* the surge of love when their eyes met. It was all tainted. "How can I *know*?"

Jameson held his gaze. "I can't tell you that. All I can say is that I felt something—a spark, a connection—before we set off on this crazy adventure. The first time I met you."

"I felt it too." Xander was the first to look away. "It was just lust. At first, anyhow. Anything after that is suspect."

Jameson sighed. "I still *feel* it."

Xander nodded. "I do too. But I need some time." Time to sort out what was real from what had been foisted upon them by Quince's well-intentioned but ultimately destructive actions. "You've used pith before?"

"Not myself. With clients."

"How long does it take for the effects to wear off?"

"I don't know. It varies with the potency and purity of the drug. How often it was administered. At what dosage."

Xander forced the words out, as if his heart wasn't breaking. "If you had to guess. How long… until I know if what I feel is real?"

Jameson shook his head. "It doesn't work that way. Pith changes you, physiologically, and we don't know when Quince stopped dosing us. Or if she even did."

"You have a better explanation for this?" He held up his hand. Part of him wanted to chop off his offending fingers.

The hell of it was he could see how much this was hurting Jameson, and it was killing him too.

Jameson's shoulders sagged. "No. I don't. I wish I did." He looked out the doorway at the evening light.

"We should get back to camp. I want to get an early start tomorrow to test this thing out." He held up the key.

"Do you know how it works?"

Jameson shook his head. "Not yet. Sort of—I mean, I *saw* it, but I don't know exactly *how* they did it? I'll have to dive into the memories again for that."

Xander frowned. "That seems dangerous."

"Maybe so. But I need to get to Errian to see what's happening there."

"We'll go together. That much I can do."

Jameson held out his hand, palm out. "Sorry, but I don't think that's a good idea. You should take some time, figure out how you really feel."

Ouch. "I… I suppose you're right."

"Besides, you need to be here for your people. Bring them with you to Errian, like we planned." Jameson's voice softened. "I don't know how long I'll be able to hold the waygate open, in any case. It's best if I find out what's going on there first."

Xander didn't care for that idea. "You shouldn't go alone."

"You're right. I'll ask Alix to go with me. He knows OberCorp better than any of us. And he might be able to help me control these memories better."

And it will keep him away from me. Xander took Jameson's hand. "Are the memories bad right now?"

Jameson flinched. Just a little, but Xander felt it. "Not at the moment, but they're always there."

"Take Venin too. He knows more about this world than you or I." Xander wondered again why the memories were so much more forceful in Jameson's head than in his own. Maybe because he was new to his skythane heritage? "Come on. Let's head back to camp. We should get settled if you want to get started early tomorrow."

Jameson nodded. He got up and strode out of the room, pausing at the doorway. "I hope you decide that there's more than just pith between us." Then he was out the door and up into the air.

Xander gave him a moment before following, wondering how things had fallen apart so quickly. "So do I."

QUINCE STARED at her lover's sleep sack, silver in the moonlight reflected off the lake. It was past midnight. The forest was quiet save for the occasional mournful call of a white-tailed whirill. The night breeze rustled through the trees, flipping the purple leaves back and forth. In the darkness, they looked pitch-black.

There was a sharp *crack* in the forest.

Robyn looked back at her and smiled.

A man dressed all in black approached the lakeside. His face was darkened with mud so that only his eyes shone white in the shadows of the forest. He carried a pulse rifle. Behind him, another man followed in his footsteps.

They came toward the camp in silence. Only the one sound had given them away.

When they were about two meters away, they raised their pulse rifles and fired shots directly into the sleep sacks.

Quince dropped off the branch where she'd perched above the camp, swooping down on one of the men like a deathhawk.

Robyn dropped from her own tree with deadly grace, even without her wings, and brought the second man down as a cloud of foam exploded from their sleep sacks.

Quince tried to get a good grasp around the man's neck, but he twisted out of her hold and pulled her off balance to fall on top of him.

The ranger was quick. She had to give him that.

Behind her, Robyn fought with the second attacker.

Quince's assailant rolled out of the way and onto his feet, but his rifle had flown out of his hands when she first jumped him.

They circled each other warily as the stuffing from their sleep sacks began to float back down to the ground all around them like snow.

Quince's pulse wound ached. She stretched her wing to try to alleviate some of the pain.

"Fucking wing men," the man spat.

"Fucking landers," she shot back.

"When OberCorp is done with this place, you'll all be working in the mines." He pulled a knife from his belt.

There was a sharp snap behind her, and then silence. She didn't dare look back. "We threw you out of Gaelan. You're the ones who should be afraid of us."

He laughed, an ugly sound. "Wait until you see what's coming. When—"

There was a flash of light, and then he was clutching at his throat. He fell to his knees, choking on his own blood, and then fell face-first into the shallow water of the lake.

"Nice shot," Quince said.

Robyn stood there with a pulse rifle, grinning. "Sometimes you have to fight dirty."

Quince nodded. "Good to have you back." She pulled Robyn in for a deep kiss. She'd missed *this* Robyn.

They separated, and Quince looked at the ruined

sleep sacks. They were heading north, into snow country. She was pretty sure she was gonna regret using them as bait, later.

They collected their carry sacks and what was left of the sleep sacks, moving down the lake twenty meters from the carnage, where she hoped they'd be able to get a few hours of uninterrupted rest. They left the rangers to rot.

I should feel badly about this. Somehow, though, Quince couldn't make herself mourn for the likes of those.

Alix watched from the shadows as Jameson and Xander set up separate tents, across a small clearing from one another.

The Gaelani camp was hidden under the trees, in case OberCorp came snooping. Not that the company didn't have ways to find them anyhow—a good thermal scan would reveal the host hidden beneath the forest canopy in short order—but there was no reason to make it easy for them.

Xander and Jameson were having problems. Alix should have been happy. It was what he'd wanted, right? And yet….

What he had done had clearly shaken Xander to the

core, his cocky know-it-all personality reduced to anger and self-doubt.

Goddammit, it's my fault. If he'd just left well enough alone, Xander—his Xander—wouldn't be broken. The man wouldn't even look him in the face.

Alix had been surprised when Jameson had asked him to come along on an exploratory mission to Errian, and even more surprised when he'd said yes.

He wanted Xander back. There was no denying that. The nine years they'd spent together had been the best years of his life. But not like this.

Jameson was a better man than he'd first judged. Maybe… maybe he and Xander were better off together.

In any case, it was done. Xander needed time to figure it out. That was something they both could give him.

Alix pulled back into the darkness and made his way to his own tent for the night.

12

SHUDDER

Morning dawned cool and damp with a fine film of dew across the top of his tent. Jameson reached up to touch the fabric. The droplets gathered together and ran in a rivulet down to the ground.

The tents were courtesy of OberCorp, another of the stashes Alix had led them to in the House of the Moon. There weren't enough for the whole host, so many of the Gaelani were sleeping on the ground. Jameson had tried to refuse his own, but the skythane of the host had insisted.

It was strange being alone, without Xander, but he respected his need to have some time to work this out. Look how much time it had taken Jameson to come around to being gay.

He sat up on his knees and put his hands together in prayer. It was something his adoptive parents had taught him, and though he no longer considered himself particularly religious, it still brought him comfort. Even if their god was a universe away—if he existed at all.

"Lord, if you are there… if you can hear me, please give Xander the peace he needs to find his way." A part of him laughed at that. The God his parents knew wasn't exactly on a friendly basis with the gays, but Jameson believed that whatever was out there, whatever higher power or being might exist, that it would be more accepting than that. "Amen."

He crossed himself and pulled on his clothes. It was going to be a trying day today, all the more so without Xander by his side.

Last but not least, he pulled on the sun sigil Quince had given him, that day on Oberon before they had stepped through the waygate. Before everything had changed.

Today things would change again. Today he would start to take back his own kingdom. To become Lyrin, King of the Erriani, in truth.

He was struck then by a vision of such clarity and potency that he *knew* it must be true.

. . .

DAEDUS, King of the Erriani, strode onto the golden balcony of the House of the Sun holding Elyra's hand. They raised their clasped hands, the King of Errian and the Queen of Gaelan, and the assembled host cheered.

"On this day, the Erriani and the Gaelani are one!"

JAMESON BLINKED. It had happened before. It would happen again.

He wouldn't lose Xander without a fight.

PATCHES OF FOG clung to the surface of the lake, extending tentative tendrils toward the banks. A flock of *creach* feasted on the bodies of the enforcers a couple dozen meters down the shore, cackling and tossing shreds of meat into the air before snapping them up with their red beaks.

Quince had volunteered to take watch. She was much more practiced at it than Robyn. She turned away, her mouth curled in distaste at the feasting.

The first rays of the sun crested the trees across the lake, dissipating the fog, and somewhere in the forest behind them, something howled.

Robyn looked up at her from one of the hastily repaired sleep sacks.

"Did you get any sleep?" Quince stood and stretched, enjoying the touch of the sun on her arms after a cool night.

Robyn wriggled out of her sack. "A little." She glanced at the sky. "You should have woken me. I would have taken a turn."

Quince shook her head. "I was happy to have the time to think." She dug into her carry sack and pulled out some auxen jerky and her canteen. She offered some to Robyn.

They sat with their backs against a redoak tree and munched on dried meat.

"What about?"

Quince was silent for a long time. "The boys. I wish we could have let them come to each other in their own time."

Robyn put a hand on her knee. "It was the only way. There was no time to waste."

"But what if they find out?" That was what kept Quince up at night—the long-term consequences of her actions. She and Robyn had long discussed the possibility of *encouraging* a relationship. "It might split them apart."

Robyn chewed on a chunk of meat for a long time before replying. "Then we'll just have to hope they never know."

That was about as unsatisfactory an answer as Quince had ever heard. "Nothing to do about it now, I suppose." Quince took a long drink from her canteen. "Want me to refill yours?"

Robyn nodded, handing hers over. "I'll pack up the camp."

Quince took it and made her way along the water's edge. The trees grew right up to the waterline, their roots climbing above the water before diving into the muddy soil below. Small yellow fish darted in schools among them, scattering in a golden flash as Quince passed.

In less than ten minutes, she found what she sought, a small brook that tumbled down the hillside above the lake, bringing fresh, cool water from the mountains to the west.

She knelt, filling the canteens one after another, scanning the forest around her for signs of movement.

There were whipcats in these foothills. Usually they left people alone, but Quince was rusty on her Titania wood lore. It didn't hurt to be careful.

A flock of forest impreans exploded from the trees overhead, flying in agitated circles over the lake.

Quince felt it before she heard it, the ground beneath her feet shuddering. She grabbed one of the redoak trees next to the brook and held on as the earth shook and a grinding rumble filled the world.

Water splashed out of the brook and the waters of the lake lapped the banks hungrily as the tumult grew, setting Quince's teeth on edge. *What the hell?*

Then as quickly as it had begun, it was over. The world stilled, though the birds still soared in distressed circles over the water.

Quince made her way back to the lake, toward Robyn and the campsite. A few trees were down, but it was nothing like the devastation caused by the storm after the shift.

Maybe it was an aftershock. After all, the world had been torn in half thousands or hundreds of thousands of years before. It wouldn't fit back together perfectly. There was bound to be some settling, as unnerving as that was.

"Robyn, you okay?"

"Yeah," the queen's voice came back. "Just a little shaken up."

Quince climbed over the roots of one of the redoak trees and saw Robyn at last.

"What the hell was that?" Robyn glanced at the birds in distrust.

"A quake, for sure. Not certain what caused it,

though. Are those common here?" She didn't remember it being so.

"Not at all." Robyn pulled on her carry sack. "Then again, this is no longer Titania. The old rules may not apply."

Quince snorted. *That* was an understatement. "We should move on."

"Let me check your wound first." Robyn pulled Quince's wing down gently. "I have *rinroot*. It's an astringent and a natural antibacterial." She pulled a small bottle from her pack and dipped her fingers in, then spread it on the wound. "You feel up to flying?"

Quince flexed her wings. "I think so. It's a superficial wound."

"You were lucky." Robyn strapped on her bi-wings.

Quince took one last look around their campsite. "Let's go."

Robyn spread her bi-wings and launched herself into the air over the lake.

Quince came up next to her, her own wings pulling her forward through the sky, away from the site of the battle and toward something even more frightening.

Jameson stood in the middle of the clearing holding the key, trying to figure out how to summon a waygate.

He'd seen it and felt it in his memories, but now, faced with the actual thing, he was at a loss.

He knew, or thought he knew, *how* it should be done. He pictured the place he wanted to go—a small white sand beach south of Errian that he'd "seen" in one of his memories—and tried twisting the key.

Nothing happened. The key remained steadfastly quiescent, its amalite finish swirling languidly under his grip.

The four of them—Xander, Alix, Venin, and Jameson—were surrounded by the host of Gaelan, men and women standing arm to arm under the trees around the small clearing. It was a risk to be out in the open. He'd heard at least two hoversports pass over their hidden camp the night before—but he didn't want to risk interference with the waygate from trees or other impediments. Besides, the host would take to the air soon enough, and there would be no way to hide *that*.

"Not working?" Xander had been distant since the day before. Jameson understood that, though it pained him. He was still *all in* with Xander, even if the man didn't feel the same at the moment. Xander would come around. He hoped.

Jameson opened his mouth to reply.

The ground began to shake, and instinctively he crouched as the quake kicked up dust from the floor of the clearing and shook leaves and cones off the surrounding trees, sending them bouncing across the grassy space.

The shaking continued, setting his teeth on edge, until it suddenly stopped and the woods were silent again. It was over in less than thirty seconds.

"What the hell was that?" Xander asked, looking more angry than scared.

Jameson smiled privately. To Xander an earthquake was probably just one more impediment, one more way the world chose to get in his way. "We just slammed two worlds back together." He dusted himself off. "We can't expect them to be bug free just yet."

Alix nodded. "We're still in beta test, after all."

Jameson shook his head. He *liked* this guy, their earlier dust-up notwithstanding. You weren't supposed to like your partner's ex. It just made things more complicated.

"Try it again," Alix said. "Xander, come here."

Xander frowned but did as he was told.

"Okay, stand in front of Jameson. Jameson, put your hand on Xander's chest, like you and I did before."

Xander undid his shirt.

Alix looked away.

Jameson put his hand on Xander's warm chest, feeling like an interloper.

"Okay, Xander, breathe in deeply, like I showed you both the other day. Then out. In, and out." He watched them a moment, then nodded. "Jameson, you feel that?"

Jameson nodded. "I don't see how—"

"Just try it."

"Okay." Alix had helped him before. It couldn't hurt to try. Jameson closed his eyes. Under his touch, Xander's chest rose and fell. The calmness there belied the turmoil he must be in. He wanted to shake Xander, to make him understand that, pith or no pith, they belonged together. That it wasn't too late to talk about this.

Instead, he focused on breathing, matching Xander's, in and out, in and out, until it was like they were two parts of one organic machine.

"Now," Alix said softly, "reach out for that memory. The one where you used the key to open a waygate. Do you see it?"

Jameson tried to remember the details. He'd been Elyra….

ELYRA STRETCHED HER BLACK WINGS, holding the key aloft. It was warm to her touch. She reached inside.

The key began to glow, and it hummed, too, the vibra-

tion traveling up her arms. In her mind, she pictured the place she wanted to go.

She could smell the sea, hear the sound of the waves crashing against the massive stones of Torr Talam, near Errian. Hear the cries of the imprean as they soared over the sea, looking for fish among the waves.

She pushed the image into the key, and the air before her split and tore, opening a doorway between the House of the Sky and the Argent Sea. Still holding the key, she leapt off the balcony and into the rift, to where her lover awaited her.

JAMESON OPENED HIS EYES. "I think I know how to do it." He pulled his hand away from Xander's chest. Xander buttoned his shirt, and for a moment, his eyes were filled with such longing and naked *need* that it was all Jameson could do not to pull him close.

Then it passed, and Xander turned away, the light gone out of his eyes.

Jameson sighed. It was like there was a pane of plas between them now. "Bring the Gaelani to Torr Talam." Once he knew how things stood in Errian, they could plan their next step. "I will check there every day at sunset, starting in three days. Maybe we can avoid a war with OberCorp, if we're lucky."

Xander nodded, but he didn't turn around.

He needs time. Perhaps this scouting excursion would let Xander work through the doubts that were plaguing him. *Damn you, Quince, for doing this to him. To us.*

Jameson held the key in both hands. He closed his eyes, feeling for the place he'd just seen in his memory. Torr Talam, on the Argent Sea just south of Errian. A half-moon beach of white sand, backed by stark black cliffs. An ancient white tower standing on an outcrop overlooking the sea.

He fixed it in his mind, and envisioned *pushing* it into the key. Using both hands, he twisted the sphere in opposite directions.

It shouldn't have worked. The key was a solid piece of amalite, as far as he could tell. It should have been impossible to twist, and yet twist it did, the surface swirling in agitation, looking like a miniature gas giant. When it reached 180 degrees, it thrummed with power in his hands.

A collective gasp rose from the crowd.

He opened his eyes to see a waygate open from the ground up, the edges spreading in fractal symmetry across the air until it was about two meters high and four across. A cool beach breeze blew through, and water lapped across the white sand toward the forest side. *I did it.*

Torr Talam loomed over the scene, built out of white stone. It was cracked and crumbling, but still magnificent. He wondered what it had been like in its heyday, and who had built it. Humans, or something else?

He raised his arm. "Thank you all for taking me in when I came to Gaelan the first time. I will welcome you in Errian soon!"

The assembled host cheered.

Jameson hoped he could deliver on that promise. He turned back to Xander. "Take your time. I'll be waiting for you."

Xander nodded, his lips set in a tight line. "Keep yourself safe," he managed at last, and turned away to disappear into the crowd.

Jameson watched him go. "Come on," he said to Alix and Venin. "I don't know how long it will stay open."

They picked up their belongings and followed him through the waygate, striding onto the beach.

Jameson turned around, searching the crowd on the other side for Xander. There was no sign of him.

He sighed. With a twist of the key, he closed the waygate.

· · ·

XANDER WATCHED the waygate shimmer and collapse as Jameson peered through the portal looking for something. Someone. *Him.*

He regretted not saying goodbye. Who knew what would happen during the next few days, to either of them? He couldn't help himself. He was suspicious of *those* feelings too. A few weeks earlier, he had looked upon Jameson with disdain, and then he'd fallen hard. He should have *known* there was something else at work between them. Something like pith. Xander cursed himself for an idiot.

"Let's get going!" he hollered, sharper than he intended. "We want to cover as much ground as possible today." It was a good four- or five-day trip from Gaelan to Errian by wing at the best of times, and these were not the best of times. Plus he had an army to feed, and they only had enough food with them for a couple days.

Xander shook his head. It was too much to worry about right then. He had to deal with one thing at a time.

He pulled on his carry sack and looked around. Everyone else was waiting on him. "Let's fly!"

13

STORM WARNINGS

As Quince and Robyn proceeded north, the land beneath them began to change.

The Sléibhte Mora, the mountains that ringed what had been the western boundary of Titania, were covered in clouds, but the valley below and the Riamhwood remained sunny.

The trees of the wood changed first, shading into golden hallerwoods as they entered the northern climes. They passed over one of the minor tributaries to the Orn, and the land below became more varied, long foothills extending from the mountain toward the east. A smell like cinnamon was strong in the air.

Along the way they talked, filling in the time they'd been apart.

"What was it like, living among the landers?" Robyn asked, her arms beating tirelessly, though she must have been fatigued. The bi-wings required different muscles than skythane wings.

Quince frowned. "They're just people, like us." She thought about it, about her time in Oberon City. "It was… I don't know… confining is probably the best word? They spend so much time indoors, and when they're not inside, they are mostly stuck on the ground." She gestured at the land below them. "I learned to be like them. To access their systems. I spent most of my life inside, behind a desk."

Robyn snorted. "I find that hard to believe."

"It's true. Sometimes I would get out of the city, though. With Xander…. Davyn."

"Xander is fine. He seems to have forgotten his old name, so I suppose Xander is as good a new one as any."

Quince nodded. "With Xander and Alix," she clarified.

"How did they meet?"

Quince sighed. She'd never told Robyn the full story. In part because she'd considered it dangerous to put such information in writing, but she had also been too chicken-shit to do it. "I lost Xander for a time."

"I remember. You said he was adopted."

"Well, yes. No. Not exactly." She took a deep breath

and closed her eyes. The warmth of the sun felt so good on her wings. Maybe she could delay just a moment or two longer—

"I know that look."

Quince's eyes sprang open.

"There's something you're not telling me." Her eyes were narrowed. Robyn knew her too well.

"Okay. You have a right to know." She sighed. "When Xander was about eleven years old, his parents were killed by a thief in the Slander. Before I knew it, he was gone, taken in by one of the Syndicate bosses. A man named Rogan." She glanced over at Robyn. The queen was silent, her lips pressed into a thin line.

Quince went on. "Rogan… he's the kind of man who likes boys. Likes to… likes to use them."

"What did he do to my son?" Robyn's voice took on a dangerous edge.

"Things I won't talk about. Even now. He can tell you, when you see him again. If he wants to." She pursed her lips, thinking about Rogan and the way he'd treated Xander. "Things he'll pay for, when the time comes."

Robyn was silent for a long time.

Quince couldn't imagine getting that kind of news about her own child. Well, maybe she could. Xander had been like a son to her too, especially after she'd fled Titania with the boys. It had nearly killed her.

"Did Alix work for him? For Rogan?" Robyn asked at last.

"No, nothing like that. Alix ran into Xander once, on the street. Something about Xander stuck in his mind. He tracked the boy down and bought out his contract from Rogan. Bought him his freedom." She didn't mention the electrical charge Rogan had inserted into Xander's head to insure the boy's compliance. Enough was enough, for now.

"Why didn't *you* save him? Find him? Prevent the whole thing from happening?" Robyn's question caught her off guard, though in truth she had asked it of herself often enough.

"I—"

"What were you so busy doing while he suffered? Enjoying *lander* culture? Sleeping with *lander* women?"

Quince closed her eyes again, unwilling or unable to look Robyn in the eye. "I failed him." It was a whisper.

"Yes. You did." Robyn surged ahead, and Quince let her go. She was angry, and she had every right to be.

Quince had never told anyone the real reason she'd never gone after Xander. She'd thought he was dead, too, killed with his adoptive parents. She'd gone on a two-year binge of sex and alcohol and pith abuse. She'd wallowed in the depths of her shame, blaming herself for losing Xander.

When she'd found out that he still lived, that he had suffered those years of abuse and pain because she'd never gone to find him, she'd felt even worse.

It was the secret shame she'd live with for the rest of her life.

Yes, Robyn had the right to be angry, and she only knew half the story.

JAMESON WATCHED as the waygate shrunk to the size of a pebble and disappeared. He sighed and put away the key, making sure it was snuggled tightly in the bottom of his carry sack.

His troubles with Xander would have to wait. They had work to do.

Jameson stood and pulled the carry sack onto his back and looked around for the first time at the place they'd landed. He was immediately filled with memory vertigo. Images flocked past him, making him unsteady as the barrage took its toll.

"Breathe," someone said, and a warm hand supported his back. *Alix.*

Jameson closed his eyes and concentrated on his respiration. In and out. In and out. He focused on the memories, each in turn, and they began to slow.

One was a child running across the sand to the warm waters of the sea.

In another, she lay on the beach, looking down at her lover, a woman with blonde hair and golden wings.

A third featured a young skythane man with a spear, scanning the azure waters of the Argent Sea.

He sorted through each one, letting them wash over him and dissipate like waves on the sand, and then they were gone.

"You okay?"

"I think so." He opened his eyes. "It was easier, that time."

Venin nodded. "Listen to this one. He knows what he's doing."

Alix shrugged. "Just part of my training." He turned away, scanning the sea and the land around them.

Jameson was starting to understand why Xander had been drawn to Alix. "Thank you."

He wondered how far the memories went back, how much information he could access if he just learned to control it. How it might change him. Jameson shook his head to dispel the thought and looked around.

Torr Talam loomed over him. The white tower was thick around the base and seemed to be made of a single piece of stone. Cracks and fissures, dark with age, ran from the base up toward the top of the tower, and the waves crashed across its base. It sat at the end of a jetty of rock, looming over the bay like a guardian.

They stood on a white sand beach, surrounded by what he could only call a jungle. The plants here were a mixture of purples and greens and yellows, tall trees that reminded him of palms and short bushes covered with heart-shaped leaves and bright green "berries." Vines thick as his wrist wound up the trees, abloom with flowers, no two quite the same. Some were bright yellow. Some were shaped like trumpets. Others were parti-colored—purple and blue, or shaped like orchids.

A loud buzzing *thing* meandered up top one of the flowers and stuck out a long black tongue. It had a fuzzy abdomen, and its carapace was a metallic purple, glinting in the sunlight.

"It's a *zimbee*," Venin said, following his gaze. "They're harmless."

"Is there anything dangerous in this jungle?"

Venin nodded. "The *martach*. It's also called the jungle cat. Six legs, each tipped with claws. It'll disembowel you before you even know it's there. Unless you're unlucky and it decides to save you to feed its brood." He scratched his chin. "There may be other things too. I've only been here once."

Jameson shuddered. "Let's get going, then." He had no desire to become dinner for a six-legged cat. He'd underestimated the local wildlife once before. He wouldn't do it again. "Errian should be just north of here."

Alix put his bi-wings on.

They took to the sky and turned north, following the coastline, staying close to the trees in case they needed to seek cover quickly.

There should have been skythane patrols, especially this close to Errian, but they encountered no one on the way.

After about fifteen minutes, they came across another white stone watchtower, similar to Torr Talam but smaller, which stood out on a promontory that jutted into the sea. Jameson signaled for his companions to set down just inside the tree line of the jungle. He hoped there were no jungle cats this close to the sea.

He needed information. Did OberCorp control Errian like they had Gaelan? If so, how? How strong was their occupation force?

Or was he just being overly cautious?

They watched the tower for half an hour. The sun climbed into the sky, and it was already becoming uncomfortably warm and humid. Jameson *hated* humidity.

No one came or went. There was no sign it was occupied, though someone could certainly be concealed inside.

"I should go take a look." A shiver of fear raced down his back, but he suppressed it.

"Absolutely not." Venin stepped in front of him and blocked the way. "We're expendable. You're not. You're the King of the Erriani. You have to try to remember that."

Alix nodded. "He's right. It should be one of us."

"I can take care of myself." His fear turned to anger. He didn't need these two to protect him. He tried to push past Venin, but Alix grabbed his arm and hauled him back. Jameson was reminded again how strong the lander man was.

"Don't be stupid. If I let you get yourself killed, I'll never hear the end of it from Xander. What you *can* do is see if you can access any memories of that place." He punched a finger in the direction of the tower. "Anything that might help me out if I'm going in blind." He stowed his bi-wings.

"Why you?"

Alix grinned as if it should have been obvious. "Lander. Ranger. Got it? If OberCorp is running things, I can get in without suspicion." He looked down at his skythane clothing. "Okay, with less suspicion. If it's your guys… well, then you can come rescue me."

"I suppose that makes sense."

"So what have you got? How does this whole memory thing work?"

Jameson shook his head. "I wish I knew. Sometimes they just come to me. Sometimes… nothing."

"And now?"

Jameson stared at the white tower. His memory flocks were stubbornly quiescent. "This time? Nothing. Sorry."

"S'okay. We'll just do this the old-fashioned way. Keep an ear out in case I get into trouble." With that he sauntered out from under the shade of the trees and strode confidently across the intervening space, following the rocky ridge that led out to the tower.

It was surrounded by water on three sides, the waves lapping at the bleached rock.

An imprean flew up over the top of the tower, and Jameson *remembered*.

Jeron stood behind him, his warm hands on Theos's shoulders. The sun was rising over the Argent Sea, the waters all a shimmer with its pink light. A single imprean soared above the waves, her white wings lined with gold by the sunshine.

Jeron nibbled his ear. "Do you really think war is coming?"

Theos shook his head. "The landers are stuck on their own half of the world."

"I meant with the Gaelani."

"They have their own kingdom in the west. Why should they make war on Errian?"

Jeron hugged him tightly. "War is never rational."

"Jameson," Venin shook his shoulder. "Wake up!"

Jameson blinked. The vision had been *intense*. He could still feel Jeron's touch on his back, between his wings, and the warmth of his mouth on Jameson's… *Theos's* ear. "Sorry, what?"

"Memory lapse?"

"Yeah." Jameson adjusted his pants surreptitiously. He didn't think Venin noticed.

"Alix is signaling us."

Jameson looked out at the tower and nodded. "Let's go see what he found." He was relieved the lander was all right.

Mostly.

· · ·

Xander led his host on toward Errian, mostly following the course of the Orn. It was a beautiful day, mismatched to the darkness of Xander's mood.

He needed time. He was sure of that much. But letting Jameson and Alix go on ahead without him, into who knew what kind of danger, grated on him.

They'd had to do it. There were more important things than his own needs.

The host passed over Ballifor at midday, the seared patch of the Riamhwood a poignant reminder of the battles fought and those still to come. Hard to imagine losing your village and everyone you grew up with in an instant.

So far they'd seen no other signs of OberCorp's presence. Xander wondered if any of the satellites or Titan Station had survived the shift. Perhaps the station was floating alone in the lonely void, circling Oberon's moon without a planet to orbit. If so, OberCorp would be flying blind—one potential advantage for the skythane.

Alia approached him as the sun passed over them into afternoon. She paced him silently for a while, providing quiet companionship. Xander appreciated that. It was nice not to be alone.

Below them, the Orn wound its sinuous way through the Riamhwood. The purple foliage was particularly lush there in the river basin, and here and there were skythane villages—smaller settlements of Gaelani. Ballifor had been one of those too, before the lander bomb destroyed it.

As the host passed over the small towns, more Gaelani men and women joined them, in ones and twos and threes.

"I've never seen the like of this." Alia looked around at the gathered skythane.

Xander nodded. "I grew up on Oberon. The few of us there kept pretty much to ourselves." The skythane there had been more of a novelty than anything, one that many sought out for sex and the thrill of the *different*. Xander had taken full advantage of that fact, after Alix.

"That must have been hard."

"In so many ways." He grinned to himself.

"Are you… how are you doing?" She glanced at him and then looked away, as if he were too fragile to survive a frank gaze.

"I'll live." Although even that was uncertain. They'd unleashed forces there that might be very difficult to contain. The divide that had separated the two worlds had also set certain limits on aggressive behavior between the landers and the skythane. Now that the worlds were one, things might escalate quickly.

"If I might ask, Your Highness—"

"Xander."

"Xander. What happened between you two?"

Xander sighed. "Are they all talking about it?"

Alia pursed her lips and looked away. "You let him go without as much as a kiss."

He should have anticipated this. People were asking questions. Thinking their leader was a pith-addled mess would help no one. "We had a disagreement on how to proceed," he said at last. "Jameson wanted to go ahead, and I needed to stay with the Gaelani."

"I guess that makes sense. Much more sense than some of the other rumors floating about."

"Other rumors?"

"That you both took pith together."

"Ah." It was out. So much for having time to process it alone. "It wasn't exactly our choice."

"I'd guessed as much." She looked ahead. "Where will we stop tonight?"

"I want to make the House of the Stars tomorrow. We can gather some food in the old orchards there."

"The hunters are gathering what they can as we go. There are six teams out collecting auxen and whatever else they can find, animal or vegetable."

"We'll manage…." There was a strange droning in

the air. Kind of like thunder, but more continuous. "What in the Split is that?"

In the distance three black specks appeared.

OberCorp. "They're coming!" Xander shouted to the skythane closest to him. "Split up…. Don't give them easy targets! Get down below the treeline!"

The dots resolved into hoversports, coming straight at them. The sleek matte-black craft were flat with rounded, aerodynamic corners, and could each hold five or six enforcers. They bristled with pulse weaponry on top and bottom.

Their direction and speed left no doubt. They were on a course to engage their enemy.

Xander signaled for Alia to follow him.

The lead ship zipped through their formation, its pulse laser finding easy targets. One, two, then three skythane were hit, plummeting yelling toward the ground. Their screams were abruptly cut off.

As the second and third hoversports arrived, the host had scattered in a hundred directions.

The first one swung back around, and Xander opened fire on it from above with his pulse rifle. He missed it by fifty meters. *Getting rusty.*

Its own weapon fired back, and he escaped by tucking his wings and diving toward it. *Looks like they no longer care about keeping me alive.*

The gunner couldn't get a good fix on him. He was coming in too quickly.

The wind whistled past him, along with pulse bolts like straight lightning. The howl in his ears was intense.

He had to time this just right, or he'd miss the mark and be vulnerable to the hoversport's lower weapons.

The hoversport veered, but he followed, and he had speed on his side. He came down on top of it like an avenging angel and swept up his wings to slow his descent at the last possible moment.

The other hoversports sprayed pulse fire all around him, but his focus narrowed to just this one. Just this place, riding this hoversport, as he grabbed the cannon turret.

The gunner must have realized what was about to happen, because the turret started to descend into the ship, but he was too late.

Xander pointed his pulse rifle down into the ship under the turret and fired three shots. He let go and soared into the air as blue light wreathed the ship, splitting it apart at the seams and exploding into a thousand or more pieces that rained down into the river below.

More skythane were falling from the sky as the other two ships picked out individual targets. But his people had seen what he had done.

Soon they were dive-bombing one hoversport and then the other.

The first one quickly went down in a stream of fire and lightning, and a victorious shout went up from the skythane.

The second shot off away from the fight, but one of the skythane had already reached it. It was Alia.

She held up her arm and let out a great cry, and then fired into the heart of the beast.

She leapt off and spread her wings as it abruptly changed course and slammed into the forest at full speed, sending up a huge cloud of smoke and a hail of dirt and pieces of vegetation.

It was done. First blood had been drawn.

The skythane gathered. Xander sent them to look for the bodies of the dead.

Some would never be found, but at least they could honor the bodies and spirits of all the fallen. It was only a fraction of his people, and yet they were far too many.

He swore he would seek revenge for each and every one.

It was to be war, after all.

14

BATTLE LINES

IT MUST have been a massacre.

Jameson looked around, his mouth twisted in a grimace of disgust. The stairs inside the tower and the bell chamber at the top were splattered with dried blood, some of it still sticky to the touch.

Alix paced the chamber, peering at the trails of dark red, kneeling here and there to look more closely at something.

Jameson pulled his wings in tightly lest they touch the bloody stone walls of the tower. "What happened here?"

"It's just a guess." Alix pointed to a clump of feathers in the blood against one wall. "There were probably three or four skythane here. The lander force ambushed them, coming in at night."

"How do you know it was landers?"

"I don't, for sure. But there are burns in several places that look like they came from pulse rifles. Do skythane usually carry pulse weapons?"

Venin shook his head. "Not before now." His nose wrinkled in disgust at the sight. "Of course, I can't speak for the Erriani."

Alix nodded. "I'd guess one or two made it out the window and were shot down as they emerged."

Jameson felt sick. He forced down his nausea. This was no time to be a weakling. His people needed him. What had been done here… it was unforgivable. "Is there… do we need to do anything else in here?"

Alix must have seen his distress. "No, I think we've seen all we need to see. Come on."

He led the others outside.

Jameson breathed deeply of the clean sea air, trying to wash away the iron-tinged smell of so much blood.

Alix clapped him lightly on the shoulder. "It's never easy, seeing the aftermath of death and war."

"Are we at war?" Venin asked.

"I don't know what else to call it." Alix looked up the coastline. A cluster of white towers was visible in the distance. "Errian?"

Jameson followed his gaze. "Yes." A flurry of memories vied for his attention, but he closed his eyes and steadied his breathing. Then he chose one among the multitudes.

The city of trees.

Slender white towers, the dead stalks of a native plant called turbien. Strong as concrete, they soared above Kylan's head like a forest of bone-dry trees, somehow majestic and terrible all at once.

He shook his head. They were just natural things. Bigger than anything he had back in his own village, two day's flight from the Erriani capital. But still, just plants.

One day, he'd get used to this place, but for now, he was a country boy on his first day in the big city.

"They're plants." Jameson's voice was soft with awe.

Venin nodded. "They grow them whenever they need a new building. Each one takes about a year to reach maturity. Then it blooms and goes into a quiescent state."

"That's amazing."

"We should get out of sight. There might be Ober-Corp patrols." Alix led them away from the tower.

Jameson cast one last sad look at it.

"I figure it will take us about a day to get there on foot," Alix said as they reached the cover of the trees. He started packing away his glider.

"We can be there in less than an hour if we fly." Jameson tilted his head. "Why walk?"

"You want what happened in there to happen to us too?" Alix pointed at the tower.

He had a point.

"Besides, we have the element of surprise. Once we get there, we'll need to figure out what the OberCorp force is up to and what they've done to the Erriani."

"*My* people." Jameson said it more forcefully than he had intended. Seeing the aftermath of the slaughter in the tower had really shaken him up. It was his fault. Maybe if he'd come there faster… "What about those cat things?"

"Martach. We'll just have to be careful. If we're going on foot, we'd best get started." Venin pulled on his carry sack. "I'll lead the way. I'm the only one who's been here before." He shot an apologetic look at Jameson. "Your memories excepted."

The space under the trees was dark. Jameson sighed. "Lead away. I still haven't gotten full control over them. That all right with you, Alix?"

"Yup. Follow the wing man."

Venin snorted. "Come on, then. I want to reach the outskirts of Errian by nightfall."

Jameson dreaded what they'd find there. He was still shaking from the scene inside the tower, but he had a responsibility. It was one that might have been thrust upon him unwilling, but he'd come to embrace it. If only Jessa and his parents could see him now.

Alix put a hand on his shoulder. "You should practice with that key thing."

"But you just said—"

"Pick a spot about twenty meters ahead and take us there. It will be good practice and might save us some time."

Jameson nodded. "I can do that."

"Besides," Alix said with a lopsided grin. "You never know what we're gonna find in Errian."

XANDER'S PEOPLE gathered the dead, those they could find. There had been at least thirty casualties.

He sent Alia to organize a bonfire, and they cut down redoaks and scavenged deadwood from the riverbanks and built a wide platform in the forest.

One by one the bodies of the fallen were lain on the raised wooden dais. Their friends and family came by to put flowers on the bodies, to say a quick prayer to the gods or a quiet last goodbye.

Xander circulated among them, saying a kind word here, pulling a grieving widow or son or father to him for what little comfort he could offer.

When all had said their last words to the dead, he climbed up on the platform and looked out at the gathered throng. The forest clearing was lit by torches. He held one aloft.

"We suffered today as a nation," he said, so softly that the crowd moved forward to hear. "We lost friends. Family. The world is changing around us, more rapidly than any of us thought." He looked down at the body of a young man, beautiful in repose, his legs crushed by his fall and one wing torn nearly in two. His voice caught in his throat, and he had to turn away before he could go on. "When I came to Gaelan, you accepted me. You fought for me. And now I've brought you to this." He put his arm over his face, afraid to let them see him cry. He would *not* cry.

The platform vibrated under his feet, and then someone pulled his hand gently away from his face.

Alia gave him a sad smile and squeezed his hand. Then she turned to address the crowd. "It's because of this man that we took back Gaelan. It's because of him that we still have a world to stand on, and because of

Xander that we were able to knock those bastards out of the sky."

There were murmurs of assent.

She stood back. "Tell us what we need to do next."

Xander lifted her hand and kissed it, mouthing "Thank you" to her. He'd been thinking about this for hours. As a group, they were too vulnerable. Here in the forest, with torches ablaze, they prescnted a sitting target, but this was a necessary catharsis for his tribe. "We will honor the dead and send them skyward." He held his torch aloft. "Then we will split apart. Our enemy is strong, but it is the strength of a giant. If we attack him as one, he will stomp us into the ground. But if we come at him from many directions at once, like gnats, he won't know where to look, and we will overwhelm his brute force with cunning."

People in the crowd were nodding,

"Tonight we will go from here in bands of no more than five. We will make our separate ways to Torr Talam, south of Errian, three days from now, spreading the word to the Gaelani and Erriani who live between here and there. And if we find the landers in Errian, we will strike."

Errian. Where Jameson had gone.

"Xander!" one of the women shouted.

"Xander! Xander! Xander!" The crowd took up the chant.

Xander raised his hands and signaled for quiet. "Now is not the time for rowdy anger. Now is the time for respect. For silence. For honoring our dead." He turned to gaze once more to the fallen. He remembered what his mother had said in Gaelan two days before when they sent the dead to their maker. "By the light of Gael, we commit the dead to the sky." He touched his right fist to his chest, twice.

Then he knelt and climbed down from the platform. At his signal, five others took up torches. Together, they stepped forward with Xander and lit the pyre.

"May their ashes climb to find their peace," Alia intoned.

"In peace they reside," the crowd replied with one voice.

The flames leapt high, aided by an oil ground out of berries from the *paraba* bush.

One by one, the bodies disappeared into flames, including the young man who lay there so peacefully.

Xander closed his eyes and turned away. *I didn't even know your name.*

He would find a way to avenge the boy, nonetheless. He would avenge them all.

. . .

JAMESON FOLLOWED Venin on the trek through the jungle. It was hot, a clinging tropical heat that soaked through his clothing.

Every few minutes, he would find a spot ahead and create a waygate to move them forward. It was getting easier with practice, though once he almost dropped them into a pond.

They stopped often to drink at the streams they crossed. The water tasted bitter, probably full of minerals that a decent filter would have taken out. There were times when he really missed civilization.

The land here was a series of rolling hills that stretched from the water inland, west toward distant Gaelan. The jungle offered a dense canopy that kept them well hidden from any eyes above—great red-trunked trees with wide heart-shaped purple leaves that Venin called red shanks. Vines wrapped around them with flowers in a riot of colors, and unknown *things* slithered or crawled through the underbrush. So far, nothing had challenged them, but the sun was just reaching its peak, as glimpsed through the crowding of leaves. They still had a long way to go.

Jameson wished they could take to the open sky. More than anything, he wanted Xander to be with him. Jameson missed his cocky manner and his unexpected flashes of direct honesty, even if he was often a pain in the ass about it. He missed his touch….

Alix came up to walk next to him as they skirted a clearing, staying under the cover of the red shanks. "How are you doing?"

Jameson glanced warily at him. He still wasn't sure he trusted Alix.

But he'd also helped Jameson with his memories and had come to help him liberate Errian, so Jameson decided to cut him a little slack. "I'm all right. Sweating like a Tander's World miner, but I'll live."

Alix snorted. "How about the memories?"

"Still there." He could feel them pressing at the back of his skull. It wasn't too bad at the moment, but then again, there were no landmarks here to trigger them.

"Good." Alix was silent for a long time.

Jameson glanced over at him. The ranger was handsome and strong. His stubble, now half-grown into a beard, only accented his masculinity, and there was a determined grit to him that was appealing.

"Can I ask you something?" Alix said at last.

That didn't sound good. "Sure. Shoot."

"Did Xander ever say anything about me?" He caught Jameson's eye and then quickly looked away. "I know it's weird, asking you that."

"That's okay." It *was* weird, but the poor guy had no

one else to ask. "Yeah, maybe once? He said you were a really good guy who rescued him from the Syndicate."

"He did?"

Jameson nodded. "I think he missed you terribly, until…."

"Until you came along. Got it." He spat.

"You guys coming?" Venin had gotten ahead of them. He gestured impatiently.

"Yeah, we're…." Jameson's mouth fell open. A dark shadow fell over Venin, and then the man was gone.

"Venin!" Jameson instinctively made a waygate, jumping through to where Venin had been standing and slamming it closed. Alix ran after him.

Jameson looked up. Venin's legs were kicking as something black, multi-legged and monstrous dragged him up the trunk of a red shank tree.

He dropped his carry sack and pulled out his pulse rifle. "Guard yourself," he called to Alix. "I'm going after him." Jameson launched himself into the air, pulling himself up to the canopy with his powerful wings.

He looked around and caught a glimpse of Venin once more. The thing pulling him along a wide branch looked like a furry spider with a catlike face. It had to be a martach.

It was as nimble as a squirrel among the tree branches. Venin's body was limp in its spindly forelimbs.

Jameson flew in pursuit, slipping past overhanging leaves. He hoped there was only one of the things.

When he caught sight of them again, they were much closer. The cat-spider thing was dragging Venin's body into a sticky-looking nest, made of broken branches, bits of leaves, and a black connecting substance.

Jameson took aim and fired at the thing, managing a glancing blow across the top of its thorax.

It let go of Venin and spun toward him, leaving Venin's body on the high branch. Without warning, it leapt at him, spinning out a black thread behind it.

Jameson pulled back and hit the thing with three pulse shots in rapid-fire order, ripping off its head and forelegs.

It fell just short of him and swung down into the forest, smacking into the trunk of one of the shank tree. Its body shuddered and then was still.

"Holy fuck," Jameson whispered and shoved the pulse rifle into his belt. He surged forward to retrieve Venin's body. There was a nasty bite mark, angry red, on his neck.

A memory pushed into his head, but he shoved it back. There was no time for remembering. He needed to get Venin out of there in case there was another of these creatures nearby.

As he swept Venin's limp form into his arms, the nest exploded with activity. Miniature versions of the thing—kitspiders?—that had attacked them poured out of the hole, leaping toward them.

Jameson leapt off the branch and flew away under the canopy.

One of the nasty little things jumped at him, landing on his shoe. It was about the size of a cat, and it scrambled to get purchase and to crawl up his leg.

He shook it and kicked at the thing viciously with his other foot, dislodging it and sending it tumbling to the ground far below with a loud *rowrsqueee*.

Venin was heavy. Jameson couldn't carry him far by himself. He opened a waygate back to where he'd left Alix.

Alix had his own pulse rifle drawn.

"What the hell was that?" Alix asked as he landed.

"Some kind of spider thing. I killed it, but it had babies." Jameson closed the waygate and scanned the trees, but there was no sign of the little horde.

Alix pulled out a knife.

"What are you doing?" Jameson asked. "He's still alive."

"I know. I want to suck out as much of the poison as I can. Set him down here and hold his shoulders."

Jameson did as he was told.

Alix made two quick, practiced cuts across the wound and then leaned down to suck the poison out of it and spit it out onto the ground. He repeated this five times before he was satisfied.

Then he pulled his canteen out to clean the wound with water. He wrapped one of his shirts around Venin's neck as a tourniquet. "Not too tight, or we'll cut off the blood to his brain. That's all I can do. Duck!"

Jameson put his head down and felt the hot discharge of Alix's pulse rifle. He turned to see one of the kitspider things twitching on the ground, split in two.

"Let's go!"

Jameson grabbed his carry sack and pulled it on, and they took Venin between them and ran as fast as they were able.

When they'd put some distance between themselves and the site of the incident, Jameson slowed down. "Wait, I can get us out of here."

"The key?"

Jameson nodded. It was risky. He only "knew" a few places from his memories in and around Errian, but it was better than being eaten alive out here by cat-spiders.

They laid Venin down gently on the ground. He moaned softly, which Jameson took as a good sign.

He pulled out the key again and held it up. He closed his eyes and remembered the center of Errian.

Tall white towers rose up all around him, and the crater wall was a black rim around the edge of the city. When he was sure he had it, he twisted the sphere. It vibrated, and the waygate opened up before them, showing the streets of Errian.

There were sounds of battle on the other side, the rumble of amalite engines and screaming both in rage and fear.

Alix and Jameson exchanged a glance and looked back behind them.

Three more of the kitspider things were falling from the trees.

They grabbed Venin and leapt through the waygate, slamming hard against one of the white towers.

Jameson flipped the key, and the waygate sliced closed, cutting one of the kitspiders in half. He shoved the key into his carry sack and looked around.

They'd jumped right into the middle of a battleground.

Xander led his small party down the Orn, keeping a watch out for hoversports. Several times they dropped into the forest to avoid them, but either the enforcers on board didn't detect them or they were bound for somewhere else more important.

He'd spread his host thin and wide to protect them. It also made foraging easier, as each cell would look after itself. If he were honest with himself, he was also happy to be shed of the responsibility of them all. He was no born leader. He was more of a lone wolf, and being looked to as the answer to everyone's problems made his scalp itch.

Quince and Kadin had both talked about *prophecy*, but he was really just bumbling around, hoping he'd do the right thing. Whatever that was.

When they reached the House of the Stars, a landmark he knew would provide them shelter, they circled it several times, looking for any signs that it was occupied.

The sun was close to setting, and he was exhausted from the fight and the long day of flight.

Maybe it was a bad idea to go to such a recognizable place, but he didn't know much else of this world, and it was where he'd first started having feelings for Jameson. He needed to revisit it, to see what he felt now.

He set down in the courtyard. It was as empty and forlorn as the first time he had come here. Moss grew in the cracks, and a cool wind blew up from the sea.

He peered inside the castle through the doorway. The main hall was empty. "Hello?" His voice echoed through the structure, but there was no reply. "I think we're safe."

Alia and the others—Harrol, Rix, and Zenia—followed him inside.

"There are some old orchards out there—"

"Let's see what we can find for dinner," Alia said. They nodded, dropped their carry sacks, and followed her outside.

Xander shot her a thankful look. He'd hoped for time alone.

He climbed the stairs to the round room with the balcony, where he'd taken his first flight with Jameson. How much had changed since then.

He stepped outside and put his hands on the railing. It was still warm from the sun, despite the chill wind. He remembered the hug he'd gotten from Jameson when they'd come back to earth.

You taught me how to fly. Jameson's words drifted back to him.

Down below, in the garden, the other skythane had spread out to look for food. The golden statue of Erro stared up at him, beautiful in the sunlight. Erro, like the name Quince had used for the whole world.

He had found Jameson lying there at the base of the statue, weak from contact with it. Held him in his lap—Jameson had fit so perfectly there.

He looked down at his fingernails. It was all a sham.

Angry now, he turned away and reentered the castle, storming down the stairs.

He would get things ready for his camp mates. That was a good way to work off his angry, nervous energy.

By the time they returned, he had a small camp set up in one corner of the room. It was full dark outside now, and the rays of Titania's moon Bandia shone through one of the casements.

He wondered what had happened to Hermia and Lysander, Oberon's moons. Were they still tethered to the combined planets' gravitational well? Or had they flown off into the dark void of space after the shift? He presumed the former, as they had survived the last shift, seven hundred and fifty years before.

"We found a few things." Alia held up some big redfruit.

Rix held up a handful of dirty tubers. "Once we wash them off, they'll be delicious," they said. "Wish we could risk a fire. They're great cooked."

"We'll make do," Xander said. "Harroll, anything?"

"Yeah, some hoarberries." He grinned. "They look pretty ripe too."

"I still have a little dried bread left." Xander opened his pack. "A feast fit for a king."

Alia nodded. "Kind of, by default."

Xander chuckled. She had a point. "Let's eat."

They shared their findings. Rix was as good as their word and washed off the tubers in a nearby stream.

They fell into conversation, Rix, Harrol, and Zenia with their heads together on one side of the fireplace and Alia and Xander on the other.

"You did well back there." Alia chewed on some of the hard bread. "At the ceremony."

"Thanks. They needed a reason to keep going."

She stared at him for a long moment, then went back to her meal. "I know this is hard for you," she said softly.

"You have no fucking idea." He wasn't cut out for this. A couple weeks earlier, he'd been a freelancer for OberCorp, with a life that made sense and a clean place to sleep every night. Now he was all kinds of screwed up.

She snorted. "You haven't been keeping it so secret." She looked straight ahead. "You were much happier when Jameson was here."

"You know why I can't be with him right now." He bit off a piece of his bread. It was getting hard, but it still tasted all right.

"Yeah, I do." Alia sighed. "Quince. You know she was only doing what she had to—"

"Don't defend her. She could have just asked for what she needed."

"Maybe so." She bit her lip.

He glanced sideways at her. "Look, I'm sorry. I don't mean to be an ass."

She laughed. "It just comes naturally to you?"

He couldn't argue with that. "Maybe so. Do you think I was wrong to let him go?"

Alia shrugged. "You had your reasons."

"But do you think I was wrong?"

"Look, people fall for each other in many ways. Sometimes they're in a forced marriage and come to love one another after years. Sometimes it's that whole crazy love-at-first-sight thing. I've fallen for someone I spent a lot of time with, just because I got to see a side of him I'd never known before."

"None of that's like being drugged into love."

"Maybe not. But if you close your eyes, is Jameson someone you can see yourself with in twenty years?"

Xander tried. And goddammit, he was.

He shook his head in frustration. "It doesn't matter. I can't *trust* my feelings. That's what kills me. Maybe he is the *right one*. But how the hell can I know for sure? How will I ever know it's not just a drug-induced emotion?" He threw the redfruit core in his hand across the room. "*That's* what Quince took from me."

"You okay?" Rix asked from the other side of the fireplace. Their eyes were narrowed in concern.

"Yeah, sorry. Just let my anger get the best of me." He closed his eyes, thinking back to the first time he'd seen Jameson, when the man, a *lander*, walked out of the immigration center. Adorable in his conservative suit. And later, at Xander's storage unit, his brown eyes sparkling with indignant anger.

He'd thought Jameson just needed shaking up. Well, they'd gotten that, and a helluva lot more.

Alia put her hand on his arm.

He looked up at her, questioning.

"You'll figure things out."

Xander snorted. "Easy for you to say."

"Maybe so. But I've seen you tested, Xander. You're one of the good ones." She squeezed his shoulder and stood to go talk with the others, giving him time alone.

He picked up one of the peeled tubers and bit into it. It was crisp and just a little sweet. He sat back, determined to enjoy the little space of quiet time he'd been granted, away from the maddening fray of love and war.

RESTLESS

It had to be past midnight.

Jameson and Alix had fallen into a steady rhythm over the last few hours. Find a skythane refugee fleeing the OberCorp attack, open a waygate and shove them through to Bolcà Isle—the island several hours out into the Argent Sea that he'd seen in one of his visions. Then hop across the city through another waygate once the OberCorp forces found him.

The island was far enough from Errian to provide momentary safety, and had ample water in its volcanic crater lagoon.

He'd sent Venin there first, and had given him instructions to get the refugees settled. The man had woken up groggy but otherwise seemingly undamaged by the martach's venom, thanks to Alix's quick action.

Errian had taken heavy damage. Jameson had counted at least fifty hoversports, slipping in and out of the city, making strafing runs against the population. The ships' pulse cannons were set to stun—apparently, they wanted to corral the populace, not kill them, but when your adversary was airborne, casualties were inevitable.

One of the skythane flew by, a young woman with red wings.

Jameson opened a waygate between them, and suddenly she was flying through it and into Alix's arms. He caught her with the ease of long practice.

Her face lit up with fear.

"It's okay. We're here to help you."

Jameson closed the waygate and opened another leading to Bolcà Isle. "People are waiting for you there." He pointed to the waygate.

"Who are you?"

"Lyrin, King of the Erriani." He squeezed her hand. "Now go!"

She nodded, white as a sheet, and fled through the waygate.

Jameson snapped it closed as soon as she was clear.

"Jameson!"

His head snapped around to where Alix was pointing.

Two of the hoversports circled around toward them, coming in hot and low.

Jameson grabbed Alix and together they tumbled through a newly created waygate as an explosion blew flames through from the place they'd just left. They landed in the shallow pool of water in front of the waterfall, and the flames snuffed out as the gate snapped shut.

"Shit, that was close." Alix was soaked.

"I'm so glad you're here to help." Jameson trudged out of the pool.

"Not that I'm doing much."

"You kidding? You just saved both of our asses back there." He scanned the city.

"Glad to do *something*, I guess." Alix joined him, and Jameson was acutely aware of the man's sweaty, masculine *presence*. "Where now, boss?"

Jameson pointed. "Things seem kinda heavy down there, by the water."

Alix grinned. "Back into the fire."

QUINCE AWOKE IN THE DARKNESS. They'd found shelter under a grove of *wempoles*—short, squat trees that had thick canopies of wide purple leaves and fragrant white flowers the size of two open hands, which smelled like vanilla and honey. Silver moonlight filtered through the leaves, creating a beautiful filigree pattern across the dead leaves on the forest floor.

Robyn was fast asleep next to her.

Something had disturbed Quince's sleep.

Since there were only two of them, they had decided it was more important to move quickly and to get sleep where they could than to post watch. Quince doubted OberCorp had penetrated this far north. There was nothing there for them to take.

Something rustled in the darkness. Quince sat up, looking for the source of the noise. There were animals in the forest. She stared into the moonlit darkness.

Two human eyes peered back at her.

Quince tapped Robyn's shoulder, then shook her, but Robyn remained asleep, as if she'd been drugged. Quince reached for her knife.

Whomever it was stepped forward into a beam of moonlight.

Quince gasped. It was Morgan.

Quince put down the knife and jumped up to embrace him. He put his arms hesitantly around her.

"You're here." She held him out at arm's length to

get a good look at him. "How is it possible that you're here?"

He looked the same. A freckled waif with floppy black hair, solemn faced and fragile. She wasn't fooled. She'd seen what he could do. "Not here."

Not here? She was touching him. She could feel the warmth of his skin in her hands. Confused, she knelt to look him in the eyes. "What do you mean?"

He pointed.

She looked over her shoulder to see herself asleep in her torn and tattered sleep sack.

"I'm dreaming." She turned to look at him again. He looked as normal as ever. "Why are you here?"

"They are coming. In seven days."

"Who? Who's coming?" She was sick and tired of these cryptic communications—dreams and visions, short responses to her questions that really told her nothing.

"The Ithani. You must hurry." He leaned forward and kissed her forehead. "I need you."

"Why can't you come here?"

He shook his head. "Can't leave. They won't let me."

"Who?" Someone was holding him hostage?

"The others, like me."

"Morgan, what are you?"

For an answer, he spun around and flung his arms

into the air. They extended into wings, beautiful iridescent multicolored wings. Then he dissolved into nothing.

Quince awoke. She sat up and looked wildly around.

Morgan was gone.

She shook Robyn gently, and this time she woke up. "What's happening?" She glared at Quince through half-lidded eyes. "It's the middle of the night."

"We have to go. We're running out of time."

"Time for what?"

"Morgan was here, Robyn. He spoke to me."

Robyn sat up. "Where? I don't see him." She rubbed her eyes.

"I think he's a nimfeach. Or something similar. Remember how we met?"

Now Robyn looked fully awake. "How could I forget?"

Quince remembered the nimfeach she'd seen in the forest, outside Ballifor. The alien creature who had told her she had a destiny. The beautiful butterfly who had set her on the path she followed to this day, more than twenty-five years later. "I don't know how, or why, but I swear to you he was here. He said something… the Ithani… are coming. Does that mean anything to you?"

Robyn shook her head. "Not at all, but if you say we

have to go, we'll go. Though I was hoping for a few more hours of sleep."

"Thank you." Quince leaned forward and kissed her. "Gods, how I've missed you."

In less than fifteen minutes, they'd eaten a cold meal, packed their camp, and had taken once again to the skies under Bandia's silver light.

Jameson huddled behind a broken wall, his back pressed against the strangely yielding surface.

Alix was crouched next to him, scowling.

The sun was just peeking over the crater walls that framed the eastern end of the city, which Jameson figured was left over from a massive meteoric impact, thousands—or hundreds of thousands—of years before. Water gushed over the edge of the wall where a part of the Orn plunged onto the crater valley.

Jameson was exhausted.

The two of them were huddled inside the shell of one of the organic towers of Errian. It had been sheared off by something heavier than pulse cannon fire and lay like a fallen tree along one of the city's winding streets. It had grazed another tower as it fell, and that one teetered on the edge of collapse too.

Jameson wanted to kick himself. He should have gotten there sooner. He should have used the key to make a way-gate in the midst of the city on the first try, consequences be damned. Maybe he would have been able to warn them, to organize them before the OberCorp forces arrived.

"How long can you keep this up?" Alix asked. His face was ashen.

"As long as I have to. These people need me."

"Down!" Alix pulled him to the ground as a hover-sport zoomed by three meters over their heads. It kept going.

"Come on. I want to see what they're up to now." The landers had set up a staging area in the center of Errian, in the great white plaza called First Square. Jameson had scouted it out earlier. He opened a waygate to a spot on a small tree-covered hill in the midst of the square that would give them some cover.

Hoversports were landing in the square with regularity, disgorging captured skythane in ones and twos, their wings banded at the base with metal.

One flew in from the Argent Sea, larger than the others. It settled in the middle of the square, and a skythane man got out.

Even from this distance, Jameson recognized him. It was the man of his nightmares—Danner Black—the one who had killed his mother. He looked older, gray streaking his long hair.

Behind him was a petite blonde woman, her hands tied behind her back.

"Holy crap." Jameson could hardly believe his eyes. "What the hell is she doing here?"

"Who?"

"That's my fiancée. Jessa." He leapt toward the square, but Alix pulled him back.

"What are you trying to do?"

"I have to save her! She came here because of me."

"Probably. But you're exhausted. And I'd bet the key is too."

"What?"

"Amalite works by absorbing energy around it. Heat, light, static, etc. It's like a little self-charging battery. They use it for the hoversports, and charge it up every night. I'll bet you've come close to using it up with all this activity. And yourself too, from the looks of you."

They had hustled Jessa into the largest tower now, the one that fronted the square. Jameson tore his gaze away from the plaza. "What if they do something to her?"

Alix shook his head. "She's bait. They must figure word will get back to you, or else have some way to let you know. Otherwise they will use her against you when they know you're here. It's classic OberCorp tactics."

"Like they wanted to use you against Xander."

"Yes."

Jameson sighed. "She shouldn't have come."

"Does she know?"

"About Xander and me?"

Alix snorted. "About any of it. That you like men. That you're skythane. That you're the fucking King of Errian."

"No. I don't think so." They hadn't spoken since he came to Oberon, and as far as his sexuality, how could she? He'd hidden it even from himself. He pulled out the holo of her he'd retrieved from the waystation. "I'm sorry, Jessa."

"Oooh, she looks feisty."

"Yeah, she is." He grinned. "She was a reporter back on Beta Tau, and brought down one of the most corrupt businessmen on the planet. Got her bumped up to anchor."

"Where she couldn't do it again."

Jameson stared at him. "Shit, you're right."

"Look, we have the advantage now." Alix flashed him a grim smile and squeezed his arm.

For some reason, the gesture made Jameson feel

warm all over. It was nice having this man in his confidence. "What's that?"

"We know she's here. They can't be sure that we are."

Jameson nodded. "The element of surprise. Though this whole disappearing skythane thing must have them worried."

"Let's see if that key has at least one more bit of charge in it. Take us back to that island of yours. Then we can figure out how to get her back."

Jameson glanced back at the tower. There was a damsel in distress there, and it was his fault. "I'll be back," he said softly. He put away the holo and opened the waygate. It seemed slower than before, but it did open fully.

They stepped through, and he let it wink shut behind them.

Xander couldn't sleep.

His mind kept circling around the strange logic puzzle he'd set for himself. Was he in love with Jameson because of the pith, or in spite of it? When the effect wore off, would he still feel the same? Would it wear off? If it didn't… what would he do then?

Not only that. Alix was back too. The man whose

loss he had mourned over the better part of a year, before he'd closed that door tightly behind him.

Alix was just a friend now. *Right?*

Xander understood why Jameson had taken Alix with him. In Jameson's place, he probably would have done the same. With Xander questioning their bond, who knew what might have happened between them in the stress of the campaign?

There were so many things he wanted to ask Alix, though. Questions about their past. About the mission he'd been sent on to Gaelan. About Dani and Danner Black. Instead he was out there practically alone, trying to sleep in a place that held happy memories of his time with Jameson, memories that only served to torture him now.

It had to be after midnight. He was frustrated with the tossing and turning, so he quietly peeled himself out of his sleep sack and spread his wings. He was tired—exhausted, really, but his demons wouldn't let him sleep.

Alia stirred and opened her eyes, looking up at him questioningly.

"It's okay," he whispered, and she nodded and closed her eyes again.

He pulled on his pants and shirt and padded out of the room barefoot, into the courtyard outside. There in one corner, Xander had held Jameson for the first time, his wings wrapped protectively over him. A sense of protectiveness gripped him again.

He shook his head and stalked off into the gardens.

The white pathways were cool under his feet, and a light breeze blew past him, bringing up goose bumps on his skin. This place must have really been something once. Its ghosts clung to him as he made his way to the statue of Erro.

Its golden beauty was silvered by the moonlight. Erro looked down on him beneficently, his warm smile promising… something. Peace? Safety? Love?

Xander wasn't a religious man, and he had no grounding in the faith of his own people. Certainly, that face offered the hope of something, but what it was remained a mystery to him.

There was another statue in the gardens, on the far side of the House of the Stars. Gael, the moon god, the god of his own people, the Gaelani.

Xander circled around the castle to the far side of the gardens, marveling once again at the wild beauty of this place. Once this whole thing was over—assuming he lived to see the end—he and Jameson would remake this place, bring it back to its former beauty, together.

Jameson.

Xander cursed himself for thinking about Jameson

again. It was far too soon to be making any plans, especially those that might include *him.*

He looked up at the silver statue. Its surface gleamed and seemed to move like mercury in the moonlight, like the amalite key. He smiled. He'd always been more partial to silver than gold. Gold was gaudy, flashy, showy. Silver was elegant, pure.

Gael was extended as if taking off into flight, his wings swept back, a silver sphere in his hand. Like Erro, the statue was flawless, polished as if it were brand-new. That was strange enough.

He reached up to touch that sphere, and a torrent of electricity ran through his arm. *It was like this with Jameson too…* he thought before he was somewhere else.

Lyda looked around the grounds where the House of the Stars was beginning to rise.

The construction was coming along apace. The Gaelani had almost entirely abandoned Oberon now after the company had chased them across half a continent. They had taken refuge in the House of the Sky, where the landers had trouble finding or following them. No one knew why. It was as if the world itself had decided to protect them.

They had eventually crossed over to Titania, the home of their bright cousins, the Erriani.

The unexpected influx had made a mess of things for a while, scrambling half a dozen treaties that laid out the ownership of Oberon and Titania between the two tribes, but now a greater outside force threatened both. Old enmities had been set aside, and this place was being built by Erriani and Gaelani together to symbolize their newfound peace and common cause.

Men and women worked to build the wall that would contain the waygate that appeared there on a regular basis. It had to be built to exacting specifications so the waygate itself would appear on its surface.

She turned back to her own task, crafting the molds for the statues of the gods. She took inspiration from the drawings of Rohin the Explorer, one of the first skythane to venture through the waygate to Titania hundreds of years before. The first one to encounter the gods.

They showed themselves rarely enough these days, though the nimfeach, their angels, were still relatively commonplace. It was one of the nimfeach that had warned Lyda's people, the Gaelani, to flee Oberon before the Ober-Corp onslaught.

She smoothed the clay form, working to make one side of the perfect sphere that Gael would hold in his hand.

Next to her, Zain worked on Gael's companion statue —Erro, the sun god.

"He's gonna be a beaut." She admired his work. She

could see the face of the statue in inverse now, and he looked every inch the loving god. Maybe too loving. "He looks like Zim, no?"

Zain blushed. "Maybe. Think anyone else will notice?"

"Probably not. He's a great model, anyhow. Very sunny." She fancied Zain, but she wasn't his type.

Lyda sighed and went back to work on Gael.

Xander shook his head, suddenly back in the garden alone, his feet on the cool marble of the paths. The stars were arrayed above him.

Was he meant to learn something from the vision? He'd known the skythane believed in their gods, and Lyda had inferred that the *nimfeach* were a part of them too. He'd never seen one, but Quince swore she had.

What if they were real?

He was caught up in a grand play that he didn't have the pages for. There were forces at work there beyond the simple machinations of mankind, and parts of this world ancient and deep.

His was just a small piece of the puzzle.

He sighed. Nothing he could do about it tonight. Maybe he'd be able to get some sleep now, if he tried.

He looked around at the grounds. He'd just seen them when they were new, and the spirit of cooperation that had existed between Gaelani and Erriani. Somehow that gave him hope that they could be made so again, that things once broken could still be repaired.

Xander returned to the House of the Stars and lay down in his sleep sack. In no time, he was fast asleep.

CRACKS

A TALL, dark-haired man with black wings—wings!—and a sharp pointed black-and-gray beard dragged Jessa out of the transport. His long hair was pulled up in a bun.

She'd read about the winged men of Oberon, but still, seeing one in person was another thing altogether.

Then she looked up to see a wonderland.

It was a *broken, smoking* wonderland, to be sure. There were smoldering fires in several places, and the towers that were still standing were scarred with black pulse laser trails. But those towers… they were something to marvel at, even in her current captive state.

They were tall and graceful, like fluted stalks of bamboo, reaching for the sky. Each segment was a slightly different shade of white, darkening near a crease that banded the whole tower. Near the top, each tapered to a narrow band, and then expanded out again in a shape that was most like a flickering candle flame.

In the distance, a waterfall thundered over a cliff face, a white cloud of spray flying into the air from its base.

"Come on, girl." The man snarled at her. "I've got other things I need to be doing besides babysitting a lander."

She ignored him, standing her ground to look at the city before her. By the half-circle rim wall behind it, she guessed it had been built inside an impact crater. On the other side, it faced the open sea.

The man grunted and grabbed her tied arms to drag her bodily forward.

A sliver of fear clouded her vision. Angrily, she pushed it back. She would not cower before this asshole. They'd have to do a whole lot worse to her than this to make her afraid.

She *hated* being used as bait for Jamie. How did these people even know who he was? He'd been a low-level psych stationed on a backwater world before this mission, but clearly things had changed. She just wished she could figure out how.

If only there were some way to warn him.

She was hauled inside the tallest tower and dragged up five flights of stairs to an empty white room. The cord tying her wrists was cut, and then the door was locked behind her and she was left on her own.

A wide-open window was the only other feature, besides the door.

She went to the window and looked out at the plaza below.

There was a flash in a grove of trees on the small hill in the middle of the plaza—a little park in the middle of the city.

She waited a few minutes, but it wasn't repeated.

Sighing, she sank down with her back against the wall, contemplating her fate. There had to be a way out of here. She would find it and show those OberCorp jerks how stupid they were for assuming she was just another dumb blonde.

Then she would find a way to warn Jamie.

On their third day out of Gaelan, Quince and Robyn finally reached the northern edge of the Riamhwood. The trees grew out onto the northern plains in small stands for a couple kilometers, valiantly trying to extend the reach of the vast forest, but sooner or later, these vanished too, giving way to clumps of purple-gray bushes that Robyn called *norcrest.*

It was colder as well, as they left the central climes and flew toward the frozen north pole.

Quince saw the scars first. She wasn't sure what she was looking at when they appeared on the horizon. The ground there was covered in purple grasses, flowing like water under the winds blowing down from the mountains to the east. In places, the patchwork of grasslands and clumps of norcrest were interrupted by brown, jagged lines. These stretched roughly north to south and were the most prominent feature of the plains.

Robyn had no knowledge of them, so they flew down for a closer look.

The scars were ruptures where the ground had split apart, in some places thrust up on one side more than ten meters, and in others divided into a canyon-like gash across the land.

Quince frowned. "The shift?"

Robyn shook her head. "I have no idea. Maybe? Or the quake the other day."

One more weird thing to add to the pile of assorted oddities.

"Like everything else, they seem to point north." Maybe this whole trip was a bad idea. Quince was decidedly uneasy about what they would find up there.

"Have you considered what we'll do if we find him?"

"Morgan?"

Robyn nodded. "You say he needs you. But if he's a nimfeach… do you think his priorities are the same as ours?"

"I don't know." Robyn had a good point. She shouldn't put blind faith in Morgan, but something told her to trust her gut. Or maybe it was just her need to make up for how wrong she'd been about him the first time. She shivered to think how close she had come to ruining everything. "I trust him. For better or worse."

"Okay." Robyn took her hand. "I trust *you*. If you say this is what we need to do, I'll support you."

Quince squeezed Robyn's hand. "It's nice, having you to myself. Away from it all. Even if we are on a mad quest through the northern wilds."

"Likewise." Robyn kissed her, and Quince let her fear and exhaustion and anxiety drain away for just a minute. For that brief interval, she was just Quince, and Robyn was just Robyn, and the world was right.

It ended all too soon.

Quince glanced worriedly at the scar. "Let's go. I want to cover a lot more ground by nightfall."

They made good time. Quince's wing was healing, though it was still sore where she'd taken the grazing pulse shot. Around midafternoon the wind shifted, blowing out of the south, and pushed them along toward their destination.

When the sun reached the horizon, they were within striking distance of the great ice sheet that covered the north pole. It was much colder up here. Thank the gods she'd brought supplies.

The land below was starting to climb, rising from the cracked plains toward the higher ground around the pole. It was cut into deep ravines now by runoff streams from the glaciers ahead.

Quince found them a sheltered spot next to a bluff, carved out of a hillside by one of the runoff streams. The shore of the stream was littered with rounded stones carried down from the glacial moraine. The gullies themselves ran from north to south, probably flowing into the Orn and eventually down to the Argent Sea near Errian.

She wondered if Jameson and Xander had arrived there yet.

THEY HADN'T SEEN or heard a hoversport in two days, so Quince decided they were safe enough having a fire.

Robyn gathered some driftwood, and Quince lit a cheery blaze up near the side of the bluff. They sat down with their backs against the hard-packed ground, staring out over the flames at the starry sky. Robyn had snagged a plains gopher, and its body was roasting on a spit that they turned every few minutes over the fire. The smell made Quince's mouth water.

She took a sip of ice-cold stream water from her canteen. It was pure and sweet.

She handed the canteen to Robyn, who took a long drink. "I don't want to go back."

Quince regarded her. Robyn looked at peace, more relaxed than she'd been since they'd left the Mountain. "I get that." She set the canteen down and rummaged through her pack, pulling out a tri-dee holo crystal.

"What's that?"

Quince passed her hand over it, and an image appeared above its surface. "That's Xander when he was five." She'd all but forgotten she had it. It was the one thing she had carried with her always, tucked in a pocket inside her shirt. She'd brought it to show Robyn when they'd arrived at Gaelan, but Robyn hadn't been there.

Robyn took it and stared at it in wonder. "He's… he's beautiful."

"Like his mother."

Robyn turned the image around to look at it from all sides.

"There are more." She showed Robyn how to change

the image by waving her hand across it. There was one of Xander at seven, and another at seventeen when Alix had found him. Then some of them together in the Outland of Oberon.

Robyn sighed, handing the crystal back to Quince. "I missed so much."

"I did too. I sent Jameson offworld." He had been like a son to her, and she'd missed most of his childhood and growing up.

"When this is all over, I want to find a place to be with you. To slow down. I'm tired of all the pain and responsibility."

Quince nodded. "I think we've earned it." She plucked the gopher off the spit. It was cooked through. She pulled out a knife and carved the meat, and they enjoyed it together.

They talked into the night, about their separate lives in Gaelan and Oberon City, about the boys—men now —and about what might yet come to be.

Quince forgot about Morgan for a few hours, forgot about OberCorp and the shift and all the other things that had been weighing on her for weeks. For years.

The rest of the world would just have to take care of itself for a night.

. . .

SOMEONE WAS SHAKING HIM AWAKE.

Jameson groaned. His head felt like it was stuffed with cotton, and his mouth was dry. He blinked, looking up at his tormentor.

Alix's face was framed by the sun. "You okay?"

Jameson struggled up onto his elbows. He was lying under something that vaguely resembled a palm tree, but the fronds were round, with veins a deep purple mottled with splotches of gold.

"I think so. What time is it?"

Alix closed his eyes for a minute. "3:17 p.m."

On a twenty-two-hour clock, that was late after-noon. "Wait, you have a PA?"

Alix nodded. "It's running in autonomous mode, stealthed."

Jameson missed Angie, his own Personal Assistant. He'd been forced to short-circuit her when this whole misadventure had begun. He was annoyed to learn there might have been another option.

He sat up and looked around. He was surrounded by people, filling the shade under the tree and spilling out onto a white sand beach in front of a turquoise-blue lagoon. Volcanic walls rose black in the distance. *What the hell?*

Alix stood back, and they came up, one at a time, to touch him. Some placed a hand on his shoulder, others his knee. Just a gentle touch, and then each one turned away to be replaced by another.

One elderly woman, her wings and hair gray with age, kissed his forehead. "Bless you, Lyrin."

By the time the line was done, he had counted over two hundred people.

The crowd edged back to give him space.

Venin was last.

"What is this?" Jameson stared at the gathered throng.

Venin knelt before him. "These are the Erriani you and Alix saved."

Jameson's jaw dropped open. There were hundreds. The events of the night before were mostly a blur, but surely it couldn't have been this many.

He got unsteadily to his feet. It was hot. Sweat ran down his back in rivulets. He wiped his brow and searched for something to say. Now he knew how Xander had felt in Gaelan.

"Hello," he managed.

The crowd shuffled, looking at one another and back at him.

Someone broke from the pack and ran up to him. It was a boy, maybe six or seven, too young to have his wings. He reminded Jameson immediately of Morgan.

"I can't find my mam."

Jameson looked at Venin, who shrugged as if to say, *you can't save them all.*

Jameson couldn't accept that. He scooped up the boy. "What's your name?"

"Tevin."

"Well, Tevin, we're going to find her soon and bring her back to you. I promise."

Tevin nodded. "I want to come with you."

"Come with me where?"

"To fight the landers."

"Ah." Jameson looked him in the eye. "You're very brave, I see. But I'll tell you what—I have a more important mission for you. I need you here to help me take care of all these folks. Can you do that for me?"

Tevin nodded, wide-eyed.

"Your mother will be really proud of you." He set the boy down. Not for the first time since he'd met Xander, he wondered if he would ever have children of his own. To the assembled crowd, he said, "Hello. I'm Jameson."

That was stupid. *They know who I am.* Venin must have told them.

"My Erriani name is Lyrin. My mother was the Queen of Errian. I was taken from her twenty-five years ago, on the night she died." He closed his eyes. The shared memory of that dark night was still fresh in his mind. If he closed his eyes, he could still see the spurt of blood from her neck as Danner Black slit her throat.

The crowd was mumbling. He realized he'd gone quiet for a long moment.

"I'm sorry. It's been a long, well, month, but last night was particularly tiring." He rubbed his eyes with the back of his arm. "I need anyone who knows the House of the Sun well to help me plan what to do next. And if you have other information or knowledge that might help, I want to talk to you too."

The gathered Erriani looked at one another and shrugged. They had wanted something more.

He wasn't like Xander. He couldn't just deliver a rousing speech on tap. "We will get Errian back. I promise."

There was a halfhearted cheer.

Venin stepped up beside him. "Jameson is a good man. He helped shift the world to save us all—"

"He brought the landers down upon us?" one man shouted.

"He should have left them all to die," said another.

Several skythane glared at Alix and edged forward.

Venin growled. "Jameson could have left you all to die. Instead he came back to Errian. Back to his home. And he exhausted himself saving each and every one of you."

"Aren't you Gaelani?" one of the men said.

"Sevyrn Triani, sit yourself down," a calm but stern voice said. The elderly woman who had kissed his forehead stepped out of the crowd to stare the heckler down.

Sevyrn glared at Venin a moment longer before dropping his gaze to the ground. "Sorry, Mistress Halta." Then he actually sat down.

Jameson wanted to laugh.

"Get back to whatever you were doing," she called to the crowd. It began to melt away. "Vestra Halta, acting Regent of Errian, at your service." She completed a surprisingly nimble curtsey for a woman of her age, which he estimated to be in her sixties. "Don't worry about these louts." She waved them off. "They're quick to anger, but loyal as *squamwats* when you win them over."

He had no idea what a *squamwat* was, but he decided to take her word for it. He bowed before her. "Glad you're here."

She snorted. "No need for all that fuss. And don't listen to Sevyrn. You're not what we expected, that's all. Come on. We have much to discuss." She pulled him and the others along after her, into the jungle. She led them to a small clearing by a stream half a kilometer into the jungle from the lagoon.

"There aren't any of those cat-spider things here, are there?"

Vestra shook her head. "Met one of those, did you?"

"On the way to Errian."

"Lucky to come away with all your body parts, then. Martach don't usually let their victims go." She settled herself on a rock in the middle of the clearing, staring around her at the jungle. "It's been a long time since I've been to this place."

"You know this island?"

She smiled. Her missing teeth did nothing to detract from the look of pure joy on her face. "Oh yes. This is where young couples often come when they are first paired."

"Oh, like a honeymoon spot."

She nodded. "You could call it that. No one lives here, and none of Titania's larger predators do either." She put her hands on her makeshift cane and looked up at him. "You have a key." It was not a question.

Jameson looked over at Venin and Alix, then nodded.

"May I see it?"

"Um… sure." He opened his carry sack and pulled it out, handing it to her.

She held it up to the sunlight, squinting at it. "Very nice. I haven't seen one of these in twenty years. I wasn't sure any still existed." She handed it back to him. "Nor one who knew how to use it properly." She looked over the three of them, cocking her head. "I imagine there's a story to be told about how a lander, a Gaelani, and the King of Errian came to be together just in time to try to save Errian from the OberCorp onslaught?"

Jameson smiled. He liked this woman. "It's a long one."

"I have time." She sat on a log and crossed her hands over her knee.

So Jameson related what had happened since he'd come to Oberon. Had it really been just a couple weeks before?

Far from being surprised, Vestra nodded as he told his story. She did raise an eyebrow, though, when he told her what Quince had done to the two of them. When he was finished, she was silent for a long moment, with her eyes closed. Jameson thought she might have fallen asleep. He glanced at Venin, who shrugged.

Then she took a deep breath and opened her eyes. "Your arrival was well timed, given the circumstances." Her cold blue eyes searched his. "Too well timed. How do I know for certain that you are who you claim to be?"

He pulled out his sigil, the golden sun that Quince had given him, for her to examine. She cradled it in her hand for a second, then let it drop back to his chest. "Easy enough for you to have stolen that from someone." She reached up and grasped his cheeks in her old, dry hands, and something electric passed through them. Jameson fell backward through time, his memories stirring up around him again like crows. Only this time, they were *his* memories.

Looking down on Oberon from Titania Station.

Playing a game with a little boy on the shuttle to keep him from being afraid as they passed the Split.

Riding on Xander's bike as they evaded the enforcers over Oberon City.

Blasting a hoversport to bits with a pulse rifle.

Wereverens. Swamp Bears. The Lost City. The Gateway.

The memories swirled past him faster and faster, until he only got a glimpse of colors and faces. Until the shift.

He stood with Xander, holding Morgan's hand as the boy vanished into nothing.

Vestra let him go, and he sucked in a lungful of air as if he hadn't breathed for an hour.

She was staring up at him with a look of awe, her

mouth open and her face lit by a golden glow. "I didn't believe it. Not really. But you're *the one*."

"The one?"

"The one who has come to save us." She squeezed his hands. "I've studied the old scrolls all my life and thought most of it was simple clap trap. Until now." She sank down onto her rock. "Few enough of us have the gift."

"The scrolls?" There was so much he wanted to know.

"The oldest records of the Erriani."

"I'd love to see them."

"If the landers don't destroy them, it would be my pleasure to make that happen."

Venin nodded. "We had some in Gaelan, but they only go back a couple hundred years."

One question burned in Jameson's mind above all others. "Did you know my mother?"

Vestra took his hand again, her own shaking. "I did. The night she died was the most terrible one of my life. The bells rang out, and I ran into her chambers to find her dead on the ground, her throat slit from ear to ear." She mimed it with a gnarled finger. "I can still see it after all these years. It was a terrible thing."

"I remember."

"You were gone as well. But you were far too young

at the time. How can you remember it?" She looked away, as if remembering something herself. "You have the gift as well."

"Quince told me about it, but it was like I could see it in my own head. Like I really remembered it myself."

"You were touched by the gods."

He laughed at that. "That's the same thing Quince said."

"She was right. She was one of my pupils. She also spent long hours in the archives, studying the scrolls."

"So, what happened after my mother died?"

"I supposed you would ask. Her husband, King Jerroll Madainn, thought the Gaelani were responsible for the attack, and he swore to find and bring you home. No one knew what Quince and the Gaelani queen had done, then." She sighed. "He started war with the Gaelani, and it raged on for seven weeks. So many terrible things done in the name of a misunderstanding."

"More of a deception." He could still see Danner Black's eyes as the man slit his mother's throat.

"Yes, in fact, though we didn't know it at the time. Danner Black was a confidant of the king, and we didn't discover the betrayal he had perpetrated until much later. There was a bloody war, and many Erriani and Gaelani perished. But it came to an abrupt end, after Ballifor."

"I've been there."

"So you know. Danner's men smuggled a new kind of weapon in from Oberon, and when we saw what he had done… the war was over. Unfortunately, the dying was not. Black's daughter, Dani, killed the king in his sleep, hoping to clear the way for her father to assume the throne."

"So Dani is truly skythane."

"Yes. She was captured, and as a punishment, her wings were cut off and she was exiled—the *Cattorah*, it's called. It was a barbaric act, worse than death, one that hadn't been done for hundreds of years. But nothing less would serve for the crime she committed." Her eyes assumed a faraway cast. "I was the Chief Archivist. In the absence of an heir, they made me Regent. I have been so ever since."

"And Danner?" He looked at her intently.

"He vanished. No one has seen him since."

"I have."

Her eyes narrowed. "When?"

"Today. He was in the plaza, in Errian." Jameson closed his eyes. "He had my fiancée. Ex-fiancée."

"Xander?"

"No. The woman I was supposed to marry. Before I came here." He still didn't understand what had possessed Jessa to come to Oberon.

"Ah. She followed you."

"I think so." Jameson scratched his chin.

She looked down at her hands. "Very interesting. So now we must figure out how to strike back at them."

"Yes. We'll have more fighters at hand in two or three days. The Gaelani are coming, with Xander. At least six hundred of them."

"After what you showed me… you aren't together?"

Jameson shook his head. "After we discovered what Quince had done, dosing us with pith… he needed some time." Damn him and his doubts.

"I see." She stood, rustling her gray wings and stretching her back with an audible *click*. "Don't ever get old, boys. It's hell."

Jameson laughed in spite of himself. "I'll keep that in mind." He closed his eyes and saw Jessa again, being dragged across the plaza by Danner Black.

"We'll figure it out, my liege." Vestra pulled a chain over her head. On it hung a golden ring. "This was your father's. I think he would want you to have it." She freed it from the chain and handed it over to him. "I have so much more to tell you. And to teach you."

He bowed to her. "I'm honored."

She chuckled. "Charmer, aren't you." She sat down once more. "There are things about Errian that only a few of us know…."

CROSSROADS

Xander looked at the world with fresh eyes. He tried to see it as the first skythane settlers might have, a new wide-open world ripe for colonization. An enigma too —the hidden second half of Oberon.

How long had the two halves been separated for such diverse ecologies to have sprung up? Or had they somehow been different to begin with?

Toward nightfall, he and his companions encountered one of the smaller Erriani towns outside of the capital. They were deep in Erriani territory now. The town was surrounded on three sides by a loop of the Orn River. What had once been neatly tilled fields were now filled with mud. They surrounded a hill topped by treehouses, whose village square was a wide, wooden platform built about ten meters above the ground in the middle of the encircling trees.

Xander couldn't help thinking that Jameson would love this place.

He decided to stop and talk to the locals, to share his news and maybe bolster their forces. Xander and his companions landed on the platform, looking around for anyone to greet them.

"Hello?" he called.

The place was a ghost town.

He looked at Alia, who shrugged. "It looks like whoever lived here abandoned the village."

"Maybe so." The silence was creepy, filled only by the wind through the trees and the creaking of the wooden platform beneath their feet. "Let's all take a look around. We'll meet here in about ten minutes."

From the central square, rope bridges led up into the trees. Xander chose one at random and started off into the foliage. The bridge swayed under his weight. The path led up to a cluster of structures—homes?—built among the branches, below the purple canopy.

He stepped into one of them. It was a dwelling of some sort, open to the air, with wide eaves above to keep out the worst of the rain. Spices were hung to dry. He rubbed one of the leaves and smelled his fingers. The leaf gave off a pungent smell somewhat akin to rosemary with a hint of cinnamon. He'd have to ask Alia what it was.

"Hello?" he called, feeling self-conscious.

There was clearly no one here. A pile of dirty wooden dishes lay in one corner, and the whole place looked like it had been hastily abandoned.

There was a shout from the direction of the square.

Xander turned and ran back the way he had come.

He clambered down the rope bridge, setting it to sway wildly back and forth.

Rix was facing off with a pair of white-winged skythane, a man and a woman who looked to be in their midforties. The man had a wicked-looking spear, and the woman held a pulse rifle.

"Hey, what's going on here?" Xander came up slowly behind Rix, his palms spread wide.

Alia, Harrol, and Zenia arrived just behind him.

"You need to leave," the woman said between gritted teeth. "We don't want you here in Taycrob." She swung the barrel of the rifle around to point at him.

"We're not here to hurt you." Xander held his hands out, trying to stay calm. *Where in the Split did they get a pulse rifle?*

"We know what you and your lander friends did to Errian."

"What happened to Errian?" *Is Jameson okay?*

"The Gaelani invaded, with help from OberCorp. That's what." The man spat. "As if you didn't know."

"Look, it wasn't us. Or my people. I'm here to help. We came from Gaelan to fight the landers."

"Sure ya did. How can we trust you? My son Arrol saw Gaelani—them with the dark wings—fighting alongside the landers in Errian yesterday."

"Danner Black and his men," Alia hissed.

Xander nodded. And probably Kadin and Dani. "Inside my carry sack, I have a pulse rifle like that one that we took from the invaders in Gaelan. Alia here has one too." He put his hands in the air. "Go ahead. Take them. Then we can talk."

Alia shot him a look. "Xander, no—"

"Just do it, Alia."

She put her hands in the air reluctantly.

The woman covered them while the man came forward to rummage through their sacks. He pulled out one and then the other rifle before stepping back behind the woman.

"Okay, see that bridge over there?" She gestured off to her left. "Single file across it to our community hall." Her hands were shaking.

"What's your name?" Xander tried his best to look nonthreatening. They were scared.

"I'll tell you when I decide if I can trust you. Get moving."

He turned around, and she poked him in the back with the pulse rifle snout to urge him along.

Xander's mind was racing. What the hell happened in Errian?

He followed Alia, Rix, Harrol, and Zenia in a single-file line. The bridge led to a circle of large trees, their branches spread out like great palms. The community hall was open to the air, shielded only by the branches and their purple foliage. It was a wide space, the floor boards shined to a high gloss.

"Sit." The woman indicated a place under the shade of one of the trees.

They did as they were told, sinking down to take a seat on the hard floorboards.

"What do you want to know?" Xander kept his hands out, palms up to show he was no threat.

"Who are you, and why are you here?"

He wasn't sure if telling them he was the King of the Gaelani would confirm their suspicions or work in his favor. He decided to fudge the truth for the moment. "Gaelan has a new king. OberCorp occupied the city for much of the last year, but Prince Davyn returned and threw them out."

The woman wiped her brow with the back of her forearm. "Things have been strange this last week. A few days ago, there was a thundering quake, and then a storm blew in as heavy as any I've seen in my lifetime." She pointed out toward the fields. "The crops flooded, and we were afraid the village would come down in the winds."

Xander nodded. "The two kings shifted Oberon to save it from a solar flare."

The woman nodded. "I'd wondered if these were the days foreseen." She looked at him strangely. "Kings?"

"Yes. Lyrin is the son of Jerroll and Andra. He went on ahead to Errian."

"So, you're a friend of the king, eh?" the man asked with a snort.

This had gone on long enough. "Something like that." He pulled out his sigil, the silver moon that hung on a chain around his neck. "I'm Davyn, King of the Gaelani."

He waited for them to be impressed.

Instead the woman started to laugh. "He's got a silver moon around his neck, and thinks that makes him a king."

Her companion was laughing too. "Look, I've got an imprean on my chain. What does that make me? King of the Birds?"

"It's true. I didn't even know it myself until—"

"Hush, son," the woman said. "You seem harmless enough. Even if you've got some delusions of grandeur." She put down her weapon. "Y'all can come out now."

On that cue, more Erriani skythane appeared as if out of nowhere, from behind trees, inside houses, even from the foliage above.

The woman put out her hand. "I'm Dorthia, and this is my husband Ravier. Ravi for short."

Xander nodded. Ravi had been his PA's name. He took her hand and stood, assaying a slight bow. "I'm Xander, and this is Alia, Rix, Harrol, and Zenia."

Something electric passed between them. Xander had a glimpse of himself and Jameson shifting the world.

Dorthia straightened, her face going white as a sheet. "In the name of the seven suns, it *is* you!" She fell to the ground, her head down. "Please forgive me, Your Highness. Do I call you that? You're Gaelani, not Erriani…." She grabbed at his boots.

Somehow he'd passed his memory along to her. He reached down and took her hand, gently pulling her up. "You had every right to question me, protecting your own people here."

"Thank you, Your Highness." She tried to curtsey, but he stopped her.

"Xander will do." He turned to the rest of the assembled villagers. "We're going on to fight the landers in Errian. Any able-bodied skythane willing to join us would be welcomed."

"Surely you can't continue on tonight." Dorthia's eyes were bright. "Stay here tonight, and we'll feed you and give you a good place to stay."

Xander shook his head. "I wouldn't want to take any of your food. You must already be short after the flooding."

"Don't be silly," she said, recovering her earlier brashness. "We have enough to spare for four more. And if Errian falls, we'll all soon be under the yoke, won't we?"

"True enough." It was getting dark, but one by one, the trees lit up with an amber glow. Xander touched one of the branches that passed closely overhead. It was fuzzy with some kind of moss that gave off the soft light. As his fingers brushed over it, sparks flew into the air, drifting in whorls along the breeze.

A big cast-iron basin was hauled out and a fire started in the middle of the hall.

Alia stared up at the trees in concern.

Ravi smiled. "They won't burn, if that's what you're afraid of. They're ironwoods, named that because the wood's basically impervious to flame and strong as iron when it's cured." He patted Xander on the back. "Come. You are our guests of honor."

Xander and his companions allowed themselves to be led to seats near the fire, where they were showered with food—nuts, cheeses, and some kind of purple meat that gave off the most amazing aroma as it cooked over the fire.

One of the handsome young skythane men, with silver wings and long dark hair to his shoulders, brought him a pitcher of ale that was sweet and crisp, like citrone. The man winked at him and turned away.

Xander knew he wouldn't lack for company tonight, if he wanted it.

He shook his head. He was still in the middle of it with Jameson, and until he figured things out, he didn't want to muddy the waters. That didn't mean he couldn't enjoy the view. The man was shirtless, his silver wings tipped with gold, and he had a near-perfect ass. Yes, Jameson would like this place.

Alia slapped him.

"What?" He rubbed his throbbing cheek.

"You're taken."

Xander sighed.

Jameson and pith. The two were inexorably mixed in his head. There had to be some way to split them apart.

· · ·

JAMESON PERCHED on the volcanic ridge, high above the crater bowl where so many of his people slept. The island towered over the ocean below. His wings extended and contracted unconsciously as he watched the rising moon.

Bandia was truly beautiful, its silver glow lighting up a path across the sea that he wished he could follow off to oblivion.

Life had been so much easier a month before, when he'd had the pillars of his old life to fall back on—work, family, and faith. He realized now that he'd practiced a lazy man's faith, trusting in others to fill in all the blanks for him. Faith by the numbers.

The real world was a lot messier and more complicated. He had a hard time seeing the hand of God in most of it, until he found quiet moments like this when he could appreciate the majesty of God's creation. This really was a beautiful world, when it wasn't busy chasing him down with spindly legs and gnashing teeth.

Jameson laughed. He'd practiced the tenets of his parents' religion all his life, until he'd left Beta Tau for his psych training on Earth and then his posting on Tander's World. It had been easy to let it go. Too easy, maybe. There were the demands of his classes. The clean, clear, beautiful logic of science and the mind, and later, the needs of his psych clients.

He wondered how the miners he'd worked with were getting along without him. Had another psych been assigned to the post yet? Did they even care? Most of them made a show of hating him and his work. They were *real men*. They didn't need to talk about their feelings with anyone, let alone a *shrink*.

Some of them, though…. There were hidden depths there, and they'd done some good work.

Still, Jameson didn't see himself ever going back.

Seeing Jessa in Errian had really thrown him. He'd already lost Xander, the one new thing he'd staked his belief on. Now that he was gone, the old ghosts of Beta Tau were here to haunt him.

What did he believe in now? What would carry him forward?

He stared out at the rising moon morosely.

Without faith and work… without Xander… what am I?

The moon had no answer for him.

Alix woke.

A breeze rustled the branches above, and a single leaf dropped down, lit by the newly risen moon, to settle on the sand next to his face.

He sat up to look around. Hundreds of skythane lay

around him on the sand above the lagoon's water line, doing their best to sleep in the primitive conditions.

Jameson had used the key to open a waygate into one of the granaries outside of Errian, with Vestra's help. They'd managed to get everyone fed and settled, but the situation couldn't go on like this for long. They had to find a way to strike against the invaders while everyone still had their strength and their anger.

He stood and stretched his arms. Then he saw the boy—Tevin?—standing in the water, looking out at the lagoon.

He looked around for Jameson, finally finding his winged form far above, on a rocky outcrop looking out toward the sea.

One problem at a time.

He approached the boy and knelt next to him. The warm water was still, save for the touch of the breeze on its surface. "Hey there, little man." He put a hand on Tevin's shoulder.

"Hello."

"Remember me? I'm Alix."

The boy nodded.

"You should be sleeping. It's late."

"I can't."

"Why not?"

"I miss my mam."

Alix nodded. "Me too."

"Where is yours?" The boy looked up at him, his brown eyes wide.

He pointed across the Argent, in the direction of the moon. "Across the sea. We haven't spoken in a long time."

The boy put a hand on his knee. "I'm sorry."

"Thanks." Alix was moved by the unexpected gesture. "We'll find your mam, Tevin. But you need your sleep. You need to stay strong for her. You understand?"

"I guess."

"Come on. I know someone who would be happy to snuggle with you." He stood and held out his hand.

Tevin took it. "Why don't you have any wings?"

"Some people were born to fly. Some of us were meant to walk." He squeezed the boy's hand and led him up to the tree line. He touched Vestra's shoulder.

Her eyes opened, and she looked up at him. "Everything okay?"

He nodded. "I have a little boy here who needs someone to cuddle with."

"Bring him here, then." She opened her arms, and Tevin settled in against her chest. She covered him with her wings. "It'll all be okay," she whispered, and winked at Alix.

"Thank you," he mouthed, and turned back toward

the broken wall that rimmed the crater.

Jameson needed him. He could sense it. The man had been torn out of his old world and thrown into this one, and then had his only certainty pulled out from underneath him. *Because of me.*

Alix had never expected to be thrust into this role—comforting the lover of his ex. But sometimes you had to choose a side, even if it went against what your heart wanted. He liked to believe he was a good person, that when push came to shove, he would do the right thing. Now was his chance to prove it.

He made his way up out of the crater valley, up to the edge of the rock wall. Jameson had probably flown up there, but there were enough handholds for him to climb. He didn't feel like going back for his bi-wings.

Even then, in the middle of the night, it was still comfortable out, with a warm, light breeze blowing in off the water. From there, he could see glimpses of the Argent, twin to the Gildensea that bounded Oberon City.

One of these days he was going to have to reckon with Lena. He'd made his first break from her in Gaelan, when he'd refused to help Dani with her plan to use Xander for her own and OberCorp's ends. Sooner or later, he'd have to confront her.

Somehow, though, his mother always had the last

word.

He clambered up the rocks, getting stuck only once when he had to detour around a sheer rock face. At last he pulled himself up to stand next to Jameson. The full view was amazing, with the skirts of the island below and the moon rising over the waters of the Argent.

"Top of the world up here." Alix put a hand on Jameson's shoulder.

"What? Oh yeah. Kind of is, isn't it? Wait, did you climb up here?"

Alix shrugged. "I needed the exercise."

Jameson's shoulders were sloped, and he seemed distracted. Alix couldn't help but notice how beautiful and sad he looked. His bare shoulders glistened in the moonlight, and his slender form made Alix want to grab him up and hug him, protect him from the great big world.

His savior complex at work again. He shoved such thoughts aside. "Mind if I sit with you?"

"Suit yourself. I'm not likely to be very good company."

"I'll be the judge of that." He sat on the hard rock, dangling his feet over the waves below. The ocean breeze cooled him off, feeling good on his bare legs. "What's keeping you up? You should be sleeping, getting ready for tomorrow. We have a lot to figure out."

Jameson snorted. "Says the man who's sitting here awake at my side."

"Touché." He stared out at the water. Better than staring at Jameson. "You did an amazing thing last night, there in Errian."

"I was just doing what I had to."

"But why? You owe *nothing* to those people. You're Jameson Havercamp, offworld psych. You've never even met any of them before."

Jameson looked at him. "Are you serious?"

"You have to admit, it's a fair question. Why do you even care?" Their thighs were almost touching. Alix tried not to notice.

Jameson held his gaze for a moment, then looked away. "You wouldn't understand."

"Try me."

Jameson sighed. "Because I have to believe in *something*," he said at last.

"That sounds like a terrible reason."

"I told you that you wouldn't understand."

Alix laughed, releasing some of his tension. "Oh, I understand it completely. I just think it's a shitcrap reason."

"What do you mean?"

"Look, I'm the last one to talk to when it comes to faith, to 'believing in something.'" He stared out at the ever-changing patterns of the waves again, determined to do this right. "I *believed* in Xander. But beyond that, my whole life has been a search for direction. My mother works for OberCorp. When I grew up, she expected me to be a company man. I tried. I really did. But I hated every moment of it."

Jameson nodded. "I can't see you in a suit."

Alix shuddered. "Neither could I. So eventually I quit. I joined the rangers branch of the enforcers. I thought law and order was something I could *believe* in."

"I get that."

"Yeah, but I found out that OberCorp doesn't give shit-all about anything besides itself." He paused. He hadn't meant to share this much, but Jameson seemed to bring it all out of him. "I was too embarrassed to tell Xander. I was the first stable thing to come into his life after the Syndicate. So I told him I was going away with friends on a camping trip in the Outland. I didn't know it was going to be a year-long assignment." He'd been an idiot not to let Xander know where he was going. He should have found a way to let Xander know he was okay. "Now I don't even believe in my old job. So, I get it."

"What *do you* believe in now?"

Alix laughed. "Funny you should ask." The answer had surprised even him. "You, actually. I don't buy this bullshit about you needing something to believe in. I think you already found it, the moment you and Xander shifted the world."

"I don't know about that…."

"Look at you, Jameson. You're *all in*. And it's killing you, because you don't know if Xander is too." He picked up a rock and tossed it toward the sea. It hit the side of the island and skittered down, bouncing three or four times before vanishing into the jungle. "Let me ask you something. If Jessa were standing right here before you, and she begged you to come home with her… would you go?"

"No." Jameson said it with a vehemence that seemed to surprise even him.

"Why?"

"Because I'm needed here. Because this is where I finally feel like I belong. Because Xander…."

The word hung in the air between them for a long moment.

Jameson looked so lost. So vulnerable.

Alix knew that he could reach out, pull Jameson gently to him, kiss those lips in that beautiful lost face. That Jameson would respond. That his *need* was great enough to overcome his reluctance.

Sometimes a life balanced upon a single choice made, or not made.

Jameson was beautiful to him in that moment, beautiful beyond measure, his golden wings lined in silver, the wind playing with his hair, his warm brown eyes clear and sad. His naked *need*. It was like a drug.

Alix closed his eyes. The moment passed. "He loves you, you know," he said at last.

"Xander?"

"Yes. He doesn't know it yet. Or he's not certain if it's just the pith. But I watched you two. I know him. We spent nine years together, after all. He'll come around." How it cost him to admit that. His heart was as cold as the void.

Until Jameson threw his arms around him. "Thank you. Gods, I needed to hear that." Jameson laid his warm face against Alix's chest.

In that moment, Alix knew he had made the right choice. His heart warmed, just a little. "Gods, plural?" he asked with an arched eyebrow as they separated.

Jameson smirked. "When in Rome…."

18

——————

NEW DAWN

Jessa waited. Hours went by, and nothing happened. Well, that wasn't entirely true.

Someone knocked on the door, and when it opened, she was served a tray of some kind of MRE. The taste sucked, but it was hot and had calories.

The enforcer who brought it—a uniformed guy with curly black hair and blue eyes—was handsome. Although her parents frowned on her using her beauty for personal gain—church doctrines and all that—she'd gotten good enough at it during her broadcasting career. She still found it distasteful, but hey, nothing ventured….

So she tried to flirt with him.

He stood there to watch her eat but wouldn't respond to any of her overtures, subtle or overt. Either he was well trained or he was gay. She knew the effect she had on men.

She had known a few gay men back on Beta Tau. They weren't persecuted or anything, though everyone whispered about them when their backs were turned. One had been the choir director at church. Jessa hadn't seen what the fuss was. He was a good man who looked out for everyone else. Why should she care where he put his cock?

But in this situation, it was… inconvenient.

When he left, she used the remaining afternoon light to scout the room.

It was strangely shaped. The walls were curved, more organic than geometric—hard but not brittle. The texture reminded her of the rind of a pomegranate.

There were dust shadows in several places on the floor. This room had been furnished until recently. That meant this place probably hadn't been built as a prison.

The walls rose out of the floors seamlessly. In fact, she couldn't find any trace of nails or screws or even molecular bonding. It was as if this tower had grown out of the ground in one big piece. *Stranger and stranger.*

She stood at the window and looked out at the city below.

The buildings were all the same—variations of the

tower she found herself in. They looked like white asparagus. Giant, elegant asparagus.

If they *were* like plants, maybe she could cut her way out. If the "rind" walls weren't too tough. There had to be a way to do it—or else how had they made the doorways?

Jamie was out there somewhere, and he probably needed her. The poor man was hopeless in outdoor situations. Their one camping trip in the Heartwood had been a disaster. She would need to rescue herself first, though, if she had any chance at saving him.

She sat against one wall and pulled off a boot. It had an iron shank in the heel. If she could free that, she might be able to use it to cut a hole in the wall, given enough time.

She broke off both heels. If just one were broken, it would raise too many questions, but she was pretty sure none of these men would notice that she had shrunk three inches. They'd probably just take it as proof of their dominance over her.

She snorted.

She stuffed one of the heels in her pocket and set to prying the shank out of the other.

She'd have to wait until after they brought her dinner. That would give her all night to cut herself an escape hatch.

At last she had her tool ready—a long thin piece of iron, attached to the heel, which she could use as a handle. It wasn't ideal. The edge wasn't as sharp as she would have liked, but it would have to do.

When the knock at the door came, she was ready. The shadows started to lengthen outside. She had hidden the materials from her activity in her pants pockets, and she artfully arranged her shirt to cover them.

She hoped it was Mister Cool, Calm, and Collected again. If she got someone a little more interested and a little less disciplined, it could cause problems for her plan.

She wasn't disappointed. This time her meal was a meat and gravy MRE with something that looked like rehydrated cranberries, but tasted like coleslaw. She forced herself to eat it. *Gotta keep up my strength.*

"Why are you guys keeping me here?" she asked conversationally as she chewed on the strange meat.

"Sorry, ma'am. I can't tell you that."

"Because you can't? Or because you don't know?"

"Sorry, ma'am. I can't tell you that."

She was halfway convinced he was an android.

"What is OberCorp doing here?"

"Sorry, ma'am—"

"You can't tell me that. Got it." She finished the

meal, washing it down with the water he'd brought in a plastic glass. Maybe if she could hide the glass, she could use it to make a sharper tool.

She handed Mr. 3C the tray. "Thank you. That was every bit as good as the meals they serve at the Galaxion Hotel on Beta Tau." She licked her lips for emphasis.

He smiled blandly. "I'm going to need the glass as well, ma'am."

Of course you do. "Here you go." She handed it over to him reluctantly.

"Thank you, ma'am. I'll see you at breakfast."

"What, no blanket and pillow?"

He ignored her and swept out of the room with more flourish than was strictly necessary.

Nailed it.

She waited half an hour, near as she could figure, and then pulled out her new tool. She decided to try it on the wall behind the door, past the curve. Hopefully it would take her into another room and not out into a hallway. She had no idea how long it would take to cut a Jessa-sized hole, but hopefully she had all night.

She chose her spot and pressed the shank against the wall to test its strength.

It sunk in like a knife into butter.

Startled, she pulled it back and stared at the spot where it had been.

The small hole she'd made slowly closed up. In two minutes, it was as if she'd never breached the wall. She touched the surface. It was as smooth and hard as all the rest.

She tried again, this time tracing a long line after plunging the shank into the wall.

It split apart, making a small opening.

Her room wasn't completely dark, although sunset had come and gone outside. The walls, ceiling, and floor gave off a soft, white glow.

She peered through the hole. The room beyond looked about the size of the one she was trapped in. It was furnished—a bed, a dresser, and a chest, along with a rug on the floor.

She watched the new hole close up again. This time it took a good ten minutes. It started with activity along the edges, as the substance seemed to boil, though it was completely silent. Then small filaments shot out across the distance, anchoring themselves on the far side of the hole.

They thickened, throwing out more, creating a gridwork that looked like fine lace. The material around the edges then grew over the new framework—the bones, she supposed—and eventually filled in the hole as if it had never existed.

This kind of tech—or whatever it was—was incredible. The applications alone were worth billions. Or would be, if OberCorp ever figured out what it had on its hands here.

She went back to the window to look at the city. It was beautiful at night, a true city of ivory towers. She shuddered at the thought of it being cut up for research and sold.

It was time to get herself out of here.

She went back to her chosen spot and cut a two-meter gash in the wall from the floor. The hole parted silently, and she slipped into the next room.

She was still too close to her own room, so she decided to move a few more down before trying one of the doors.

First, she pushed her shank through the wall in one corner to make a keyhole through which she could check out the next room and listen for any activity.

The room looked like a storage room, full of wooden racks. It was also empty.

Behind her, the hole into her room was starting to heal.

She stopped to check what was on all those shelves.

It was mostly kitchen implements—ceramic pots, earthenware mugs, wooden cutlery. She also found knives, handmade with handles of the most beautiful purple wood, their blades sharp enough to split a hair.

She chose one of these to carry with her.

Strangely, it didn't have the same effect on the walls as her iron shank.

She pushed the shank through into the next room and withdrew it to listen.

Voices.

"…absolutely right. She's giving us three days."

"Three days? Do you think that's enough time?"

"Yes. We think Havercamp will strike tomorrow or the day after, latest. Once we have them all in one place, we'll call in the cavalry."

Havercamp. They were talking about Jamie. They had to be.

"You sure the MB will take out the whole city?"

"We tried it a few years back on one of their villages. Place is still a slag heap. It will do the trick. Then we can round the rest of the wing men up and figure out how to get back home."

The hole was closing up.

Jessa sat back against the cool white wall and considered what she'd just heard. They were laying a trap, for Jamie and the wing men. She had no idea who the wing men were—the travel guides had never mentioned a whole city full of them—but if Jamie was with them, they must be decent folk.

She had to get out and find a way to warn him. She didn't want to go back, and she couldn't go forward.

Decided, she pushed the shank through the floor and took a look around at the room below her.

Another empty space, this one maybe a bathroom? There was a long trough on one side and washbasins on the other, all made out of the same glowing white material.

She cut herself a hole and dropped silently through to the floor below.

Someone was shaking Quince's shoulder gently. She opened her eyes, staring blearily out at the world.

Robyn was peering down at her. "Quince, wake up," she whispered.

"What? Is something wrong?" Her left leg was cramped something fierce.

"No. Sit up and be quiet."

Quince did as she was told, rubbing her calf. Beyond the now-cold ashes of the fire was a wonder. She caught her breath.

Out on the plain before them was a herd of *aux*. The magnificent animals stood two meters at the shoulder, covered in shaggy white fur. Their six legs shuffled complacently as they munched on the short grasses that covered the plain.

There must have been a hundred of the beasts.

One of them looked up at her, its golden eyes big as her fist. Its horns made almost a complete circuit around the side of its skull. The animal had to be at least thirty years old to boast such a rack, ancient by aux standards.

"They're beautiful," Quince whispered. Her breath came out in a fog.

"They're good luck." Robyn kissed her. "I thought you'd want to see them."

Quince nodded. "You're beautiful too."

Robyn laughed, shaking her head, her black hair fanning out like a waterfall. "I'm a mess. Camping does *not* agree with me."

"I beg to differ." Quince pulled her back for a long kiss. "I've missed this. Us."

Robyn nodded. "But we have work to do before we can enjoy or long-delayed reunion, don't we?"

"Unfortunately—"

Quince was cut off as something startled the aux, and they began to gallop away down the valley, kicking up a cloud of dust.

Quince laughed. "I wonder what frightened them?"

As if in answer, the ground began to rumble and

then shake. The bluff they camped against began to rain down dirt and pebbles.

"Come on!" Robyn pulled her unsteadily to her feet, and they stumbled away from the cliff.

A huge rock tumbled down where they had been seated, smashing their fire pit before rolling on past them down the hillside.

"Holy hell!" How close they'd been to being crushed.

The rumbling subsided to a dull grumble, and then the valley was silent again. "Something's happening. We need to go." Quince scrambled back up the slope, looking at their campsite. It was buried under a foot of soil and pebbles, but nothing was too badly harmed.

They dug out their packs and the poor, tattered, and now dirt-covered sleep sacks.

She pulled out her heavy winter wear from her pack —fur-lined boots, a fur jacket, and warm wool leggings. "No idea how long we'll have to spend on the ice."

Robyn shivered, doing the same. "Hopefully not long. I was made for warmer climes."

"You and me both." Soon they were packed and ready to fly.

They climbed up to the bluff where Robyn could take off on her own. Quince breathed in the cool morning air. "Are you ready?"

"Let's go. The sooner we get this quest over with, the sooner we can go home." Robyn leapt off the cliff and soared into the air, climbing on thermal updrafts.

Quince followed her, and soon they were soaring over the valley where the aux had been.

A kilometer north, half of the little creek was gone, replaced by a deep crevasse. The runoff from the glacier dropped into the new crack in the world in a spectacular waterfall that fell away into blackness.

Quince and Robyn exchanged a look. "It's getting worse." Quince had a sick feeling in the pit of her stomach. They were too late. "Come on. Let's get going." Quince turned toward the glacier and set off to find Morgan.

"What do you think you're going to find?"

"Is there a mountain at the pole?"

Robyn nodded. "It's as big as Deireadh an Domhain —the Mountain. Or as big as it was."

"To answer your question, I have no idea. Morgan is there, I think."

"Where did you find him, again?"

The land below sloped upward toward the glacier wall, ice-blue on the horizon. There was a thunderous sound as part of the glacier calved, dropping an avalanche of ice onto the foothills below.

"Xander came across the boy in an abandoned farmhouse on Oberon. We were fleeing OberCorp at the time and had been separated." The sun was warm on her wings, but the air around her was cold. She was glad of the fur coverings to help keep her warm. "I thought at the time that it was suspect. Too convenient. That farm had been abandoned for at least a hundred years, according to Xander."

"Sometimes I think this whole world is too *convenient*." Robyn chuckled.

"How do you mean?"

"Look at it. Two halves that are near mirror images of each other. Two perfect mountains, like giant pyramids. Sometimes I wonder if this world didn't evolve so much as it was *built*."

Quince chewed on that for a while. In truth, she'd had similar thoughts herself. No known human technology could have split a planet in half, at least not without catastrophic results. Let alone shift it into another universe. "You think something once lived here that had that kind of ability?" She shivered at the thought. How insignificant would humankind—lander or skythane—be in the face of power like that?

"Maybe." Robyn's grimace must have mirrored Quince's own. "And if that's true—if the waygates and the mountains and all the rest are part of something greater, what does that make your little friend Morgan?"

She's not part of the plan. Those were the words Morgan had spoken when she lay near death's door, according to Jameson. So, what was the plan, and were the humans on Erro a part of it?

"I don't know." Storm clouds were gathering on the western horizon. "Something he said, to Jameson and Xander—he has his own agenda. And yet… he said I wasn't a part of his plan. But he still reached out to me for some reason."

"Good or bad?"

"I don't know. But let's say there is something greater afoot. The only way we're going to find out—and have a chance at steering things our way—is to find Morgan."

Robyn nodded. "Just be ready for disappointment."

Quince laughed darkly. "I always am. And I'm rarely let down."

XANDER HUGGED DORTHIA. "Do you have somewhere safe you can evacuate the village to?" He looked worriedly at the sky. "OberCorp has already sent troops inland. If Errian has truly fallen, they may turn their eye toward subjugating the provinces."

She nodded. "We can go to the hunting grounds—about three hours inland. They're hidden under the jungle. They won't find us without sending troops in on the ground. That is, the ones that don't follow you. You're taking half the village with you."

"For which we are grateful."

She put a hand on his cheek, looking him in the eye. "Take care of them. Send them all back to me when the fighting is over."

"I will do everything in my power." He bowed to her.

"Charmer." She kissed him on the cheek. "Go with Erro."

"You too." To the rest, he called, "Let's fly!"

Fifty skythane took to the air. He planned to keep them low to the ground, ready to dive below the treetops if a hoversport approached. He hoped to make the rendezvous spot at Torr Talam by nightfall.

Somehow, so slowly it was almost undetectable, he was getting used to this whole leadership thing. What he still wasn't used to was being alone.

How it had come to that in such a short time, he didn't know. Well, actually he did. It was the pith.

He looked at his nails. The double moons were still there, like a stain he couldn't wash off. He'd never been afraid to be alone before. He was a lone wolf and proud of it. Maybe it was time for him to learn to be alone again.

. . .

Jameson had spent the better part of the morning working with Alix to figure out who they had among the two hundred or so survivors of the attack on Errian. According to Vestra, the city was home to several thousand skythane, not counting the villages that dotted the countryside for a couple hundred kilometers out from the city walls.

Many of the city's people had likely escaped to the countryside.

About half of the skythane on the island were fit enough to fight. He sent them with Alix to do what the ranger could to put together a fighting force, separated into ten flights of skythane.

Jameson retreated to the clearing they'd used the day before, which had been turned into a sort of war room. Plans were being sketched out in the mud near the creek side.

Vestra and Venin were there, along with a young skythane courier named Alvyn who said he knew the city like the back of his hand.

"We should go now and find Jessa." Jameson pointed at the assortment of reeds that represented the main buildings of Errian. "They took her inside the big tower—"

"We call it the Castain." Vestra put a hand on his arm. "It's the seat of Errian's government. Some also call it the House of the Sun."

"The Castain, then."

"First of all, there's no guarantee that she's still being held there." Venin sounded exasperated. "And there's the fact that she's probably being used as bait to catch you."

They'd been over this ten times already. Jameson sighed. "She *needs* me. I can't just leave her there. Look what they did to Robyn."

"I can find her."

Jameson turned to find Alvyn standing behind him, a hand on his chin, scratching the tiny bit of stubble there.

"No, I won't allow it. It's too dangerous."

"I can do it. I know the city better than anyone. Send me in, and I'll find out where she is."

"No way. I'm already responsible for too many deaths."

The boy crossed his arms and glared at Jameson. "That's total crap, and you know it."

"Excuse me?" Granted he'd only been king for a little while, but he was pretty sure his subjects weren't supposed to speak to him like that.

"Look, you've saved over two hundred of us already, but like it or not, Errian's not *your* city. Well, maybe it is now. But not like it belongs to us. I grew up there. My family is there. My *annama* is still there."

"*Annama?*"

"Soul mate." Vestra nodded. "The boy's correct—he has as much a right to fight for Errian as any of us. When are your Gaelani friends due to arrive?"

Jameson shook his head. "It depends. Xander is bringing a host of fighters from Gaelan. They may have to stop and forage on the way." He counted back the days. "Tonight, at the soonest?" They had made plans to meet at Torr Talam at the end of the day, where Jameson had arrived via the waygate.

The thought of seeing Xander again made him both excited and nervous. Had Xander had time to think through the whole pith thing? Emotions and their causes were difficult things to pin down, and Xander wanted an easy answer.

Jameson feared he'd be sorely disappointed. "I'll see if he's there at sunset."

"So, you'll send me?" Alvyn looked overeager.

"If I do, promise me you'll find out where she is and get back out to wait for me. No heroics."

"Promise."

Jameson wasn't sure he trusted the boy to keep his word. He remembered what it was like to be a hot-headed teenager.

He looked at Venin and Vestra, who nodded. "All right. But I want you back at the waygate spot just before sunset."

"Yes, sir."

Jameson chuckled. That was more like it.

He pulled out the key and opened a waygate to the inside of a half-destroyed building where he'd taken refuge during the battle. "Good luck." He clapped Alvyn on the shoulder.

"I won't need it." Alvyn winked and jumped through the waygate.

Jameson closed it behind him. "The gods save me from overeager teenagers."

"Not exactly what you expected when you arrived from offworld, is it?" Vestra grinned.

"Not in my wildest dreams."

They went back to planning the assault on Errian as Jameson kept a nervous eye on the sun.

19

MORGAN

Jessa huddled inside the dimly lit room, waiting for her pursuers to pass her by. She had chosen her entry carefully, hidden behind a hedgerow of bushes with heart-shaped purple leaves and orange flowers. The cut she had made in the building wall was already starting to heal. She'd kept it small and low to the ground. As long as no one looked behind the hedge for a couple of minutes, she'd be safe.

It had to be late morning. She'd been on the run since before dawn. Her feet were sore. The boots hadn't been designed for use without heels, and they were killing her ankles and toes. Still, they were better than going barefoot.

She closed her eyes, said a quick prayer to God, and

crossed herself. Not that she was particularly religious, but it never hurt to hedge one's bets.

She looked around the small space she found herself in. It was about three meters in each direction, with a door on one end. More shelves—these people loved their storage.

She scanned the contents. They looked like food canisters. Maybe the back room for some sort of store, or food storage for the building's inhabitants? It was cool inside, cooler than it ought to have been. Maybe these buildings—plants?—were able to regulate their internal chamber temperatures?

She was starving.

Who knew if this food was human-edible? The flying people—wing men, her captors had called them—seemed human enough except for their wings.

She decided it was worth a try.

If it killed her, at least that was one problem solved. Or maybe all of them.

She opened one. It was filled with a white powder that smelled like flour. Okay, so good sign, but not something she wanted to eat right out of the can.

Another had some kind of oil, while a third had what looked like a dried fruit. She picked one of the shriveled things up and popped it in her mouth.

Not bad. It tasted like a kind of musky, cinnamon-y

apple. She ate a few more before moving on to the next one. This one seemed to hold a type of dried meat. She tasted a piece—it was mostly salty, with a gamey flavor. It reminded her of venison.

In another rack, she saw something she recognized. Wine bottles. They were sealed with wax plugs.

She used her knife to pry out a plug, and washed down the jerky with a sip of the dark red wine within. The bottles looked like they had been hand-blown.

The wine was full-bodied, fruity—it reminded her mostly of blackberries—and it had a kick. She stopped after a few sips, wary of getting herself drunk, or worse.

When she had found enough to eat to sate her appetite, she used a canvas sack she found in the back of the room to take some food for the road. She also took one more bottle of the wine, whispering a thank-you and sorry to whoever's stores she was raiding. She figured they were probably too busy to care at the moment.

She went to the door and opened it a couple centimeters to peer out into the room beyond.

It was a stairwell. It appeared empty, and she didn't hear any sounds, so she eased out from the storage room into the brightly lit space.

This was one of the smaller buildings. She guessed it was probably a residence. There were certainly no indications of retail activity. She peeked into each of the other rooms on the ground level, five in all. Kitchen, bathroom—that seemed to be universal—and two other storage spaces.

She climbed the stairs. On the second level, she found three bedrooms. All appeared to have been abandoned hastily. The furnishings were simple but handcrafted—carved from wood, mostly—and the linens seemed to have been handmade as well.

In one of the closets were several pairs of handmade leather boots.

She pulled them out excitedly, matching them against the sole of her own broken shoes.

One of them was fairly close, just a little bigger than her current ones. She pulled off her boots and pulled on the new ones, lacing them up tightly. "Oh man, that feels good." She whispered another apology to the owners and tucked the other pairs of boots back in the closet.

She climbed the stairs again and came out in a single room that appeared to be the top of the structure. It held three window openings. She chose one at random and stepped up next to it to peek outside.

The crater wall that surrounded two-thirds of the city thrust up into the sky before her, black striated rock laced with clumps of moss and something fernlike. The waterfall she'd seen earlier cascaded down the cliff face. *West.*

The next window looked south, over a tangle of white buildings, a lake, and something that looked like vineyards. That explained the wine, at least.

The last one, the one looking northeast, held the biggest surprise.

A line of wing men, hundreds of them, were being herded past the building, toward the crater wall. Something shiny bound the base of each of their wings.

Enforcers in black uniforms prodded them along, using shocksticks to keep them in line.

Many of them were bleeding or had broken wings.

One of the wing men looked up and caught her eye.

She dove back behind the safety of the wall, her heart racing and her breath coming in short sharp gasps. *What in God's name are they doing to those poor people?*

She went back to the window that faced west. The line extended now toward a black hole at the base of the wall.

Then she saw him. A young wing man, making his way on foot from the south, toward the building where she stood.

He was going to run right into the enforcers, unless she did something.

Jamie would have to wait. Maybe the man could

help her find him. The voices of her prisoners had said he was working with the wing men.

Decided, she ran down the stairs, intent on saving at least one of the beautiful angels.

ALVYN SLIPPED from hedge to bush for cover, working his way toward the center of Errian. He'd planned to find some of his own people. Surely there must be some hiding out among the wreckage? It seemed like half the towers in Errian were cracked or fallen.

He'd hoped, too, to find Neamiah, his *annama*.

The place was empty as a cemetery.

He'd used the sewers under the city to move from place to place at first, but this next bit required a jaunt aboveground.

He glanced up at the sun. He guessed he had about five hours left to find out where this woman, Jessa, was and get back to the rendezvous spot.

He was still trying to figure out the new king. The man was barely older than Alvyn. He seemed to be both Jameson and Lyrin, and both skythane and offworlder. He wasn't sure how that was possible, but Vestra trusted him, and he had saved over two hundred Erriani from the invaders.

Before the invasion, he'd never even seen a lander. Now they controlled his city. His home.

He checked to make sure the street was clear, ran for the cover of another building, and ducked behind a heartbrier bush. He was about to make his next dash when a hand reached out from the building behind him and hauled him through the wall.

He landed on his ass. "Hey!" he shouted, looking up to see a lander woman. Blonde, blue-eyed, holding something that he thought was a knife at first, but it wasn't sharp. "You're…. Jessa."

Her eyes went wide. "Are you working with *them*?" Now she was holding a knife, kneeling and pressing it to his neck.

"With them? Who?" *The landers.* "No, no, of course not. Jameson sent me to find you."

She lowered the knife and sat back, looking stunned. "Jamie sent you?"

He nodded, rubbing his neck. "I know Errian better than anyone."

"How did he know I was here?"

"He saw you. When the lander thugs brought you in." He sat up. "Why did you drag me in here like that?"

"I saw you from the room up above. You were running right into a mess of enforcers."

"Enforcers—landers?"

She nodded. "They're taking your people—the wing men—to a cave or something."

"Skythane. Only lander assholes call us wing men."

"Sorry." She blushed. "What should I call you?"

Alvyn thought she was about the most beautiful woman he had ever seen. He gulped. "We're skythane. You… you said they were taking skythane somewhere?"

"Come on. I'll show you." She helped him up.

"I'm Alvyn, by the way."

"Jessa. But you knew that. Come on."

She led him up the stairs.

They reached the summit, and he looked out to see the tail end of the line of captives entering the cavern mouth. "Oh no." His heart dropped.

"What's in there?"

"That's where the old mines are." At best, they were using the caverns there as a secure prison for his people. At worst…. He decided not to mention the forge.

"We have to tell Jamie." Jessa read the fear on his face.

"We can't reach him until nightfall. Unless…." Maybe there was a way. "Are you afraid of flying?" It was a long shot, but Bolcà Isle was only a two-hour flight. He could do it by himself easily, but with the added weight, it would be a challenge.

"If it gets me to Jamie faster, I'm not afraid of anything."

"How did you cut through the wall?"

She grinned and held up a piece of metal. "My shoe shank."

"Must be made of iron. It's what we use to shape the *corrinders*." He took it from her and looked it over.

"The what?"

"These buildings. This could be our ticket out."

"How?"

"How do you feel about sewers?"

THE ENDLESS WHITE of the snow was blinding to Quince. The cold was starting to get to her too. They'd been flying for hours, and the mountain ahead of them seemed to be taking forever to grow larger.

The storm clouds were moving in too, sure to provide some respite from the blinding reflection of the sun off the ice pack below, but Quince worried about being caught in a blizzard. They didn't have the equipment for it. She would have killed for a good ice tent.

They had to reach the mountain before the snow came.

She wished they could have postponed this journey until a better day, with more preparation, but Morgan's voice still cried insistently in her head. They were running out of time, and she knew it.

She wondered what the boys were up to. Had Jameson taken his rightful place in Errian? Was Ober-Corp moving against them? She should be there with them.

But she *had* to help Morgan.

"Damned cold place to spend an afternoon." Robyn shivered. "You sure we're going to find this *Morgan* before the storm moves in?" Robyn glanced nervously at the eastern sky.

At least she's here. Quince followed her gaze. The clouds there were heavy and sullen, sending their first emissaries overhead in the form of high, thin cirrus clouds. "I hope so. We'll be in a heap of trouble if we don't."

The whole world was uneasy. Tremors and quakes, strange weather, nervous animals. Maybe it was all a result of the shift. That made a sort of sense, as the two halves of Erro settled back in together and their weather systems and ecosystems collided and combined. Not to mention their human contingents.

It felt like something more to Quince.

The land below was splintered, the ice cracked and thrust up into strange faery castles, canyons, and miniature mountain ranges.

Some patches were the faintest blue, while others were drenched in purple by algae that seemed to thrive on frozen water. It spread out across the ice fields in some places for a dozen kilometers, its bloom creating stunning fractal patterns.

At last, the flanks of the mountain appeared before them. It was a monstrous beast, easily the match of Deireadh an Domhain, the vast Mountain that had fallen when the world had shifted. Its rampart sides went up and up, sheer black walls dusted with snow and ice.

"It's huge," Robyn said. "How are we going to find him? It's like looking for a single hoarberry in all the Riamhwood."

Wind teased Quince's hair. The ice storm was closing in. The western sky was a mass of dark clouds, topped by sunlight as the sun sank toward the crest of the cloud front. "He'll find us." She caught an updraft and began to climb, keeping a keen eye on the mountain. Robyn followed.

As they climbed, Quince could see that this mountain was relatively new, geologically. It was full of angles and sharp edges, the rock not yet worn down by the hands of time.

Mankind had the ability to make a mountain, she supposed, though it would mean a huge investment in time and materials. But if whoever had built this one had also split the world, something like this was likely child's play for them. *Whatever* they were. She shivered from more than just the cold.

"Quince! Up there!"

She looked up at the mountain, but all she saw was wind and snow blown from the mountainsides. "What?"

"I thought I saw a flash." She shook her head. "It's gone now. Probably just a glint of sunshine reflected off the ice."

"No, I see it too." It was Morgan. It had to be.

The storm was closing in, covering the western flank of the mountain. Icy wind tugged at her, trying to knock her off course. "Come on. We have to get to safety."

Robyn nodded, though her doubts were plain on her face.

Quince strained toward the flash, her wings pulling her forward, fighting with the angry wind. She glanced back at Robyn, who was having a hard time of it with her bi-wings. "You can do it."

"Don't waste breath on me." She shot Quince a look that was either angry or determined. Or both.

A huge gust sent Quince spinning through the air.

She spread her wings and slowed her headlong

flight, pulling forward once again toward her destination.

She glanced back, and to her horror, Robyn was no longer there.

"Robyn!" she screamed above the wind. There was no response.

Quince looked all around for the woman she'd crossed a world for, twice. The wind was howling by then, making it hard to see more than ten meters in any direction.

Quince flew as close as she dared to the mountainside, searching for any sign of Robyn.

At last, she found her.

Robyn had made it to the mountain slope, but far below their goal. She lay sprawled on an ice shelf, her bi-wings cracked and broken.

Quince didn't stop to think. She dove toward the shelf, not caring anymore about Morgan or the quest or the fate of this gods-cursed world. Without Robyn, none of it mattered.

She fought her way through the oncoming storm. A gust slammed her, but she pushed back with her wings, even though her wound hurt like hell in the ice and exertion.

It seemed to take forever to reach Robyn's body. Not

her body. *Robyn.* She was not a corpse. Quince would not let herself think that way—

Robyn would be all right. She *had* to be.

At last Quince landed on the ice shelf and knelt beside her beloved.

"Robyn, are you okay?"

The queen lay absolutely still in the snow, one of her legs bent at an awkward angle, a trickle of blood coming from her mouth.

"No no no no…." Quince knelt and picked her up gently, lifting her body from the snow.

Robyn's face was pale. Quince put her cheek next to Robyn's mouth.

She was breathing. Faintly, but breathing nonetheless. *Thank the gods.*

"Quince."

She turned so fast she almost lost her footing on the treacherous perch.

It was Morgan. He threw his arms around her, acting every bit the eight-year-old boy he seemed.

It was impossible. The flash they'd seen had been much higher up the slope. How could he be down with them so quickly now?

How could he be there at all? He couldn't have survived the shift. She'd seen it.

None of that mattered. "Morgan, she's hurt."

He let go of her and nodded. "Bring her inside."

Inside?

There before her was a cavern entrance. One that hadn't been there a second before. She was sure of it.

She shrugged and followed him into the darkness, away from the howling winds outside.

JAMESON WAS deep in conversation with Vestra, discussing the best way to get his forces into Errian and disable the OberCorp force, when Alix tapped him on the shoulder.

Jameson turned to find Alvyn waiting to speak to him. The poor kid looked exhausted.

"Alvyn! How did you get here?"

Standing there with him was his onetime fiancée. "Jessa! Oh my God, you're here!" He swept her up in his arms, hugging her tight.

She hugged him too. "You have *wings*," she said in his ear.

"That's not all that's changed." He let her go. "Alvyn, how did you get back so soon?"

"We flew. Well, I flew. Is it okay if I go get something to eat and drink?"

"Of course. You must be worn out."

"A little." Alvyn gave him a grateful smile and ran off.

"We have a lot to talk about." Jameson took Jessa's hand. He'd given this a lot of thought since he'd seen her the day before. In truth, once he'd accepted his fate on Erro, he'd never thought he would see her again.

Now that she was there, he owed her an apology and an explanation. "Tell me how Alvyn found you. Did he help you escape?"

She laughed, and Jameson remembered how much he loved that sound. "I'm not the kind of woman who needs saving, Jamie…." Her voice trailed off. "Jameson, I mean."

He sighed. He understood it. She needed to put a little distance between them. He supposed it had been inevitable since he'd pledged his heart to Xander. It was just a matter of time.

"I should have remembered that. Like the time we were lost on that camping trip in the woods, and you were the one to guide us out."

She smiled thinly but didn't reply.

"So tell me how you got here. What happened in Errian?"

She explained how she had decided to come after him when she'd sent him a message and it had come back undeliverable. She'd sent an inquiry to the planetary authorities, but no one had known where he'd gone.

They walked down to the lagoon, where he procured some bread and water, and strolled along the black sand, the sun warm on their faces. Jessa got a few strange looks from the skythane they passed, but no one said a thing.

At last, they found a quiet cove, a kilometer down the beach from the camp. Jameson handed her a loaf of bread. "It's not much, but it's better than nothing." They sat down and shared a simple meal, drinking water from his canteen to wash it down.

Jessa chewed the hard bread. It had a good taste, but it was tough and a bit mealy.

She tried not to stare at Jameson.

He was no longer her Jamie. That man was gone, melted away by this strange world. In his place, this new man sat before her. He had filled out, looking much stronger and more athletic than her Jamie ever had.

He had wings too. Beautiful, glorious golden wings. He looked like a red-haired angel.

He was different in demeanor as well. Her Jamie had been cautious, sometimes to his own detriment. Conservative in his actions. Slow to make any important decisions.

Jameson, on the other hand, was sure of himself, decisive. It suited him, to be sure, but she was having a hard time letting go of Jamie.

"So… the wings?" She had news for him. She would share it. She promised herself she would, but first, he owed her an explanation.

"It's hard to explain." He blushed.

She snorted. "I've just flown halfway across the Common Worlds, stormed the offices of an OberCorp CEO, been taken hostage, escaped, and soared over the ocean in the arms of a wing… skythane man. Try me."

He sighed. "I didn't mean for any of this to happen."

She nodded. "I believe you." He had always been honest with her. Well, about most things.

"The guild sent me here to investigate a shortage in a drug I use—used in my practice. It's called pith."

"I remember."

"What I didn't know is that I was chosen for the task by someone who lived here on Oberon." He looked out over the lagoon, as if searching for something.

He'd never been reluctant to talk about personal things with her before. That, more than anything, told her their relationship had changed.

At last, he ran his hands along his thighs, sighing, and looked back at her. "I was adopted. *That* was a shock. My parents never told me. I came from Oberon…."

She listened with growing amazement as he told her what had happened—the mad flight from Oberon City, the separation from Xander, the attack of the wereveren. How he'd come into his wings. She still couldn't quite believe he had wings.

"Can I touch them?" she asked, staring at them, at the way the sun changed the colors of his feathers as he shifted.

Jameson nodded. "Go ahead."

She stood and approached him. His wings spread out, startling her.

"Sorry." He blushed again.

She reached out to touch his left wing. Some of his feathers were half a meter long, and they were soft and smooth. And warm. "You love him, don't you," she whispered as she stroked his feathers.

"What?"

"Xander. You're in love with him."

His wings slumped. "How did you know?"

"We've been friends, and more, for a long time, Jameson. You can't hide much from me. Where is he now?"

"He's coming to Errian with a force of Gaelani—those are his people."

"More skythane?"

"Yes. Jessa, I'm so sorry—"

She laughed bitterly. "I guess I should have known."

That seemed to surprise him.

She sat back down on her rock and stared at the lagoon disconsolately. "You were always… sensitive."

"That's hardly proof—"

"Let me finish. I know ours was an arranged union, but I was genuinely happy when I found out it would be you. You're kind. Sweet. Considerate of others. When you talk to someone, you *really* listen. You don't know how rare that is."

"Still—"

"I'm not stupid. I saw. When some guy would walk into the restaurant where we were having dinner and your head would turn. The way you used to look at Jerrod in the church choir."

"I did?"

"Yes. It was pretty obvious. You really didn't realize?"

He scratched his chin. "I mean, I guess. I just thought everyone felt that way." He looked down at the sand. "My parents weren't exactly accepting and open-minded about the whole homosexuality thing."

She nodded. "Things are changing, even on Beta Tau."

"So, you're not angry?"

She thought about it. "No, I'm definitely angry. But being angry and trying to change something unchangeable are two different things. I *did* chase you across half the Common Worlds, you know. And I certainly didn't expect… *this.*"

Whether she meant his wings, his sexuality, or his newly assertive personality, even she didn't know. Probably all three.

"I deserve that."

"Yes, you do." She stood and offered him a hug.

He accepted it with a grateful smile.

"Jamie… I have to tell you something."

"Oh crap. You have a crush on Vestra, right?" He grinned.

"What?" She laughed. "No, I mean I overheard something while they had me held captive." She tried to remember the exact words. "One of the men said something about an MB."

Jameson frowned. "I don't know what that is."

"He said they were going to wait for you and the other wing men… skythane to attack. Said it would take out the whole city, like some village they used it on a few years back."

Jameson's face went pale. "Ballifor."

"What?"

"I've been there. It's a village that was destroyed by some kind of bomb. Nothing left but a sea of fused glass."

Jessa shivered. "That sounds bad."

"We won't let it happen. Come on."

"Not gonna let a girl catch her breath, are you?" She liked his new decisiveness, but she'd been hoping for a good night's rest after her forced captivity and daring escape the night before.

He gave her a halfhearted grin. "I have one more surprise for you." He pulled her back the way they had come.

She grumbled. She had always hated surprises.

IT WAS late afternoon by the time Xander and his companions reached Torr Talam, the white tower, and the sheltered beach Jameson had chosen from some unknown memory.

As they approached the sea, he was startled to see the size of the encampment there. Much of it was hidden under the jungle, but there were clearly far more than the six hundred skythane he'd brought from Gaelan. Double that, at least. Dark and bright wings,

Erriani and Gaelani intermingled. If nothing else, this threat had united the two skythane nations like nothing else in recent history.

He landed on the beach, folding in his sore wings. He'd given them quite a workout these last few weeks. Sometimes he really missed his hoverbike.

Xander strode under the jungle cover, looking for whoever had taken charge. In one clearing, a group of men and women trained, some kind of hand-to-hand combat that used both ground and air as its battleground.

Another group seemed to be in charge of food preparation. The smell of meat and some kind of local spices made his mouth water.

A man with dark hair and wings ran past, and Xander grabbed his arm.

He looked up at Xander and immediately fell to the ground. "Your Highness," he said. "Forgive me. I didn't see that it was you."

"It's all right. Get up, please. You don't need to do that in my presence."

The man stood hesitantly. "If you say so, Your Highness."

Xander sighed. This was never going to end. "What's your name?"

"Fynx, Your Highness."

"Fynx, who's running the camp?"

"That would be Mylin, Your—"

"*Xander* is fine." *Mylin.* Why should he be surprised? He'd assumed she would go with the rest of the Gaelani to the caves, but she had a gift for this sort of thing, young as she was. "Where is she?"

"Last I saw her, she'd set up headquarters in the white tower." He pointed back toward the beach.

"Good man. Back to whatever you were doing."

Alia was smirking at him. "You should just let them call you 'Your Highness.' You make them really uncomfortable with all this *just be casual* nonsense."

"They make *me* uncomfortable," he grumbled. "Who's the king around here, anyway?"

Everyone looked at the sky, the ground, anywhere but at him directly.

"I see how it is." He sighed and rolled his eyes at the sky. "Okay, let's go find Mylin. She'll put all you ingrates to work."

The skythane who had come with him from Taycrob nodded, and more than a few of them grinned or snickered.

Ungrateful bastards, every one. He stormed back through the jungle toward the beach, climbing over fallen trunks and under vines.

Back on the beach, he made his way to the tower,

leaning in through the open doorway that faced inland. He heard Mylin's voice.

"…thirty more over to the practice field. We have to be ready to fight."

Xander's eyes adjusted to the dim light inside the tower. It was a wide, round room with a staircase cut into one stone wall. She'd turned it into her own personal war room with a makeshift table made from a couple logs lashed to a large, flat piece of wood. She was staring intently at a piece of parchment, mature beyond her sixteen years.

"I should have known you'd be the one to take charge."

She looked up and the severe expression on her young face transformed to a smile. "Xander!" She squeezed around the table to hug him. "You made it."

"I see you've been busy." He arched an eyebrow.

"Oh, I'm so sorry. You can take over. I just—"

"Hey, you're doing an amazing job from what I can see. Why would I mess with that?"

She laughed. "Thanks. Did you have any trouble getting here?"

"A little. We worked it out. Speaking of which, I brought you some fresh recruits. Can you find a place for them?"

"Of course. Nim, can you get these folks settled?"

An Erriani man in his late forties stood at her side, grinning at her through his salt-and-pepper beard. "Your Highness." He bowed to Xander. "All right, folks, follow me. We've got plenty for you to do."

Xander kissed Mylin on the cheek. "You are truly amazing. How many strong are we?"

"With these…." She counted silently. "Thirteen hundred and seventeen, give or take."

"Holy…." He bit his tongue. "That's incredible. Any trouble with OberCorp so far?"

She shook her head. "They seem to be holed up in Errian for now. We've been keeping an eye on them, but so far they haven't made any forays out this way."

There was something wrong about that, but Xander couldn't put his finger on it. A little too "come and get me," maybe?

Alia broke in. "I'd love to get something to eat. How are we on supplies?"

"Fair so far. Many of the outlying villages sent people and food. I think they're still shocked at what happened to Errian. Once they found out we'd been through the same, it opened a lot of doors. Come on. I'll take you four to get something in your stomachs."

She led them back toward the beach. He let Alia and Mylin catch up and fell back to take time to think.

They were *there* now. Errian was just a short flight

away. They'd have to make a move soon or risk being discovered and attacked.

And yet, the OberCorp forces had to know they were coming, after the battle over the Orn. Why hadn't they at least scouted out the lands around Errian?

Something was *off*.

He'd see Jameson soon, at nightfall, and they could talk about it then. He glanced up at the sun through the purple leaves overhead—it was late afternoon.

Sometimes he missed his Personal Assistant too—back when he'd known if it was 4:57 or 5:15 just by checking inside his own head. And how he missed his ionic shower.

On the other hand, he hadn't needed a sleeper to knock him out in weeks.

He took a deep breath. He wasn't sure he was ready to see Jameson yet. What if he felt a rush of feeling for the man? How would he know if was real?

Worse yet, what if he felt absolutely nothing?

Sometimes he thought his old self had it right. Love no one. Trust no one. Rely only on your own wits and fortune.

Then the only one who could let you down was yourself.

20

REUNITED

Quince followed Morgan into the mountain with Robyn in her arms. She was experiencing a strong feeling of déjà vu. Morgan once again provided the light, his hand glowing.

A deep sense of foreboding filled Quince's heart, a fear of what was about to happen.

She looked behind her. The passageway was sealed, the door to the outside world gone.

She shoved her fear down deep. This was why she had come, to find Morgan. And at the moment, nothing was more important than getting help for Robyn.

The light went out as suddenly as it had appeared,

and Morgan's hand guided her against the wall in the inky darkness. "Shhhh."

She stood immobile, holding Robyn in her arms, and waited for whatever Morgan was warning her against.

His hand was warm on her arm.

Her eyes adjusted slowly to the darkness, or maybe the darkness was changing. Bit by bit she found she was able to see the walls of the cavern, smooth like the cavern in the Mountain. Had it really been just six days before?

Then she saw it, or became aware of it, something moving down the cavern toward them.

It was ethereal, a construct of gossamer wings and rainbow colors, drifting about half a meter above the cavern floor. *Nimfeach*. She wanted to step out into the cavern, to greet it. It emanated goodwill and warmth as it approached.

Morgan's nails dug into her arm, and she held back, hugging Robyn and the cavern wall.

It passed within half a meter of her face but seemed unaware of her. It continued up the cavern toward the place where they had entered, now just a solid rock wall.

It stopped, seeming to cast about for something. Then it turned and shifted.

The rainbow colors were gone, leaving behind a

small, shriveled black *thing*. It glowed with a golden light now, and as it floated past, she got a good look at it —six spindly black legs, a long, tapered, purple-and-black striped thorax, dark iridescent wings, and a head with oversized, multifaceted eyes. As it reached them again, it stopped and turned to look directly at her.

Those alien eyes seemed to bore into Quince. They pulled at her, like the compulsion before, but without the warm and fuzzy feelings. This time it was a demand.

She squeezed her eyes shut, praying to Erro that the creature would let them be.

When she opened her eyes at last, it was no longer there, and Morgan's hand was glowing again.

"What was that?" she whispered, hoping to never see its like again.

"*Nimfeach*. One of the protectors." He let go of her.

"Is it gone?"

"Yes. It came to check the waygate after I opened it."

Quince frowned as that sank in. "So… where are we?"

"Far beneath the surface. Come on. I will take you somewhere safe."

Beneath the surface. How were they going to get out of there, if Morgan decided not to help? Quince shivered, thinking of the thousands of tons of rock sitting overhead, ready to collapse with the next quake.

Against her better judgment, she continued to follow him down into the bowels of Erro. What else was there to do?

They continued walking for about fifteen minutes before the tunnel leveled out and came to a juncture. Morgan led them off to the left and then into a dark room. He closed the door behind them, and it shifted to become part of the stone wall, leaving no hint of their passage.

He put a hand on the wall next to where the door had been and the room lit up, a soft golden glow like that of his hand.

The room was sparsely furnished with a set of what looked like cabinets on one side.

Morgan touched a hand to the floor and lifted it up, and the floor *followed*, forming a wide table. It looked fragile as ice. "Put her down here."

Quince looked around. She'd given up most of her options when she'd followed him inside. They were at Morgan's mercy now.

Gently she set Robyn down on the edge of the table and took off her carry sack, setting it aside. Then she laid Robyn's unconscious form on the table.

Immediately the table began to change its form, stretching upward with multiple white extensions to envelop Robyn's body.

"What's it doing?" Quince asked, alarmed, and reached for Robyn's arm.

"It will make her whole again." He pulled her arm back gently but firmly. "Trust me."

Quince was finding that hard to do, despite her recent warm feelings toward the boy. Or whatever he was.

Morgan touched the floor again, conjuring up two chairs. "Sit. We will talk."

Quince set down her own carry sack and sat down, surprised to find the spindly ice chair quite comfortable. She tried not to look at the table, which had entirely covered Robyn's body by then, as if it were eating her alive. She shoved those thoughts away too.

"You called for me," she said at last, and was surprised to see Morgan squirm in his chair.

"I did. I… shouldn't have. It's not part of the plan."

Morgan had spoken of "the plan" once before, when her own life had hung in the balance. "But you did call me. And why me?"

He nodded. "Part of me called. And because you listened."

"Part of you? Morgan, what are you?"

In response, he stood and put out his arms. A rainbow glow extended around him, forming beautiful wings, like she'd seen in her dream, the night by the lake. Like she'd seen in the tunnel just minutes before.

"You're a *nimfeach*." She wasn't as surprised as she should have been. She'd suspected it for some time.

But he shook his head. "Only part. I am part human too. Like you."

All at once, she understood. "Someone made you, didn't they? To guide us? To get us to do what you wanted us to do?"

He nodded, looking miserable.

"Like… the *sneach*?"

He shook his head. "The *sneach* were failures. Hybrids that didn't follow the plan."

Quince shuddered. He meant human experiments. Or experiments on human subjects, at least. "What's the plan? Whose plan?"

In response, he stood and walked to the far wall. His hand touched the surface and it turned transparent, like fog and frost retreating from a window.

Quince stood and went to join him.

They were looking out on a vast open space, full of white pods eerily similar to the table that now encased Robyn. There were thousands of them, lined up in even rows.

In between the rows were dozens of golden *nimfeach* going from pod to pod like worker bees.

"What are they?"

"Ithani. They return."

. . .

Jameson gathered Vestra, Venin, Alix, and Jessa by the lagoon as the setting sun fell past the rim of the volcano. He swallowed hard as he brought out the key. This was the first time he would see Xander since they'd parted near the waystation. The intervening time had only made Jameson more certain of his feelings for him.

Who could say if it had done the same for Xander?

At the moment it didn't matter. There were more important matters to be dealt with.

He took a deep breath and summoned a waygate, connecting one beach to the other. He gestured for the others to go through and then followed them, snapping the waygate shut behind him.

Xander was there waiting, along with Alia and a young girl. It took Jameson a minute to recognize her. "Mylin!"

She grinned. "Welcome to Torr Talam."

"Good to see you made it." Xander's voice was flat and professional.

Jameson's shoulders drooped. "You too. Any… trouble getting here?"

"Not really. We picked up a number of Erriani on the way. They've told me about the situation in Errian."

"Good. That'll save time." He swallowed again and

then pulled Jessa forward. "Xander, this is Jessa. My… fiancée."

Xander's eyebrow went up at that.

"Nice to meet you." Jessa held out her hand.

Xander shook it firmly. "You came looking for him?"

She grinned. "I couldn't let Jamie here get in trouble." She squeezed his arm.

Jameson felt the temperature on the beach drop by ten degrees.

"Come on. We can talk in Mylin's office." Xander turned and led them to Torr Talam, his shoulders stiff. Only his wings betrayed any emotion, quivering slightly.

Jameson shook his head and followed Xander into the tower.

Xander grumbled under his breath.

This was *not* how he'd wanted the reunion to go. Although he wasn't sure what he *had* wanted, either, but meeting with his own ex and Jameson's… fiancée? Ex? When he was still unsure of his own emotions? He felt queasy.

He ducked into the tower's cool darkness. He wasn't used to these gray areas in life. Since he'd been freed from Rogan's grasp, he'd taken firm control of his fate, first with Alix and later without him. He'd told himself he was done with love. Done with dependency on others. He didn't need anyone to take care of him.

Now Jameson was back, and he looked as good as before. Better maybe. Absence makes the heart grow fonder and all that, but how was he to trust his *own* heart?

When Quince returned, she was going to have a lot to answer for.

Xander turned to address his guests, putting his hands on the table. "This is about the closest we have to a war room. Mylin has been running the camp from here."

Jameson nodded, stepping up to the makeshift table. "This represents Errian?" He pointed to a group of spiral shells on one side of the table.

"I'd say a frontal assault is best." Xander pointed at the southern edge of the *city*. "We have more than a thousand skythane now, but if we keep them here too long, we lose the element of surprise. Plus, food will start to be a problem."

Mylin jumped in. "We have enough to feed everyone for a couple days, at most."

"What kind of food?" Jameson studied the table.

"Fish from the sea, animals we've been able to hunt

or trap. Some of the villages sent stores as well."

"I can help with that."

"Your Highness?"

"The waygates. I can get us food or access to it." Jameson turned to look at Xander. "But we have another problem."

"I think we have enough fighters to overwhelm the invaders." Xander had spent the last few hours figuring out who to send where and how to use Jameson's advantage to take down the invaders without much of a fight.

"Jessa overheard Danner Black when she escaped." Jameson's knuckles were white as he grasped the edge of the table.

Xander hissed. "He's here?"

"Yes. Remember Ballifor?"

Xander nodded. "But I… oh shit." Quince's village had been reduced to slag by some kind of lander tech.

"They know we're here. They haven't come to find you, have they?"

Xander shook his head. "We thought they were just hunkering down, consolidating their hold on Errian."

"I think it's clear. Errian's a trap. We have to find another way."

"How long do we have?" Xander frowned.

"Jessa overheard them say three days." Jameson sounded short with him.

Xander whistled. "What if we took the fight to them in Oberon City?"

Jameson looked up, his eyes narrowed. "What do you mean? We'd be using swords against plasma weapons."

"Not necessarily. What if we convinced Rogan to fight them for us?"

"The Syndicate?" Jameson scratched his chin. "And why in the hell would he do that?"

Xander's grin widened. "Because we have a room full of pith to trade for it?" He'd been thinking about the OberCorp pith storage room back in Gaelan for a couple days, wondering how it could be put to use.

"That… that could work." Jameson held his gaze for a moment, then looked away. "One of us would have to go back to Oberon City to talk with Rogan."

Xander nodded. "I'll go."

"No. Absolutely not." Jameson shook his head fiercely. "I'm not letting him anywhere near you again, not after what he did to you."

Xander's mouth dropped open. "I—"

"Forget it. You're not going to play the martyr. I'll go. After all, I can take him to the pith to show him what we have to trade."

"Um, guys.…" Alix put his hand on Xander's shoulder.

Xander wondered how the two had gotten along these last few days. "What?"

"So, just to be clear, we're talking about starting a gang war, in the middle of Oberon City, to stave off a regular war?"

"Only until they agree to back down." Xander leaned against the old tree. "I think it's our only play."

"What if I had another?" Alix had a gleam in his eye.

"Like what?"

"What if I talk to my mother?"

That was a surprise. Alix *never* talked about his family. Xander didn't even know he had one. "Your mother?"

Alix met his gaze, looking deadly serious. "Ask her to call all this off."

Jameson asked the question they were all thinking. "Who the hell is your mother? The head of OberCorp or something?"

"Yes." He smiled grimly. "I may be the only one who can get her to listen."

WHEN THE MEETING BROKE UP, Jameson pulled Xander aside. "Walk with me?"

"Sure." They crossed the beach and headed into the

jungle in silence. They traversed the small stream that burbled its way down toward the sea and found a quiet space among the trees to talk.

Jameson looked around nervously for any of those spider-cat things before sitting down on a fallen log. "How are you?" He was unsure if he should hug Xander or leave him be.

"Still working things out." Xander wouldn't meet his gaze.

Jameson looked down at his hands—the double moons were fading as the nails grew out, but they were still visible. "I missed you."

Xander snorted. "Looks like you've had lots of company."

"What?"

"Jessa, your fiancée, traveled a hundred light-years to find you." Xander turned away. "And Alix doesn't seem to hate you anymore. Should I be worried?"

"I don't know. Should you? If you don't care about me anymore, I don't see why it would matter." It came out more sharply than he intended.

"You're not denying it."

"Denying what? Look, nothing happened. With Alix or with Jessa. I'm here. Waiting for you."

Xander's shoulders stiffened. After a long moment, he said, "I'm not ready."

"Fucking typical." Jameson looked away. It seemed he was less patient than he'd hoped to be. He took a deep breath. "Look, I'm sorry. I'm going to go. I'll take Alix to Oberon City and see what we can do, but I don't want to leave it like this between us. The last time was hard enough."

"What do you want from me?"

"Xander, look at mc."

Xander turned reluctantly to face Jameson. His face was tight with pain.

It killed Jameson to see him like this. "Whatever there is between us, or whatever there will be, I care about you." He shook his fists in the air. "*Fuck it.* I love you, Xander Kinnson, even if you don't love me back." He put his arms around Xander and pulled him close, feeling Xander's resistance. "I'll keep waiting for you, even if it kills me." Jameson kissed Xander's cheek and let him go. He squeezed Xander's hand one more time and turned to walk away.

"Be careful," Xander whispered.

Jameson stopped, squeezing his eyes shut to hold back the tears. His insides were twisted, like he'd been split down the middle by a massive blow, his guts burned to ash. But he couldn't let Xander see it.

"I will." Then he left Xander behind, hoping somehow, someday, his skythane would change his mind.

21

XANDER AND JESSA, SITTING IN A TREE

"WHAT ARE the Ithani?" Quince had a pretty good idea, but she wanted to hear it from Morgan himself.

"They were the masters of Erro, the ones who planned to spin it here, to this new place."

"Why?"

"To escape their enemies, the Dhagani." He touched his hand to hers, and she was in the middle of a war.

AN ENTIRE PLANET BURNED. Ships raced past one another in the black depths of space, exchanging fire. A sun went supernova, spewing superheated plasma into the void.

. . .

Morgan let go. "It raged on for two thousand years after the Ithani discovered the Dhagani homeworld. Millions were killed on both sides."

Quince struggled to take it all in, breathing quickly. The human race had yet to encounter another sentient race in its spread across this corner of the galaxy. Then again, the portion of the Milky Way so far inhabited by humanity was vanishingly small.

"What were these dog… dagh…."

"Dhagani. They were diminutive in size… like me. They were easy to kill in battle."

"They don't sound so fearsome."

"They were masters of macro-tech. In the end, they sent a bomb that destabilized our sun."

"The flares!"

"Yes. The Ithani think it was meant to make the sun go supernova, but that something went wrong. Only because of that chance of fate did they survive."

"What about the Dhagani?"

"The Ithani retaliated against them. By then they were few, but they were no longer willing to stay their hand. The Dhagani homeworld was destroyed, pummeled into a radioactive wasteland, but the damage had been done. The Ithani scientists found a way to move the homeworld to a new place, a universe where they could complete the next step in their evolution."

Quince rubbed her chin. "And the *nimfeach*?"

"We are the servants of the Ithani, here to prepare the way. When the first shift went awry, it fell to us to find a way to complete it. The Ithani couldn't withstand the energies of the shift unshielded."

"How long have they been waiting?"

"A little more than a hundred thousand years."

Quince whistled. "Why couldn't you just come to me? Or tell me, in a dream or something?"

"They watch me. The others don't trust me. You had to come here."

"Why are you telling me all this? I have no interest in the Ithani. They can evolve to heaven or hell, for all I care."

"The Ithani were almost freed once before. But the part of the world you call Oberon was spun back to your universe before they could be awoken."

Quince's mind raced. Seven hundred and fifty years before, when Elyra and Daedus had stood in the same place where Jameson and Xander had been, in the room under the Mountain.

"How did you survive?"

Morgan frowned. "I am a key. After the world shifted, I came back here."

It made a certain kind of sense—Morgan was the reason Xander and Jameson had been able to shift

Oberon at all. Then it hit her. Why the Mountain had collapsed. "It was you."

He nodded. "We did not wish to allow it to happen again. This time our masters will be freed."

Without the Mountain, there was no way to spin the worlds apart once again. No way she knew of. And the broken rocthane key, which they had assumed Dani or Kadin had broken… it had been Morgan all along.

She backed away from him, seeking to flee, but there was nowhere to go.

He was no child. She'd known that for some time. Still, he'd seemed childlike, in need of protection. But this….

"What… what happens when the *Ithani* awaken?"

"They will use the heart of the world to complete their transformation."

The heart of the world. "The amalite?"

He nodded solemnly.

"But that would destroy Erro…."

"Yes." He seemed small now, once again the child Xander had taken him for.

What if he *was*? He could have left her and the rest of the skythane—the rest of the human race on Erro—in ignorance. Or he could have left them to die in the cold after luring them here. *Unless…*

"You're not like them anymore, are you?"

Morgan shook his head, his eyes fixed on hers.

"Something changed you." She knelt before him and looked into his big brown eyes. "How did they *make* you? The other nimfeach?"

He looked away. The pain in his eyes, in his posture tugged at her soul, but she stayed firm. "Tell me."

"There was a boy. In Egeus. He was starving. Near death. They promised him life and he… accepted."

Her eyes narrowed. It was horrid, what they had done, stealing a boy's life. But too much rode on what happened next for her to get sidetracked. She shoved her disgust down into her gut.

"This boy, what was his name?"

"Tanner."

Quince closed her eyes. "Is he still… in there?"

"Yes. We're one now. He is me."

Her eyes widened and her breath caught. "What?"

"We have become one, and I/we are no longer sure about the *plan*."

If Morgan was telling the truth… "Tanner?"

The boy nodded.

She pulled him into her arms and hugged him fiercely. For all the things that he was, he was also still a boy. A part of him, anyway. A boy who had called out to her for help.

If half of him was human, they had a chance. Maybe he did too.

She let him go. "Can you… the nimfeach part… let him go?"

The boy shook his head. "We are one."

"Did you have a name before too? The nimfeach part?"

The boy's face tilted, and he nodded slightly. He touched her face, and a light went through her, filled with reds and golds and a taste like cinnamon and chocolate.

"That's… gonna be hard to pronounce. What should I call you?"

He smiled weakly. "Morgan is good."

Jameson opened a waygate back to Bolcà Isle and sent Vestra and Venin back through to prepare the Erriani there, and to bring them to Xander under cover of darkness. Jessa decided to stay with Mylin to see what she could do there.

Mylin saw them off. "Good luck." She reached up to kiss his cheek. "I'll look after him. So will Alia."

Xander was nowhere to be seen.

"Thank you." Jameson closed his eyes, wishing it

were Xander who would accompany him, instead of Alix. "Take care of yourself too, little sister."

She grinned and hugged him. "I wish I were."

He kissed her forehead, then gestured for her to stand back.

Next, he opened a waygate to Gaelan, to the room where all the pith had been stockpiled. He and Alix stepped through the gate, and Jameson let it close behind him.

"Let's get this stuff moved." The place was strangely quiet, empty.

Alix pulled him back. "Hey, are you okay?"

Jameson shook his head. "I hoped… I wanted it to be different. Maybe he doesn't love me after all, but that doesn't matter at the moment." Like hell it didn't, but he couldn't deal with it now.

Alix held his gaze for a moment. "I get it. Come on. Let's get this done."

Jameson was grateful to Alix for understanding. He opened a new gate, this one to the caverns where he and Xander had taken refuge. Alix crossed over to the other side, and one by one Jameson handed the crates of pith that OberCorp had stockpiled across the waygate. In fifteen minutes, they had transferred it all to its new place for safekeeping.

Jameson took ten vials and stuffed nine of them in

his carry sack. *At least I figured out the pith shortage.* It seemed like such a small victory in the scheme of things, but it was something.

He stared at the last vial for a moment before putting it in his pocket. This little thing, the cause of so much trouble for the Common Worlds. For Oberon and Titania, the landers and the skythane. For him and Xander.

With Alix at his side, he closed the waygate and opened one more, to the one place in Oberon City that he remembered most clearly, the storage unit where he and Xander had gone just before they fled the city.

"Ready?"

Alix grinned. "Not really. You?"

"As good a time as never." They stepped through the gate, one after the other, and Jameson closed it, shoving the key into his carry sack for safekeeping.

Alix looked around. The place had been ransacked, the door still in tatters from the enforcer attack.

"Xander's secret bunker," Jameson said by way of introduction. "Where he kept his stash of clothing, food, and weapons, in case he ever needed to flee."

Alix looked at Jameson, raising an eyebrow.

"You didn't know about it?"

Alix shook his head. "Not until this evening. Either he rented this place after I left, or…."

"Or he never really felt safe, even when he was with you." Jameson had seen it many times before, in abuse cases. The abused were always ready to run, because they were always sure they'd have to, one day. "It's no reflection on you. What he went through with Rogan…."

"Maybe not. But I always thought he felt safe with me." He spat. "And now you're going to make a deal with the man who abused him."

"I know. It feels wrong. But we have no other good plays, and it was Xander's idea, after all. If you can't convince your mother—"

"You better get going. I'm going to take my PA out of stealth mode. I'll give you the location as soon as I get a lock, but in about five minutes, this place is going to be swarming with enforcers."

"Good luck." Jameson held out his hand, but Alix pulled him in for a hug. "I think we would have been good friends, if none of this had happened." He let go of Jameson, closed his eyes, and placed his fingers on his left temple, pressing in and muttering "Code alpha-gamma-379106, pass code black angel." He blinked. "I'm in. Tracking Rogan."

"No rush or anything."

"Got him. We're in luck. He's at the Castle."

"The Castle?"

"It's a Syndicate stronghold outside the city. I can slit it to you—"

"We burned out our implants. Didn't Xander say there was a tracker chip here somewhere?"

Alix dug through the bins that were thrown about the back of the storage unit.

"Running out of time."

"Got it." He pulled out a small silver disc and pressed it to his temple for three seconds. Then he handed it over to Jameson. "It will blink faster and faster until you reach the target. Fly east and then follow the tracker." He grinned. "I also downloaded some black-ware into it. Press and hold the button for five seconds when you get close, and it will disable the house's security routines for a good five minutes."

"Got it." Jameson turned to go. As he stepped over the wreckage of the roll-up door, memory tugged at him, and he turned to see Xander standing there, looking invulnerable, a black-winged angel. He blinked, and it was Alix again.

"Godspeed." Alix waved him off.

"You too." Jameson turned away again and leapt in the air, making for the far side of the city.

. . .

ALIX WAS off by about four minutes. He used the extra time well, sending messages to Braid Seneford, Sera Thorpe, and several other OberCorp board members, laying the groundwork in case his mother stubbornly refused to see things his way.

It took nearly ten minutes for the hoversport to find him, and by then, he was sitting lazily on a crate, chewing an old Nutrisynth bar he'd found in one of the crates. The enforcers poured out of the craft, pulse rifles at the ready, but he made no move to oppose them. Instead he put his hands in the air and stood still as they surrounded him.

"Alix Preston, you are under arrest, under the laws that govern Oberon City."

"I won't resist." He threw the wrapper aside. His hands were pulled behind his back and locked with stim cuffs. He was careful not to push too hard against them. He didn't relish the shock they would produce.

They hauled him into the hoversport, and it lifted smoothly into the air, carrying him back toward Ober-Corp headquarters.

He wondered how long it would take for word to filter up to Lena Preston.

The prodigal son had returned.

· · ·

FOR THE FIRST time in weeks, Xander really missed his implants and his PA. The planning was done for the assault on the OberCorp forces in Errian. Now all they had to do was wait.

He sucked at waiting.

If only he could spin up a few tunes in his head to distract him. Something by the Preachers, rough rock with a smooth beat. Or something by Anellia, with her soothing triple harmonies, something only extensive genetic body modification had allowed her to achieve.

Instead he sat on a high branch of an ironwood tree in this strange jungle, looking up at the stars. Wondering what the new day would bring.

"Xander, is that you?" It was a woman's voice.

He glanced down at the ground. It was too dark to make out much, but he could see she was a lander. Jessa.

"I don't really want to talk."

There was no reply.

He sat back against the trunk of the tree and stared out at the rising moon. Bandia shone silver light across the treetops, washing out all the color and leaving things cleaner, simpler. He wished it would wash over his heart as well.

The tree shook. "What the hell?" He peered down to find a pair of eyes staring back at him.

Jessa levered herself up onto the branch, looking around her. "Wow, it's really beautiful up here."

"I *said* I didn't want to talk." He was surprised that she showed no fear. Landers usually preferred to stay closer to the ground.

She ignored him. "This world is much wilder than Beta Tau. Did you know there are cat-spiders in this jungle that can eat people?" She shuddered.

For his response, he stared off into the star-filled sky, refusing to engage with her. Two could play this game.

"You're being an idiot, you know."

He stared at her. "*I'm* being an idiot? So says the woman who followed her crush halfway across the Common Worlds."

"That was love, not stupidity."

"Looks about the same from here."

"Touché." She dusted the bark off her hands. "I've known Jamie since we were kids. I always knew we were supposed to get married. As I grew older, I knew… or guessed… other things too."

"So, you knew?"

"That he was gay?" She sighed. "I suspected. Or at least bi. But he was my friend long before we were supposed to be something else to each other." She took his wrist, then saw the scar there. "You burned out your implants?"

"Yes. When we were on the run."

"I wish I could show you what he was like. Back then. I have pictures, but they're all in my head."

He nodded. "I miss being part of the grid, sometimes."

"Yeah, I can imagine." She edged closer to him on the branch. "Look, I don't know you. But I can see why Jameson chose you. You're—pure?—I don't know. You're real. No bullshit."

"Really? You can tell all that just by looking?"

"I'm a good judge of character." She took his hand again. "I'll say it again. You're being an idiot."

"You don't know what you're talking about." He pulled his hand back and wrapped his arms around his chest.

"You're scared your feelings for him aren't real. You were hurt before, when Alix left you, and now that you've been dosed full of pith, you think you can't trust what you feel for Jameson."

"How do you—"

"Alia and I talked. She's worried about you too. She said you're waiting to see if you feel the same when the pith wears off."

He took a deep breath. "That's true. Or that's part of it." He set his hands in his lap, searching for the best way to explain it. "I was abused as a child, by the man Jameson is going to see."

"Oh." She looked pained and put a hand on his.

So, she didn't know *everything*. "When Alix came for me—he bought out my contract—I thought I loved him. But I know now that it wasn't love. When I saw him again, I was relieved. Not in love. He was my savior, and I transferred everything over to him—all my hopes and fears. I *needed* him to be my protector. When I lost him, I thought my hope died too. And then Jameson came along."

"And you trusted in the future again."

He thought about it for a moment. "Yeah. I guess I did. But it was all a mirage, a drug-induced fugue."

"Are you sure? Are you willing to lose him just to prove your point?"

"What do you mean?"

She ran a hand through her blonde hair, smoothing it back. "Look at it this way. Every day people meet and fall in love. Sometimes it's because they miss the train and take the next one, only to bump into someone they've never met before. Sometimes they are in an arranged marriage for years, and suddenly truly *see* the person before them. Other times they bond over drinks at a bar on a space station." She squeezed his hand. "My point is that it doesn't matter how they get there. It's the end result that matters."

"I don't know—"

"How do you feel about him right now?"

"It's not—"

"Right now. *Do you love him?*"

He shuddered. "Yes. But—"

"*But* nothing. Do you love him? Or are you going to be an idiot and let him go?"

"I…." He didn't really know how the stuff worked. Maybe it *had* permanently altered his brain. Maybe he loved Jameson only because his mind had been warped. But did it even matter?

I love Jameson.

Maybe it didn't. "I don't understand. Why would you want to help us? You must be furious at him for keeping a secret."

She smiled wanly. "Jamie and I had a long talk. I will always care about him. But he's not *supposed* to be with me. You're the one he needs." She kissed his cheek. "Just promise you'll take care of him."

Xander laughed. "I can do that. I think. If he'll still take such an idiot back."

She grinned. "He will. He's a bit of an idiot too." She looked down at the ground far below. "Mind giving me a ride down? *Up* was hard enough, and it's gotten a lot darker."

"Of course." He swept her into his arms and carried her down to the ground, grinning the whole way.

I love him.

He didn't need his implants to hear the music in his head now.

22

THE PRODIGAL SON

QUINCE AWOKE, feeling more refreshed than she had in weeks. She lay on her side in a white bed, as utilitarian as the rest of the room, and yet supremely comfortable. The material conformed to her shape, cradling her the same way she cradled Morgan.

The lights in the room—dimmed when she woke—brightened as she sat up and put her feet on the cool, smooth white floor.

She was clean too, as if she'd just taken an ionic shower, and her clothing looked like it had been laundered and repaired. She could get used to this place, looming alien threat notwithstanding.

Quince turned around and gasped.

Robyn lay on the table, once again exposed to the

world, but still as death. A pile of clothing sat on a pillar next to her.

By Gael's blade. Robyn had *wings* again.

Quince leapt up and practically ran to her side, putting a finger on Robyn's carotid artery. If the bastard place had killed her….

Robyn's pulse was strong.

Her green eyes flickered open. "What happened?" She sat up, looking around wildly. "Where are we?"

"Hey, it's okay. It's just me. You're safe. Morgan saved us." She leaned down to kiss Robyn. Their lips met, and it was as sweet as ever.

Then Robyn pulled back. "What's… wait… holy Split, I have wings!" She tried to twist around to see them, and they fluttered in agitation. "How in the three hells…?"

"This place. Morgan said he'd fix you, but I never imagined he could fix *that*."

"Oh my gods, Quince. I have my wings back. I have my wings back!" She danced around the small room, and there were tears in her eyes. "I thought I was crippled for life."

Quince pulled her close. Robyn's heart beat next to hers. "It didn't matter to me."

"I know. But it did to me."

"I know." Quince couldn't imagine losing her wings. They might as well have thrust a dagger into her heart.

When they separated, Robyn's cheeks were wet. She wiped them with the back of her arm. "What is this place?" she asked, looking around.

"It's the home of the nimfeach, and their masters. It's why Morgan called us here." She sat Robyn down on the bed.

Morgan watched them from where he sat, on the bed, back to the wall, his knees tucked under his arms.

Quince explained what she'd learned, and at her request, Morgan showed her the Ithani in their cavern far below.

Robyn pressed her hands against the transparent surface, taking it in. "They've been here all this time?"

Quince nodded.

"How sad for them." In the great open space below, the nimfeach made their rounds among the pods. "Buried here under the ice for a hundred thousand years, waiting for their spring."

Quince frowned. She saw things differently. "When they awaken, Morgan says they will destroy the world."

Robyn looked at her. "That could be a problem."

Quince laughed ruefully. "Yeah, it could. Question is, what do we do about it?"

They both turned to stare at Morgan.

He shook his head. "It's too late now. You have to save those you can."

"How?"

"Send them back."

"To Titan Station?" Quince shook her head. "Even if we knew how, without another shift, there's no way to evacuate so many people from the world."

Morgan looked miserable.

Quince sat down next to him and hugged him. Whatever he'd started out as, he was at least half-human now, and she could see that part of him was scared. "We'll figure something out." She laughed ruefully.

"What?" Robyn asked, crossing her arms.

"Looks like we're gonna have to find a way to save the world *again*."

JAMESON FLEW EAST, following the *beep beep beep* and *blink blink blink* of the tracker. He kept low to the ground, hoping to avoid detection, though he was sure his outlandish (by Oberon City standards) clothing didn't help. He knew he wasn't the only skythane in the city, but there were precious few.

He turned a corner and was almost battered by an oncoming freight hover. He flattened himself against a wall as the thing lumbered by, his feet perched on a small ledge.

This would have been easier if he'd had a point of reference outside the city.

Oh damn. Of course he did. The immigration center, where he'd first landed on Oberon.

He flew on to the Slander, where he was less likely to be seen when he opened the waygate.

The traffic slowed down as he skirted the edge of the decrepit district, leery of tripwires or traps that might have been set for his kind. Even up here, the putrid smells from the streets reached his nose, and he wrinkled it in disgust.

The company allowed such misery to flourish at its doorstep, filth and poverty and criminal behavior that went far beyond anything on Beta Tau. For all its faults, his homeworld took care of its own.

My homeworld. This was his place of birth. Maybe once all this was over, he'd find a way to do something about the way its people were treated.

Jameson found a dark rooftop on the edge of the Slander. He looked around to be sure there was no one nearby and opened a waygate to step through.

The immigration center was abandoned. Not much need for it without anywhere to go to or come from.

It was midafternoon on this side of the world. Beyond the last bits of the city, the rolling green hills of the Estates stretched for thirty kilometers, surrounded by orchards. Great mansions sprouted from the hills out here, and of all of Oberon, this place reminded Jameson the most of Beta Tau.

He stayed below the trees as much as he could, flying from orchard to orchard in short spurts. Once, he startled a crew picking big green fruits from trees with leaves as large as his arm. He waved and flew on, hoping they wouldn't report him.

At last he closed in on his target.

It was a large mansion made of red stone, standing three stories tall in some places. A castle indeed. It was surrounded by vineyards and had wide balconies that looked out over the rolling hills of the estate.

Jameson found a perch in a tree close enough to see the place. The tree was covered in fuzzy yellow leaves, providing ample cover from above and below. He settled in to watch and wait for nightfall.

He pulled out some dried bread and cheese he'd brought with him to tide himself over while he waited. He missed processed food and carbonated sodas, especially fizzpop that had big chunks of alco-sugar that burst in your mouth. He was about sick to death of keff and water.

After about an hour, as the sun began to slant toward the horizon, he was rewarded. Rogan himself strode out onto his balcony, tying up his red silken robe, to gaze across the vine-covered hills.

The Syndicate bosses were no better than OberCorp. They lived like *this* on the backs of the people in the Slander, and they did horrible things to their charges. Jameson wished he could snap the man's neck for the way he'd treated Xander.

Not yet. They needed him. The fate of many more innocents rested on those fat shoulders.

Jameson waited until after nightfall, when the light bled out of the sky and the stars appeared above but before the moon rose. He leapt from his perch into the sky, and a short flight brought him down silently onto Rogan's balcony.

He pressed his chest flat against the wall next to the doorway and peered inside.

A young boy, maybe ten, sat on a wide bed, shivering, wearing a space marines costume, his bare feet hanging over the edge of the bed.

A cheery fire lit the room, but the sight made Jameson's blood run cold.

He waited for fifteen minutes to be sure there was no one else in the room. Then he pushed the button on the tracker chip for five seconds, hoping Alix knew what he was doing.

Fingers crossed. He stepped inside, signaling the boy to be quiet.

The boy's eyes went wide.

Jameson knelt before him. "It's okay. I'm here to help you." The boy had bruises on his arms and neck. Jameson swore to himself he'd make Rogan pay. "Go out on the balcony and stay there until I come for you."

"I'm… I can't." The boy pointed to his temple.

"Dammit. Okay, it may take me a day or two, but I'll take care of that." Putting a bomb inside a child's head. "Now go."

The boy was white as a sheet, but he nodded and ran out of the room.

Jameson took up a place behind the door and waited. It felt like an hour but might have just been fifteen minutes.

The door creaked open, and Jameson grabbed the man's fat wrist. He had just enough time to see Rogan's startled face before he opened a waygate and threw him through, joining him half a world away as it slammed closed behind them.

ALIX WAITED IN AN EMPTY ROOM. Well, not entirely empty. There were two white chairs and a plas table to keep him company.

But the walls were blank, and the floor was an industrial-grade beige carpet used in corporate offices across the Common Worlds. The only nod to color was the brass doorknob.

He'd been a constant source of disappointment to his mother. His "homosexual proclivities," while certainly not unusual in Oberon City, precluded him marrying a woman and siring an heir, which had displeased his mother. It was a little crazy, as she ran a multisolar corporation and not a kingdom with bloodlines of succession, but the line between the two was fuzzy these days. Plus, it's not like he couldn't adopt or father a child by other means. There were many ways around the problem, of course, but Lena Preston seemed to take his sexuality as a personal affront.

She had clawed her way to the top of the company over three decades, deposing the previous chairman in a bloodless coup with all the precision of a zakka strike. As she had so often told Alix, she intended to leave it to him when the time came.

Alix had no interest in running a multisolar conglomerate, even a small one like OberCorp. Yet his half-hearted attempt at rebellion had come to nothing. He closed his eyes, remembering the day he'd told her.

. . .

"I'*M NOT COMING IN TOMORROW.*"

She looked up at him from her desk, ruthlessly organized and severely plain. "Everyone needs a day off, now and then." She closed her eyes, mouthing something to her PA. Then she looked back up at him. "What is it this time? Trip to the Outlands with… Xander?"

There was always that pause when she spoke Xander's name. A not-so-subtle reminder that she would never entirely accept him as Alix's equal.

He shook his head. "I've joined the rangers."

She slammed her fist down on the desk. "Absolutely not. I need you here. You still have a lot to learn about running the company."

Alix sighed. "I'm not cut out for this. This is *your* *life.* I want to be out there, dealing with people, with the real world, not this swirl of ones and zeroes." If he squinted, he could sense the data streams slipping through the air around him.

"*This* *is your life. Your future. I've fought all my career to give this to you.*"

"Are you happy?"

That stopped her. She cocked her head at him as if she didn't understand the question. "Happy? I'm… I am content *with the work I do. I am happy to know that I am one of the few people on this half ball of rock who could do this kind of job.*"

Alix sat down and took her hand. "But are you happy?"

She looked down at her hands. "I don't think that really matters."

"Last month, I stood under a waterfall in the Outland, the cool creek pouring over my skin under the summer sun. Xander kissed me, and I experienced such a moment of unexpected and total bliss… I realized that I was happy for the first time in years." He took both of her hands in his. "Don't you want that for me?"

Her eyes were misty. "I remember being happy once. There was a boy in Philo…." She closed her eyes and took a deep breath. "But we all have to grow up sometime. As an adult, you can't always be happy."

"Or ever?"

She let go of his hands. "Two years. You can pursue this little dream of yours for two years. It would be good for you to see the rest of this world, from the ground up." She sat back and crossed her arms. "Maybe it's time I met this Xander of yours."

There was no pause. Something had shifted. He nodded. "Maybe so. But I don't want him to know who you are. Or about… this." He gestured around the executive suite.

"Ah, now who are you ashamed of?"

"You. Always you." He kissed her cheek. "Thank you, Mother."

"Two years."

ALIX CHECKED WITH HIS PA. His two years would be up next week. Close enough for corporate work.

He wondered if she'd had a hand in sending him away from Xander with Dani Black. He wouldn't put it past her. Lena Preston did what it took to get the job done, even at the expense of her own son.

The door swung open.

"Hello, Alix. I've been waiting for your return." His mother was perfect, as always, her business suit just the right length below the knees to assert her power and her cool femininity. Her red hair was tied up in a neat bun, and her face was pale as snow and as cold. "You look like you were out in the wilds a couple months too long."

He scratched his beard and smiled. "Price of the job."

"Come on, then. We'll get you cleaned up. Then we can talk."

"I'd rather talk now."

"Don't be silly. Nothing important's going to happen in the next two hours, and I will not stay in the same room with you when you're smelling like that. Come back to my suite with me." She turned and left the room, expecting him to follow.

After a moment, he did, cursing under his breath. Thirty seconds in her presence and he was back under Lena Preston's thumb.

As he left the room, the two enforcers stationed outside started to fall in behind him.

His mother waved them off. "I can deal with my own son alone, thank you."

"But Ms. Preston—"

"Enough. I've made up my mind." She snapped her fingers. "Coming, Alix?"

He followed her, but he was already figuring out how to go around her to do what he had to do.

GAMBITS

Quince was rearranging her carry sack, filling it with the strange food bars Morgan had supplied. The technology at work there was amazing, and not only because of what it could do.

Humans had food replicators and advanced medical tech. They could duplicate many of the things that Ithani tech could do, although she suspected that shifting an entire world into another universe was still beyond the capabilities of the human race.

No, what was truly amazing was the fact that it all still worked after a hundred thousand years.

The food bars were nondescript—like sugar cubes, but larger—but each one tasted different, a whole meal in a mouthful. She'd tried one that was something close to chicken soup, and another that was like nothing she had ever tasted before. The closest she could come was beef and chocolate ice cream. Which sounded absolutely terrible in theory, but her mouth still watered for it.

"Come with us," she said to Morgan. They had decided they needed to find Xander and Jameson. Maybe together they could find a way to stop what was coming.

He shook his head. "I can't leave. I've already spent too much time away from the others. They'll start to suspect."

"How many *nimfeach* are there?"

"Just over a hundred. Every few hundred years, we are absorbed and rebirthed. We gain the memories of our predecessors."

Quince nodded. "Inherited memory. Like some of the skythane. You must have rubbed off on us."

"Yes."

That simple statement caught her off guard. She knew they had experimented on children. Morgan was proof of that. What else had they done? She suspected there was a whole lot more behind it that he wasn't saying, but she didn't have time to explore it.

"You can send us to Errian?"

"Not from here. We have to go outside."

She shivered. The sight of the naked *nimfeach*,

without its beautiful rainbow aura, still haunted her mind.

He took her hand in his. "I will keep you hidden."

She nodded. "You ready?"

Robyn had been repacking her own bag. "Ready if you are."

Quince pulled her close and kissed her. "Whatever happens…."

Robyn nodded, wrapping her new wings around Quince. "Whatever happens."

Quince pulled on her carry sack and turned to Morgan. "Let's go."

In response, the boy threw himself into her arms.

She hugged him fiercely, remembering there was still a lot of Tanner in Morgan. When she pulled away, she knelt next to him. "Hey, we'll figure this out, okay? One way or another."

"Okay."

Robyn knelt next to him too. "What did you mean when you said you'd rubbed off on us?"

Morgan squirmed. Clearly talking about it made him uncomfortable. "It's part of the plan," he said at last.

"The plan." Quince looked at Robyn. "The shift was the plan." Her mind raced with the implications. Jameson and Xander had been needed, according to the prophecy, to shift the world. Those two, connected, and no other. And long before them, Elyra and Daedus. "Morgan, are Xander and Jameson… are they part Ithani?"

He stared at her for a long moment. Then he nodded.

"By the Split!" Robyn stood and started pacing around the room. "This whole plan… it was a fucking *breeding program*."

Morgan looked scared.

"We're not angry with you. But we need you to tell us. Have the *nimfeach* been… preparing skythane for the shift?"

He nodded.

"For how long?"

"Since you came to Erro."

Quince sat back on her ass on the bed, stunned. For a millennium, her people had been used by the Ithani, forged into a key for the lock that bound them. *We're as much a tool as the rocthane.*

She wondered how much Ithani she had in her own blood.

She looked up at Robyn. "If Xander and Jameson are special… if the Ithani part of them is strong…."

"Maybe they can find a way to talk to the Ithani. To stop them before it's too late."

"We have to go." To Morgan, Quince said, "How much time do we have?"

"Five days."

She hugged him once more. "We'll come back for you."

He nodded solemnly.

"Now send us to Errian."

JAMESON LOOKED AROUND THE CAVERN, his eyes slowly adjusting to the blue light that filled it. The last time he'd been there, it had been with Xander, when they'd shared a few stolen hours after the shift. The last time they'd really been alone.

Once again the memories flickered in his head, but he forced them down ruthlessly.

Rogan lay on the dusty cavern floor below him, staring at him with a mixture of anger and fear. "Who are you? What did you do to me?" He looked around wildly. "What is this place?"

"Don't recognize me?" He leaned down so Rogan could get a better look at his face in the blue glow from the ponds.

Rogan's pig face squinted up at him, and then he let out a snort. "It's you! The one who was with Xander."

His features shifted to anger. "Where's my fucking pith?"

For his answer, Jameson pulled the vial from his pocket. "Here you go."

"That's nothing."

"A quarter-million crits isn't nothing."

The man struggled to his feet, pulling his bathrobe closed and tying it off, trying to regain a little dignity. It was a lost cause. "You promised me in on the pith trade." He snatched the vial from Jameson's hand.

"Turn around."

Rogan turned, and a gasp escaped him at the sight of crate after crate of the drug. "Holy shit." He sank down on his knees to grab the nearest crate and pried it open with his hands. "This is… all of this is pith?"

"Enough to keep you supplied for years, if not decades, I'd imagine."

"And it's all mine?" Rogan turned to stare at him.

Jameson shook his head. "I want something else first."

Rogan glared at him. "We had a deal."

Never mind that Rogan would break a deal as easily as breathing, if it suited him.

"Let's consider your current situation." Jameson ticked off the facts on his fingers. "You have no idea where you are. You're all alone here with me, a man who is younger and stronger and faster than you, and who could dump you in the middle of the Gildensea in five seconds if I decided it was in my best interest." He held out his arms. "So, what do you say we renegotiate the terms of our agreement?"

Rogan was silent for a long time. The moment stretched past what Jameson felt reasonable, and still there was no discernible reaction.

Finally, he started to shake. A laugh sprung up from his fat stomach, exploding from his mouth in a rumble.

What the hell?

"I like you, Jameson Havercamp." He continued to laugh.

"How did you—"

"I did a little research after you left Oberon City. It always pays to know who you're getting in bed with."

Jameson stared at him.

"You have balls, boy. So what do you want?"

"We'll supply you with pith for the next three years. We just need a little firepower in return."

"What kind of firepower?"

"The kind that can take on OberCorp?"

His eyes narrowed. "That's a big boat to rock. And how do I know we'll even be able to sell to the Common Worlds again?" He looked around at the beautiful caverns and scowled. "This isn't exactly home, is it?"

Jameson laughed in spite of himself. "Maybe not. But we'll set that right too."

Rogan looked at him with newfound respect. "You have a deal." He extended his hand. "What do you need?"

Jameson took his hand, privately wishing he didn't have to touch the man. "Put some pressure on Ober-Corp. Lay siege to their headquarters and make them nervous." He pulled out the vials of pith he'd secured in his pocket earlier and handed them to Rogan. "A show of good faith."

Rogan accepted them greedily, casting a regretful glance at the rest.

"I want one more thing. The boy. The one I saw in your room."

"Taylor?" Rogan grinned. "Ah, so you have a taste for them too."

Jameson's stomach turned. "Have him ready for me the next time we meet. That means I want the little bomb taken out of his head too."

Rogan's fat hand tugged on his chin. "Deal. There are always more where he came from."

Jameson shuddered. He pulled out the key and opened a waygate back to Rogan's estate. He was careful to put it in the garden where the man wouldn't have anyone waiting for him.

"How much for one of those?" Rogan eyed the key.

"You couldn't afford it." He resisted the urge to kick Rogan's ass through the waygate. He shuddered again at the thought of the Syndicate having a key, though it probably wouldn't work for landers.

Rogan grumbled but allowed himself to be escorted through.

Jameson snapped the waygate shut as soon as he was gone. He felt dirty, but Rogan's time would come.

He opened another one back to Xander's camp along the Argent Sea.

ALIX CHECKED HIS CHRONOMETER.

"It's 7:03 p.m.," Erissa whispered in his ear. He'd missed his PA.

Jameson had agreed to check back with him at midnight, and every six hours after that, at the storage unit. He didn't see how he was going to make their first check-in, but he'd figure it out somehow.

Two years in ranger training and deployment had changed him. He wouldn't just nod and do what she demanded.

She palmed open the door to her private residence, and he stepped into the most luxurious apartment in all of Oberon. Unless one of the Syndicate bosses had something nicer.

The flat was enormous, spread over an entire level of one of the arcos. The top one, of course. It was floored with bamboo, imported from Earth at tremendous cost. Floor-to-ceiling force windows showed an early evening sky. On one side, the waters of the Gildensea glittered under the silver light of an alien moon.

She led him to her sitting area, taking a seat on a white granth-leather couch. The rare feline species had been hunted to near extinction a century before on Pleiades Six's only inhabitable world and the ice cats put on the endangered species list. Hunting them was a crime punishable by death.

Those couches sure didn't look a hundred years old.

Alix took a seat in an armchair across from his mother. Lena Preston crossed her legs and stared at him. A servitor brought her a crystal glass filled with something golden. Brandy would be his guess.

"Where the hell have you been?" she said at last, taking a sip.

"Until last week? Locked up in a work camp on the Split. But surely you knew that."

Her eyes narrowed. "Of course."

She was hard to read, but he'd learned through trial

and error over a lifetime. She was surprised. She hadn't known.

"I mean, since that time. Since that damnable event." She set her drink on the synthglass table next to her chair. Ripples of colored light radiated out across its surface.

"With Xander."

She scowled and pushed herself up, taking her drink with her, to stand by the window. "Those wing men are plotting, even now, to take us down. It was a mistake not to wipe them out when we had the chance."

That brought him to his feet. "You don't mean that. They're not like that. Xander's not like that. What happened to make you hate them so?"

She didn't reply.

"Mother…."

"There was a man. One of them. I met him in Philo."

He came to stand next to her, looking at the darkening sky. "You've never told me this before."

"It was a brief affair. One that ended painfully."

"So one skythane man breaks your heart—"

"He raped me." She said it as calmly and coolly as if she were commenting on the weather.

"Oh my God. I'm sorry, Mother. I didn't know."

She looked at him and shrugged. "How could you? It was a long time ago, before you were born."

"Still, they're not all the same."

"They're animals. Savages. None of us are safe while they rule half the world."

He closed his eyes. She would never change. It explained so much, though.

"The stars are different," she said softly, catching his attention once more.

"What?"

"The goddamned stars." She turned to face him, and the mask slipped a little. She was afraid. "Where in the seven suns are we?" She put a hand on his shoulder. "Titan Station is gone. The whole of the Common Worlds is gone."

"We're in Titania's universe now. Surely you know that. You sent us there to take over the pith supply."

She turned away. "I did. That seems like a long time ago, now." She put her hand on the window. It fuzzed, sending a ripple outward from her hand. "I didn't believe this was possible."

"It's not too late to change course, you know. Call back the rangers and enforcers from Errian."

She looked up at him and put a hand on his cheek. "I'm sorry, darling, but I can't. The board would fight me on it. They're running scared, sure the barbarian hordes are going to come after us, now that we share a world." She shook her head. "They're not wrong. We have to see this through now. Danner Black made sure of that when he dropped the bomb on that town of theirs. And the occupation of Gaelan only took us farther down that road. It's them or us now."

Alix groaned. "It doesn't have to be. I know these people. I spent a year among them. Hell, I *lived* with Xander for nine. We can still stop this." He took her hand. "I still love him. Even if he doesn't love me." That was a bitter pill to swallow, but there it was.

"I wish I could. Truly. But we may never get back home, to the Common Worlds. I'm only acting to secure this new world for you, for our kind." She took a deep breath, and her mask came down again. She pulled her hand away from his. "In any case, you're home. You'll stay here, of course, until we can figure out other arrangements."

"That can't be how this ends. Mother. Mother!" He tried to stop her, but she moved out of his reach.

"I'll see you in the morning. Zenix will see you to your room."

"Goddammit." It had been a long shot, but he'd been sure he could change her mind. "Zenix, where's my room?" he asked the house AI.

"This way." A series of lights lit up the floor.

He took one last look out at the Gildensea. Xander and Jameson were somewhere across that expanse of water and its twin, the Argent.

Alix sighed. He had one more play to make. If that fell through, he'd have to find a way to get word to Jameson that he'd failed.

24

BREAKTHROUGH

MORGAN LED them out of the small room where they'd spent the last day.

Quince looked back once more at the transparent wall. She shivered at the thought of what lay beyond it.

When they were in the hallway, he put his hands up along the doorway, and the wall reappeared there, unbroken.

Damn, that was cool.

He led them back the way they had come, as far as she could tell—up a long, featureless passageway. They weren't intercepted, and after a time, Quince began to relax. It looked like they were going to make it out okay after all. Not that their odds over the longer term were all that great.

She took Robyn's hand, and it was warm in her own.

Part of her ached to be out of the confines of this dark warren, back in the clear skies of Erro. Part of her was afraid to leave Morgan—*Tanner*—behind.

They reached the end of the tunnel, a blank wall where they had come through the waygate earlier. She knelt next to the boy. "Come with us."

He shook his head. "I need to stay here, or they will suspect. I can try to slow things down."

"Are you sure?"

He nodded.

She pulled him to her breast and hugged him tight. "We'll come back for you. I promise."

He slipped something into her hand.

As he let go, she held it up. It was another key. "You will know what to do with it." Its surface swirled like mercury, and it was bigger than the one Robyn had given her, so many years before. "You have to go. They will come soon."

She looked at it for a second, and then tucked the key away in her carry sack.

Morgan touched the wall with both hands, and a new waygate appeared. The towers of Errian, bathed in the light of late afternoon, awaited them.

She knelt and kissed Morgan on the forehead and

stepped through the gate. Now she just had to find Jameson.

Robyn followed right behind her, and the gate winked out of existence a second later.

"What's that doing here?"

Quince turned to see a hoversport sitting in the middle of Errian's main plaza.

She looked around. The city was in shambles. Ober-Corp had already come.

"Fly!" she yelled to Robyn, and leapt into the air.

Something slammed into her back. Her body sizzled with electrical current, and then everything went dark.

JAMESON LEANED back against an old wormwood tree whose branches reached out over the little stream that ran through the Torr Talam camp.

He'd checked for Alix twice at the old storage unit in Oberon City, but there'd been nothing—no one and no note.

Night had fallen over this stretch of Titania now, and he needed solitude.

Xander had been so cold to him before he'd left. So closed off. Like when they'd first met, before things had blossomed between them. Now Jameson was shattered.

For once, he was the one ready to go ahead, to stop running.

Xander was the one who didn't want to be with him anymore.

Jameson picked up a pebble, slinging it down the stream. It skipped a few times and then sank below the water, leaving no trace of its passage.

"Hey, I was looking for you."

Jameson looked up to see Xander in all his beautiful glory, his black wings spread against the evening sky.

"I didn't feel like talking with anyone." He stood and stretched his own golden wings, a challenge of sorts. How quickly he'd gotten used to them. "This seemed like a quiet place for a little contemplation, but I can go find another." He got up and started off up the stream bank.

"Wait."

"Why should I?" He turned on Xander, and his voice came out angrier than he had intended. "Just so you can tell me you don't want me, again? I get it."

"No. I mean… I don't—"

"Why can't you just trust this thing between us? Wherever it came from, however it started?" He took a deep breath, calming himself. This was not how he'd wanted this to go. "I flew to Rogan's estate, outside of

Oberon City. I cut a deal with him to try to save our people, all the while knowing what kind of monster he is. What he did to you. And all I wanted to do was to kill him, to grind that fat face into the dirt. All I want to do is to protect you. To be with you, and you won't let me in—"

"Would you just shut the hell up for once?"

Jameson stared at Xander. The hairs stood up on his arms, and the adrenaline rush sent a thrill up his spine.

"Look, I came to find you because I had something to tell you." Xander took a deep breath, then forged ahead. "You're right. It doesn't matter how we got here. I *just want to be with you.*"

Jameson was stunned. He opened his mouth to speak.

"Just hear me out. More than that, I don't even care whether it was pith or fucking fate or just the chemical attraction that brought us together." He ran his hand through his dark hair. "Damn. I'm shit at all this. What I'm trying to say is—"

Jameson pulled Xander close and kissed him. "I think I got it." Their bodies entwined, and Jameson dragged him to the mossy ground next to the stream.

Xander whispered, "I love you."

Jameson grinned. "About fucking time." Though he

was still pissed about all the runaround. He'd just have to take it out on Xander's poor body.

He unlaced Xander's shirt and his own, and pulled Xander down to kiss him again.

His hand went inside Xander's pants. Xander was excited and ready for him.

Soon they were both transported to a world with no one but the two of them, and they didn't need a waygate to get there.

Xander was flying.

As they moved in perfect sync, he felt a surge of love for Jameson. This offworlder who was really skythane. This man who had broken past all his barriers, one way or another.

As they climaxed together, his spirit soared.

He was far above Erro, his wings no longer black, but an iridescent rainbow of colors. He felt different, looser, freer. His thoughts raced in an alien tongue, and Jameson, next to him, was the same, like two glowing butterflies.

To him, Jameson was beautiful.

The sun rose in the distance, but it was an angry sun,

bloated past its normal size. The heat hit him immediately, and the air started to boil.

Below, the forests burst into flame, and the lakes began to steam and evaporate.

He pulled Jameson to him as the heat became unbearable, and then vision ceased.

XANDER SAT UP, rubbing his eyes.

What the hell was that? Another memory? It had felt so real. He was sweating profusely.

Jameson sat next to him, looking dazed.

"Did we just see the end of the world?"

Jameson looked up at him. "You saw it too? The sun and the flames…."

Xander nodded. "The last thing I felt was you in my arms." He pulled Jameson close, not caring that they were both sweating. "I was… we were something else."

"I know. I've seen them before. They lived here once."

"On Erro?"

Jameson frowned. "I think so. They were the ones who split the world…." He shivered in Xander's arms.

"Hey, it's okay. That was a long time ago." He stood and pulled Jameson up with him. "What matters is the here and now. You and me. Come on!" He padded into the stream, where the water was deepest, and rinsed himself off.

Jameson followed and soon was splashing Xander playfully.

Xander splashed him back and then pulled him close. "I've missed you, robin."

"I've wanted to hear you say that for days and days." He kissed Xander, and Xander's heart hummed.

"I see you two have finally made up?" Alia was staring down at them from the shore. "It's about time. Come on. We need to finish planning for tomorrow." She turned away. "And put your clothes on. You're creating quite a distraction."

Xander watched her go. "Think they really need us *right now*?"

Jameson laughed. "I don't see what difference another fifteen minutes will make."

Alix had spent the last three hours trying to find a way to crack the grid block Lena's AI had on the apartment. Clearly she wanted him out of the game until it was all over, but he'd learned a few tricks in his time with the rangers.

He ran a patch app that would fool the AI, making it seem like he was in his room sleeping.

Then he tackled the grid issue. Oberon's grid ran on a super high frequency network, and the blocker kept him from accessing it. With enough power, though, he could build an amplifier that would pierce the block, and then he could send whatever he wanted across the grid.

He stripped the wiring out of one of the lamps in his bedroom, and used a couple strips of metal from his mother's collection of ancient machinery. She was gonna kill him for that one. He found a roll of insulating tape to cover the wires. Next, he pried open the access panel on the grid transmitter and patched in the whole mess. He plugged it into the power source and sat back to examine his handiwork. It was an unsightly jumble, but thankfully his mother had left him all alone in the apartment while she attended to what she was calling "the skythane mess."

Alix tested his connection. He could reach Oberon City's grid, but the signal was still intermittent. He needed a bigger antenna.

Alix looked around, and his gaze fell on the white leather couches. They were made offworld, on a fairly primitive planet. Maybe…. He used a kitchen knife to cut open one of the seat pads, and sure enough, there were rows of metal coils inside, so he pulled a few out and twisted them together. Soon he had a stronger antenna, strong enough to reach the grid.

Success. He sent out two instructions. One to get a messenger to meet Jameson at the storage unit at noon, and one to advance another plan he was working on.

Then he set to overriding the lock code on the front door. That took another hour or two, as he tried several different hacker apps to try to tease out the lock code.

In the end, he resorted to brute force, disabling the lock through a rapid-fire series of commands that pried at the lock until it finally slipped open. It was less elegant, but in war sometimes you had to be a little rough. It would also set off an alarm, but he planned to be far away from there by the time anyone came to investigate.

Sure enough, a siren started blaring behind him. He had about thirty seconds to get to his old hoverbike before the system shut down the building.

Alix ran down the hall and plunged into the dropshaft that would carry him down two levels to the family garage. He slammed into the floor, knocking the breath out of his lungs, and gasped for air as he pushed himself forward toward the bike. Alix pulled himself onto it, sending the command via his PA to open the window.

Taking in a long, ragged breath at last, he gunned the engines as the plas slid open.

It stopped and started to reverse. Lockdown was coming.

He shot forward, put his head down, and rammed through the closing panes of plas, shattering them outward as he raced toward freedom.

JAMESON OPENED the waygate to check for Alix one last time, at midnight, not expecting anyone to be there.

A young man waited for him, wide-eyed, wearing a helmet, elbow and kneepads, and standing on a hoverboard. "Jameson Havercamp?" he asked, staring at the world through the waygate, his mouth falling open.

"That's me. Who are you?"

"Alix Preston sent this for you." He handed over a package, trying his best to behave professionally in a circumstance that should have left him speechless.

Jameson took it and opened it, reading the terse message.

No dice. It's war. I will do what I can.

There were also two pairs of communicators, one marked "Alix" and the other "untraceable—for Rogan."

"Thanks," he said to the messenger. "I'd give you a tip, but I don't have any wetware."

The boy laughed. "That's all right. This is the coolest thing I've ever seen—"

His voice was cut off as Jameson closed the waygate.

"What did he say?" Xander asked, frowning.

Jameson shook his head. "We go to battle with OberCorp tomorrow. Gods help us all."

25

IN THE DARK

Quince awoke in darkness. She was lying on something soft.

Oh gods, I can't feel my wings. She flailed about, trying to touch them.

"Shhhhhh," someone whispered, taking her head in their hands. "It's okay. You're okay."

She stilled. "Who… who are you?"

"My name's Neamiah."

It was pitch-black. She kept waiting for her eyes to adjust, but she couldn't see a thing. "What is this place?"

"The old mines."

"Mines?"

"Yes, in Errian." The voice sounded petulant, as if that should have been obvious.

"You're Erriani."

"Of course." A long pause. "Aren't you?"

"No. I'm Gaelani."

"Oh. I didn't know they had captured any of your people."

Neamiah's voice wasn't exactly feminine and not entirely masculine—maybe they were one of the tweeners. "Are there more of us here?"

"Two more."

"I'm Jenner," said a voice to her right.

"I'm Toree."

Those voices were more recognizably masculine and feminine.

"No one else?" Where had they taken Robyn? They must have been captured by rangers or enforcers.

"No, sorry. Are you missing someone?"

She nodded and then realized they couldn't see her. "Yes. We were separated."

"I'm sorry," the voice Quince recognized as Toree said.

She sat up. "What's wrong with my wings?" She could feel now that they were there, behind her.

"There's some kind of nerve blocker. To keep us from flying." She felt Jenner come up and sit next to her. "Here, feel mine."

Quince found his shoulder. She followed it to where

the wing joined his back. There was something cold and hard wrapped around the base of each wing. "Motherless bastards."

"What?"

"Those are military grade nerve cuffs. They must have been preparing for this for a long time." To have them, and in sufficient quantities for a whole city….

She had underestimated OberCorp's thirst for Titania and its riches. "What is this place?"

"It's the mines—" Neamiah sounded exasperated with her again.

"I mean right here. Where we are being held?"

"Ah. It's a storage room. The mines are full of them, cut out for cold storage when the ore went dry."

"They didn't bring my carry sack in here, did they?"

"No. You were just like this when they brought you."

Damn. If they searched her bag… time enough to worry about that later. "I'm going to trace the contours of the room."

"Go ahead."

Quince stood hesitantly in the dark. She felt her way to the first wall. It was rough, but generally vertical. Feeling along the wall, she bumped into someone. "Sorry."

"It's okay," Toree's voice said.

Quince slipped past her and found the first corner.

The next wall was narrower and had nothing unique about it, at least that she could tell by feel.

The third was long, and this time she called out and Jenner moved out of the way. This wall was smoother. There were places that might have held shelf brackets for storage, spaced as evenly as they were.

On the fourth wall, there was a change.

It was imperceptible at first, something her instincts noticed but her mind didn't. It brought her up short.

She stood there, stock-still, for a long time.

"What is it?" Neamiah asked from behind her.

"Something…." She pulled herself up on her toes, trying to feel the difference. Cool air blew on her face. "There's an opening up here. I can feel moving air."

"It might just be a crevice."

"Might be. Or it might be something bigger. Can one of you give me a boost?"

"I can." It was Toree. The woman came up behind her, touching her shoulder. "Put your foot here. I'll lift you up."

Quince did as she was told, and then she was ascending. Toree was *strong*.

Quince felt along the wall in front and just above her. Nothing, just blank stone. The air was coming from higher up.

The wall was rough enough there to allow a few hand- and toeholds, though she had to find them by feel. "I'm going to climb higher."

"Okay. I'll try to support you as far as I can."

Quince took hold of the wall and pulled herself up half a meter. She put her other hand up, and there it was.

"There's an air grate up here," she whispered, fearing there could be someone on the other side. "They must have put in ventilation for these storage rooms."

"Maybe so." Neamiah sounded uncertain. "These caverns haven't been used much over the last hundred years."

Quince felt around the edges of the grate. If she could move it, she could probably fit through the opening. She pulled herself up to where she could reach the grate with both hands. It was recessed into the wall.

"What's happening up there?" Toree asked, sounding anxious.

"If I can get this grate free, I'm going to go for help."

"Help from who?"

"The King of Errian."

"There is no King of Errian." Neamiah now sounded downright annoyed. "The last prince was killed twenty-five years ago. When they captured us four days ago, Errian had a regent, not a king."

"Lyrin Madainn has returned. I've seen him myself." She worked at the grate. It was loose on one side but wouldn't move on the other. What she wouldn't give for a pulse rifle right about then.

Wait. She felt the side and found a piece of metal sticking out at a forty-five-degree angle from the edge of the grate. Could it be a release?

She tugged on it. It was slow to move, but finally it did, and the grate came loose and fell past her toward the floor. "Watch out," she hissed, nearly losing her grip.

The grate clattered to the ground.

"Everyone okay?"

"Except for the heart attack you just gave us," Jenner said, but she could hear him stifling a laugh.

"Good." She tested the sides of the opening. She should be able to make it through, though the dead weight of her wings wouldn't help. "I'll go find help and come back for you."

"Go quickly," Neamiah called. "Who knows what the landers have planned for all of us?"

"I will." *Damn, I hope this shaft doesn't get any narrower.* Like many skythane, she had a *thing* about dark and enclosed spaces.

Quince dragged herself into the shaft, her legs dangling over the edge for a moment before she pulled them in behind her. She needn't have worried. The shaft was only about a meter and a half long.

She found the grate releases on the other side, and in a moment was through, but she hadn't counted on coming out the other side headfirst. Quince decided to turn on her back and pull herself out, grasping at the rocks above the shaft entrance.

She felt like a butterfly coming out of its chrysalis as she heaved herself out of the hole, her wings dragging behind her like dead things. It took her a good twenty minutes to extricate herself, bit by bit, while clinging to the rock for dear life.

Quince had no idea how far down the ground was, but had to guess it was the same as on the other side—two to three meters. Not enough to kill her, but she could break a couple bones if she fell the wrong way. She eased herself down a handhold and foothold at a time until she was holding on to the lower lip of the vent entrance.

She should be okay if she dropped straight down and let her knees take her weight. "One, two, three…." Quince let go and dropped.

JAMESON RUBBED HIS EYES. He'd managed to get a little sleep after a couple hours reacquainting himself with Xander. What a reunion that had been. He was relaxed, if tired, and ready to take on the day. With the sun due to rise at any moment, he had one more card to play before the battle was joined.

Morning light shone through Torr Talam's casements, brightening the round white room.

"Are you sure he'll cooperate?" Xander was staring at the battle plan, his wings twitching in irritation. They had to be ready to fall back at a second's notice if Ober-Corp should follow through on its threat to bomb Errian.

Xander had been doubtful about Rogan's part of the plan all along, and given his experience with the Slander boss, he had every right to be.

Jameson took a deep breath and shrugged. "For now, yes. He wants the pith. I think that will keep him on a short leash, at least until he realizes we may never get back to the Common Worlds."

"Would you want to? Go back, I mean?" Xander was looking over the map in their "war room," making last-minute adjustments to his battle plan.

"Not really. There's not much left for me there." He closed his eyes. "I wouldn't mind seeing my parents again. One more time." His adoptive parents had treated him as their own son and had never told him he wasn't theirs. Sure, they were religious and conservative, and who knew what they would make of his wings and the rest of it, but they had always been there for him. He had a hard time accepting that they were gone forever.

Xander nodded. "I feel like I don't even know my own mother, and she's here." He looked northward. "I wonder what they found?"

"Quince is getting an earful from me when she comes back. Assuming we all make it through the next day alive." He kissed Xander. "I should go."

"Be careful of Rogan. The man's the devil."

"I know. And he has his eye on this." Jameson held up the key.

"He knows about it?"

"It was kind of hard to hide it when I used it to drag him halfway around the world." He stepped away from the hollow tree and opened a waygate to Rogan's estate, being careful to choose a different exit point than before. "I'll see you soon." He stepped through and closed it behind him.

He was in the courtyard of the estate house. It really was a beautiful home, three sides surrounding a central courtyard and a well-trimmed garden.

He leapt into the air and landed on Rogan's balcony. "Rogan, I'm ready to collect on my part of our deal."

The double doors swung open, revealing the Syndicate boss with his young slave. "Here he is."

Taylor had a big bruise across the left side of his face, and he limped as he walked toward Jameson. His eyes, though, shone with hope.

Jameson growled under his breath. "You've done as I asked?" He took the boy under his wing. Taylor clung to him.

Rogan nodded. "And a lot more."

Jameson wanted to knock that sick smirk right off the man's face, but for the moment, he had to restrain himself. The time would come soon enough.

"We need you to move against OberCorp, now. Lay siege to the corporate office. But keep casualties at a minimum."

Rogan's sly grin said he'd been itching for this chance for years. "We'll have our men in place within the hour. Do you want us to bring the building down?"

Jameson shook his head. "We just want to scare them, for now."

"We're good at that."

Taylor shivered under his touch. "Here." Jameson handed the man a communicator, one of the pair Alix had sent him for this purpose.

Rogan took it and looked at it suspiciously.

"Where will you be?" Jameson asked.

"The empty warehouse where we first met. I'll set up operations there."

Jameson nodded. "Understood." He picked the boy up. "We're going to go somewhere far away from here."

"Away from him?" There was a damp spot in the boy's pants.

"Yes, far away." To Rogan, he said, "I'll be in touch soon."

Then he leapt off the balcony, forming a waygate in midair, and took the boy to safety.

Quince had landed badly on her left ankle in the fall, and it hurt to walk on it. Not that she had any choice at the moment.

There was little light in the long cavern, apart from some kind of glowing fungus that ran in seams along the walls. It wasn't much, but it was enough for her to find her way.

The floor was rutted, probably by the passage of wheels over a long period of time, taking whatever they had mined here out and—later—bringing goods in for storage. She figured if she followed the ruts, they would lead her out of the caverns eventually.

There were hundreds of rooms there, each one locked. She'd quickly determined that there were no captors in the mines with them. The skythane had been locked inside and apparently left to die.

At each one, she knocked and told the frightened men and women inside that she would help them. And as each one was left behind, she despaired of being able to do anything for them at all. Still, she had to try.

She hadn't found Robyn, either. That weighed heavily on her heart. Where had she been taken? Quince didn't think Robyn could bear to lose her wings again.

A deep rumbling sound gave her enough warning to duck into an alcove as the whole tunnel began to shake, showering her with dust and pebbles.

They rattled across the floor, and the air grew heavy. There were screams and cries from behind the doors.

It calmed down after a moment.

The quake reminded her that there was a larger game at play here than just landers versus skythane, and time was running short.

Somehow, she would find Jameson and Xander, and they would help her set things right.

She did catch one lucky break. As the tunnel reached a fork, where the light was brighter, she noticed a rusted metal door that was slightly ajar.

She pulled it open. It required considerable force, but she managed to get inside without falling on her ass.

In the dim light, she could see stacks of personal belongings. There were carry sacks, shoes, jewelry, and even some children's toys, including a little carved wooden doll with a sad face that just about broke her heart.

After some digging, she found her own carry sack. She pulled it out into the brighter light of the hallway. Inside it was the key that Morgan had given her. She breathed a small sigh of relief.

She returned to the room, searching along the back wall to see if the jailers had left anything else behind.

On a dark shelf, she found another key—a human one this time—for the nerve cuffs she was wearing at the base of each wing. She matched the key to the magnetic lock. It took a little contorting, but after a minute they fell away, one after the other, returning feeling to her wings.

Quince felt like she was being poked by a thousand pins and needles, but that sensation was preferable to not feeling them at all. She spread them out behind her and felt better about her chances.

The fact that all these things, and even the key to the cuffs, had been left behind did not bode well for the trapped skythane. What did OberCorp have in store for them?

She resumed her walk, trudging up toward the source of the new light. It was sunlight—she could see that now. She was almost at the exit.

The light resolved itself into a series of bars. "Fuck

no." She hurried forward, hoping her eyes had betrayed her.

No such luck.

The tunnel was blocked by a sturdy metal gate, which had been fused shut.

Quince reached the gate and rattled the bars. They were too close together to squeeze through. The gate was firm and barely moved when she shook it with all her might.

She sank down to her knees, exhausted and sad. She had failed.

JAMESON LANDED in the clearing that was the heart of the activity in the skythane camp. He sought out Vestra, finding her serving food to a bunch of the troops—a cooked grain that looked unappetizing. He figured it must be great for the body.

"Vestra, this is Taylor. He's been through a lot the last couple of days. Can you take him under your wing and see that he gets fed and finds someplace safe he can sleep?"

She nodded. "Of course. I was just getting ready to eat, myself."

Jameson knelt next to the boy. "Vestra here will take care of you. You're safe now." He tried to hug the kid, but Taylor pulled away. Well, he *had* been traumatized. He'd seen abuse cases before and knew it was going to be a long time, if ever, before things would be *normal* for him again.

Jameson patted the boy's back, wondering if this was how Xander had been…. Had he been this young when Rogan had taken him? He would give that bastard what he deserved, one of these days soon.

"Go with Vestra. I'll come check on you later."

"She has wings too."

"Yes, she does." He shot a grateful glance at Vestra. "Thanks." He turned to go find Xander.

Vestra's hand on his shoulder held him back.

"What?"

She looked up at him, her long gray hair tucked neatly behind her ears and her face as serious as he had ever seen it. "Be careful out there. And bring back our people."

He kissed her on the cheek. "I'll do everything I can."

Xander watched Jameson and Vestra from the entrance to Torr Talam, as Jameson handed off a child to her.

"How'd it go?" he asked, his gaze still fixed on the boy.

"As well as can be expected."

"Who's the kid?"

"He's… he's like you were, once."

"Ah." Xander's hand tightened on the edge of the doorway, the knuckles showing white. He closed his eyes. So many kids like him. So much damage. He hated that they had to work with Rogan, *again*. He would have liked nothing better than to rend the man limb from limb. The boy was so young. So innocent. *Like me once indeed.* "What's his name?"

"Taylor." Jameson was looking at him curiously.

Taylor. One more name for the list of crimes the Slander boss had committed. He sighed heavily. "I'm glad you helped him." It wasn't lost on him that Jameson had felt the same impulse for Taylor as Alix had for him, once upon a time.

He hoped Alix was okay. "Are we ready, then?"

"Yes, as ready as we'll ever be. Give me an hour lead time."

"I wish I could come with you." He pulled Jameson close and kissed him. "What if something happens? I just got you back."

"They need you here." He stared into Xander's eyes.

"Besides, you're better at the big inspiring speeches than I am."

For his response, Xander kissed him again. Besides, he was right. Jameson was shit at public speaking.

The earth shook underfoot.

"Damn, that was some kiss," Alia said, arriving at the tower.

Xander let him go, and Jameson shook his head. "I don't like it. These quakes can't be good for the mines where they stashed the Erriani." He gave Xander one last peck on the cheek. "We'll see each other soon," he whispered.

"Go bring 'em home."

Xander watched as Jameson opened a waygate to Errian. He'd gotten really good at it. Xander would have to ask Jameson to show him how it was done, when there was time.

Shaking his head, he went off to rally the troops.

QUINCE OPENED HER EYES. She had to get up. To do *something*. There had to be another way out, or something else she could do. It couldn't end like this.

She levered herself up. At least the pain in her ankle had lessened.

"Quince?"

She spun around to find Jameson standing there, on the other side of the gate, with three other skythane. She squinted—it was Venin, Alia, and another man she didn't recognize. "You found us!" She put her hands through the bars to touch him, but he pulled away.

"I'm glad to see that you're okay. How did you get here?"

"It's a long story, and we need to talk about it. Soon. But first we need to get these people out of here." She rattled the gate. "I can't get it open."

"That's okay." He pulled out the key. "I have another way in. Stand back." He twisted it, and a waygate opened up between them. Two of them, actually, one on either side of the gate. Jameson stepped through, and his companions followed.

Damn, it worked. "Gods I'm glad to see you." She hugged him, but he was stiff in her arms.

"Did you find Morgan?"

She nodded. "You haven't seen Robyn, have you?"

"Sorry, I haven't."

"Okay." She wondered why he was being so cold to her. Something had happened. They'd have to sort it out later.

"You know Venin and Alia. This is Tobin."

"Where are the guards?" Alia asked, looking around the tunnel. Her wings twitched with nerves or anxiety.

"There aren't any."

That seemed to send a shiver up Jameson's spine. "We have to hurry, then. We don't have much time."

"What's coming?"

He touched her shoulder, his eyes clouding with compassion, the first real emotion he'd shown. "Ballifor."

She remembered. The high-pitched whine, the bomb that had wiped her village off the map. Her whole past had been erased in the time it took to blink.

She staggered, but Jameson caught and steadied her. "Where are they?"

"Follow me." She led him back down the tunnel to the first of the improvised cells. He frowned at the pile of personal belongings. "They banded our wings with nerve cuffs."

"Nerve cuffs?"

"They cut off the connection to the brain—makes them useless." She shuddered.

"Gods, that's horrible."

"Can you use that key to get inside the cells?"

"They're in cells? No. I have to see the place before I can open a waygate to it."

"Well, then, did you bring something that can break locks?"

"Will this do?" Jameson held up a pulse rifle.

"Yes. Hope you have more than one."

"We do." Venin and Alia held up theirs.

She banged on the first door. "We're here to get you out. Stand back!"

Jameson aimed the pulse rifle at the lock and squeezed the trigger. The lock shattered.

He pulled the door open and handed the rifle to Quince. "Take the others and open all the doors. Send them to me and I'll get them off safely." He pulled out the key and opened another waygate. He was sweating.

"It costs you to use that key."

He nodded. "A little, each time. I'm rested—I can handle it. Go!"

She did as she was told, running to the next door.

26

WAR

Alix walked into the boardroom in a new suit, freshly showered and shaved, his hair neatly trimmed. He'd asked for the meeting at 5:00 p.m., and here it was a quarter after.

The board members looked up at his entrance…. Everyone was there but his mother.

He buttoned his jacket, taking his place at the head of the table. He'd been brought up by Lena Preston. He knew how these things were done. "Thank you for meeting with me at such short notice. I'm Alix Preston, Lena Preston's son. Many of you have met me before."

"What's the meaning of this?" Braid Seneford looked annoyed at being called in for a meeting in the evening hours. The man knew damned well what it meant. Alix had warned him in advance.

Still, he played the game. "I have a proposal for the board. An offer of an alliance with another entity—"

The double doors flew open with a crash. "Why is this board meeting being held without the OberCorp CEO?"

Alix spun around to smile at her. "Welcome, Mother. I was just suggesting that the board reconsider our current… entanglement with the skythane."

"That situation is fully under control and should be contained within a couple hours—"

The whole building shook.

Alix leapt out of his chair and raced to the window. He looked down in time to see a fireball blossoming from the base of the building. "Under control, huh?"

She came to stand by his side, her face going pale. "What have you done?"

He ignored her, turning to the board. "We seem to have company."

Xander stood at the top of Torr Talam and looked out over the gathered skythane host. They were now over fifteen hundred strong.

He looked over at Vestra, to his right.

She nodded at him. "Go."

He raised his arms. "Are you ready?"

There was a great cheer.

He raised his fist. "Let's fly!"

The first wing took to the air and swung toward Errian.

They had practiced the methods he'd shown them to bring down the hoversports, taking them from above. Each wing carried two pulse rifles—as many as they'd been able to collect and bring from Gaelan. Which on the whole really wasn't very many, but they would do what they could with what they had.

They had planned to stagger the wings to make the attack look bigger than it was, and everyone had been instructed to pull back when Xander sounded a horn given to him by one of the Erriani skythane.

Maybe Jessa was wrong. Maybe she'd overheard their enemies incorrectly. Yet they had to act as if it were the dead-on truth.

The second wing took to the air, and Xander joined them. Gaelani fighting alongside Erriani. It had taken an external threat, an existential one, to bring their two peoples back together. Now they were strong, forged like the tip of a spear in the fire.

As more wings took flight behind them, he led his host of skythane toward Errian.

. . .

QUINCE BLASTED off the lock from the last of the cells, flinging the door open and searching desperately for Robyn inside.

"Thank the gods," an elderly woman said, ushering out a little girl. There were ten others in the crowded room, and it smelled of human excrement.

She'd found Neamiah, Toree, and Jenner in the tenth cell. Neamiah was beautiful, a tweener with golden eyes and hair. They had hugged Quince tightly.

None of them was Robyn.

Quince cursed under her breath. She shepherded the group up the tunnel. "You're going to be safe now." Up ahead, she could see the waygate. The edges of it flickered. She hoped Jameson could keep it going for another couple minutes.

She could see a turquoise lagoon sparkling on the other side.

One by one, the refugees crossed through, and then the last one was gone.

"We did it."

The waygate snapped shut, and Jameson swayed.

She caught him and steadied him. "We did it. Now get us out of here, and you can rest."

He nodded and held up the key.

The ground shook, harder than before, knocking him off his feet. The key went flying.

Quince caught it.

The shaking increased.

"Jameson, how do you use this thing?"

There was a crash in the distance. She knelt beside him. He was trying to get up, but the earth was moving under all of them, and he looked so tired. "Picture the place in your head that you want to go. Then twist it and *push*."

Push? Push what? She held up the key.

"Quince, you have to try!" Alia squeezed her shoulder. "This place isn't going to hold together much longer."

Where to go? She pictured the last place she'd seen before ending up here—the plaza in the middle of Errian. It would be in the middle of enemy forces, but anything was better than being crushed to death here.

She twisted… but nothing happened.

"Like this!" Jameson shouted. He put his hands around hers, and all of a sudden she felt it in her head. "Now *push*!"

She pictured the plaza again in front of the Castain. She *pushed*, and the waygate opened. *Thank the gods.*

She dragged him through onto the flagstones of the plaza. The others dove after her, and then the waygate snapped closed as a hundred thousand tons of rock collapsed where they had just been standing.

She looked up to see a Robyn being stuffed into a hoversport.

"They've taken over the ground floor." The enforcer looked nervous, his helmet held in his black-leather-covered arm.

The Syndicate had never made such a bold move before, and most of the OberCorp forces were currently engaged on the other side of the world.

Alix smiled.

Lena Preston shot him a look. "Hold the second floor. Get a hoversport to the roof to evacuate us."

"Ma'am, I don't think that's a good idea." The enforcer glanced out the window, gulping. "They've got land-to-air pulse weapons. You're safer here for the moment."

"Goddammit." She took a deep breath. "Go. Keep them out."

The whole building shook for a good thirty seconds. Lena dove under the conference table. "What the hell is that?"

The rumbling subsided.

"This can all be over," Alix whispered, kneeling beside the table.

"It will be, soon enough." His mother crawled out from under the table and pushed him aside, brushing off her skirt. "Helena, get me Danner Black."

"Mother, what the hell are you doing?" He glanced at the board members. They were huddled at the back of the room, as far away from the windows as possible.

"Danner, are the wing men in position?" Lena cocked her head, listening to the response. She was all business. "Let me know as soon as you're ready to fire."

THE FIRST WING was approaching Errian. Xander had to trust that Jameson had gotten the captives, and himself, safely out.

The hoversports began to lift off from the ground one by one. There were at least twenty of them, each with superior armament to his own forces.

"Onward skythane! We fight!" he shouted and blew his horn.

The skythane host began to dive out of the sky toward the approaching enemy craft.

· · ·

Danner Black dragged a skythane woman into one of the hoversports a hundred meters away from where they'd landed. Even at that distance, Quince recognized her mate. "It's Robyn!"

The hoversport hatch slammed closed.

"We have to stop them."

"How?" Alia pointed at the teams of enforcers running toward them.

"They're not after us. They're running to the other hoversports!"

Above, skythane appeared from the south, hundreds and hundreds of them.

The ground started to shake once again.

"Come on! Bring Jameson along!" She stood and ran toward the nearest hoversport, overtaking the crew of three that was running for the hatch. She jumped on the first one's back, bringing him down hard to the pavement.

He spun and caught her across the chin with his fist, but she grabbed his uniform in her fist and lifted him up, smashing his head down hard against the ground.

The other two fell, taken in the back by pulse rifle fire.

"Thanks," she said to Alia.

"No problem. Come on." Alia put her hand out and lifted Quince to her feet.

Together they ran to the hoversport. Venin and Tobin carried an exhausted Jameson between them.

"I hope you know how to fly this thing." Alia strapped Jameson in the back as Quince climbed into the cockpit. It was a tight fit.

"It's been a few years, but this is child's play." She ran through the system checks as Alia squeezed in beside her.

"These things weren't built for skythane, were they?"

"Not really. Hold on." Quince powered up the hoversport, and the craft lurched into the air. "You all good back there?"

Venin flashed her the okay sign.

"Hold on. Here we go!"

Robyn struggled against her bonds. Her wings were useless, hanging behind her like dead things. Her mouth was gagged, but eyes burned with anger.

"You comfortable back there?" Danner Black grinned at her. He hadn't changed all that much over the years, though his hair was a little grayer than she remembered it.

"Lemf me ouhhhh."

"Sorry, can't do that. You're my new insurance policy." He fired up the controls of the hoversport, and the transport hummed to life. "Just in case we run into any trouble."

She growled at him.

"The little bird has claws. And wings. I'd love to hear how you got those back. I might just have to cut them off again when this is all over." He lifted the hoversport off the ground. "Your son and his army will be here soon. We have a little surprise planned for them."

Her mind raced. What was he planning? Draw in the skythane and then…

The blood drained from her face. *Ballifor.*

She pulled again at the bonds that tied her hands and feet, desperate to get free.

Jessa managed to land without breaking either of her legs. She considered that a personal triumph.

Xander had loaned her Alix's bi-wings. She'd never used them before, but they were fairly easy to get the hang of. She knew she'd be no good in the sky, but down here on the ground she could do a little damage for her new winged friends.

She stripped off the wings, letting them drop to the ground.

Crews of enforcers were running for their hoversports as fighting exploded in the air.

She pulled two pulse pistols out from where she'd tucked them into her belt. She might not be able to fight in the air, but she could help keep some of these craft on the ground.

"That's for Jamie, you bastards," she said, taking down two of the enforcers who had just reached the opening hatch of their hoversport in quick succession.

Who said boys had all the fun?

"MA'AM, THEY'VE made it up to the seventh floor." The explosions rocking the building had become constant.

Lena hesitated.

Alix seized the moment. "Members of the board, I move that we adopt the terms of the agreement with the skythane forces, and furthermore that Lena Preston be removed as CEO of OberCorp for leading this company to the verge of destruction."

"How will that help?" Sera Thorpe asked.

"The skythane are working with the Syndicate. If we sign the accord, the fighting will stop."

Braid Seneford raised his hand. "I second the motion. Before the Syndicate kills us all."

"All in favor?"

One by one, all the board members gave their assent.

"I further move that I, Alix Preston, be made the next CEO of OberCorp."

"Seconded."

"All in favor?"

The vote was once again unanimous.

His mother glared at him. "This isn't over."

"Erissa, please isolate Lena Preston from the grid."

"What? You can't do that. I demand a hearing with the board."

"Please take Ms. Preston to a conference room for holding," he told the enforcer.

The man nodded. "My pleasure, sir."

"Erissa, give the order to Mr. Black to stand down. I'll let the Syndicate know that we're laying down our arms."

"Done, Alix."

He took a deep breath. It was over.

27

ENDINGS

"Almost there. Almost there!" Danner Black had a bad habit of speaking to himself.

Robyn had found a sharp place on the edge of her seat, and was methodically working her way through the rope that bound her hands. If she could just get them free…

The man had been happy enough to explain his plan to her—draw the skythane into Errian to take back the city and then wipe them all out in a single blow. The hoversport carried a meso bomb big enough to level Errian and a good bit of the surrounding jungle, he'd been happy to tell her.

Robyn had no idea what a meso bomb was, but she'd been to Ballifor. Or where Ballifor had once stood.

Quince was down there somewhere. And Xander and Jameson. And most everyone else she knew or cared about.

She pushed down on the sharp place harder, sawing her arms back and forth. Just a little bit more….

Quince flew after the lone hoversport, keeping her distance. It passed out over the Argent Sea, the midday sun glinting off its metallic shell. When it slowed and turned back toward Errian, she watched it for a couple moments to see what it would do.

Below it hung a shiny black disc, unlike any armament she'd ever seen on one of those craft. She had an idea what it was, or at least what it could do.

Ballifor was never far from her mind.

At last she opened a communications channel to the other craft. "Danner Black, we have our weapons trained on your hoversport. Please bring it back down to the ground."

"Sorry, can't do that." It was *his* voice. Danner Black. That voice was burned into her memory. She closed her eyes and saw Queen Andra's face as he slashed her throat. "I have someone close to you here, Quince. Wouldn't want to take a chance at hurting her, now would you?"

"I can't let you destroy Errian." She closed in on the other craft, so they were facing each other with just fifty meters between them.

"Quince, he's going to do it. It's just a matter of *time*." Robyn's voice.

Something about the way she said time…. Quince muted the com. "She needs time."

"Clear out of the way, Quince. I have a city to destroy."

"I was there."

There was silence on the line.

"When you killed Andra. When you sliced the throat of the Queen of Errian." Keep him talking.

"You weren't…."

"I saw you. I saw it all."

THE BATTLE RAGED OVER ERRIAN.

Skythane were taking the lessons Xander had taught them, teaming up to land one of their own on top of the nimble craft to deliver a death blow.

Xander crashed onto one of the craft, pointing his pulse pistol down and firing. It swerved, throwing him off, but it was too late. The hoversport was wreathed in blue lightning, and it exploded just before it crashed into the crater wall.

It was a rough fight.

Six hoversports were down, but so were close to fifty of his own men and women.

He spun around to find his next target, and to his surprise, the remaining hoversports began to disengage, turning back toward the Argent Sea.

One by one they fled, and the skythane cheered.

What was going on? His heart raced. *This is it.* They needed to get out of here. Xander sounded the horn. "Retreat!"

The word was passed along quickly, and like a flock of birds, the skythane fled the city, wheeling away in a sudden exodus.

THE HOVERSPORT FLOATED IN MIDAIR.

Quince was talking to someone. Danner Black?

Jameson was fuzzy on the details. He was still wiped out from the effort he'd expended holding the waygate open in the mines. The longer he held it, the more it seemed to drain him.

Something buzzed in his pocket.

"Rest," Venin whispered. "You've worn yourself out."

Jameson shook his head. "It's Alix." He managed to pull the two communicators out, activating the one that was buzzing. "Alix."

"It's over. I've taken control of OberCorp." Alix's voice floated out of the little speaker. "Call off the dogs."

He came through. "Okay… give me a sec."

"You sound exhausted."

"You have no idea." He switched communicators. "Rogan, can you hear me?"

There was a pause. "This is Dawson."

Dawson. Jameson remembered the little prick, the man who had threatened them after their first encounter with Rogan. "Tell Rogan to stand down."

"No one tells Rogan anything." He could hear the smug satisfaction in the man's voice.

"Then tell him if he doesn't, I'm tossing all those cases of pith into the Orn." Jameson cut the connection. "Alix?"

"I heard it. Way to stand up to a Slander boss."

"Thanks." Jameson closed his eyes.

"He's wiped out," he heard Venin say before he slipped back to rest.

"I knew you were there. I should have…." That was the last thing Danner Black said to Quince over the com.

She tried to reengage him, to keep him talking, to

stop him from releasing that deadly weapon on Errian. He didn't respond.

She shared a worried glance with Alia.

Danner Black ignored her.

"Quince, look!" Alia pointed at the other craft.

Black's hoversport started to lurch back and forth in the air, like a drunken enforcer.

ROBYN FELT the last strands of the rope part, freeing her hands.

"Commander Black, you are instructed to stand down."

"Who is that?"

"This is Erissa, representing the new acting CEO of OberCorp, Alix Preston. You are instructed to stand down."

"Fuck that. We're going to finish this, now." He reached for the red button to shoot the meso bomb off toward its destination.

It's now or never. Robyn lurched forward and knocked him off course. Her feet were still tied, but she managed to slam him into the console.

The hoversport lurched wildly to the right and then the left.

She saw a flash of light below. Black had a knife strapped to his boot.

Robyn pulled it out as he struggled to sit up. She grabbed his hair and pulled his head back. "This is for Ballifor." She sliced the knife across his throat and he screamed wordlessly, the sound coming out in guttural gushes as he grabbed his throat.

Blood burst from the wound, and the craft began to spin wildly.

She had to get out.

The hoversport was off balance now and careening toward the waters of the Argent Sea below.

Robyn scrambled toward the back, fighting the g-force, and ripped at the red emergency handle with her hands. She missed it.

She tried again, and this time she grasped it and pulled, sending the hatch flying out into the sky.

She hesitated. Her wings were clipped. She couldn't fly.

Still, it was better than going down with the ship.

She leapt.

Robyn's form appeared at the hoversport's hatch. Her wings were bound.

"Holy Split…." Quince turned to Alia. "Keep the ship here. I have to get her."

"What? I don't know how to fly this damn thing either."

"It's easy. Just hold this here." She put Alia's hand on the hover control. She climbed to the back of the hoversport. "I'm executing a manual override of the hatch control," she told the others.

Jameson nodded. His skin was gray, but his eyes were wide-open. "Go get her, Quince."

She popped the hatch and leapt out into the open air, seeing Robyn do the same. The other hoversport was lurching toward the sea below. Quince dove after her.

She was right behind her. *Moonrise help me, it's going to be close.*

She tucked her wings in and dove.

Robyn wasn't flailing. She fell, peaceful as a babe, her eyes closed.

The wind whistled in Quince's ears as she arrowed toward the water.

At last Quince was below Robyn's falling form. She spread her wings and came up to catch her, just twenty meters above the water. "Need a lift?"

"Holy Split, you cut that close. I thought I was going to die."

"Is Black…?"

"He's gone. Just like Andra Madainn."

The hoversport hit the water as Quince gained altitude. It plunged in, swallowed whole in a second.

Ten seconds later, the sea began to boil below them, and a huge column of water burst from the surface, showering them both. Dead fish floated to the surface, and the water turned red.

Gods, that was close. Quince shook off her wings and lifted them up to their waiting transport.

The war was over.

XANDER WAS FRANTIC.

The fighting had ended. He still didn't understand entirely why. There had been a big explosion out at sea. He'd seen the spume of water from there.

The skythane, who had fled at his call, were now landing all around the plaza, but one of them was missing.

"Have you seen Jameson?" he asked everyone he passed.

No one had.

The entrance to the caverns where the captive skythane had been kept was collapsed. What if Jameson was still trapped inside? *Gods, I wasted so much time.*

The whine of a hoversport snapped his attention up

into the air. A single craft was coming in from the east. *Another attack?*

It came in slowly, settling down to the ground, a little wobbly.

"Everyone stay back," Xander called.

The hatch opened, and out stepped Venin, supporting an exhausted-looking Jameson. "Thank the gods." Xander ran forward to embrace him. "You're alive! I was afraid—"

"Thank my pilot, Quince. She's the one who got us out of the mines and confronted Danner Black."

Xander turned to see Quince and his mother coming out of the hoversport.

Robyn had wings. He let go of Jameson and embraced Robyn, then held her out in front of him to look at her beautiful black wings. "How is this possible?"

"Your little friend, Morgan."

"He's alive?"

Quince nodded. "We found him, at the north pole. Where Robyn got her wings back."

Xander had been furious with Quince for what she had done to him. To Jameson too. But now…. He hugged her too. They could talk about it later. "I'm so glad to have you back."

She searched his eyes and nodded. "You know, don't you?"

"Yes."

"We'll need to work things out between us, but right now… is there somewhere we can go to talk, just the four of us?"

"About?" He was ready to celebrate their victory, saving Errian even at such a high cost.

"About what's coming next."

He frowned. "Isn't it over?"

"This is." She looked around at the damaged city and its inhabitants, and at all the Gaelani who had come to its defense. "This could have been a tragedy. But… something worse is coming."

"What is?"

"The Ithani."

Xander had no idea what the Ithani were. "Is it urgent?"

"Yes." She looked flushed.

"I want Alix, Vestra, and Mylin in on this too, and a couple others. Shall we say, three hours?"

"That will give us time to get some refreshment and get the cleanup started here." Jameson looked at his city. "Quince is right. It could have been worse. But it's still going to take some time to rebuild."

"Can you manage a waygate for us? I'd like to have this meeting somewhere away from prying eyes and ears."

Jameson nodded. "Get something in me, and I can probably do it."

"Look at you, thinking about sex at a time like this." Xander kissed Jameson to silence his protests. "Yes, we'll get you fed." To Quince, he said, "Back here in three hours?"

"Perfect. We'll see you then."

JAMESON LET himself be led away from the hoversport. He was dead tired, but it seemed more would be required of him before all this was through. At least he'd managed to rest, just a little, during the hoversport flight.

Had he dreamed that conversation with Alix?

Xander led him over to the little park in the middle of the square, under the shade of the trees. Venin came with them. Xander eased him down against the trunk of a black-barked tree, topped with round purple leaves the size of his hand. They fluttered in the wind.

Venin laughed. "You know what this is?"

"What?" Jameson looked around at the tree.

"It's a púca tree. They don't usually grow at this low of an elevation. Someone must have planted this here on purpose."

"Púca tree?"

"It's where pith comes from."

Jameson touched the bark. It was black as pitch and smooth to his touch.

"I'll get you two some water and something to eat." Venin bowed and turned away, leaving Xander and Jameson alone.

"No rest for the weary." Xander looked as tired as Jameson felt.

"Or the wicked." He slipped his hand under Xander's vest, eliciting a yelp as he tweaked Xander's nipple.

Xander pulled Jameson in for a kiss. "I was so scared I'd lost you for good."

"I know." Jameson felt safe. Home. "Don't ever leave me again."

Xander laughed. "That might be difficult to promise."

"You know what I mean." He took Xander's hand and looked him in the eye. "This—what we have—it's real. I don't care how it came about."

"Me neither. Now finish your meal. You need to get some rest before we're called back into action."

Jameson did as he was told and lay back in Xander's lap. He closed his eyes. No matter what else was yet to come, he was with Xander.

There was nothing that the world could throw at the two of them that they couldn't handle.

EPILOGUE

DANI BLACK listened to the radio transmission, uncomprehending. The OberCorp people were telling her father to stand down.

Errian was supposed to have been destroyed by now, and yet, there it was, on the horizon, still standing.

Danner had sent her off to witness the destruction from a distance. Overprotective as always. Didn't he know she'd already been through one war?

Then his hoversport began to toss and turn in the air. Something was *very* wrong.

She zoomed in, getting a better picture on her screen. There were two hoversports there, facing off, but her father's craft was spinning out of control.

She watched as someone flew out of the first one and someone from the second one intercepted it.

Quince and Robyn. She was sure of it.

Then the sea exploded.

Her father was dead.

"Gods damn them!" She pounded her fist on the console. She should have killed Quince when she had the chance. She wouldn't make the same mistake again.

"Zim, run a manual override of that hoversport's com systems." She had blackware of her own. She needed more information, and this was the best way to get it.

"Ready."

She listened in as the other hoversport landed in Errian, and her enemies were reunited.

She listened until Quince and her friends moved out of range.

The north pole. Interesting. If one skythane could get her wings back there, why not another?

"What are you thinking in that dark little mind of yours?" Kadin looked worried.

"How do you feel about taking a trip with me?" She kissed his cheek. She knew the effect she had on him. He liked a woman in uniform.

"Sure. It will be good to put this all behind us."

She shook her head. "It's not that kind of trip. We still have work to do."

Kadin frowned. "What kind of work? The war is over. We lost."

She kissed him again. "It's never over until the enemy is dead."

GLOSSARY

Alia: Guard in Gaelan

Alix Preston: Xander's ex, a lander man missing for a year

Alvyn: Young Erriani man who "rescues" Jessa

Amalite: Raw ore found only on Oberon that serves as Common Worlds power source

AmSplor: Exploration division of the Northern American Union

Andra Madainn: Queen of the House of the Sun, Jameson's mother

Anellia: Pop singer capable of singing in triple harmony

Angela Havercamp: Jameson's adopted mother

Angie/Angela: Jameson's PA

Annama: Soul mate

Arcatus: Interstellar ship Jameson came in on from Tander's World

Arco: Vast buildings where most of Oberon City's citizens are housed

Argent Sea: Titania's sea

Ari: Quince's PA

Arracha Grain: Native grain grown as a staple on Oberon

Auxen: Forest herbivores in the Riamhwood

Aux: Larger cousins of the auxen, they live on the northern plains

Ballifor: Small Titanian village where Quince is from

Bandia: Titania's golden moon

Banga Tree: Low, wide Titania jungle trees that resemble barrels

Beta Tau: Jameson's homeworld

Bi-Wings: Artificial wings used by the enforcers on Titania

Blackware: Illegal apps/software/code

Blade File: Electronic file format

Blueoak: Native Oberon tree

Bolcà Island: Island in the Argent Sea

Boxcorn: Genetically modified square corn ears used as base for foods/fuels on Oberon

Braid Seneford: One of the OberCorp board members

Cafflite: Oberon equivalent of coffee

Camspecs: eyeglasses with a built-in tri-dee camera

Castain, the: The "castle" in Errian, also called the House of the Sun

Cattorah, the: A ritual removal of a skythane's wings, usually as punishment for a severe crime

Chit: Portable cash chip

Christianist: Throwback religious sect that hearkens back to conservative "Christian" values

Cirq: Bio-interface in the temple that allows users to access the grid

Citrone: Native yellow fruit that grows on vines on Oberon

Colifir Tree: Red native tree that grows by rivers

Common Worlds: Loose-knit government of human worlds

Conjunction: Alignment of one of the moons of Oberon with the planet and sun

Corrinder: The plants used as building stock in Errian

Creach: Scavenger birds on Titania

Creeper Vines: Native silver ground vegetation on Oberon

Crits: Credit/money

Croyol: Fungus that burns without smoke

Daedus Madainn: Prior King of the House of the Sun

Damella Sléite: Prior Queen of the House of the Moon

Danielle (Dani) Black: One of the lander enforcers in Gaelan, daughter of Danner Black

Danner Black: A skythane pith trade runner who helped instigate civil war between the skythane

Dark Market: Black market on Oberon, run by the Syndicate

Daro: One of Dani's lander guards

Davis: Zefron's son

Davos Madainn: Prior King of the House of the Sun

Davyn Sléite: Xander's Gaelani name

Dawson: Rogan's henchman

Dax: One of Rogan's enforcers

Deathhawk: Deadly bird of prey native to Titania

Deca: Oberon's tenth month

Deireadh an Domhain: The Mountain

Demetrius River: Southern tributary to the Theseus

Deterrent Field: Rope that is used to create a field to deter the local wildlife, especially wereveren

Dhagani: The enemies of the Ithani

Dillan Farrai: Quince's brother

Distortion Field: Shield generated by a small device that blocks electronic surveillance

Distortion Zone: Zone of electronic interference at the edge of Oberon

Dorthia: Erriani woman who lives in Taycrob

Drimm the Dragon: One of Titania's constellations

Earth-Standard: Timekeeping based on Earth's clock/calendar

Egeus: City on Oberon

Elyra Sléite: Prior Queen of the House of the Moon

Enforcers: Men who work as the muscle of the Syndicate

Errian: City of the Sun (as in House of the)

Erriani: Citizens of the House of the Sun

Erissa: Alix's PA

Erro: Sun God; also the Ithani name for the whole world

Ethilium: Growth hormone that stimulates the development of wings in the skythane

Faery Caves: Caverns in Titania's mountains, often lit by glowing blue ponds

Faery Ponds: Blue glowing ponds in the caverns on Titania

Fizzpop: Carbonated sugar-alcohol drink popular on Beta Tau

Fynx: One of the Gaelani skythane at Torr Talam

Farris: Assistant to the Prison Master

Feather Trees: Trees native to Oberon

Fennow Root: Natural antiseptic

First Wave: First human colonists on Oberon, also called skythane

Fynx: Gaelani man in the war camp

Gael: Moon God

Gaelan: City of the House of the Moon

Gaelani: Citizens of the House of the Moon

Galaxion Hotel: Interstellar hotel chain

Gildensea: Oberon's sea

Glow Sphere: Portable light source

Governor: Governmental head of Oberon

Governor's Residence: Vast estate where the Factor lives

Granth: Feline equivalents from Pleaides Six, valued for their leather

Great Division: Period after skythane refugees were chased out of Oberon to Titania

Great Retreat: The flight of the skythane settlers before the landers and Ober Corp

Grid, The: Oberon's data and communications network

Gridcode: App, programming code, etc.

GSN: Great Sky Network, one of the Common Worlds news services

Gumba Tree: Tall, leafy native tree often used as a windbreak for farms on Oberon

Hallerwood: Golden-leaved trees native to northern Titania

Hachmoss: Yellow moss native to Oberon

Harrol: One of Xander's companions on the way to Errian

Heart Fungus: See Croyol

Heartbrier Bush: Titania bush with heart-shaped leaves and orange flowers

Heartwood: Forest on Beta Tau

Hermia: One of Oberon's two moons—red-colored

Hesies: Xander's past life

High Slopes: Northern district of Oberon City, where the Spaceport is

Hippolyta: City on Oberon

Hoarberries: Little blue berries covered in a sweet white "frost"

Hollyhock Trees: Trees found in the valley of The Mountain

Honey Ale: Titanian alcoholic drink

House of the Sky: Ruins in the center of Oberon

House of the Stars: Royal retreat in the center of Titania

Hover-Plat: Transportation platform used to move small amounts of goods

Hoverbike: One of the main methods of personal transport in Oberon City

Hoversport: Hover craft used for human transport

Ice Pine: White tree native to the northern climes of Oberon—the Rim Forest

Imprean: Carrier pigeon-like bird used to carry messages

Ironwood: Tall trees in Titania that are impervious to flame

Ithani: Original inhabitants of Oberon/Titania

Jameson Havercamp: Psych from Beta Tau who comes to investigate pith shortage on Oberon

Jenner: Erriani person trapped with Quince in the mines

Jessa: Jameson's fiancée on Beta Tau

Joseph Havercamp: Jameson's adoptive father

Kadin Tamain: The chamberlain of the House of the Moon

Keff: Titanian equivalent of coffee—tastes like herbal tea and coconut.

Knacks: Oberon insect pests

Landed: To be stripped of your wings, usually as punishment for a criminal act

Landers: Second wave human settlers

Lyda: Sculptor of the statue of Gael at the House of the Stars

Lydia Madainn: Prior Queen of the House of the Sun

Lyrin Madainn: Jameson's birth name

Lysander: One of Oberon's two moons—golden color

Martach: Six-legged jungle cat on Titania

Mattis Vinder: An OberCorp headquarters employee

Meso Bomb (MB): Bomb that works by averaging out the molecular content of everything within its radius

Midcity: Heart of Oberon City

Mikelos: Miner on Tander's World

Morgan: Mysterious child Xander finds on Oberon

Morgan Kinnson: Xander's foster father

Mora Mountains: Titania's mountian chain, Sléibhte Mora

Mountain, The: Location of one of the gates between the two worlds, close to the House of the Moon

Mugjuice: Oberon beverage made with pith

Mylin: Young skythane girl who helps Xander

Neamiah: Erriani person trapped with Quince in the mines

Nerve Cuffs: Handcuffs that cut off the nervous system

Nim: An Erriani man at Torr Talam

Nimfeach: Butterfly-like creatures on Titania

Norcrest: Small purple bush found in the plains north of the Riamhwood

Northern Glacier: At the north pole on Oberon

Nutrisynth Bar: Nutritional bars Xander likes

OberCorp: Corporation that controls most of Oberon —The Oberon Mining Corporation

Oberon: Also known as Split—the half world where the story takes place

Oberon City: Capital of Oberon, with about two million residents, most living in arcos

Obieberry: Native red-stippled fruit on Oberon

Orn: Main river on Titania

Outland: Desert and wilds beyond Oberon City

Paraba Bush: Titania shrub that has berries that can be ground for oil

Philo: City on Oberon

Pith: Psychoamoratic drug derived from the sap of the púca tree in Titania

Plas: Versatile artificial material with the hardness of diamond and the malleability of plastic

Pleiades Six: One of the worlds of the Common Worlds

Plascreet: Variation of plas used in heavy construction; a concrete analog

Pocans: Edible white fungus that resembles a string of pearls and tastes like chocolate and bread

Preachers, The: Rough rock band

Psych: Therapist

Psych Guild: Association of Psychs

Psychoamoratic: A drug with aphrodisiac qualities

Púca Tree: Tree which pith comes form

Pulse Laser: High-powered blast-pulse weapon used on transport ships

Pulse Pistol: Small pulse weapon

Pulse Rifle: Large pulse weapon

Pyramus Mountains: Mountain range along the Eastern edge of Oberon

Quince Farrai: Xander's skythane friend who joins the quest

Rangers: OberCorp soldiers used in military campaigns

Ravi: Xander's PA

Ravier: Erriani man who lives in Taycrob

Red Sands: Desert covering the southern part of Oberon

Red Shanks: Big red-trunked trees with large heart-shaped purple leaves, native to the Titanian jungle

Redfruit: Fruit native to Titania

Redoak: Tree native to Titania

Rentz Class Cargo Carrier: Heavy lifter that carries amalite ore up from Oberon to interstellars

Riamhwood: Forest on Titania

Riding Armor: Body armor Xander wears when riding

Rift: The split that divides Oberon and Titania

Rim Forest: Forest on the northern half of Oberon

Rinroot: A natural antibiotic on Titania

Rix: One of Xander's companions on the way to Errian

River Apples: Native Oberon water fruit

River Cat: Small scavenger the size and temperament of a raccoon

Robyn Sléite: Queen of the Gaelani and mother to Xander, and Quince's former lover

Rocthane: Access key to bring the worlds together

Rogan: Syndicate boss who has history with Xander

Rohin the Explorer: One of the first skythane to find Titania

Scurf: Domesticated, one horned herbivores on Titania

Second Wave: The second set of human colonists, also called landers

Sera Thorpe: OberCorp board member.

Seven Weeks War: War between the Erriani and Gaelani twenty-five years before

Sevyrn Triani: One of the Erriani skythane Jameson saved

Shift: Moving Oberon into Titania's space

Silverbark: Tall, thin tree with silver bark, leaves, and a dark stripe on the northern side, native to Oberon

Skythane: First wave of human colonists, who have wings

Slander, The: Slums of Oberon City

Sleeper: Sleep drug patch

Slit: Transfer funds or information electronically

Sneach: skythane term for orphan—mischievous spirits who cause trouble or death

Split: Nickname for Oberon; also used for its broken side.

Squamwat: A small domesticated animal that imprints on its human owner and shows absolute loyalty

Standing Stones: Guardian statues outside the faery caverns on Titainayes

Stim: Stimulant

Stim Cuffs: handcuffs that can deliver an electric shock

Swamp Bear: Harmless forest creature

Symbol of the Two Gods: Tapping your right fist against your chest twice

Syndicate: Crime ring that controls the Slander

Synth Meat: Meat grown in a vat from a cellular culture

Synthglass: A more expensive form of plas that radiates light when touched

Taycrob: Small Erriani village of tree houses

Tamara Fine: OberCorp's head of PR

Tander's World: Mining colony where Jameson was stationed

Tartanga Tree: Oberon riverside trees with broad, tri-partite silver leaves

Teanna: Skythane woman in Gaelan

Tevin: Erriani boy Jameson saves from the invaders

Tharsis: Home to one of the Tander's World miners, Mikelos

Thera: Prior Queen of the House of the Sun

Theron Sléite: King of the Gaelani, Xander's father

Theseus River: Main river in Oberon

Titan Station: Receiving space station for visitors to Oberon

Titania: Half of the planet on the other side of the rift

Tobin: Skythane man with Jameson in the mines

Toree: Erriani person trapped with Quince in the mines

Torr Talam: Tower in the time of Elyra and Daedus

Traxon: A smaller, light gravity Common Worlds planet

Tri-dee: 3-D video, video player

Tubers: Native Oberon edible plant—can be eaten cooked or raw, like a jicama

Turbien: Plants used to grow the towers of Errian

Tweener: Someone who is nonbinary or gender fluid

Vassir Honym: Prison master on the Split

Venin: Guard in Gaelan

Veril: A small rabbitlike creature that lives in the Ri-amhwood

Verrim: One of the Ithani from Jameson's memory

Vestra Halta: Acting Regent of Errian

Virgo Sléite: Prior King of the House of the Moon

Water Cane: Native Oberon edible plant

Wempole: Short, squat trees with wide purple leaves and fragrant white flowers the size of two hands that smell like vanilla and honey, found in the northern Ri-amhwood

Wereveren: Birds that transform at night into lethal pecking machines

Wetreeds: Native plant with numbing properties

Wetware: bio implants that allow humans to interface with machines and the grid

Whipcat: Deadly feline equivalents in the mountains of Titania

Whirills: Titanian bird that lives in the Riamhwood

Wing Man: Slang for the skythane

Wrenwood: Tree from Titania whose wood burns without smoke

Xander Kinnson: Skythane who works in Oberon City, embarks on a quest with Jameson

Xiini: One of the Ithani from Jameson's memory

Zain: Sculptor of the statue of Erro at the House of the Stars

Zakka: Poisonous reptile in the Red Sands

Zaxxim: One of the Ithani from Jameson's memory

Zefron: Stranger on Titan Station

Zenia: One of Xander's companions on the way to Errian

Zenix: Lena Preston's house AI

Zim: Dani Black's PA

Zimbee: Large, harmless pollinator on Titania

ABOUT THE AUTHOR

I live with my husband of 28 years in a Sacramento, California suburb, in a little yellow house with a brick fireplace and a couple pink flamingoes.

As a writer, I've always lived between *here and now* and *what could be*. Indoctrinated into fantasy-sci fi by my mother at the tender age of nine, I devoured her library. But as I grew up and read the golden age classics and modern works, I began to wonder where the people like me were.

After I came out at twenty three, I decided it was time to create stories I couldn't find at Waldenbooks. If there weren't many gay characters in my favorite genres, I would reimagine them myself, populating them with men who loved men. I would subvert them and remake them to my own ends. And if I was lucky enough, someone else would want to read them.

My friends say my brain works a little differently - I sees relationships between things that others miss, and get more done in a day than most folks manage in a week. Although I was born an introvert, I learned to reach outside himself and connect with others like me.

I write stories that subvert expectations, and transform sci fi, fantasy, and contemporary worlds into something new and unexpected. I run both Queer Sci Fi and QueeRomance Ink with Mark, sites that bring people like us together to promote and celebrate fiction that reflects us.

I was recognized as one of the top new gay authors in the 2017 Rainbow Awards, and my debut novel "Skythane" received two awards. In 2019, I won Rainbow Awards for three other books, and became full member of the Science Fiction and Fantasy Writers of America in 2020.

My writing, whether queer romance or genre fiction (or a little bit of both) brings LGBTQ+ energy to my stories, infusing them with love, beauty and power and making them soar. I imagine a world that *could be*, and in the process, maybe changes the world that is just a little.

ALSO BY J. SCOTT COATSWORTH

Liminal Sky: Ariadne Cycle:

The Stark Divide | The Rising Tide | The Shoreless Sea

Liminal Sky: Oberon Cycle:

Skythane | Lander | Ithani

Liminal Sky: Redemption Cycle:

Dropnauts

Other Sci Fi/Fantasy:

The Autumn Lands | Cailleadhama | Firedrake | The Great North | Homecoming | The Last Run | Spells & Stardust Anthology | Wonderland

Contemporary/Magical Realism:

Between the Lines | I Only Want to Be With You | Flames | The River City Chronicles | Slow Thaw

99¢ Shorts:

The Emp Test

Audio:

Cailleadhama (May 2021) | Homecoming | The Stark Divide (Winter 2021) | The River City Chronicles (Fall 2021)

www.ingramcontent.com/pod-product-compliance
Lightning Source LLC
Chambersburg PA
CBHW060754210726

48292CB00013B/108